The good die and the bad live on

The good die and the bad live on

Jonathan Dennis

authorHOUSE®

AuthorHouse™
1663 Liberty Drive
Bloomington, IN 47403
www.authorhouse.com
Phone: 1-800-839-8640

Published by AuthorHouse   06/27/2012

ISBN: 978-1-4567-8419-5 (sc)

Hope you enjoy the memoir of a football legend

Gordon Banks

1

"The first day that I met you I was looking in the sky
When the sun turned all a blur and the thunderclouds rolled by
The sea began to shimmer and the wind began to moan
It must have been a sign for me to leave you well alone"

From "Sleeping Village" by Black Sabbath

Beautiful girls have a special power in life. It's indisputable that they can do and say things no one else can and in a way no one else could. It's why they are loved and why, occasionally, they are hated. It's as natural as breathing in and out.

My name is Matt Malone; on my first day at university I found the most beautiful girl on campus was also on my course. I didn't need to see the rest to know that. Like her, I was an undergraduate at Birmingham University and reading History.

Her name was Liv and I never thought she'd look once in my direction but it didn't stop me looking in hers; gazing would be a more accurate way to describe it, I suppose. I tried to keep a critical eye open, seeking any imperfection to seize upon to make her seem somehow less attractive and more accessible but she was simply, flawlessly beautiful. She had straight, long dark hair; depending on the light it could even look black. Her skin was pale and delicate, unblemished as far as I could tell, although I rarely got close. Her exquisite little mouth seldom seemed to threaten a smile but she looked thoughtful rather than sad and her lips were often slightly parted when she listened in lectures but would close when she committed her thoughts to paper. Occasionally she would bite gently on her bottom lip with her front teeth in a faintly sexual gesture. Whenever I looked at her, I was careful to avert my attention by a few degrees if I sensed she was about to look in my direction, so while I couldn't say with any certainty, I felt her eyes would be dark and I knew they'd be as mesmerising as the rest of her. She usually wore a pensive look that I took for deep concentration and, because I liked her, I chose to see it also as an indication of intelligence. I saved my most concerted gazing for the insufferably turgid lectures on WWI given by Dr Brown, where I saw even Liv lacked the reserves of patience to concentrate fully.

As unattainable as she may have seemed, since she was alone so much I very easily daydreamed that our great romance might start once I'd contrived to install myself in the seat beside her on a regular basis. She was almost always in lectures before I arrived, sitting a few rows from the back, to one side or other. It was pretty much where I'd have sat if I'd not been so keen to observe from a distance and in truth, a little too bashful to plant myself too close. On the single occasion I'd entered the room late and found only a seat next to her available, we hadn't spoken and she hadn't once looked up to catch the friendly smile I was studiedly wearing.

By the end of November we'd been at uni for two whole months and were making our study choices for the following spring term—I gave exhaustive thought to making the right choices—meaning sharing at least one of Liv's seminar classes so I'd get the chance to get to know her.

I lived in Swafforth Bank, one of the university's oldest halls of residence and built in an uninspiring utilitarian style. Those who lived there were nicknamed Swankers. There were eight T-shaped, three storey blocks, each containing nine flats of five students. It was one of a number of halls on a large bank called 'The Vale', and being at the top of the hill, it was a brisk twenty-minute walk from the main university campus. There was also a large lake, The Vale's most interesting feature. At the top exit was the main road, which led into the city centre and at the bottom, a road which led to the union and university faculties. Swafforth had originally comprised four blocks arranged around a grassy quadrant with a few oak trees. I lived in a ground floor flat in block two and from my window I looked directly onto the middle of the square; I longed for the summer when it would be full of people picnicking, sunbathing or kicking a ball around. Four further blocks had been added later and were arranged haphazardly around the outside of the quadrant and consequently didn't seem part of the main community.

My best friend was Dave, a football mad Geordie studying Chemistry. We shared a flat with three other guys who pretty much kept themselves to themselves although we socialised with Calum, a decent bloke who played hockey for the university. Aside from me, Dave was the only one in the flat not to have a side parting—his mid length ponytail put him five years behind or some way ahead of the current fashion.

All five of us had taken a year out after leaving school; I'd failed to dredge up the energy to go travelling and ended up working on a building site for nine months, which didn't seem half as exciting as what the others had done.

Besides Liv, the other main focus of my attention (studies being a distant third) was my football team. On our third day at Swafforth, Dave and I had made our way to the launderette for the first social club meeting and volunteered to run The Swankers football team.

How we got to know each other was incidental but I found I had far more in common with the guys I played football with than most of the people on my course.

Socially we became a tightly knit group quickly getting used to how closely we all lived to another. Mike lived across the hallway from us and Digger lived directly above Mike. Two Nottingham lads, Fats and Chris shared a flat in block one; we called Chris 'Ghost' because he often turned up looking so pale and sorry for himself. From my room I had a clear view of Fats' window and if I could see he was up late, I'd often pop over to see him.

The other players either lived with one of these guys or were known to us from our courses. Terry, one of the few friends I'd made on my course had joined the team. He was tall, wiry, with red hair and stereotypically fiery temperament.

Thanks in part to Terry, we developed and enjoyed a reputation for being an edgy team and few games passed without some incident or other. While it had always seemed insignificant perhaps something more serious was bound to happen sooner or later. On the first Saturday of December we met our match, a crack outfit of Biochemists. Throughout the first half Mike and Dave had been hacked at a number of times and Terry had found an opponent ready to trade blows on and well off the ball. With the scores level at half time I gave the best rallying cry I could to my team and resolved to set the best—you may quite understandably think it the worst—example I possibly could. I only had to wait about five minutes for my chance as half our team poured forward in an attempt to score and the ball broke to the opposition winger. He set off at a gallop along the touchline and I tore across the pitch towards him, intending to send man and ball into the middle of next week. Perhaps I had second thoughts for a split second and lost my timing; or maybe it was simply bad luck; maybe I just got what I deserved. Whatever it was the outcome was catastrophic; I arrived in front of the guy from square on, my left foot raised to hip level and he never broke stride, crashing through my standing right leg and smashing my knee to pieces. Five minutes or what felt like a week later an ambulance arrived and took me to the local hospital.

Two days later I was lying in a hospital bed having been transferred, thanks to my dad's health insurance, to a private ward where the nurses were a little prettier and a little less qualified. I was preparing myself for the removal of my new best friend, the morphine drip stuck in my arm. The blood drain in my knee had already gone and the nurse was gently mocking me for the tears in my eyes.

"I'll come back in a couple of minutes to take the drip out of your arm—give it a few clicks in the meantime and you shouldn't feel too much," she said.

I gave her what I imagined was a stoic smile. The drip was set up so the painkiller was only injected at safe intervals but I couldn't really tell when it went in and when it didn't. I had some very hazy memories of the day and night following the operation when I'd first come around, mumbled something down the phone to my mum, felt the pain, hit the button, went crazy for a few minutes, slept, woke, felt the pain, hit the button, went crazy, slept, woke . . . you get the picture. I was ever so slightly panicking at the thought of losing my passport to mind clearing heaven, god alone knew how long term users were supposed to get off heroin if it was anything like this.

Before I knew it, the nurse was back and had sent me cold turkey in a matter of moments. She told me the surgeon and physiotherapist would see me later that day. As it happened the surgeon, Mr Fairbank, arrived at exactly the same moment as my parents. It was smiles all around as he breezily talked us through the procedure and what would happen over the next few months.

I'd ruptured my anterior cruciate ligament and torn the cartilage. On discovering this, Mr Fairbank had decided to stitch the cartilage and replace the ligament with part of the tendon connecting my kneecap to my tibia. The same injury had ended Brian Clough's playing career and finished Gazza's chances of becoming the best footballer in the world, but a few years on the operation had become a routine procedure. The chances of my becoming the best footballer in the world had already been slim but I had some intensive physio ahead to get strength back into the knee and an even harder nine to twelve months if I wanted to have any chance of playing sport again. For now my knee felt grotesque and horrible and the extent of my ambition was to one day walk to the toilet unaided.

For those few days in hospital it felt as if real life was in suspension. I was touched by the endless stream of visitors I received—all bearing chocolate gifts which I piled high in my bedside cabinet ready to leave to the nurses when I left. In the end I got my appetite back before I left so the bounty I left behind was a good deal more meagre than I'd originally intended. Dave came to see me with Mike and gave me the full low-down on the rest of the match—we'd scored twice late on to win. They left a card signed by the football team and another from the girls who lived upstairs from us. Donny, my brother came a couple of times and read most of the magazines people had brought from cover to cover. He also smuggled in a KFC for which I was eternally grateful. My parents were there every day or night despite the two-hour drive from London. All in all it felt like the whole world had stopped to service my every need and that was at least some comfort for the excruciating pain that had been a constant companion.

On my fourth and final night in hospital, I had a confused but vivid dream. Remembering it the next day, I thought it was probably due to the last remnants of the morphine kicking around my system.

. . . I was in my room and the sound of the door closing woke me. I peered into the blackness and a human shape formed slowly in my vision at the foot of the bed—somewhere in the back of my mind was a vague feeling of recognition of the robed and hooded figure.

"What are you doing here?" I asked, even as I rose from the bed and followed her out of the double French doors leading onto my first floor balcony. Broken as my knee was even in the dream it didn't need to support me as I simply floated down from the balcony and into the thick woods at the back of the hospital. Twigs broke across my face as I pushed onwards through the trees, drawn on by my guide until I stopped at the edge of a wide clearing in front of

girls from upstairs had all been in to check on me I felt as at home as I had for the previous six weeks.

Dave brought me in a cup of tea about six and sat down for a chat. He'd spent a white Christmas back home in Newcastle with his folks and being back from uni for the first time, had been the star attraction for a procession of grans, nans and aunties. I too felt pretty well disposed towards him for the way he showed such interest in and sympathy for my position—he winced throughout my description of the operation and had a lengthy go on the wobble board I'd been given by my physio to aid my recovery. He even asked with a concerned expression if I minded the rest of the flat going out without me for a couple of hours, to reacquaint themselves—I was genuinely touched.

The girls popped in before they went out to hear about the operation and later, when I was on my own again, I imagined them all talking for hours around a pub table about the terrible things I'd been through.

2

"I've seen you twice, In a short time,
Only a week since we started"

From "Name of the game" by Abba

Monday, 17th January

With all that had been going on, behind as I was with my studies, perhaps Liv should have been the farthest thing from my mind. Instead, when I arrived fifteen minutes early for my first lecture, I made deliberately for her usual seat thinking I'd have a few minutes to work out how to make an opening. She came in barely thirty seconds after I'd settled. She walked to her usual spot and spoke her first words to me.

"What are you doing here?" Fuck, was I imagining the annoyance in her tone? "You know this is where I sit." This was a direct accusation; I blushed with embarrassment and thought she'd seen through me but finally she said, "I'm kidding." Crimson, I gave a laugh of relief to show I understood the terrific joke, but somewhere deep inside I felt a twinge of excitement that she'd actually spoken to me at last. She hovered at an awkward angle while she took out a silver clipboard, pen and paper. My eyes followed her hands into her bag but saw nothing in there that didn't come out.

Fuck it, I thought, it's a new term, I'm allowed to introduce myself. I took the plunge.

"Matt," I said, offering my hand, inane grin fixed on my face, trying hopefully to project happy, relaxed thoughts I didn't feel.

"Nice to meet you Matt," her smile capturing exactly the look I was trying for. She paused for a moment before deciding to add, "I'm Liv."

9

"Nice to meet *you* Liv," deliberately echoing her choice of words (well they say imitation is the sincerest form of flattery) and looking into her eyes in a mock serious gesture which hardly fitted the situation. People were around, our fingers parted, but slowly it seemed to me. I concentrated like never before in one of Brown's lectures and for the next fifty minutes history unfurled before me with such clarity, it reminded me why I'd chosen the subject in the first place.

At twelve o'clock, as everyone hurriedly packed away their pens and folders, I made contact with Liv again—I raised my eyebrows, gave a cheeky smile and dipped my head slightly forward and down. To her credit she didn't appear to take it as the ritual mating call of the serial rapist but simply smiled back and left.

Tuesday, 18th January

You often see unrealistic scenes in Hollywood films where one person sees an ex or potential partner in a bar or restaurant and tries to make them seethe with jealousy by laughing wildly with the crushingly dull person they're invariably stuck with. I always hate these scenes but here's mine anyway.

I sat in the coffee bar with Dave and Calum; it was eleven thirty and early for me to have already had a lecture. It was equally unusual for Dave to have a free hour mid morning, but it was a regular thing we did. Calum had similarly few hours to me and was there, I supposed, because we hardly saw him outside of the flat since we'd made friends at the start of the first term.

The conversation centred on our respective parents' clownish behaviour over Christmas and was mildly but not raucously amusing. I happened to glance at the door and see Liv enter; I was pleased to see she was alone. I was usually keen to point out a nice looking girl but on seeing Liv, for once I didn't want to share. I felt my heart quicken in my chest and my face redden. She was like a solar eclipse I couldn't look at directly, but I kept track of her course, along the cafeteria line to the till and then to a seat by the window. Knowing she was close and that she could look over and see me with two of my smarter friends, started to make me feel a little like showing off and before long, I launched into an animated impression of my father having his customary tirade preparing the Christmas dinner.

All the while I was laughing, trying desperately to keep the guys looking as visibly amused as I was. There was barely enough laughter to justify me dragging it out but since there was no way back and Liv might have been watching by now—it felt like everybody else was—I continued with a wholly inaccurate falsetto impersonation of my mother telling him to get more turkey on the plate and less in his mouth. Self-consciousness hit me very suddenly and combined with the laughing and the feeling that if Liv had been watching at any stage, she'd hardly have taken away a favourable impression, I became incredibly hot and flushed. This was confirmed within a second as Calum pointed out, "Matte-o you've gone so red!"

"Yeah, it's really hot in here," I said, grabbing my collar and flapping my shirt like a fan. I am a serial blusher and knew nothing would work.

I let the others take the lead in the conversation for a while, breathed deeply and studiedly avoided looking around for Liv. I'd completely lost track of time when Calum said, "You're going to be late aren't you, it's five to twelve?"

He was right, my crutches would see to that and I was annoyed no one had said anything earlier. My annoyance and the fact I hated turning up anywhere late would normally have meant I'd have given the whole thing a miss but it was the first seminar of the new term and I could hardly miss it. I remembered the appalling comedic scene I'd created for Liv's benefit and again had to fight the instinct to give the seminar a swerve.

I was sure my crutches would mean I was in the clear as far as an excuse for my lateness was concerned but I wasn't let off as lightly as I'd hoped when, at ten past twelve, I knocked and entered Dr Robertson's tightly packed office.

"Mr Malone, you've decided to join us after all; we were speculating you might have guillotined the whole idea!" The room erupted at this topical shot across the boughs; the course title was, *'Characters of the French Revolution.'*

All I could do was laugh along and offer up my crutches and an apologetic look as I took the nearest available seat. Like most of my school teachers Robertson appeared to have taken an instant if mild dislike to me. Some I'd won over, some I hadn't and other times I'd had too much fun taking the piss to notice. I was lost in these thoughts while I unpacked my pen and file and it wasn't until I looked up at the sound of my name at the end of a question that I realised I was sitting bang opposite Liv. She, like the rest of the room, was looking at me waiting for me to answer

Robertson's question—like the rest of the room she probably also knew what the question was which gave her an advantage over me.

"Errrmmm, I'm sorry I didn't quite catch the question," I stammered, looking apologetically once again at Robertson. I could feel his dislike of me hardening with every second he had to look at me.

"I was merely wondering if you could give those of us who haven't had the pleasure of meeting you before, a brief picture of how and why you are here in Birmingham and here in this particular study group," Robertson replied curtly.

"Ah sorry, of course. Well I chose Birmingham because I was born here and history because it was one of the few subjects I was fairly good at at school. I studied the French Revolution as part of my A-Level course and found it very interesting." I don't know what made me say I'd chosen Birmingham because I was born there—although I really had been born there, I'd originally wanted to stay in London. I think maybe I thought it gave me some sort of advantage over everyone else in the room—to them I looked like a local boy somehow and this was cool. I guess I don't know how my mind works in times of stress. Anyway it was enough for Robertson to move on and back to the subject in hand. Evidently I had missed the opportunity to find out more about how and why Liv had decided to study *Characters of the French Revolution,* but I would have bet against her having admitted to any Brummie roots.

I decided to say as little as possible for the next two hours, spending a significant amount of time wearing a pained expression and rubbing the side of my knee to try to extract some semblance of sympathy from my colleagues. There was no evidence to suggest it worked. I packed away slowly at the end of the session so I would be the last person in the room with Dr Robertson and could start to rebuild our shattered relationship. The small talk was pretty meaningless but I fancied at least he was insightful enough to see I was merely trying to make an attempt to build bridges and I hoped he'd appreciate that.

My mood wasn't good. I felt bad enough to spend four hours in the library looking into the early career of a wretched bore called the Comte de Mirabeau. It felt like more bridge building with Robertson so I persevered. That night, before our regular drink at the hall bar I lay on my bed exercising my tired and stiff knee listening to Eliot's music through the wall. Despite four hours of academic knuckling down earlier in the day I picked up my books once more before Erica, the ray of sunshine from upstairs, popped her pretty face around my door and declared in her brightest tone, "It's ten o'clock!" meaning why wasn't I up and ready to go?

"Two minutes," I said, holding up two fingers and she disappeared up to Dave's room to knock for him. Erica was an incredibly cutesy blonde girl; way out of my league like Liv but thankfully not my type anyway so it wasn't so much of a headache. Nevertheless it was always great to be seen with her and she was entertaining company. Her friend Clare was much more my type; quiet and more of a thinker, pretty in a less obvious way than Erica—once you'd familiarised yourself with her unusual beauty it was easy to get hooked. She always seemed happy to accept she was overshadowed to an extent by Erica in terms of the attention they got but I suspected I wasn't the only one who always checked her out first. Clare was less sure of herself than Erica and from time to time I imagined myself exploring her hidden depths and charming her to within an inch of her modesty.

I can't remember exactly how I came to know Kenny although it was probably football related; he was a north London born Pakistani and fervent Tottenham supporter. I don't even know if we hit it off straightaway but we got pretty close some time early in that first term. He wasn't typical of the type of person I usually got to know—loved as he was by everyone and I thought at first quite prone to various affectations. We were both from London and we shared a kind of vague private joke at the expense of anyone who wasn't. I know he looked up to me and I enjoyed the adulation without really thinking that maybe he looked up to others too in the same way. We all loved his unique way of looking at things and the laughs he gave us without ever trying to be funny and Erica, Clare and I were particularly close to him. Many times I looked out of my window to see if his ground floor light was still on past one o'clock, an hour or two after we'd all said good night for the evening and if it was I'd wander over, tap on his window and climb through. One afternoon he came home from town with a seventy-pound lava lamp; and this a day after he'd secured a two hundred pound extension on his overdraft. Another time he'd daubed luminous paint all over his walls and ceiling, leaving him unable to sleep.

Wasting his money on such non-luxury items as these probably explains why he resorted to eating bread sandwiches to save cash in the final week of the autumn term—thick slices being the filling. This might make him sound like a character who'd end up on the cutting room floor even of Hollyoaks but Kenny was only partly village idiot. The rest of him was honest, open, generous and intelligent. I respected his opinion on a great many things, most notably football which was our greatest common love. He spent most of his student grant, overdraft and loans attending every Tottenham game he could but even this didn't put me off. We were very different; where I could be opinionated, confrontational and outwardly confident, he was quiet, ultra relaxed and prepared to concede on any point if he thought it mattered less to him but he certainly had an inner resolve and determination which almost no-one quite knew was there.

The night was much like any other; we bought drinks and took them through to the games room where there was a pool table, table football and a couple of quiz machines. After mixed success on each Erica, Clare and Kenny came back to my room and we talked for an hour or so with the TV on. By the time the girls left it was approaching one o'clock and Kenny asked if I wanted him to go. I'd really wanted to speak to him about Liv. I knew he had next to no practical experience with girls but this made him pretty optimistic whenever you spoke to him about your chances with anyone and it was just what I wanted to hear. He made us some tea and then made himself comfortable on my easy chair, covering himself in my spare duvet.

While I couldn't give Kenny any details about Liv other than what she looked like, he was very upbeat about my chances of hitting it off with her. We talked football for a while, to the point where neither of us was awake enough to make much sense. Kenny would be making his first visit to Sweden that week to see Tottenham play Malmo and he was pretty excited about it. I knew as much about Sweden as he did about women but I wanted to be as optimistic about how good the trip would be. When Kenny left it was gone two thirty and after brushing my teeth and making a final check on who was up in the square I fell quickly into a restful sleep.

Wednesday, 19th January

My alarm woke me at ten fifty the next morning. Wednesday was normally sports day but that was out for me for a while so I hauled myself out of bed solely for my French language subsid lesson. I got back to my room at about one thirty and no one seemed to be around—Kenny was on his way to Malmo, Dave was at football and Erica and Clare were awol. I noticed a big yellow spot above my top lip that had escaped my eye that morning. I squeezed it, annoyed that the two passably fit girls in French would undoubtedly have already entered a black mark against my name. It was unlike me not to have scrutinised a mirror with sufficient care.

I climbed into bed and quickly nodded off, awoke in the dark, masturbated into the only suitable object I could reach (a sock) and went back to sleep. At about seven I was woken up by a knock on the door.

"Yo!" I shouted as I caught sight of the sock.

Dave opened the door slowly and found his attention drawn to the sock flying through the air towards the bottom of the wardrobe.

"Just tidying up for you!" I laughed, hoping I wasn't giving anything away.

"No need on my account," Dave laughed. "Still coming into town?"

"Yeah, I'll make the pub but Bakers might be a bridge too far, who's coming?"

"Not sure if we're going to Bakers anyway. Fats, Chris, Vern . . . Digger might see us down there, Jez, Mike, Mark . . . Erica, Clare . . . maybe Timmy Steel."

"Is that a joke?" I asked, raising my eyebrows.

Dave smiled; Tim Steel wasn't my favourite person.

"No, he said he might pop down with his flatmates. He's alright, he was asking how you were today."

"Yeah, I know but keep him away from me once he's had a shandy."

"Once either of you have had a shandy you mean. I've got some work to do but I'll be ready to go at eight thirty—Mike's booking the cabs. Everyone's meeting here."

Dave went and I put on some music to fit my mood; I changed CDs a few times and found nothing really did.

I came back from the pub later with Mike, Erica and Clare, everyone else choosing to go to Bonds—a nightclub I'd wanted to go to for ages. I was pretty pissed and I wanted to be on my own for a while so I told the others I was going to do some work before bed—it can't have been convincing but no one quibbled. They all went back to Mike's and I let myself into the flat. I could hear someone talking in the kitchen so I went straight to my room. I sat on my bed and felt alone and for the first time I was conscious of being genuinely upset that my leg was so fucked. I forced myself to go through my physio programme and that at least gave me something to focus on for long enough to get over the worst feelings. I lay back on my bed feeling sad and then thinking about Liv briefly.

Without realising I was asleep I was awoken by faint tapping on my window. For a second I thought of the dream I'd had when I'd been drugged and in hospital and I felt a twinge of excitement that I might still be dreaming. When I pulled back the curtain I saw it was Clare and a positively beaming Erica with their faces pressed closely to the windowpane. I was so pleased to see them, I wondered instantly why I hadn't asked them back in the first place. I handed my keys through the window and they let themselves in. Luckily I was still dressed and there was a book near the bed that I could plausibly have been reading for the past hour. While Erica cleared some space on my desk Clare went to make some tea and, at my insistence, steal some chocolate digestives from Eliot's cupboard.

For no particular reason, I remember that night with near perfect clarity; playing a knock out game of naming Eastenders characters; Erica lying on my bed with her head on the thigh of my good leg; me wishing it was Clare lying there instead of sitting cross legged on the easy chair. I remember feeling a satisfying conceit that I had such great friends, who clearly were so happy to be in my company they'd leave the pub early and stay up late with only me to entertain them. I felt untouchable. Like Al Capone.

I skipped my lectures for the rest of the week and concentrated on my leg exercises.

3

"My eyes have seen the glory
Of the sacred wunderkind"

From "These things take time" by The Smiths

Monday, 24th January

At ten thirty the following Monday, I clambered into a cab and made it in for a Modern History lecture; more Dr Brown rambling on about the social implications for women of The Great War. Liv came through the door a minute or so after I'd settled. I raised my eyebrows and gave a slight nod of recognition.

"You're back then," she said.

This is a bit friendly I thought, unprepared.

"I thought you might have broken your other leg."

Jokes too; my mouth went dry.

"No, just laziness I'm afraid. I had a doctor's appointment one day but I couldn't face the journey in and out on Thursday—didn't think anyone would miss me!"

"Hah! I didn't say I missed you."

"Ouch, kick a man when he's down why don't you?"

"Sorry, I was kidding." She gave me a rare and perfect smile; I had to keep her talking. "It's actually nice to have some regular company up here, even if it's only because you can't make it closer to the front. What did the doctor say—is the prognosis good?"

"It was just a check up really, make sure I'm doing my phsyio and I haven't done anything stupid like fall over drunk. For some reason they're convinced the only thing students do all day is drink. He said I was doing fine though."

Liv appeared to be searching the room for something or someone. I was losing her. Silence. I searched my mind for something I could ask her.

"So . . ." I started.

"What did you do anyway, was it broken?" she interrupted.

"No, I snapped one of the cruciate ligaments in my knee. There's two of them, they provide the stability in the joint, especially when you're turning sharply or twisting." I cursed inwardly; like she needed to know that. I had to get her back to some common ground.

"So what did I miss?" I asked.

"McCandless talking about Mussolini. I left a copy of my notes in your pigeonhole," Liv replied.

I was taken aback by this casual act of kindness. "Shit, thanks for that, that's really kind, erm . . . I hope I can do the same for you sometime." I was bowled over. "Although you won't be able to read my writing of course," I added, making it all too clear how bowled over. I tried to get a picture of a twerpish Hugh Grant in a seemingly endless stream of British films out of my head.

"Same here I'm afraid so I typed mine up for you," Liv smiled, understandably very pleased with herself.

Bowled over and trampled into the ground. "Well thanks again," and then, from nowhere, "can I buy you a coffee . . . lunch even . . . after the seminar tomorrow perhaps to say thank you?"

"Tomorrow's out for me I'm afraid, how about a coffee after we finish here? I don't tend to eat lunch much to be honest."

"Yeah, that's cool for me," I said, hearing every pint of blood in my body thundering in my ears.

Too excited to concentrate on the lecture, I spent the next fifty minutes working out my budget for the next nine weeks. For some reason I find it the best thing when I absolutely have to eat up some time and the games on my mobile phone aren't an option. A minute before the bell, I cursed myself for not spending the time working on conversation ideas.

I packed up slowly, indicating to Liv that we should let the crowd go, presenting my crutches in mitigation. As we walked over to the union building, I asked Liv about where she was living and what her halls were like. She had a similar set up to mine by the sound of it but in an all girls' hall called Garforth a bus ride from campus. She shared with four other girls who made her life bearable and living hell by turns but she was pretty happy overall as far as I could tell. She didn't give too much away. The worst thing she seemed to have against any of her flatmates was that one of them insisted on always calling her Olivia in spite of the fact Liv had never indicated she was known as anything other than Liv.

I enjoyed the conversation and it was only after countless replays in my head that night that I appreciated how interested she had seemed in me and how many questions she'd asked. I went to secure the last table in the coffee shop while she bought the drinks. I got a real buzz from sitting alone at the table waiting for the most beautiful girl on campus.

"Sorry, you sugar?" Liv broke in on my reverie.

For a few moments my mind was lost and I looked at her blankly before coming to the inevitable realisation I was being asked something but I had no idea what.

"Sorry?" I asked, smiling apologetically.

"Can I get you some sugar?" she repeated.

"Oh, just one please." I said, before realising she'd have to go back to the counter. I thought I saw a crease of annoyance flicker across her brow and wondered if I should have gone without.

We covered a lot of ground in those forty-five minutes and Liv let me pay for a second cup of coffee. In her final year at school she'd been withdrawn from Roedean at the head mistress's request, only to be reinstated after a significant donation from her father. She wouldn't elaborate on the details but I was hopelessly impressed and resolved to find them out if I could ever get her drunk enough. She'd got straight 'A's of course—History, Psychology, English and Ancient Civilisations—"That would have been quite an achievement a few years ago," I'd joked but she didn't laugh. Musically she named a few standard bands and a few I wasn't as sure about. When I mentioned I had a penchant for old school punk she easily reeled off a few names, but she had to concede she wasn't familiar with the finer works of Peter and the Test Tube Babies. I promised to play her *'The Mating Sounds of South American Frogs'* one day. The whole conversation went about as perfectly as I could have hoped but the clincher was our shared passion for Charles Bukowski. She preferred his poetry while I only really had the patience for his novels but I wasn't going to hold it against her.

We'd both taken a year out after finishing school, me to spend nine months working on a building site fixing aluminium panels to a suspended ceiling (not my original intention but marvellous fun in the end), her to travel alone through Asia and South America. It was no effort for me at all to bring to life the characters I'd been lucky enough to work with—Claffy, Rigney and best of all, Crackerjack, the permanently coked up fiend I'd been teamed up with once I'd learned the ropes. He'd coined in upwards of five hundred pounds a day for three months and slipped me a fifty on the night of the Christmas piss up for making it all possible through my semi-autistic knowledge of the location of any one of a hundred different panel types on the massive site; I'd find them for something like minimum wage and he'd put them up for three pound a go. Once he'd shown me how, I put up almost as many as him—he picked up the three pound per panel and I got as much overtime as I wanted.

Last but not least we'd probably spent a few freezing midweek nights on the same terrace at Selhurst Park supporting the Super Eagles and chanting the names of heroes past and present—my favourite when I'd been really young had always been Eric 'the Ninja' Young with his trademark black headband. Liv refused to admit she was joking when she said her heroes had been Tomas Brolin and Lombardo.

How quickly can a person fall in love? Always faster than the other person is all I know. Fast, hard and forever is how I always do it.

4

*"There's things I haven't told you, I go out late at night
And if I was to tell you, you'd see my different side"*

From "We don't care" by Audio Bullys

Tuesday, 1st February

By the Tuesday of the following week when we met for an afternoon coffee, I'd done my homework, Lady Luck playing her part, and found Palace were playing Birmingham City that Saturday.

I could hardly believe Liv's response when I popped the question.

"Wicked!" she exclaimed. It was the most uncool thing I'd yet heard her say and easily the most exciting.

Having got her acquiescence, it quickly dawned on me I'd not thought beyond this point in the conversation. Thankfully Liv was less overawed by the prospect of our first date and changed the subject naturally.

"Have you thought about what options you'll choose next term?" she asked me.

I hadn't. "No," I said, "sounds like you may have though . . ."

"I definitely want to do *'Lost Tribes of The American Plains'*, I put my name down for it last term but didn't get on."

I'd already done it in term one, an opportunity for quality face time with Liv was gone. Still, I had to salvage something. "It's brilliant, really quite moving at times reading some of the first hand accounts. Everyone who did it absolutely loved it. Apparently Dr Scott is thinking about doing an extended course in future."

"Why moving?" Liv was looking at me quizzically.

Confused by the question I stammered, "Wwwell . . . it's just pretty mind blowing to think that cultures that survived and grew for thousands

21

of years, cultures that adapted so marvellously to their environment were wiped out in a historical blink of an eye to satisfy the immediate needs of a marauding invading force." She indicated I should continue with a nod of her head. "And the buffalo too, they were driven to extinction." I was done; I'd had a crack at sounding informed but having missed about a third of the seminars I was struggling.

Liv paused a few seconds, just long enough to make it clear she was not convinced. "I guess so," she said, clearly about to court controversy, "but the Indians warred, raped, pillaged and plundered for as long as they were winning then quickly played the defenceless passive peoples' card when the tide turned against them. If the boot had been on the other foot they'd have wiped the settlers out to a man, any way they could. The problem is the way history is taught panders to the liberal belief that whoever is stronger and better equipped must necessarily be morally bankrupt while any local savages, be they in the American west or the middle of Africa, were part of some idyllic utopian society. The world only moves on when the big guys with guns get the motivation to get out of their own backyard and shake things up, driven on by necessity or tempted out by a perfectly rational greed for more. It's man's way—what more is there to say?" She had such a wicked smile on her face by the time she'd finished her mischievous little tirade.

"You can't pin all the blame on us poor men," I said cheerily, trying to lighten the atmosphere. It was a serious miscalculation on my part.

Her smile vanished instantly and she looked malevolently into my eyes, boring a hole through the back of my skull with her stare.

"You shouldn't flatter yourself that I was referring to *men*, I meant mankind." She hadn't loved my joke.

There was silence for a few moments and I felt quite perturbed, confused by her reaction. This sudden atmosphere between us had come from nowhere. We're friends I thought, this can't matter, but try as I might I couldn't think of any way to dispel it. I looked around the room for inspiration and then I felt her eyes on me. After a moment's pause I looked at her, with as conciliatory an expression as I could muster. She wasn't about to speak.

"Where shall we meet next Saturday anyway—for the football?"

"I don't think I can make it after all, I remembered I have something planned next week. Sorry."

She didn't look very sorry. She looked coldly triumphant.

"Fuck," I said quietly, feeling sick. "That's a shame, we'll have to catch them the next time they're up." I felt crushed.

"Definitely." She wasn't even looking at me now. I could feel her fury and it paralysed me.

"Liv, I gotta run—well, crutch—see you next week?" I asked hopelessly.

"Mmm." She nodded, looking away.

Having made my excuses I left, fighting the urge to look back at her sitting there and surrender the last of my dignity. When I did look she was in conversation on her mobile phone and looking placidly out of the window.

I'd arranged to get a lift back to halls with Mel, a girl I'd had a crush on for months, at five o'clock so I hung around campus for another couple of hours before meeting her at the clock tower. I had hoped to extend my afternoon coffee with Liv most of the way to five—the best laid plans and all that . . .

Mel lived in a flat of five girls on the top floor of Kenny's block. She was pretty highly strung but great company, especially on the odd occasions she was able to relax. I'd never really understood the fuss about the Red Hot Chilli Peppers but something about hearing '*Under the Bridge*' in Mel's company changed my perspective overnight. Her dad was a self-made millionaire who ran a small telecommunications company somewhere near Leeds, her sister was apparently far better looking, intelligent and happy and she rarely mentioned her mum. Mel wasn't a conventional beauty—in fact I was the only person I knew who found her particularly attractive. She had a real edge to her personality; I always had to be careful not to say the wrong thing and I enjoyed the challenge. She had dark curly hair, slightly buck teeth and ever so slightly hamsterish cheeks. Her eyes sparkled though and her smile really drew you in. She was a great storyteller, something I hadn't really come across in a woman before, and while she gave off a super confident air I loved that I saw her vulnerability. Having so much money she was also lucky to have a great sense of style and while she slobbed around her flat in the most shapeless, outsized clothes one could imagine, whenever she stepped outside she was immaculate. This was nearly something we had in common—I would never be described as immaculately turned out but if she ever made any positive comment on what I was wearing it made my day.

I always found a lot of girls tend to let you get closer to them if they're sure you're not interested in anything more than friendship. I adored Mel and had wanted her since the moment I first saw her but I'd been fairly successful—or so I thought—in keeping it hidden from her. Now I was so keen on Liv, I was happy my relationship with Mel was such that she wouldn't see anything amiss in me telling her how much I liked a girl I'd met on my course. Mel looked too happy—dare I say relieved?—to hear all this and she looked straight at me, ruffled my hair and playfully pulled my cheek back and forth teasing in a baby voice, "Isn't it sweet—little Matthew's got a crush on a girrrrrrrrl?"

Actually it was still two crushes and right now it was Mel's warm fingers on my face that were making me blush. I'd known her pretty well from the start of uni and this was one of the very few times she'd initiated any physical contact and it always made me feel special. I had an inkling she'd had some emotional trauma in the recent past although she hardly gave up any detail. It didn't detract from her attraction for me and made it easier for me to forgive her frequent distance. Everyone else wrote her off as a spoilt, neurotic, self obsessed show off.

"What are you doing tonight?" Mel asked, sounding far too casual for it to be simply a casual enquiry.

I felt an unerring sense my plans were about to change. "Not sure, what were you thinking?"

"There's a karaoke competition at Garforth, the first prize is a trip to New York."

My mind was going at about two hundred miles an hour; Garforth was where Liv lived and turning up there (by coincidence!!) with the other girl of my daydreams represented quite an opportunity. Basically my chances of the perfect evening were doubled—I could end up celebrating Mel's success over a few late, private cocktails, maybe even commiserating abject failure; who cared which? Cocktails and privacy were the keys to success. I didn't know if she could sing or not, I didn't much care; this was the sound of opportunity knocking . . .

. . . *I can almost smell Mel's specially made up hair as she buries her tearful face in my chest and sobs her gratitude for my support . . . she'd never even thought of asking anyone else, did I really think she was the best? She'd been thinking of me when she'd sung. Liv didn't know what she was missing, "you're so sweet, I'd never play so hard to get . . . why don't you see me to my door, no I meant my bedroom door . . ."*

Then again if it were to be Liv's lucky night . . .

. . . I could arrive with Mel looking positively radiant in my company, be spotted by a repentant but irresistible Liv who is careful to keep a discreet distance until Mel makes her way to the stage, at which point she shimmies over and takes the still warm seat next to me. The booth we're in is tight and Liv really is very, very close. I like it. We chat, she giggles, we touch and as Mel finishes her song—the daydream reel breaks down as I can't think of a song she would sing—we are obviously friends again, much more than friends in fact. I realise Mel's not the one for me—her role in all this is all too clear—to bring Liv and me together. I don't quite know how or how quickly it happens but Liv and I leave together, holding hands; Mel looks happy enough to see us together but I'm sure I see a tinge of envy in her eyes. Liv's fancied me for ages apparently and she was so worried when I left so suddenly after coffee and then when she saw me come in with Mel . . .

So I decided on going to the karaoke with Mel. And it didn't really turn out exactly as I'd imagined.

Mel had said she'd give me a knock at about seven fifteen. A couple of minutes before then I heard a knock, but it wasn't Mel who I heard say, "Hi" as Colin, my least favourite flatmate, opened the door. It was Phil, another guy who definitely had a thing for Mel and one who had done a far more effective job of leaching onto her. His big attraction, as far as I could tell, was that he was more than happy to attend their shared politics lectures and photocopy his notes for her, provided he could drop them round in person on a seemingly daily basis; there were occasions when I suspected he didn't even have any notes. He was as badly dressed as me—my excuse being that only oversized combat trousers actually fitted over the metal brace I was still wearing after my operation. He was like a provincial peasant who had discovered consumer credit but not how to use it; thankfully Mel wasn't shy of letting him know on a regular basis. As he came into my room I saw tonight's ensemble; plain and untucked orange Ted Baker shirt at least a size too big, Eisenegger ski jacket three sizes too big and some ice wash Armani jeans that could only have come from Macro. The finishing touch was what looked like some old school shoes; Mel wasn't going to be short of material.

"Hi Matt, Mel's in the car waiting," he said, clearly as thrilled as I was about the extra company.

"Yep, give me two minutes and I'll see you in the car," I said, struggling up from the bed, hoping he'd have the nouse to get into the backseat of Mel's Astra without me having to tell him when I got out there. I took my time straightening my hair and clothes because I was pissed off at Mel for bringing that idiot along. I even popped my head round Dave's door to let him know Phillage, as we'd christened him, was playing gooseberry for the evening with the express desire of fucking up my far more realistic chances.

"Might be worth a laugh, tell her I'll be down about nine," he said with a malicious grin.

Dave had pissed himself when I'd mentioned the karaoke to him. Although they were both northerners and had a similar sense of humour Dave and Mel didn't get on. Neither was particularly confrontational but on the few times they'd met, usually at my instigation, they had argued constantly.

I got to the car and, predictably enough, Phil had made himself comfortable in the front seat. Behind his back I raised my eyebrows and shook my head at Mel, not trying to disguise my annoyance. Rather frustratingly he wasn't making much of an effort to hide his own pique at having to clamber into the back. As I passed my crutches to him in the back seat, I playfully jabbed at his paunch and asked him if he'd got anything else for Christmas. This was intended to remind him that he wasn't really in the running for anything more than useful school work chum to Mel; have to be cruel to be kind sometimes, I told myself.

"Hiyerrrrrr!" Mel beamed at me and leant over to give me a quick peck on the cheek. She obviously knew she was playing catch up for inviting that twat along. I noticed she was pretty heavily made up for the evening and it wasn't really doing her any favours. I felt another tinge of annoyance as I thought it unlikely Liv was going to feel particularly jealous when I turned up as part of this motley crew.

"Alright?" I replied, trying to sound like I was pissed off but trying to hide it. "Just us three?" I asked with more edge.

"Yeah, it starts at eight."

"Good good, only forty minutes to complete the five minute drive—some congestion expected en route?"

"No, I just want to make sure we get a good spot—I want you two sitting right at the front so you can lead the applause." The conceited cow wasn't even half joking.

"So what are you singing?" I asked, not caring, trying to keep Phillage out of the conversation for a while longer.

"*'Flashdance'*," she replied, as we pulled out into the road running through The Vale.

"Quality," Phil chirped, trying to sound like a geezer, probably trying to sound more like me I thought with a smile. Poor fool probably had *'Layer Cake'* down as his favourite film.

Now Phil had jumped in, I thought it was a good moment to instigate some chilly silence. Unfortunately the nervous energy coursing through Mel meant silence was about as likely as a smooth gear change. She asked me what I was going to sing. Thankfully I knew my crutches would preclude any chance of me actually taking part tonight but I played along for now.

"I don't know—I was thinking of *'Maybe I'm Amazed'* by Paul McCartney. It's the only song I know older than *'Flashdance'*." Fuck knew where that had come from.

"What?" Mel asked, sounding genuinely intrigued, ignoring my slight.

"It's an old song. He wrote it about Linda—the wife with two legs."

"Never heard of it," Mel said, shaking her head. "What about you Phil?"

"No way am I singing anything." I'd made him look like a square even though I had no intention of singing either; things weren't going so badly after all. "Unless I get really pissed and I'll probably end up doing *'Under the Bridge'*," he laughed. One of Mel's favourite songs; why didn't he ask her to marry him now and have done with it for fuck's sake? Whatever happened tonight I wanted to see Phil up there singing—Anthony Kiedis he was certainly not. I guessed the thirty quid I had in my wallet would be sufficient to get Phil pissed enough to make an ass of himself.

"Dave said not to go on too early as he might pop down later on," I said, trying to penetrate Mel's super confident air by telling her the last person she'd want down there might be coming along.

"Wonderful," she answered sarcastically and I felt a pang of guilt.

"I doubt he'll make it, I think he's got a full day tomorrow," I backtracked, trying to repair some damage.

For the few minutes it took to get to Garforth, I gave it my best shot to make some pleasant small talk with Phil. I felt sorry I'd been in such an obvious bad mood after Mel had asked me along to her big night. When we arrived, Mel parked right outside in a disabled space and I wondered if I should question as to whether or not this was why I'd been invited. I didn't have the chance anyway as Mel virtually sprinted out of the car, turning at the front door to the bar to remote lock the car a split second or two before Phil had shut the door. We both looked on as she disappeared into the bar, Phil doing the honourable thing and walking in with me, holding the doors open and then even going straight to the bar for a round—more guilt!

Although it was far from empty, Mel had found some seats at the front, probably because no one else wanted to sit there, to the right of the mini stage that had been erected. Either side of the stage were two large screens on which the audience would be able to read the words to each song, I wondered if we'd have to move the table so we wouldn't obstruct anyone's view of the screen.

I sat down with Mel and she seemed happy enough, all nervous smiles. She kept looking all round the room; I assumed she was trying to imagine what it would be like on stage and how many people would be watching. For the first time I thought about what she was going to sound like; *'Flashdance'* seemed like a strange choice unless she was pretty confident in her voice. If she was going to be awful it was going to be embarrassing for her but more importantly what would it be like sitting right at the front and being her main supporters?

"I'm going to go on after about forty five minutes so I don't look too keen," Mel told us.

I sipped my pint and nodded. "Sounds like a plan," I said sagely.

"And then we'll come on and do *'Five hundred miles'* and one of us has to win," Phil added. As a mood lightener I didn't think it was so bad but Mel gave him a pretty cold look. And with that the real business of the evening began.

Something Mel had told me about the evening had me slightly confused. "They're giving away a trip to New York for winning tonight?" I asked.

"No way, this is only the first heat. They'll have a competition at each of the halls and then a final at the union for the grand prize," Mel said. She seemed a bit better informed all of a sudden; I'd clearly been tricked.

"So why didn't we just go to the Swafforth Bank night?" I asked.

"Matt, I wanna *win* that trip—if I don't qualify tonight I'll go to all the nights until I do." She was looking at me as if I was the stupid one.

"I see. I probably won't be doing *'Five hundred miles'* every time," I replied, turning away, exasperated. I didn't know if she was planning on taking her fanclub to each event or whether we were just the only ones mug enough to make the away leg.

The next half an hour or so was filled with each of us pointing out a few of our course-mates, one of Mel and Phil's even looked like joining us at one point. I could tell even they didn't much like him and thankfully either my glowering or Mel's general evasiveness drove him away. I watched him intermittently for the rest of the night and ironically it looked like he might have been a useful person to have had on side since he seemed pretty pally with the guy who turned out to be the evening's judge and compere.

If I'd been in any doubt about how good the evening was going to be I was soon put right when the compere bounded out and straight into Bon Jovi's *'Living on a Prayer'* without so much as a, "Hello, how ya doing Garforth, wanna get rocked?" What he lacked in raw talent he more than lacked in energy—by the end of the song when he knew he should have been really revving it up he was practically dead on his feet. I guess he had another ten halls and another ten nights to perfect the act.

Next up was some bumpkin, who looked like he'd come straight from lambing. His thick Yorkshire accent gave something to *'American Pie'* Don McLean or Madonna never could and there wasn't a dry eye in the house when he sang Miss a-Harrogate Pie right at the end. A cute girl sang something by Girls Aloud gamely if not brilliantly and then halfway through the next act—another girl, singing without trace of irony, *'Shut Up'* by the Black Eyed Peas—Mel leant over and whispered that she was going to go up next.

I couldn't believe she wanted to compete with the dross we'd seen so far—perhaps she thought she'd seen all the competition she needed to but I didn't think it was such a smart move.

"What happened to waiting forty five minutes?" I asked.

"Bugger that, I can't wait now I'm here. I'll flippin' wet meself."

It seemed as good a reason as any so I kept quiet.

Mel approached the compere at the side of the stage but was clearly disappointed to learn there was already a running order and she'd have to wait for the next two acts. So we sat through *'Mr Brightside'* and *'Walking on Sunshine'* and then Mel was called up to sing *'Flesh-dance'*—"ooh, kinky!" the compere (or could that be Frankie Howerd with us from beyond the grave?) said. In spite of myself I joined Phil in some concerted whooping and cheering as Mel walked the short distance to the stage.

When she'd told me she was singing *'Flashdance'* all I could really remember were the chorus and the video—both pretty upbeat, lively affairs. What I hadn't remembered and what became apparent as soon as the music began was that the intro to the song was simply a couple of notes from a synthesiser letting the vocal hold the tune on its own over the top. Mel's voice wavered chronically as she began and I felt my face redden with embarrassment for her and, looking around, I could see a few hands in front of mouths concealing cruel comments to friends about the poor girl dying right in front of them. And then the song really started and the transformation was breathtaking—and not just for those of us watching who desperately wanted it to happen. With every word Mel got stronger and louder, gaining more control of the song and she began to relax and enjoy herself. By the end the whole place was caught up in the performance of a song they'd sneered at being sung by a girl they'd moments ago been so prepared to see fail.

I never stop being impressed when I think of Mel that night and how she'd been so brave in stepping up there and bearing her soul. I saw why she'd been so confident but she'd been prepared to fail and fail in such a style as I knew I'd never have had the guts to do. It was almost enough to make me want to get up there and sing myself. But I didn't of course. I just told her she'd rocked, wishing I could have put into words exactly what I really felt about her at that moment. But I couldn't do that either. Even Phil did a better job than I could when he leapt up, hugged her and kissed her cheek. I wasn't even jealous, I was just glad someone was emotionally eloquent enough to do it. No one came close to her all night in terms of singing or performance. She didn't win though; the evening hadn't been about being the best singer. I don't even remember who did win; perhaps I somehow deliberately erased it from my memory in disgust. Mel was so upset that thankfully she never went along to any of the other competitions—what put the seal on that was the special mention and even more special prize she was awarded at the end of the night as one of the 'plucky losers'.

Mel was pretty down and wanted to get home, Phil had wandered off with a couple of guys from his course (not before treating the audience to a worthy rendition of *'Walk This Way'*) and predictably, there'd been no sign of Liv all night. Mel and I made a bit of small talk on the way back but I was happy enough to sit in silence as I reckoned neither of us was particularly in the mood. I asked if she wanted a coffee before she went back to hers but she just thanked me for coming with her and went inside. As soon as she'd gone I realised even her miserable presence was better than nothing and I wanted badly to talk to someone. It was ten forty and Fats and Kenny's lights were both off despite it being too early for either of them to be in bed. I considered knocking on Mel's door anyway but I decided I might be tempted to get a bit emotional—I had that pre-depression feeling of suppressed panic in my gut. People can smell that feeling on you I think and they always know when to be out, too busy to talk or so offhand that you can't get anything off your chest. Probably just as well.

I went into my room with a cup of tea, which I left on the desk to cool while I went through my knee exercise programme. I put on Radiohead but couldn't really get into it. I took this as quite a good sign—maybe I wasn't so depressed after all. I was pacing slowly and carefully around my room without the aid of a single crutch—progress! After just six weeks I was walking unaided. I smiled without feeling much emotion at all. Perhaps I was actually *too* depressed for Radiohead if I didn't feel happy now. I changed the CD and went to sleep with the light on. When I awoke, for the second time that day I decided to do some work. About two o'clock I checked for signs of life at Kenny or Fats' window and again saw nothing so I turned off the light and went to bed.

Not long after, before I'd even been to sleep, I heard some voices outside and there was some tapping at my window. I pulled the duvet tight against my chin and stared hard at the curtains willing whoever it was—Kenny, Erica or whoever—to go away. Pretty soon silence was restored and I screwed my eyes tight shut and tried to pretend I was Magellan's second in command on the approach to Cape Horn.

. . . The next time I heard tapping at my window I got up, right up and found I wasn't in my room at all anymore. Looking out I saw there was no one at the window—all I could see by the weak moonlight was a path leading up to and into some thick woods. At the point at which the path met the edge of the woods she was waiting for me to come. It felt familiar. I opened the window and jumped down the ten or twelve feet to the ground. My fingers briefly touched wet grass as I bent my knees on landing. I started slowly but deliberately down the path—I wanted to go but my body was fighting the

31

instinct. She waited for me to get somewhere near and then moved off into the woods; I lost sight of her momentarily. She was some way into the woods, waiting for me to follow again. As I moved on, I felt the trees close tight behind me removing any trace of the path I'd taken. I followed, losing track of time, unable to think of anything but trying to keep up with her. I could feel my heart thumping in my chest, my head—my ears full of the sound of the blood rushing through me. Other times all I could hear were the deafening, terrifying sounds of the forest. She never seemed to run but I did, carefully at first, but once I started I couldn't stop; I kept running deeper and deeper into the woods. The sounds of my rapid breathing and the branches, twigs and leaves being crushed and broken before and beneath me were somehow more comforting than hearing the forest itself. She'd disappeared but I kept running; whether towards something or away from something I could no longer tell. I stopped even looking for her, or where I was going, I don't even think there was a path, the moonlight had all gone and I crashed through more and more branches—thick heavy braches that hurt me—through thick and thorny bushes that cut me to rivens—until before I knew it I wasn't running anymore at all. I had crashed through the very edge of the forest and out into an endless blackness that swallowed me. My feet no longer found solid earth beneath them, I fell and fell, arms pin-wheeling, screaming and spinning . . . as I looked, falling backwards there she was peering over the edge at me . . . Was she laughing?? I kept falling . . .

Wednesday, 2ⁿᵈ February

I awoke with a start, in a cold sweat, the edge of the duvet bunched tightly in my hands under my chin, an unfamiliar noise spooking me further. I slowly came to the realisation that it was pitch black and I was terrified. I sent the lamp on my desk crashing onto the floor. I followed the lead with my fingers and turned it on where it lay. With the light on I looked vainly for the source of the noise before I realised it was slowing down with my breathing—I'd been panting, out of breath. I looked at the clock; it was two minutes to three—I couldn't have been asleep more than ten minutes.

Sitting on the edge of my bed I let the cold restore my senses and listened to the silence return. What to do now? I was too scared to think about closing my eyes. What was I afraid of? Waking up like that again probably. I opened the curtain with an outstretched arm and edged towards the window to see if Fats' light was on—it wasn't. As I pressed my face against my window to look for Kenny's, I saw his light go out. I knew Kenny wouldn't object to me waking him up but when I considered it, I realised it wasn't really company I needed. I just wanted out of the flat.

I pulled on my combats and the rest of my gear and quietly let myself out. This'll be good exercise for the knee, I thought grimly. As I left the few blocks of Swafforth Bank behind and joined the main campus road, I felt the icy wind attack my hands gripping the crutches. I didn't want to turn back now and probably wake everyone up so I continued down the hill towards the lake. The hill, the wind and the crutches rapidly wore away my resolve to make it all the way to the dark and muddy lake and I settled onto a bench fifty yards or so down the road where I could still see Swafforth Bank and its silent windows. I'd thought I wanted to be alone with my thoughts but on this too my determination quickly dissolved and my sole thought was about the cold—I'd forgotten I was supposed to be analysing my dream and my reaction to it. With my imaginary tail tucked between my very real freezing cold legs I gave up and headed slowly back up the road towards the flat, taking the long way and staying on the road rather than cutting through block three. Again I became aware of an unfamiliar noise, this time getting louder as I walked up the hill. Up ahead, a car careered through the entrance from the main road into the campus, tyres screeching wildly, momentarily louder even than the thumping bass of the stereo. Adrenaline pumping, I practically threw myself behind a bush a few yards off the road and stayed there, on the cold, hard ground, feeling the bass pulse through me as the car sped past. It was obvious how well my rehab had gone as I tucked the crutches under my arm and hurried back to the flat, glad to be so close. In my room I slumped back against the closed door and undressed, leaving my clothes all over the floor. Exhausted by my adventure, I fell asleep as soon as my head hit the pillow.

Thursday, 3rd February

I came out of the lift on the fourth floor of the Arts building already a couple of minutes late thanks to the taxi driver going to the wrong flat. Passing the student pigeonholes, I noticed that for only the second time in four months I had some mail—I guessed from one of my tutors cancelling a seminar or trying to rearrange it for nine o'clock on Sunday morning. Consequently, I only picked it up when I went back after lunch with Dave—if I'd known what it was I'd never have been so casual. I was sitting in my American History lecture when I read Liv's note. I wondered if there was any significance in the choice of card—a pair of sparrows sitting on a snowy telephone wire. Maybe she wanted us to fly away somewhere together.

Matt

Turns out I can make the game Saturday after all. If you're still planning on going drop me a note before Friday (not coming in Thursday by the way) and let me know when and where I should meet you.

Hope to see you Saturday.

Liv x

ps sorry if I was ratty the other day—you know how it is sometimes! pps I wanted the birds on the card to be eagles—these were the closest I could find.

I was touched by Liv's gesture. I was tempted to reply immediately but I knew I should carefully consider every word of my response so I decided I'd take my time and drop it into her pigeonhole before I went back that evening. I wasn't fussed about looking too keen—if anything I wanted Liv to get the impression that I *was* keen now she'd gone out of her way to apologise and get our date (well what else was there to call it?) reinstated. Unable to get into town to scour the shops for the perfect card, I had to go to the shop in the student union before my last lecture of the day and see what they had to offer.

On my way to the shop I bumped into Calum. Buoyed with confidence, I shared my good news with him and he decided he'd come with me to the shop and look at the cards, all the while offering me his advice about what I should write back to Liv.

My hopes weren't particularly high but fate was smiling on me, as almost the first card I saw was cut in the shape of a ninja; Eric, I thought! This was perfect as it fitted the football theme and would be a neat reminder of the first time I'd spoken to Liv. I hid the card so no one else would see it before I picked it up; I didn't want to go through the whole story with Calum so I just kept looking and bemoaning the lack of choice until he disappeared to meet one of the peckers from the hockey club. On closer inspection I found the card somewhat less than perfect after all—the message inside read, "Happy birthday from the ultimate swordsman." I didn't think Liv would be offended by such ribaldry but I'd be crossing out the message in any case.

I spent the hour when I should have been hearing all about Bismarck's plan to unify Germany, in the library trying in vain to frame the perfect reply. Anything that seemed like it might be funny became too contrived as soon as I'd written it down. In the end I settled for levity and brevity.

Liv

Great news you can make it Saturday, let's meet at 1.15 at the uni station. My mobile number is 07970 180297 if you have any problems.

Matt x

ps hope you like the card, took me hours to find it!

A split second after I'd sealed the envelope, I wondered if I should have added something about there being no need for her to apologise for the other day—would she notice the omission? I wrote her name on the envelope and cringed at my sub human scrawl, was I somehow blowing my chance? I deposited the card in Liv's pigeonhole and looked forward to an agonising couple of days wondering if she might call to cancel—would she even bother to call?

I looked at the time. It was late and I had missed my cab. This is going to be fun I thought as I dialled the cab office to explain why I'd missed my cab and ask them to send another one as soon as possible. I gave them a story about a seminar overrunning and it being completely unavoidable—did she know what it was like when these professors got onto their favourite topics? When the miserable creature failed to have a bar of it I asked her if she knew that this was the first time I'd failed to make one of the taxis the firm had sent to me twice a day for the past three weeks. I was genuinely fucked off by the end despite my only excuses being entirely fabricated—after all she didn't know that; she was basically calling me a liar and an unreliable one at that. She eventually relented and agreed to send another cab when I said I'd pay the fare for the one I'd missed and ensure that in future I'd let the office know if I wasn't going to be there for a pick up.

Back at my flat there was only Eliot in but Mel had dropped me a note about going into town that afternoon. I went over to her flat to see if she was back from town. I caught her locking her front door on her way out of her flat.

"Hiyerr," she said with a smile. She looked harassed.

"Hiya, anything wrong? You look a bit . . . harassed," I added by way of explanation.

"I'm in a bit of a hurry. I have to get to the library to get a book out for an essay that has to be in tomorrow."

"No probs, did you go into town in the end?"

"No, I just washed my hair and watched TV all afternoon—Phil's been over all afternoon telling me how fantastic he thought the karaoke was. Look, do you want to come into town tomorrow, I just need to pick up a few things, then we can go for a drink or something?"

Fuck it, did I ever? Suddenly I'm fighting them off, I thought. I made a show of thinking about whether I could spare the time to join her but I didn't want her to start thinking about other options so it didn't last too long.

"Yeah, I could do with picking up a couple of bits and bobs." "Bits and bobs?" I shuddered, not an expression Cary Grant ever made the mistake of using in front of a lady. "You don't mind me slowing you down though do you?" I asked, offering my crutches in supplication.

"No, I'm only going to pick up some pants before I run out again."

I thought this was more information than my question warranted. I wondered if Mel was trying to drop some sort of hint by buying her knickers in front of me. I thought it would be sensible to see the knickers first before making a final call on this.

"I'll give you a knock about ten thirty ok?"

"Yep, see you about eleven," I answered, trying to be funny.

Friday, 4th February

We got into town for about midday, which in terms of timekeeping was standard for Mel. After an embarrassing few minutes trailing Mel while she chose her underwear, she finally settled on one pink, one blue and one white set. Feigning complete disinterest I did notice that she doubled up each time on size twelve knickers, her bra size I already knew was 34c. There was nothing overtly sexy about her choices; she was definitely the sort of girl who wouldn't be showing her knickers off to anyone unless she was pretty sure of a certain depth and permanence of feeling.

She held up the blue set to me, "What do you reckon?" She was deliberately trying to embarrass me.

I looked away. "If I see them now it'll spoil it later," I said, trying to return the favour.

Mel blushed and looked away. I regretted it of course but I felt a bit resentful that for the rest of the shopping trip Mel was a little cold. I knew Mel could be sensitive at times but I didn't really feel I'd done much wrong.

After a more atmospheric lunch than I'd been hoping for we made our way back to Mel's car. Taking advantage of some uncomfortable silence, I opened some mail I'd grabbed on my way out that morning. I wouldn't have bothered if Mel had been a bit chattier but I wanted to show I had more on my mind than trying to atone for my misdemeanour. When I told her the letter was from Hannah, my ex (she'd asked) she seemed even more put out. In spite of my physical tiredness and the emotional drain of the last few hours, when we got back home I asked Mel if she wanted to come in for tea; she'd taught me never to offer a 'Yorkshire lass' coffee.

"Would you mind coming up to mine, I can't face Dave right now?" Mel said. This was probably the first time since I'd known Mel that I wasn't about to jump at such an offer—and the offers were pretty rare. But she looked like she had something on her mind and with no polite way I could refuse, I followed Mel upstairs.

Normally I never made it any further than the kitchen in Mel's flat—her bedroom was always too untidy for visitors—but this time we went straight to her room. She left me sitting on the bed, looking through her CDs while she made tea for us.

As she came back in her room, catching me looking at the lyrics to Michael Jackson's *Thriller*, she said quietly, "We need to talk Matt. What did you mean earlier when you made that remark about not seeing my knickers?"

I couldn't believe she was being serious. "It was a joke Mel, a joke. What do you mean what did I mean?"

"Sometimes I feel you want to be too close to me, you seem to expect something of me I can't give you, I don't know, maybe it's me . . ." she left it hanging for me to fill in the gaps. I wasn't in a rush to speak.

Eventually I just gave it to her straight. "Mel it's not you, I do like you a lot. We've been friends since we both got here and I do sometimes feel close to you and I thought—think," I corrected, "you feel that too . . . sometimes anyway, when you can actually bear to relax. Which is not often enough if you ask me. I've never asked you for anything or put any pressure on you to do anything you don't want to have I?" It was a rhetorical question; I wasn't ready to stop. I was tired, not up for the situation and handling it badly but I was on a roll. "Sometimes I look at you and it really puzzles me that you never let anyone close to you. It's what you need to stop you being such a closed book. That's what I believe, and if I've given it away by my actions or words somehow that I think it should be me you get close to, God knows it wasn't deliberate. If you want me to apologise for it, then fine. I apologise."

"Matt, I think you'd better go," she said quietly. No tears yet but they were close. My anger completely dissipated—hadn't I just been trying to cover up the depth of my true feelings all along?

"Mel, I don't want to go, not now, not knowing I've upset you." Without thinking I took her hand in mine for the first time and looked through my own teary eyes into hers, wondering what I should do next.

I didn't have to think for long. Mel leant closer to me than ever and offered her cold lips to mine. A week ago I'd have been in heaven but as I kissed her back I realised I'd been articulating something I no longer felt. Absurdly, I suddenly had the feeling I wanted to keep myself for Liv. Another part of me—the part that always wins in a man—wouldn't even let me consider not kissing Mel having wanted it for so long. I pulled her to me and gently squeezed her in a way that most of the women I'd been with before had all more or less appreciated. I'd never been to bed with a girl so soon after a first kiss, still less one I'd recently stopped being attracted to. I was so oddly detached throughout, knowing this was going to be our first and last time together, that there was never a danger of it being over quickly. By the end I thought I might have to fake it the way I guess she may have done already.

When it was over, no declarations of love followed, Mel reached for a glass of water, we lay down and I held her as long and as tenderly as I could until I fell asleep.

The room was dark, I could see through a crack at the top of the curtains that it was dark outside too. Mel was asleep beside me, snoring softly, facing the wall, as far from me as the single bed would allow. I could hear muffled conversation and then laughter from the kitchen; although Mel didn't get on well with her flatmates they all got on with each other pretty well. I needed the toilet but I needed not to see Mel's flatmates even more, for her sake as well as mine. I rolled over and went back to sleep. Back to a dream I hadn't remembered when I awoke.

. . . I'm thirteen, it's night and it's the middle of January. The garden is freshly covered in snow and I have turned off all the lights behind me so I can see into it without the lights reflecting in the window. At the bottom of the garden the bushes are quivering from time to time as if disturbed by something deep within them—or behind them. I think I see one then another dark shape come shooting out and over to the other side of the garden, then nothing. I'm excited and I can even feel myself smiling with the fun of it all. I keep staring deep into the darkness at the end of the garden desperately looking, hoping for some more movement. From the side of the house the huge black shape of a man appears suddenly, shockingly at the window, inches from me, only the glass of the door between us. I know he wants to do me harm and it hits me that I am alone in the house. I curse myself for turning off the lights and thereby somehow making it inevitable that he came for me. I bolt, tearing at breakneck speed through the hall towards the front door hopelessly aware that my legs feel heavier and weaker with every stride—the front door gets no closer. Behind me the terrible smashing of the glass in the backdoor, the handle being turned, the door scraping against its frame as it is ripped open. I know I'll never make the front door, I collapse and bury my head in fear as I hear him step in from outside into the house where I should have been safe . . .

A grunt and a kick from Mel woke me, so close to hurting my recovering knee I felt seriously like hitting her back. I was quickly embarrassed as I saw her naked and hunched form lit only by a sliver of moonlight that cut through the top of the curtains. I had most of the duvet—in a pose that had become familiar since my dreams had started, I had much of it balled in my fists and clasped tightly under my chin. It transpired this had all happened in a flash and the shock of it had woken Mel with a start. I'd earnt the kick because she thought at first I had done it deliberately to wake her up.

"Sorry, bad dream," I said thinly.

"Yeah, you look like it," she said, less than brimful of sympathy. "You'd better go I think."

"Mmm, what's the time?" She just pointed at the clock four inches away but behind me. It was ten twenty. "You free Sunday if I pop round—I'm off to the football tomorrow?" I asked her.

"My parents are coming Sunday, better make it next week—Monday or Tuesday."

"No problem, I'll give you a shout—if you're free Sunday evening though, give me a knock, yeah?" I was trying to sound breezy without giving the impression I was desperate to get out of there. Somehow I knew she was regretting it already.

I finished pulling on my clothes. She watched me so we were both occupied. I concentrated on putting on my shoes like I was Richard Reid. Before I left I kissed Mel once on the lips and once on the forehead. I held my crutches in my hand trying to be quiet and speedy. The tiny waves we exchanged at the door could have signified anything—anything at the time and anything for the future. I hadn't got a clue.

Having snuck out of the flat like an invalid cat burglar I thought I'd give Kenny a knock on my way past his front door. He didn't answer the door himself but his flatmate Jon knocked on his door for me and decided to join us for a three way conversation for twenty minutes—thanks mate, exactly what I didn't want.

Eventually he went and Kenny asked me how I was.

"Just shagged Mel," I said. Simple as that. As crass as that. I knew I wouldn't be sleeping with her again so perhaps I was simply trying to put some emotional distance between us.

"Really? That's good isn't it?" Kenny asked, seeing something in my face that confused him. "It's not good?"

"As it turns out I don't think it is particularly good, no." I wasn't seeing a whole lot of understanding on Kenny's face so I launched into the unabridged version.

"She started off having a go at me; fancying her, putting pressure on her to be more than friends blah blah blah. Next thing we're getting on with the whole dirty business. It wasn't much fun to be honest, I just couldn't get up for it."

"You couldn't get it up?" Kenny shrieked loud enough for the whole building to hear.

"No, I didn't mean that you twat, I just meant I wasn't *particularly* up for doing a good job—she still came three times. I don't know what was going on in her head but it wasn't love."

"Maybe it will get better now you've got the first time out of the way?"

I realised I was talking to a rank amateur who was giving me an approximation of what he thought were the right things. It struck me he was probably a virgin.

"To top it off I'm supposed to seeing Liv tomorrow for the football; Birmingham—Palace."

"Should be a good match—City have got a couple of ex-Tottenham youth players." Kenny back on more familiar ground.

"Yeah, but now I feel I've fucked up my chances with Liv. I didn't leave Mel's in a happy state. All that time spent chasing after Mel and I finally get to brandish my poker just as the fire's gone out." I smiled at this impromptu if imperfect metaphor.

"There's no pressure with Liv though is there? I mean this is the first time you'll have seen her for a date. Is it even a date?"

"On my side I'm counting it, for her who knows? I just wanted it to be an easy, relaxed day so she could see what a happy, carefree all round good egg I am. Now I'm going to have this shit hanging over my head. I could kill Mel for this." Even as I said it, I wondered why I was trying to blame Mel for any of this.

"You'll be fine. If anything you can go out Saturday knowing Mel's not the girl for you—that's got to be good hasn't it?"

Perhaps he had something there. "Fair point, shall we crack open that bottle of Galliano you've had sitting on your shelf since November?" I said with a hollow grin.

A couple of hours later I rolled out of Kenny's and headed back to my room a little or lot the worse for wear I couldn't tell.

All I wanted was for this sourest of days to be over. I was dead on my feet as I trudged back to my room, but somewhere between brushing my teeth and getting into bed I became wide-awake and stary eyed. What I'd done with Mel had been a mistake and I couldn't figure out why. I wondered if we'd be able to get past it and stay friends. I had a sick feeling in the pit of my stomach because I'd probably lost that too.

"Fuck!" I said aloud to make me feel better. I don't know why I thought it might help. It didn't.

I began to think about the nightmares I'd been having recently—only two or three but it was the first time I could remember having them since I'd been a little kid and spent too long engrossed in my sister's Encyclopaedia of monsters. I was too scared to look alone at the page with the black and white drawing of the vampire on it but ever so thrilled when I did. Aside from the blood dripping from his fangs, he was the spitting image of Patrick MacNee. In my dream he'd come out of the wardrobe in my bedroom at the head of a whole troupe of ghosts and ghouls. He was the only one who scared me. Nothing happened in the dream apart from that that I could ever remember.

My nightmares now were obviously stress related; the slow and painful recovery from my operation had taken more out of me than had been immediately apparent.

I thought about Liv for a while too and how it'd be when we met up at the station. Already I wanted her to be the girl I'd be with for the rest of my life, just as I'd wanted Mel to be a few short days ago. In the short term I just wanted the date to be a laugh, for her to think I was funny, easy going and in great shape considering my injury. I wasn't billing myself as the trophy boyfriend so I had to work with what I had; listening skills and an unstinting keenness to impress.

I turned on my side and drifted sadly to sleep.

Saturday, 5th February

I awoke from a long and deep sleep to the ringing of my mobile; my room bathed in bright sunlight. I struggled pathetically to free it from my jeans pocket and answered it without looking at the caller identity.

"Morning."

Why is she shouting so loud? I asked myself.

"Did I wake you up?" Liv sounded confused, maybe even put out.

She's the one ringing me up at some ungodly hour, I should be the one sounding put out, I thought.

"Yeah, you did as it goes," I said, trying to sound anything but put out. I wanted her to know she could call me *anytime*. "What time is it?" I stifled a yawn.

"About quarter past twelve, will you make it ok for one o'clock?" Now she sounded really put out.

"Fuck, quarter past twelve?" I shrieked, leaping out of bed not catching myself before my knee exploded in pain as I put my foot hard on the floor. "My alarm must have not gone off. Fuck. Sorry. Of course I'll make it, the cab's booked for twelve forty five, I guess I'll just have to skip breakfast," *and beg the cab company to send me someone at short notice*, I didn't add. "I'm not going to be late for my first date with the most beautiful woman in town," I said, hoping Liv would appreciate the Bukowski reference as much as the compliment. I was surprised at how easily it had slipped out.

"Cool." She was composed again thank God. "I was just ringing to see if you wanted me to bring you a scarf, I have two up here—one says Super Eagles, the other one Eric the Ninja's Super Eagles." She was even laughing now.

Panic. "Er well . . . I thought we might well be up the City end to be honest." Fuck, that sounded so weedy.

"So????" she screamed (in a nice (well, nice-*ish*) way) "All the more reason to show our support surely. Don't want to be mistaken for one of the Zulus!"

Christ, I thought, she's serious. Suicidal perhaps. And me on crutches! "Unless of course we're surrounded by them." I needed to rescue this situation fast. "No, of course bring your scarves—if it all kicks off I can always wave my crutches in the air. I'll borrow Dave's glasses too just in case." I just couldn't say no to this girl. I was setting a dangerous precedent here and I had the feeling it wouldn't be the last time.

"And I'll bring the words to Men of Harlech." It took me a few moments to realise she was overextending the Zulu metaphor.

I wanted to reply to this with an equally clever comedic reference but I just filled the conversation gap with a laugh, a grunt and then silence, the grunts not buying me enough time to come up with anything.

Eventually I replied to Liv in a pretty weak Welsh accent.

"Ok boyo."

At least she was polite enough to laugh.

"Cool, see you at the station then, there's a train at twenty past one."

"Yep, see you then."

I closed my eyes thinking of all the things I might have said better, funnier or faster. This seemed to give me a lot to think about. Still, I consoled myself; I can't have completely blown it yet.

I rang for a cab and picked up my smartest shower gel; a 30 ml bottle of Paco Rabanne XS, part of a set Hannah had got me for Christmas a couple of years before. I was seriously pushed for time and the last thing I needed was Colin taking a shower and singing like a cunt in there; one of his rugby songs would you believe? Probably because he only owned about three CDs if you discounted the free compilation rubbish he always saved from the Mail on Sunday.

I hadn't got time to hang around so I stuck some boxers on and went across the hall to Mike's flat to see if his shower was free. It was freezing outside and Mike took an age to open the door. He was in the middle of getting ready for football and looked puzzled to see me standing there in nothing but my boxers and holding a towel. I could tell he was itching to hear what my predicament was.

"Alright lad?" he said in his grating Barnsley accent.

"Colin's in our shower and I have a cab booked for about twenty minutes time, any chance I can borrow yours?"

"You not coming to watch the game again? I don't know, I thought you'd be back playing by now. They don't make 'em so hard down south duthee?"

Despite the cold, my semi-naked state and my obvious hurry he wanted to make me sweat; and what choice did I have but to sweat obligingly for him and give him some banter?

"I can't imagine many northerners going in for the sort of tackles I go in for to be honest. There's no-one in there at the moment is there?"

"What, you mean two footed knee high lunges when the ball's been gone five minutes?"

It occurred to me he'd have made a good policeman; good at extracting confessions from innocent men anyway.

"Mike, he was asking for it. He'd made you look silly a couple of times and it got to me. Good luck today, probably see you tonight." I went to push past him.

"You needn't have retired yourself from football on my account." I don't think he meant it but it seemed a pretty tactless thing to say to me. Perhaps seeing the look on my face made him soften. "I don't know if there'll be much hot water left, where are you off to anyway?"

"Off to watch Birmingham-Palace with a girl from my course."

"I think Dave mentioned something the other day—sounded like she was out of your league!"

"Well you can rest easy, it's not that kind of date. We're just friends and yes, I'm afraid she's well out of my league."

"I'm not saying a word, hope it goes well anyway."

"Cheers mate, good luck to you too," I said as I made the bathroom at last and closed the door.

The shower was stone cold. It wasn't too bad working up a lather in my hand and spreading on my shivering body but I had no choice but to stand right underneath to rinse the soap off and then wash my hair. Cold water never seems to get you as clean as hot water. I made a mental note to ask Dave if there was any reason for this. I was just patting myself dry when Mike banged on the door and shouted that he'd heard the game might be off and to make sure I closed the door behind me. I deliberately shouted a muffled grunt into my towel by way of reply, why would I care if his game's off when I had a lovely lady to impress? I felt pretty good about myself as I stole across the hall back into the warmth and safety of my own flat. I realised as I got through the door to the flat that I'd been lucky no one had since left and locked the door behind them. I'd once got into big trouble with Colin for not locking the door when a tramp had got into the flat and shut himself in the bathroom—I made another mental note to tell the full (i.e. unrecognisably embellished) story to Liv later on. I hoped it would make me seem slightly anarchic, a little dangerous and generally at the centre of all sorts of crazy goings on. On reflection this seemed unlikely with a girl who had been expelled from private school.

I had about three minutes to get ready. Once the XS talc had been liberally applied to toes, body and undercarriage, followed by same branded deodorant and after-shave I'd used up two of my three minutes. Best socks and boxers out of the drawer, my combats already chosen, I just had to select my winningest top. It was plain and blue and suited me in a casual, non-fussy way and was expensive although no one would ever guess. I played around with my hair, messing it up the way I liked it. The cabbie buzzed a few minutes later and I was finally on my overexcited way.

We got to the station just before one fifteen and, as I paid for the cab, I noticed my flies were undone. I thanked my lucky stars I'd sidestepped that particular schoolboy error on my first date.

I looked for Liv but she wasn't outside the station so I went inside to see if she was thawing out in there. As I walked in, she was just turning away from the ticket desk and putting something into her black clutch bag. She looked up, her mouth forming that 'o' shape last seen sported by the cartoon Penelope Pitstop. I got a headrush when I saw how amazing she looked, hair tied back, a single lock falling over the left side of her face. She wore blue-black pinstriped trousers with a short brown corduroy jacket over a powder blue v-neck cashmere top. To finish (me) off she had on black stiletto heeled boots. I couldn't see how she'd possibly be warm enough but I guessed the thirty foot Super Eagles scarf wrapped fifteen times around her neck would help. Trinny and Susannah would have objected I'm sure; at least until they saw how completely it rammed home that this girl looked perfect. I tried to think of someone she reminded me of but there was no one.

"Hi, I got you a ticket." She beamed at me.

"Oh nice one, how much do I owe you?" Liv gave me a coy look as if to say I'd asked a silly question—I knew it was only a couple of quid but you never knew with students, Colin had once collected eleven pence off each of us after buying some completely unusable Tesco Value toilet roll. "Thank you," I added self consciously, "Which platform is it?"

"Number one, over the other side. I think the train's actually coming now," Liv said, handing me the ticket. I tried to think of some conversation but Liv beat me to it as we walked over the footbridge to platform one, our train already approaching.

"Where did you find your ninja card?"

"Just in the stationers on campus, they seemed to have millions of different ones."

"Did you go out last night?" Liv asked me.

"No, I went shopping in the afternoon in town and fell asleep for about three hours when I got in. By the time I woke up, everyone was out. I couldn't be bothered to go and meet them on my own so I just went over to my mate's flat for a while as he was in. What about you?"

There was a break in the conversation as we boarded the train and took seats opposite one another.

"Not so much, I opened a bottle of wine, listened to some music and did some work . . . exciting huh?"

I would have been happy with hearing anything other than she'd been up all night having Olympic standard sex with her boyfriend and it felt great to hear she'd been home alone. "No, not at all, it sounds pretty similar to my evening—apart from the work!" I joked.

"Everyone seemed to be lining up a massive night out last night and I just wasn't up for it, and I didn't want to force it, you know?"

"How about tonight?" I asked, ready to change my plans in an instant, hoping I'd have the chance. Maybe she read my mind.

"The girls on my floor are heading into town for a session—it's my flatmate Elma's birthday."

"Sounds like fun," I said, and worried in case that had sounded sarcastic, immediately added, "Late one d'you think?"

"Could be, once Mya starts she's pretty hard to pry away from the bar."

"And Mya is . . .?"

"Just one of my flatmates, does Sports Science, always up for a night out, different guy every Saturday night. You know the type, maybe you even know her, she's been around."

Christ, I hoped that wasn't a flat standard and I wondered why she'd even joked about me maybe having shagged her flatmate, surely Liv wasn't suggesting I was a tart.

"Broad Street or in town?"

"Broad Street I think, we usually end up at Bakers on a Saturday night."

"Smart, we had a night there one Saturday after football, the music's good. Not really ideal for the football team as we all had to go in pairs so they wouldn't think all eight of us were together. All got very messy once we'd made it in."

"One of the UCE rugby teams tried the same thing at Dino's in town apparently and the bouncers realised straight away, let them straight through the main door then directed them into a courtyard out back. About ten of these students ended up in this yard, realised they'd been had and thought it was hilarious until eight bouncers came crashing through the door and set on them with metal bars, hammers and chair legs—one of the guys is still in St Giles."

This little anecdote changed the tone somewhat. I'd read about the incident and I seem to remember Dave and I had just laughed because they were rugby players.

"Bloody egg chasers—does anyone really care?" I said, restoring the mood with some gentle humour.

She looked at me as if I'd just shot her Beagle. My stomach turned over as it dawned on me I'd said the wrong thing.

"If he ever regains consciousness I'll let my brother know how much his plight has touched everyone. They feed him through a tube, he may never speak or walk again." She said it ever so quietly, cold black eyes boring holes in my skull.

"Jesus I'm sorry . . . I can't believe I . . ."

I stopped talking. She was practically wetting herself, and was thumping my knee with her fist.

"I'm sorry, that was a terrible thing to do." I noticed she didn't look very sorry. "*You* believed I had a brother who'd play rugby, I should feel insulted."

I felt like I'd just been run over but I squeezed out a weak laugh. As it was I had to admit she had done me up like the proverbial kipper.

"Fuck, that was impressive. You're just a girl too, I wasn't expecting any attempt at humour—even one so weak," I said. One poor guy, whoever he was, still being fed by tubes, no longer able to register a single human emotion, the scar from a sheared radiator pipe that had been stabbed through his spinal column barely begun to heal, now forgotten, an ice breaker for a first date if you will, a footnote in our embryonic relationship—his purpose in life served. "I can see I'll have to be on my toes." Eventually some of the redness started, unhurriedly, to leave my cheeks.

We had to change trains in town to get to Adderley Park, the nearest station to the ground and it was just after two o'clock when we got up to get off the train. Liv had been totally engaging; a lot more open and relaxed than I'd seen her before and secretly, I'd much rather have stayed on the train getting to know her than go to the football. I think we'd both been so engrossed we hadn't taken much notice that the train was barely a third full until we saw the notices all over the station saying that due to the frozen pitch and failure of the undersoil heating the match had been called off.

"Fuck it," I said resignedly. We could have just stayed on the train after all; I thought of Mike shouting through the bathroom door. A few people in the station were venting similar emotions, almost exclusively in thick Brummie accents. Instinctively I touched the scarf Liv had leant me but I couldn't take it off then without looking feeble.

"What d'you wanna do?" I asked Liv.

"I have an essay on Franco to finish, I might as well go back and do that." Liv sounded pretty definite. I'd been run over again and she must have seen it. "Hey, I was only joking, why don't we get a couple of bottles of wine, go back to mine and chill out?"

It was far from the most unwelcome suggestion I'd ever heard.

"Liv, I never know if you're being serious. I can't really expect to compete with the lure of General Franco and I don't want to be the reason you fail your first year," I said, attempting coy; I was blushing but it didn't seem to matter.

Liv smiled warmly at me, "I'm open to suggestions," she said.

"I liked yours—shall we just see if we can get a cab, some of the natives look a bit hungry round here?" Even as I said that I caught the eye of a tattooed bruiser who was showing too much interest in Liv and me.

"Yeah, I've had enough of trains, there should be some numbers on the board over there."

I knew the numbers of about three cab companies off by heart but it seemed ungallant to ignore Liv's suggestion.

"Good thinking."

After fifteen furtive minutes hanging around in the comparative warmth of the station and, in truth, nothing more than a few casual glances from some of the City fans our minicab arrived—the usual ageing Nissan—and we got in.

"Weer ya gowin' to mate?" the driver asked in a thick accent, without turning round.

"Garforth Close, on the Bristol Road towards Northfield," Liv jumped in curtly, it seemed making no effort to sound polite.

I felt a lot better once we were away from the local fans who seemed to be milling about at the station unsure as to what to do next. I was anything but unsure as I marvelled at the ease with which Liv had suggested going back to her room; probably a sign she had no thought whatsoever that it could be for anything more than an innocent chat. Then again she'd also suggested getting a couple of bottles of wine; perhaps I was on the money.

"'Scuse mate, can we stop at an offie somewhere on the way back? Cheers."

All I got back was an unintelligible grunt from the driver but five minutes later we pulled into a horrendous looking housing estate, all tower blocks and dark, dingy connecting walkways, with a less than charming cluster of shops. Liv went to get wine from a steel-fronted off licence with tighter security than the Ministry of Sound. She'd insisted on going in and I hardly protested since I didn't particularly want to leave her alone with our monosyllabic cab driver. I don't know that it's possible to look monosyllabic but if you were looking for a precedent then this guy set it in spades.

I watched Liv's wasp-like waist and spike heeled boots until she disappeared through the off licence door, clearly confident despite her obvious incongruousness with the surroundings. I suddenly wished I'd gone with her, crutches or no crutches, even those twenty five yards could be dangerous for her where we were. When she disappeared inside I realised I'd been holding my breath.

"Noice 'ere innit?" The driver was leering at me in the rear-view mirror.

"Not quite like home mate," I replied, deliberately exaggerating my south London accent in an attempt to establish some credibility with a man who seemed to be testing me somehow.

"Where's that then mate?"

"South London, found out too late the match was off today," I said, pointing at my scarf.

"Get the fook outta my cab you stewdent cunt."

And with those few simple, charmless words my afternoon took a somewhat different turn.

My stomach turned, I had about a quarter of a second to decide what to do. Answer? Try to buy more time.

"Yeah?" I said trying to combine a degree of menace with more than a hint of probable compliance if that was the end of it.

"Get outta my fooking car," he screamed, throwing open his door.

"I'm getting out, take it easy," I shouted, as he ripped my door open and started to manhandle me out of the car. I tried to hold on in the car in an attempt to control my exit and save damaging my leg. He leant right into my face and as he screamed obscenities through alcohol breath, I saw he had been one of the guys who had been taking an interest in us at the station. He must have overheard me book the cab or talking about it. He filled the back door opening entirely and was as much trying to hit me as get me out as I backed as far as I could towards the other door totally unsure how the hell I was going to stop this fucker doing whatever he wanted to me if he ever got me outside. He snatched one of my crutches and jabbed it into my face, catching me just above the eye, adrenaline not allowing me to gauge how hard. He threw the crutch behind him out of the car.

"You ain't gettin' very far now are ya, cunt?" He punctuated the last word perfectly by smashing my face with his fist and hit me twice more hard before I had time to cover up at all. I felt so weak as he backed away to give himself room to pull me out of the cab by my injured leg. When he'd got my leg braced on the bottom of the doorframe he left it there ready to destroy it by smashing the door itself into it. He had the door in both hands and, seeing that I couldn't even resist enough to move my leg at all, gave himself time to pass on one last piece of joy.

"Your girl's gonna get the fucking of her life from fucking six of the Blues finest. Might let her stay all weekend if she's any good."

And then he did a curious thing. He took his hands off the door and let them fall limp at his side before swaying forward and rolling his eyes back in his head. Then his knees appeared to give way under him and he collapsed at the side of the car.

As he was prostrate on the floor, consciousness the vaguest of realities, Liv hit him twice more flush on the side of the jaw with the bottle she held in her left hand. Given that it hadn't broken I knew it wasn't red wine the guy was drowning in, and there looked to be much more than 750cl of claret anyway. I was on the point of being sick but thankfully Liv seemed to be staying amazingly calm and she merely put the wine back into one of her bags, which she then placed next to me in the car. She lifted my legs very gently back into the well behind the passenger seat, while I flopped gratefully across the other seats. She then retrieved my crutches and laid them next to me.

She leant right into the car the way the cabbie had and when she asked me if I was ok, I thought she must be an angel. I fell completely in love with her there and then. I mumbled something and closed my eyes, trying to nod slowly.

I listened as Liv closed the back door and then got in the driver's seat and started the car.

"We'll go somewhere towards home, park and get a black cab the rest of the way," she said, exuding calm. "Can you wind your window down a bit, your mouth's bleeding?"

Not wanting to open my eyes, I groped for the handle and after struggling for a few seconds the stiffness of the mechanism started to yield and I felt a stiff and unpleasant breeze hit my face. Everything was pain, sheer white-hot pain but at least I knew I was alive. Even with my eyes closed I could tell Liv was driving incredibly fast.

"He was in the station when we arrived, talking to a couple of other guys who he met off the train after us." She sounded so matter-of-fact.

"What the fuck did he hit me with?" I kind of knew the answer, hoped Liv might not.

"Just his fist I think babe."

I don't know if she knew it, it's not impossible that she did, but hearing her call me babe would have been worth another ten rounds with that bastard. That bastard who might be dead by now, I thought. I didn't care. Consequences I could consider later. I opened my eyes, there were consequences to that too. Whiter, hotter pain and spots in front of my eyes but at least I could see bits of the back of Liv's head. I closed my eyes again, happy to let her stay in charge, it felt safe that way, cool headed murderess and car thief that she was.

I slept or passed out for a few minutes and only woke when the car pulled in somewhere and stopped. We were in the car park of the Hibernian pub on the Pershore Road. Liv, still so calm and soothing, helped me out of the car and onto my crutches where I felt as unsteady as the first day I'd used them. A day later I'd had to be helped by my mum and dad to their car for the drive home, a couple of nurses telling them I'd been 'a very good patient.' Was that really just a few short weeks ago? It seemed a lifetime away.

Liv was peering at my face intently, wiping away some dried blood around my cheek, mouth and eyes. It hurt like hell but I knew that she was doing it so our next cab driver might take less of an interest in us.

"You look fine now, we'll walk back towards town and get a cab if you can manage it. Wait one second while I get the shopping."

As we set off along the road the traffic was steady enough but there were no free cabs for Liv to flag down. She walked on ahead as I shuffled along unsteadily, trying to make sense of it all in between the pulsing pains in my face. I just wanted to be somewhere safe and warm where I could talk it over with Liv. It already seemed totally unreal and I was having difficulty rationalising it at all.

I hadn't got more than two hundred yards before I needed to sit down. I knew it would be much better to get a black cab rather than ring for one but I didn't know how much further I could walk. Neither of us had mentioned going to the police and something about Liv's absolute calm told me she wasn't going to suggest it. A black cab dropping us off on the main road would be far less traceable.

There was a bench up ahead and I called out to Liv to say I needed to rest. She came back down the road to me and the expression on her face told me everything I needed to know about how I looked. She shepherded me over to the bench and a wave of nausea swept over me and I threw up violently all over the bench, losing one of my crutches as I thrust an arm across Liv a split second before to hold her back. I kept retching and emptied the rest of my guts over the floor around the bench and I felt Liv's hand rubbing me gently in the middle of back.

"You poor thing. Wait here for a couple for minutes and I'll either get a black cab or call for one from a phone box."

I spat out what was left in my mouth and stood up, determined to pull myself together.

"Can you grab my crutch? Let's move on, I feel a bit better for that." Which in truth, I did. "I'm really sorry for this."

"Babe, none of this is down to you, don't apologise. It feels awful now but we'll be back home soon and you'll feel ten times better."

Somewhere just below 'totally fucked' then, I thought. But how I loved hearing her say the word babe again! I couldn't believe how kind she was being.

"Fuck this, I'll just use his mobile," she said. "How quickly can you get to the Pershore Road, just down the road from the Hib? Oh, never mind. Forget it." As she spoke, heaven sent a black cab complete with yellow light, around the corner towards us. Liv hung up, stuck her hand in the air and waved it down. "You still ok to come back to mine?" she asked.

"God yeah. I mean, yes, yes, if it's no bother to you, I'm not exactly showing you the time of your life. I promise not to be sick again." I said, laying it on far too thick.

Just a few minutes later we pulled up outside Liv's flat. Liv paid for the cab as I got my crutches sorted. We hadn't said a single word to each other in the cab, I was simply concentrating on not throwing up, Liv had taken my hand in both of hers while she engaged the driver in some small talk. Out of the cab we stood together and watched it drive away before she led me to her front door. Just before we went in she asked me again if I was ok. She said it in the sort of tone that suggested she was concerned about more than just my cuts and bruises, I guess she meant was I ok sharing this whole experience, letting her take full charge and being an accessory to whatever it was she'd done? My mind was fucked but that was more just the amount of shit that had gone down and as for what Liv had done, from start to finish she'd been a lifesaver. Anyway I was head over heels in love, and who thinks straight when that happens?

"I'm fine I think. A bit shaken up, a bit sad more than anything else that the day's turned out like this."

"Hey, it's not over yet. And anyway, aren't first dates *supposed* to be traumatic?" Liv put her hand on my back again, something that reminded me of my mum and me being young and sorry for something. The words first date nearly didn't knock me sideways. "We'll get in the warm, have some tea and forget it all. I'm in that block over there," she said, leading the way.

"Tea?" Liv asked me as we went through the front door and into the flat.

"Please."

I followed her into the kitchen and waited while she put the kettle on and stuck a teabag in each of two mugs. She put her head outside the kitchen door and shouted to see if anyone else was in. No answer.

Thank fuck for that.

Once the tea was made Liv found two glasses and set them on a tray with the tea. She then took some biscuits from another cupboard, the third one she'd checked. People had been excommunicated for less in my flat. She handed me some frozen peas for my face.

"Should we put the wine in the fridge?" I asked.

"It's red," Liv said quickly. "D'you wanna grab my keys and I'll follow you with the tray? Mine's the last door on the left."

In spite of everything, I still felt the same twinge of excitement you'd expect as I was opening the door to Liv's room wondering what it would be like. It was smallish, about twelve feet by ten feet, with a low single bed next to the window along the far wall. On the writing desk were a neat silver iPod I-Dock, a couple of unmarked files and a single fountain pen she didn't use in lectures. The desk chair was pushed under the desk and there was another brown leather low-slung armchair, which looked a good deal nicer than the cheap, ancient easy chair I had. On the wall Liv had hung an abstract watercolour—pretty much a mess of oranges, reds, yellows and odd black shapes, which I couldn't make any sense of. I was no art critic but I knew I didn't enjoy looking at it. Once you were in the room you could see there was some space behind the door, which was filled by a grand ageing, dark wood wardrobe, which again contrasted sharply with the plywood MFI jobs we had to put up with at Swafforth. It didn't have the feel of a student room and I supposed Liv had brought some of the furnishings with her.

A clock on the desk said it was just past three and I remembered numbly where we were supposed to be. I paused, waiting for Liv to direct me where to sit.

"D'you want to sit on the bed? Can you manage to get down, it's quite low?"

"Yeah, I should be ok." I eased myself down at one end of the bed, put my crutches against the wall and pressed the peas onto my swollen face.

Liv set the tray on the floor and put my tea next to me on a small square of free desk. Then she opened the wine, "Letting it breathe," she said and pulled the leather chair towards the bed and set her tea down next to it. Hardly had she sat down when she jumped up to put on some music.

"Something mellow I think . . . old or new?"

She put on The Smiths before I could answer.

"Hatful of Hollow—their best album," I said rather self-consciously. In the last few moments I'd begun to perceive just the slightest hint of awkwardness between us. I hoped she wasn't regretting having asked me back.

"Well, it's pretty mellow isn't it?" Rhetorical question.

"Liv, I feel pretty shell shocked. I think it's been the most bizarre and frightening experience of my life and I don't know if we should talk about it, laugh about it, forget it or tell the police all about it." Well, that was a good way to ease the tension I thought.

"Was it that bizarre? Just some football thug seeing the opportunity to pick on a couple of easy targets and getting unlucky."

"You mean when we clubbed him half to death and stole his car?" I wasn't sure if she was in shock or just thought I was a fool for making such a big deal out of it.

"*I* clubbed him half to death and stole his car you mean. And his mobile—I picked it up when I went back for the shopping," she laughed.

I wasn't sure what to say; now I thought she might be a kleptomaniac too.

"I can't believe how calm you are, I feel totally . . . emotional I guess, for want of a better word."

"I've always been calm—it's a gift." Understatement was clearly another one. She changed tack. "Look, I wanted you to come back with me so we could chill out, make the day seem like it actually turned out ok. I think you got the worst of it; I just reacted out of instinct when I saw what he was doing to you. Let's finish our tea and start on the wine, you need to relax."

"I think you're right." Well, she was. "I just feel . . . emotional—for want of a better word," I laughed.

"He wasn't moving at all when we left him."

Why the fuck had she just said that after telling me to relax? I ignored it and reached for my tea.

"Nice tea," I said lamely.

"Caroline's. She'll only drink Yorkshire tea. I'll tell her you were complimentary."

We sat in silence for a couple of minutes; I was trying to clear my head of thoughts of Mel all of a sudden.

"This feels weird doesn't it?" Liv asked, and then answering herself, added, "You're the first person I've had in my room since I arrived apart from the girls."

It reminded me of the nurse in 'An American Werewolf in London', when she invites the clearly troubled American patient back to stay after his release from hospital. Liv was every bit as attractive as Jenny Agutter and every bit as charming and I felt thrilled by what she'd just said. So what if it was a little awkward, she wanted me here.

"Really?" I was glowing, but something inside was wondering why it was weird to have a guy in your room for a cup of tea but smashing a psychopathic stranger over the head (with the bottle of wine we were about to share) before stealing his car was hardly worthy of comment.

"To tell you the truth I'm not a terribly social person. I go out with some of the girls here if there's a bit of a crowd I can lose myself in, you know? Dance, drink, whatever."

"No, I understand, I'm fine with people I know but I'm not really a natural mixer either. I was dreading coming here, but I got lucky with my flatmates—only three of the four are complete weirdos." It wasn't the funniest thing I'd ever said but we both needed a laugh and it succeeded in relieving the tension.

"How's your head?"

"Better for sitting down for a while—and the tea of course."

"Ready for some wine?"

"Sure, should just take care of whatever pain's left."

She poured two generous measures of the wine and when she brought mine over she stayed and took the space next to me on the bed. The world outside might as well have stopped for the next couple of hours; it felt like I was acquiring a new best friend. More than that, like all best friends of the opposite sex, I fell completely in love with her. Every time we got to the bottom of our glasses and Liv got up to get more wine or change the music my breathing shallowed until she sat back down next to me. Every time she came back she seemed to fit just a little more snugly next to me and at times she'd hold my hand or rest her head on my shoulder. When she did this I breathed in slowly, deeply and silently, my nose as close to her soft, dark hair as I dared. I knew there'd come a time when this wouldn't be enough and I'd need to kiss her and hold her, want her naked flesh next to mine but it wasn't today; it was perfect already. And here and there we drifted into the softest of dozes.

My eyes were closed when she asked me, "What would you have done when that guy started hitting you if your leg hadn't been like that?"

She was fond of asking testing questions. "I don't suppose he'd have bothered with us if we hadn't looked like such easy targets."

"How did it start? When I came out of the shop I didn't have a clue what was going on."

"I don't know . . . we were talking and he just suddenly shouts, *"Get out of my fucking cab you student . . ."* Well, the next word rhymes with 'bunt'. Then, ten seconds later he just lost it. It doesn't seem real at all, I just feel like I'm hung-over, not like I nearly got killed. When you got back he was just about to smash my leg in the car door . . ."

"Hey, don't cry," Liv said, wiping my cheek with the back of her hand. "It's over, I wouldn't have let him hurt you."

I snapped back into my surroundings as if out of a dream, I was crying, really crying, without even knowing it and Liv's hands were holding both of mine, her warm lips now kissing my wet cheeks like my mother might have done when I was her three-year-old soldier with freshly grazed hands and knees.

"Sorry, it must be concussion or something, I'm not always such a flake. You know, your timing was pretty impeccable."

"Depends if you're an Eagle or a Zulu I guess," she laughed.

I thought about kissing her but again it wasn't the right time. I felt shaky and I didn't want to appear quite so pathetic when I went to kiss her the first time.

"You ok then?" she asked, brushing away my hair from my eye and no longer holding my hand. The intimacy receded a level. I was happy with that, I didn't want to rush anything just because I could get away with it after such a day. It felt as if I'd be here again and the longer it took me to get to know Liv the more there'd be to enjoy.

Liv backed away and sat at a right angle to me with her feet up on the bed, her light blue socks not more than half an inch from my thigh.

"Are you a Jack White fan?" Liv asked as she searched for some new music.

I thought of some CDs I'd had in my collection for years and never bothered getting into. The very fact I even had CDs made me feel old fashioned.

We talked for another couple of hours, changed positions now and again, never getting back the really intimate moments but she was great company. We demolished the second bottle of wine and even though Liv probably had sixty per cent of it I was feeling pretty tipsy. When it got dark Liv drew the curtains, put on a lamp and lit some unscented candles giving the room a cosiness that exaggerated the effects of the wine. I could have stayed forever.

Liv told me some stuff about her childhood. She'd grown up in Dulwich, where her parents still had a house they hardly used. She was an only child but had a friend, Katy, who had lived with her family from the age of six when her own parents had been killed—she didn't say how and I didn't ask. They'd attended Roedean together and Katy had achieved similar academic results to Liv. Katy had gone to Oxford to study Theology and

Philosophy while Liv had chosen Birmingham for reasons she didn't make clear. She never mentioned boyfriends and I wasn't going to probe but she seemed happy to talk about anything I did ask her. She felt she'd probably have been happier in her own flat rather than shared accommodation as she missed her piano. The only chance she got to play while she was at uni was at a local restaurant where they let her play downstairs if they were quiet during the day; she said she liked to play alone. When I suggested she might have got lonely living on her own she raised a serious eyebrow. The only times she seemed slightly evasive were when I asked her about her parents—she didn't seem too fussed about whether or not they'd come up to see her in Birmingham and I guessed they weren't ever so close.

She was a lot more interested in my parents though and I was happy to share any and every bit of information I could recall. I hadn't exactly been Borstal material but my teenage years were not likely to have been my dad's happiest times as I was generally petulant, moody and in constant need of transporting about for the minimum of thanks. I was always happier talking about—rather than to—my dad. I admired him so much; even more as I got older and became better able to appreciate exactly what he'd done for me, but I couldn't find any way to demonstrate this when he was about. Talking about him in honest and glowing terms seemed to at least be saying some sort of thank you. That afternoon I probably had more reason than ever to be grateful to my dad as I'd inherited or learnt his gift for story telling, effortlessly (or so it felt) intertwining half truths with fantastical myths to paint a picture of a childhood and adolescence simply littered with adventure, amusing mishaps and close shaves with everyone from the law to the local heavies. The wine helped, relaxing me and reinforcing how close I felt to Liv after just one afternoon together in her room. As I talked and time passed Liv again moved physically closer to me, sitting beside me and listening as I spoke softly about this and that. It was light but intimate and although there was nothing conscious within me trying to, I knew I was instilling in her some of the same feelings I held for her as I talked. Odd then that she somehow managed to ask me inadvertently about the one thing that more than anything else I believed had shaped my life and personality.

"Did you ever have a teacher you really hated or who really hated you?"

And because I'd been talking and I was a little drunk and it had been an emotional day and she'd probably saved my life and anyway, I didn't really feel like lying, I told her something I hadn't shared with anyone for more than half my life. It also helped that she'd rested her head on my chest, facing away from me so I could make sure she wouldn't be watching my face as I told her.

"Can I have a top up? You might want one too, this is quite a story; you'll probably regret asking me."

"No way, don't make it *too* racy will you? I don't want you stealing my thunder," Liv laughed, filling up both glasses from our second bottle. When she sat back down she put her head back in the warm spot where it had just been and I had to fight the urge to stroke her hair.

"Not sure racy is the right way to describe it, I was only eight years old. Are you sitting comfortably? Then I'll begin."

"Okay, as I said, I was eight years old and it was the day of the Christmas party. My best friend, Ally Mason, was not at school. Our teacher, Mrs Bailey—Baggy we called her—finished running through the register, closed her book and looking right at me, said, "Matthew Malone, I want to talk to you about a *very* serious matter." My stomach tightened and I felt sick, I had no idea what she meant. The whole class got up to walk to the assembly hall down the corridor. Just before I got to the door myself, Mrs Bailey took my arm roughly and yanked me out of line before almost screaming at me, in front of half my class, "You stand there and think about what you've been doing to Ally Mason to make him too scared to come to school on *Christmas Party day.*" She really shrieked the last few words and there was so much hate in her face I couldn't speak.

I stood there, alone outside the hall, watching the other classes file in, looking at me and not knowing what to make of my shell shocked, embarrassed face. Once they'd all gone I just stood and tried to make sense of what was going on. Ally had been my best friend since playschool, we were joint leaders of a gang called The Spitfires, we were the fastest runners, the best at football and the coolest kids in the class and I couldn't understand any of what was happening. Scared out of my wits, I remember singing along to every hymn and Christmas Carol that was sung in the assembly hall, I joined in with every prayer and said one or two of my own to the empty corridor.

Finally, one class at a time, kids began to leave the hall and head back to their classrooms, me shrugging my shoulders whenever an enquiring face looked in my direction. My own class went back to their classroom and were told to be quiet while Mrs Bailey came back down the corridor to speak to me. I can hardly remember anything of what she said, but she was so full of vitriol and bile that even if I had been able to form any sort of reply, I don't think it would have made any difference. I never said I didn't do it, I'm not sure she asked. The only words I can remember her saying over and over again were, "too scared to come to school on Christmas Party day." I look back now and I wonder how an adult in a position of responsibility could allow herself to show so much contempt for an eight year old, and all I can think is that if there were no consequences, I'd kill her even now if I could. Having destroyed me in private, she hauled me in front of the whole class and appealed there and then for witnesses to my "bullying" of Ally. I couldn't believe it when someone put their hand up—Orla Roberts her name was—and said she'd seen something. After some more public humiliation, to which I was pretty numb by this stage, the whole class got to enjoy the spectacle of me moving all my books and pens to a desk on its own at the front of the class. I'd switched off as much as I could of my brain by this point, something I'd get increasingly good at over the next few months. At some point during the morning, Ally joined the class and as he walked to his desk he looked at me casually as if to say, "What's up?" I couldn't read his expression at all, I thought he was the devil."

"He wasn't the devil," Liv said quietly, both interrupting me and reminding me she was there. She was sitting up now, holding my hand I think.

"That's it really, except that I didn't tell anyone about it through fear and embarrassment. I thought about nothing else for months until a few months later it was parents evening. Even then I didn't see it coming—when my mum and dad came home, the first thing I asked was whether they'd seen all my stars and gold stars for my work. God, my Grandma was even staying at the time—probably the only time she stayed with us in her life—and she'd been babysitting me. As soon as they got home, my dad said it was bath time and I was whisked upstairs. I remember sitting in the bath with them both standing there and shouting at me about the horror, embarrassment and shame. Unlike my destruction by Mrs Bailey, I cried and protested my innocence over and over again. I just kept repeating, "I swear I didn't do anything" over and over again—all for nothing. My dad said he was going to take me out of the school and, I remember clearly saying that I'd rather die than leave all my friends—an eight year old saying that! It didn't make them any less angry but it was the only thing

I said all night that got through at all and he left that subject once he'd said, "It doesn't sound like you have any friends!" I think if I hadn't been so much my dad's favourite, he probably would have carried it through. I was such a complete mess after a while that my dad turned on my brother and sister to vent his considerable anger. I don't remember a single word mum said that night."

"Can I have some more wine please?" I asked, exhausted.

"You hardly touched that one," Liv said to me, smiling sympathetically. "You didn't explain what had happened between you and Ally."

"That's just it. Nothing. Nothing at all. He'd been my best friend since playgroup and I'd never have done anything bad to him. No one ever even thought to ask me if it was true and I was always too . . . disorientated—there must be a better word—to say it for myself."

I laughed; I was still miles away in memory land. Bad memory land.

"You know you're the first person I've ever told that to. I think that probably merits an apology of some sort. I didn't mean to go on and on, I can't believe how fresh it all seems. You know, after it happened I went from being the centre of attention, really confident, playing football every night to nothing. I stopped playing football after school, stopped having friends, stopped trusting anyone and lost all my confidence for ages."

"Forget the apology. Why did you tell me? I mean, if you've never told anyone before?"

"Um . . . the wine, the day, the bang on the head . . . plus you asked about my least favourite teacher. I realise that's not quite what you had in mind. Sorry if I've . . ." I searched for the right words, ". . . dropped it all on you. Forget it, sorry. I was eight years old; it's not a big deal any more."

"Hey, of course it is, I'm sorry I asked you, I feel terrible. You poor thing, what a bitch." Liv placed her hand gently on my thigh.

"She was yes. How about you tell me about your favourite teacher now, lighten the mood a bit eh?"

"It'll have to be some other time; I should probably get ready for tonight. I think I heard Caroline and Becca come in a few minutes ago. I'll go and see," Liv said as she leapt up and out of the room, seemingly desperate to get away from me and the atmosphere I'd created.

I could have kicked myself; what had made me bring out all that on a first date? I sometimes had a tendency to get a bit too "deep and meaningful" with people before I really knew them. I sat in silence—the last track had finished some time ago—and had nothing to do but realise I needed the bathroom. I thought about hanging on and then remembered that at any moment, five girls would be descending on the bathroom to get ready for their night out. I still didn't want to go straightaway in case Liv wondered where I'd gone (like she'd care now!) so I just leant over and looked out of the window to take my mind off my throbbing bladder. I watched through the gloom as two girls struggled to get their weekly shopping from the back door of an old and battered Beetle to a block of flats opposite. Liv coming back into the room made me start.

"Taxis booked in half an hour would you believe?" As I struggled to think of a suitable reply to what I hadn't spotted was a purely rhetorical question, Liv continued, "I made sure there was space for you, we can drop you home on the way." She sounded so concerned once again.

"Cheers, not sure I'd fancy getting a cab anywhere on my own just now. Can I just quickly run to the bathroom?"

"Of course, Jo's in there at the moment. She's giving me shout when she's finished anyway."

"Cool, d'you want me to wait in the kitchen or something while you get ready?"

"No, don't worry, I'll get dressed in the bathroom," Liv replied. No chance of sneaking a cheeky look at her breasts then. As I smiled to myself I realised Liv was still holding my gaze, probably reading my thoughts.

Embarrassed, I thought honesty might be the best policy. "Sorry, I was just thinking I might accidentally catch a glimpse of naked flesh!" I raised my eyebrows and gave my most supplicate half smile.

The look I got from Liv in the split second before she sighed and went to her wardrobe was one of pity more than anything else. I couldn't tell if I'd been forgiven.

"That *was* just a joke," I offered.

"I know," Liv said, her back still to me.

The sharp rap on the door was a welcome distraction.

"I'll nip to the loo," I said with as much lightness as I could muster. "'kay"

As I got up shakily to go to the bathroom, I realised I was very drunk. I also knew I didn't want Liv to know this. In the bathroom I looked at myself in the mirror and slapped myself in the face a couple of times for the remark about Liv's naked flesh. I gulped some water from the tap and rubbed some toothpaste into my gums in a vague hope of there still being a goodbye kiss.

The second I re-entered the bedroom, Liv got up from a chair she'd pulled in front of a long mirror, set her hairbrush on the desk and picked up her clothes, leaving wordlessly for the bathroom.

I looked at myself in the mirror and wondered how long it would be before I could lose the crutches and get back to some sport. I'd put on some weight since my accident but nothing noticeable to anybody but me. I stayed looking in the mirror a long time, searching for something Liv might find attractive, irresistible even. I had big shoulders and an insolent toothy grin other people seemed to like a lot more than me. I sat unhappily on the bed and looked through Liv's iPod for something to put on. As I looked, a sharp rap on the door and a girl's voice shouting, "Five minutes!" as she sprinted down the hall startled me.

I wasn't going to put any music on as I thought Liv would be back any second but I kept looking through the list of artists in any case. Despite their being no CD player in the room I noticed there was a small CD rack under the writing desk in the very corner of the room. Putting one hand on the floor and leaning right under the desk to get close enough to see the titles in the shadows, it seemed about ten degrees cooler under there. There was a draught coming around the CD rack itself and as I leant even further over most of my upper body went under the desk. I felt around the back of the rack and in the very corner the draught was much stronger, the floor damp, feeling like bare, wet earth. It was pitch black so I couldn't see anything but I was shocked at how shoddily the flat had been finished. I paused for a moment and the door opening behind me made me jump and I quickly scrabbled back onto the bed, banging my head hard on the underside of the desk.

"Taxis are here," Liv said as I looked sheepishly at her.

"Sorry, I was just looking at the CDs under there," giving her an explanation she'd given no indication of wanting. "It's really damp under there, have you noticed?"

"I think the reaction I was looking for was more along the lines of, "Liv, you've taken my breath away,"" she said, ignoring my question. I was relieved to see a hint of a smile back in her face.

"Sorry." Keen not to commit to anything that wouldn't do her justice, I took in her whole wonderful form before I spoke. She was wearing a black wafer thin, lowish cut v-neck, with a multi pleated black skirt that finished a few inches above the knee, opaque, slightly shimmering black tights and shiny black round toed t-bar shoes with a three or four inch heel. The finishing touch was the small silver cross pointing to her modest cleavage. Her hair was straight down and seemed longer and even more lustrous than ever and it framed her porcelain doll features beautifully. As I appraised her she stood rather confidently, holding my gaze waiting to see if I could find the right words.

I failed miserably.

"You look perfect. Just perfect. Your hair . . . the top . . . the skirt, the shoes . . . it all just looks perfect together. But you took, like, about eight minutes to get ready, how is *that* possible???"

Sounding sincere was not a problem, if anything I was surprised not to feel even a hint of awkwardness saying all that. In fairness to Liv, she didn't seem at all fazed by hearing how stunning she looked. She still held my gaze with that half smile, inviting me to go on. She seemed pleased. I was pretty much overwhelmed but I went on.

"I should mention your smile too I guess, now I've started. When I see it, I can barely hold a sensible thought in my head."

Her gaze faltered just a little then.

"Thank you, you're very kind to say so."

"Not at all," I said, rising and emboldened. "Thank you for a great time today—well, apart from the scenes from a badly put together action movie," I said, moving towards her, "I've had a really brilliant time."

I kissed her on the cheek, my free hand taking hers. As she put her arm around my back and pulled me to her, Liv whispered, "I've had a great time too. I wish it didn't have to end just yet." My heart fluttered and I turned my head so I could feel her lips on mine. If it was possible, for the second before I closed my eyes, she looked even more beautiful now she was so close. It was as if this might be our last kiss and neither of us wanted to be the one to end it. Eventually, when Caroline knocked on the door for the third or fourth time we parted lips and, feeling like an adolescent schoolboy, I smiled bashfully at her.

"Keep those lips warm for me," she whispered, before turning to retrieve a dark grey three quarter length coat from the wardrobe.

In the cab, Liv introduced me to her friends—Caroline, Becca and Mya. The birthday girl, Elma had apparently gone in the cab ahead with Jo. We held hands discreetly for the whole journey and I did everything I could to make a sound impression on Liv's friends—the life and soul of the pre-party you might say. When we got to my flat and I got out, I gave Liv a light kiss on the cheek, taking my cue from the discretion she'd shown in the cab. As I got to the front door I heard Liv call my name right behind me.

"Smooth operator!" she said, handing me the crutches I'd left behind in the cab. It was a complete oversight of course, caused by concentrating so hard on not making an idiot of myself in front of Liv and her friends and I was about to protest my innocence when Liv's soft moist lips enveloped my own.

"See you soon ok?"

As I watched Liv walk back to the cab it dawned on me that I'd just walked unaided all the way from the cab to the flat; it wasn't far but it was the first time I'd taken a step outside my room without a crutch. And I'd just done it by accident, and pissed. The realisation hit me and I was suddenly rooted to the spot. I pushed the door open—even after our incident with the tramp we still didn't always lock it—and saw Dave, wet hair down to his shoulders, resplendent in his red dressing gown and slippers, come out of his bedroom and head down the corridor towards me.

"Alright chief?" he asked with a slightly bemused look. As he headed into the kitchen, I called after him.

The second time I shouted he popped his head back around the kitchen door, raising his eyebrows quizzically.

"I just got out of a cab and walked back here—no crutches."

"Ayyyyy," he said, like a Geordie Fonz. "Excellent—you coming to the Unspoilt to celebrate?"

"Yeah, I will, but right now I can't actually move."

"Can't you just use your crutches?"

I looked at them in my hand, my mental block clearing in an instant. "Yeah, s'pose I can."

"What's up with your face?" Dave asked as I moved into the light.

"Altercation with one of Birmingham City's finest. Tell you all about it in the pub."

Back in my room I lay on my bed thinking, trying to doze but too happy and excited. I'd practically skipped from the cab to the flat without thinking about how dependent I'd become on my crutches. It meant I was getting better and the only thing slowing me down was my own confidence.

"That's the power of love," I sang quietly. The classic Huey Lewis edition—I was with Patrick Bateman on that one. I fell asleep trying to remember if Huey Lewis was still alive.

An hour and a half later and I was having my Saturday night in the Unspoilt by Progress on Hagley Road. Dave was there with his new girlfriend, Lucinda. Mike, his flatmate, Erica, Clare and I were seated with them around a couple of small round tables. Downstairs, a couple of guys from the football team were with another group.

The day's game had been against decidedly mediocre opposition from the sound of it and Dave was talking me through his third goal.

"I sort've feinted to hit it with my left, took a touch round the keeper as he went down and walked it across the line."

"You were lucky the keeper lost his footing more like—that goalmouth was a mud bath!" Mike chirped, in reality all admiration. We talked through the game for half an hour or so, Dave and Mike saving most of the player-by-player analysis for later when the evening was well under way. This pattern had been set from our very first game when the three of us had sat in our kitchen and talked all night about the shape and make up of the team. The more tedious it became to anyone else seemingly the more we found to talk about.

Erica was desperate to hear about my day and how the date with Liv had gone—I couldn't believe I hadn't explicitly told Dave not to say anything. Her eyes got wider and brighter as she repeated every detail back to me for confirmation.

"So you don't think he was a real taxi driver?"

"No, I guess he'd spotted we weren't local when we phoned for a cab, then nipped round the corner and got his car. God knows what his plan was once he'd annihilated me."

"And Liv smashed him over the head with a bottle of wine?"

"Absolutely creamed him," I answered emphatically.

Something inside was telling me I might have been better off playing things down; there was a chance at least that the guy was now the subject of a murder inquiry. The problem was I was being asked to repeat every line of my story by a gorgeous and incredibly sweet girl and I could not bring myself to give up my control of such a captive audience.

"And you just dumped his car and went back to Liv's—how did that go?" Erica asked, a discernible glint in her eye.

"Well, we had a cup of tea, some wine, she listened to me witter on about how shocking the afternoon had been and then I came home," I said, winking to let Erica know I wasn't telling her the full story on this final detail of my day.

"And you definitely don't want to involve the police?" Mike asked, typically more concerned with brass tacks.

"As long as he's not dead and he gets his car back, what's the point?" I replied, keen not to hear the answer. "Come to think of it, I'm not sure I'd even be that bothered if he didn't get his car back—or, fuck it, if he's dead for that matter."

A pause, no one wanted to reply to that.

"Sorry, my nerves are still a bit raw. I don't know what the best thing to do is, I'm just happy to be here, standing up and alive."

"Alright lad," Mike said, sounding unusually understanding. He even clapped me on the back as he said it. "You know she might have set the whole thing up just to get you back to hers so she could have her wicked way with you."

"It crossed my mind of course but she only had to ask; it's not like I get too many offers!" As I said it my eyes caught Clare's and she looked away slightly embarrassedly.

"Who wants a beer?" Dave asked, rising.

Mike got up too to help with the round—bottled lager for the southern softie (me), three assorted bitters for the northerners, a vodka and coke each for the two sweethearts (Clare and Erica) and a dry white wine for the moody North London girl (Lucinda.)

"Dave said you walked back to the flat without your crutches earlier." It was Erica showing her concern again.

Clare and Erica shared a flat with three other girls on the top floor of our block. They were both pretty in their own, very different ways. Erica was blonde, fresh faced, unfeasibly bright eyed and very confident. She was chatty, very easy to get to know and great fun to be around, the kind of girl who you always felt flattered just to be talking to. Clare had straight, longish light brown hair, very sexy eyes and a nicely rounded bottom—she was quieter, ever so considerate, and had a sweet smile we saw all too infrequently. She was more reserved but as time went on we developed a different, more intimate closeness that was important to both of us. I'd met them briefly at the welcome drinks organised at the halls on our first night and when I'd seen them a few days later struggling with their shopping on their way back from Tesco, I'd caught them up and offered them a hand. I got a cup of tea for my trouble and sat in their kitchen chatting away for a couple of hours, joining them for a drink in the evening, which was possibly how I'd got to know Kenny. I counted myself lucky I'd got to know the three of them before any of us had become attached to other groups. The girls, Kenny and I had become especially close as we almost always stayed up later than most of the others—Dave and Mike, both being scientists, usually had early morning starts. Clare was an arts student like me and Kenny and Erica both did Commerce which meant they had even more of a doss.

I told Erica about my walk back to the flat and how I'd frozen as soon as I realised what I'd done.

"Even if you didn't do it deliberately, it's great news—you thought it might take you another month didn't you?"

"I guess you're right—and I *am* pleased—it's just you take a step forward sometimes and it makes you realise how far you've still got to go," I answered without really capturing exactly what I was trying to say.

"You'll be back playing football in no time—Mike told me not to tell you but he says they're missing you," Erica said with a conspiratorial smile. Yet another girl I was fighting not to fall for.

"I can't imagine Mike saying anything so complimentary but I'll try to get him to admit it once he's had a few more drinks," I joked.

Erica squeezed my hand as she excused herself and went to the bathroom.

As Dave set some of the drinks on the table in front of me I asked him how Terry had played.

"Mm, he did *alright,* fitness lacking a bit towards the end as always. Not really his sort of game today—no aggro for a start."

"I thought he was piss-poor," Mike chimed in as he re-took his seat. "Bin out boozing all night by the look of him."

And we were off again, solid football for the next hour and a half. Mike, direct and to the point as ever, Dave seeing positives throughout and me arguing the case for my favourites. Vern, another of our informal football committee, joined us from downstairs and gave us some new angles to debate. By the end I was adamant I should have the casting vote on who won man of the match.

After last orders Erica, Clare and I went over to Kenny's. Kenny, who had watched his beloved Spurs record a surprisingly emphatic win, had got back around ten thirty and was in the middle of cooking his characteristically idiosyncratic signature dish when we'd knocked on the door; a mountain of alphabet spaghetti over chicken nuggets.

The four of us played cards, chatted and took turns nodding off on Kenny's bed until around three o'clock when we all finally called it a night.

In no way a serious drinker at the best of times, as I entered my flat I was already starting to feel hung-over after a day of drinking and mixing my drinks. I gave my teeth a cursory brush and lay on my bed with the room spinning around me. When I first tried to close my eyes it made me feel sick so I lay with my lamp on for a few minutes letting my body and brain get used to things before turning off the light again. In the dark I concentrated on a small shard of light at the top of the curtains and before too long I was asleep and back at primary school . . .

. . . "I want to talk to you about a very serious matter," she said, infusing each word with her vicious bile.

Me singing hymns to an empty, white corridor; small eight year old voice echoing back to me, no comfort at all. Red with fear and embarrassment, my eyes full of tears I know will never drop . . .

. . . . Cold, hard hatred—first hers and now mine.

Not eight years old anymore, her hatred becoming mine, her power becoming mine.

"Do you remember?" Now I'm asking the questions of the small, frightened, pitiful creature shrinking before me. Pitiful but not pitied. Not by me.

"Let's have a Christmas carol," I say, "How about Once in Royal David's City?" as I nail her hands to the floor, not taking much care to hit the nails, just the red mush somewhere on the floor.

"While shepherd's watched, did we have that one . . . ON CHRISTMAS PARTY DAY?" I shriek into her face.

"Please, don't rush. I owe you a fucking lifetime."

I hear a piano in the room; I look but there's no one playing. I'm pleased she won't be playing that again. As I go over to it, the room blurs behind me as other dreams start to encroach. There's no hammer, no singing, no bloody teacher any more. No bloody teacher . . .

Sunday, 6th February

I woke up around eight o'clock bursting for a piss, the sunshine outside hardly blighted at all by the cheap, orange curtains in my room. In the bathroom, I inadvertently pissed on the floor for a second or two, my eyes struggling to focus on the mark. I didn't clean up when I'd finished—who the fuck was going to know? I went back to my room, convinced I wouldn't be able to sleep, wondering if it was worth trying. Thankfully I was wrong.

It was gone twelve by the time I woke up and I knew instantly it was going to be a Sunday to forget. Staring up at the ceiling, I wondered how to fill my day. I didn't want company that was certain. I'd always hated Sundays when I was younger but this was the first Sunday I could remember waking up at uni and having that sinking feeling about the long hours ahead. I was hungover and my face felt sore from the beating I'd taken the day before. I thought back four or five years to a few mad, sad Sundays I'd spent with one of the stoners from school, Luke Wilson.

I was fifteen when I fell in with Luke. He'd been in plenty of my classes at school but we'd never gotten to know each other until I fell out with his older brother and we found we had something in common. Carl, Luke's brother was a real creep who fancied himself both intellectually and physically without a genuine claim in either camp. He was big though and at times aggressively threatening, especially towards Luke. He had bleached blonde curly hair and although it never occurred to me at the time, I would best describe him as looking like a cheaply bespectacled (and blonde) Bryan May.

Luke was a waster, into his skateboard and not much else, somehow friends with a small group of kids who were a lot smarter and a lot nastier than him. Apart from Carl's antipathy towards us I can only really remember us sharing general discontent. I was missing my brother who had gone off to Manchester and I was pretty fucked up because I'd split up with my girlfriend at the end of that summer and my depressed state of mind gave us a very powerful if very temporary bond. While my problems were probably standard teenage emotional responses to short-term issues, I look back and wonder if Luke's weren't borne of real neglect, as he didn't get on with his parents either. Perhaps I sought him out just because I knew on some level that he was definitely worse off than me.

I lay back on my bed, sad at how little I remembered about Luke. I'd got my ex back within a few weeks and pretty much dumped my substitute as quickly and easily as possible. It was guilt free for me because, like a lot of sad people, he was perceptive enough to see it coming and provided me with an excuse to move on. Strange that all those years later it was possible to invoke much stronger feelings of compassion than I ever felt at the time.

I edged open the curtains and looked out on the empty quadrant. I couldn't face getting up and having a shower and I didn't want to make myself a cup of tea while I could hear Colin in the kitchen so I took the arts student's last resort and picked up a book.

Later that day, I texted Liv to say hi and thank her for a lovely day, held my phone for five minutes waiting in vain for an immediate response and then phoned my brother to arrange for him to come up the following Saturday. He was typically vague about what time he'd arrive and how long he'd stay and only offered shopping as a possibility for filling the time. Even though I couldn't wait to see him and he was always like this, I was pissed off with him. By the time I got off the phone I had a message from Liv. It read, *'Had a gr8 time 2. Last night complete disaster, tell all when I c u next. Won't be 2moro as not going in—borrow ur notes pls?? What am I saying pls for, u owe me?!! Call Tuesday, lvLV.'*

It was five o'clock, cold and dark outside and the day was gone. I was wondering if I should go and disturb anyone and risk inflicting my less than fantastic mood on them. I did a few exercises on my leg, which was agony after a day doing precisely nothing and weighed up my options.

Dave—probably working; could ask if he fancied a drink later;

Clare & Erica; the fact they hadn't been round all day indicated they were doing something better, probably shopping;

Kenny; my go to guy in these circumstances, could even be sitting on his own in his room wondering if he should disturb anyone. Like Clare and Erica, I could count on seeing him later anyway.

Fats; always good value, bound to be sitting at his desk pretending to work. Might be fun to talk to about Liv.

I leant across the bed to see if Fats's light was on; it wasn't. I thought he might be in his kitchen or off with Chris somewhere.

My last option was Mel. That she hadn't been in touch since we'd had our substandard fuck wasn't a great sign. I tried to think back, had I said I'd call her Sunday? She'd said something about her parents coming up but

I figured they'd have left by five fifteen. I could always call her and say I'd forgotten about her parents; then again what would I say? Then *again*, I couldn't just leave it forever.

I brought up Mel's number on my mobile, pressed dial and then cancel a couple of times over and finally decided I might as well let it ring. When she picked up, she sounded very hacked off.

"Hi Matt."

"Hi Mel, I think I said I'd call you this afternoon." It was a terrible opening, now she'd think I was doing it out of duty.

"Oh, ok—do you actually have anything to say?" I'd asked for that one.

"Yeah, of course," I laughed, taking it as a joke. "How are you?"

"Great." She didn't sound like she meant it. She sounded like she meant, "Shit—because I'm wasting my time on the phone to you."

"That's good, what have you been up to?"

"Not much, you?"

"Look, sorry to have bothered you ok? Do you want to call me back when you've remembered we're actually supposed to be friends?"

I gave her a second to melt and respond with an apology but I was listening to dead air. I'd blown it. Exactly why Sundays should always be exercises in damage limitation.

I looked at Fats's dark window again, then Kenny's. There was light! I decided to go and see Kenny, as he was impossible to offend or be offended by. I gave Dave a knock on my way out and asked if he was coming for a drink later on but he wasn't sure. A waste of forty five seconds.

I saw through Kenny's window that he already had a room full of company—Clare and Erica were sitting on his bed drinking tea. I bristled slightly at the thought that I'd been forgotten. A second later they saw me through the window and somewhere between Kenny's and Erica's smiles, I lost any thought of annoyance; after an eternity in a Sunday wasteland I was about to be among friends.

5

"That man took the stage, his towel swinging high,
This man was my bombers, my dexys, my high"

From "Geno" by Dexys Midnight Runners

Monday, 7th February

Mondays were by far my busiest days and when my alarm went off just before nine o'clock, my heart sank with the realisation that I now wouldn't be returning to the supreme comfort and warmth of the duvet for at least another eight and a half hours. The worst of it was that so soon after I thought I might have established a routine lunchtime date with Liv, she wasn't going to be in. As I thought about closing my eyes again, I remembered her text. Typical—the only thing that might have made the day palatable were a couple of hours with Liv, and now because she wasn't going in I was responsible for ensuring she got lecture notes.

As luck would have it I saw Gareth, one of the few guys I had gotten to know on my course, as I came out of my ten o'clock French subsid. His only notable characteristic was a dry, extremely nasty wit, which he would train on the closest and easiest target available. However much I didn't want to I always found him entertaining. Today he'd spotted Donna, a pleasant and not unattractive Sheffield girl who I'd spoken to a couple of times in a seminar in my first term. Poor Donna was afflicted by a slightly withered hand and Gareth heartlessly referred to her as Beadle—as I said, I never *intended* to laugh.

"Where's your bird today then?" he asked as we looked for a place to sit.

"Liv you mean?" I replied, trying to hide my pride. "She's not in today." Then because I was with Gareth and he would expect it, I added,

"Must have ridden her too hard last night. I was trying to go easy too." He brought out the worst in everyone, not just me.

"Really? She told me you hardly touched the sides once I'd been through her," Gareth replied with a conceitful smirk.

"Really? Beadle said you were a virgin."

In reply, Gareth tucked half his hand up his sleeve and started pawing at me with his newly deformed hand. Worried, in case anyone was watching this charade, I tried to end the conversation by pushing his hand away and turned my attention to the lecture.

"Please make love to me and my Beadle hand," Gareth was saying far too loudly for comfort, "I haven't had sex for fifteen months."

"Have you got one of the karaoke events at Farrell?" I asked, "I went to the one at Garforth last week," hoping a change of subject would shut him up.

"Oh yeah, can't get enough of making a tit out of myself on stage . . . where do I sign?"

Thankfully, Dr Brown was clearing his throat in preparation for another fascinating insight contrasting the eating habits of the British Tommy, 1914-1918 with his Boche contemporaries. In fairness to Dr Brown there was a lot more to be said on the subject than I'd thought possible. I texted Liv half way through to tell her she was missing nothing and to apologise if my notes were a bit patchy. When she hadn't replied after five minutes I started to worry that she'd be annoyed about the notes and I made sure my attention didn't waver again.

I had been planning on seeing if Gareth fancied a drink at twelve, as I had two hours to kill and he was in my two o'clock, but his pre-lecture assault had been enough to put me off. I told him I needed to go to the library and I'd meet him before two o'clock. I needed to go to the library anyway, as I had to copy my notes onto a piece of paper that didn't have shoddily drawn pictures of a tiny Beadle fist wrapped around a tiny cock on it. Gareth's artwork was probably bad enough that Liv would never have guessed what it was supposed to be but, like spending a further two hours with him, it wasn't a risk I wanted to take.

Thursday, 10th February

Liv had replied to my text, but I didn't see her again until that Thursday as she also skipped our *'Characters of the French Revolution'* seminar. She'd missed a stellar performance by yours truly. I'd always seen the French Revolution as something of a pet subject of mine and while it hadn't been a view immediately shared by Doctor Robertson, I felt it was only a matter of my putting in a couple of performances like that week's before he'd mark me out from the rest.

I was early for the Medieval History lecture; I was getting more and more mobile by the day, but even so, Liv was outside the room waiting for me when I got there. That was pretty cool because I hadn't fancied sitting in the room, continually looking round every time the door opened in case it was her; what if she'd turned up with someone else and sat with them? Over the past couple of days I'd become steadily more convinced we'd shared nothing more intimate than an exciting afternoon she'd be happy to forget all about.

"How are you—good week?" Liv beamed at me, setting my mind to rest.

"Yeah, haven't done much really. I photocopied my notes for you. The World War One ones aren't great I'm afraid as I sat next to Gareth and he just pissed about the whole time."

"I'm sure they'll be fine—wasn't it just about the differences between standard equipment between the British and German forces?"

"Erm, well he talked a lot about the superiority of German sausages," I answered.

I had her laughing already. I suggested lunch without even thinking about it.

"Sure, union will be crushed though; we could head down the road to the Gunbarrels? Sorry, I was forgetting your leg," she added.

"Don't worry, I could probably make it down there ok," I said, trying to sound accommodating but unconvincing. It must have worked.

"No, forget it, if we get in there straight after twelve, we'll be alright in the union anyway."

An hour or so later we left the Arts Faculty behind, at least one of us none the wiser as to why on earth we were studying *'The Song of Roland.'*

We walked over to the union and I enjoyed the simple pleasure of being with an indisputably attractive girl. I felt relaxed with Liv, from the first time we'd spoken there'd been no forced small talk. Or perhaps that was just how it felt there and then. In a way we hardly knew each other but it didn't feel like it, when she'd seen me outside the lecture room it was like we'd been in the same routine for months.

As Liv and I sat down at a table in the union café, she asked me if I had any plans for the weekend.

"My brother's coming up for the day Saturday, probably take him into town and do some shopping. Not much else planned at the moment, what about you?"

"That's Donny right? He's a few years older than you isn't he?"

"Yeah, six and a half years but you'd hardly guess it if you met him," I laughed.

"Does he look much like you?"

"Not really, although people say you can tell we're brothers when we're together. He got my mum's looks, I got my dad's. Which means *he* got the looks. Same build as me though more or less, we share clothes quite a lot. Well, when I have something he likes we share clothes." Liv didn't appear to get the joke.

"Is your mum very pretty then?" Liv asked me, shaking her strawberry milk.

"Well I guess I'm biased but yes, she was very pretty when she was younger and even now has the most amazing skin. She's fifty but you'd never think it."

"Like your brother."

I took a couple of seconds to understand what Liv meant by this. "Kind of—I think he just seems young because he's cute. And because he smiles a lot probably."

"Your dad must be handsome too . . . if you got his looks I mean," Liv looked at me archly, eyebrows slightly raised as if she knew she'd said something cheeky. It was as sweet a compliment as I could imagine. I smiled in acknowledgement.

"I guess he must have been ok at some point to have snagged my mum."

"So you must have been at school with your brother," Liv said, clearly still interested in my family.

"We went to the same school but there was only a couple of years when he was doing his A-levels and I'd just started that we were together."

"Same *primary school* though," Liv said, confirming what she sounded like she already knew.

"Yep, same," I nodded. "So, what are you up to for the weekend, did you want to meet up one night?"

"I'm going away for a long weekend from tomorrow morning."

FUCK IT.

"Great, where to?"

"Parents' holiday home in the South of France," Liv answered distractedly. I couldn't tell if she wanted me to probe more deeply or stay off the subject. I chose the latter, a touch deflated. Suddenly things felt a little awkward once again.

"Thanks again for bringing my crutches back the other day by the way."

"No problem at all. You didn't even need them to get back to the flat though, that's good isn't it?"

"Definitely. Only thing was, when I realised I didn't have them I was rooted to the spot. Dave had to come and rescue me."

Liv looked at me quizzically.

"I actually noticed you get out of the car without them—I didn't say anything because I thought it might be good for you to walk without them."

Well, this was a turn up. I was annoyed by what Liv had just said.

"Good for me, as long I didn't break my neck I guess."

"I knew you'd be ok," Liv answered. Just that, she *knew* I'd be ok. She had a smile and a beauty I couldn't really argue with.

All too soon Liv had to go on to her next class and as I stood up to say goodbye I asked her if she fancied meeting up on Sunday night.

"I told you, I'm away," she said, fixing me again with that quizzical stare of hers. I kicked myself for failing to remember what she'd told me not half an hour before—for god's sake I'd been hanging on her every word!

"Yeah, sorry—dibbo!" I said, pointing at my temple and sounding about twelve years old, "err, see you next week then I guess." It must have been the situation, the emotion or the combination that had made her so tender on Saturday; Liv seemed surprised I'd asked to see her again so soon.

"I'm in tomorrow morning briefly for a seminar, are you in?" she asked.

"No, tomorrow's a free day for me, enjoy your weekend."

When I'd stood up I'd been thinking in terms of a friendly kiss on the cheek, now I was embarrassed and disappointed enough to want to see the back of Liv quickly and I realised I'd lost my joviality. Sometimes it was bad to have the sort of face people think they can read like a book, but this wasn't one of those times. Seeing something in my expression, Liv came around the table, took my hand in hers and said softly, "I'm getting back late on Monday, shall I give you a call then?"

Once again, she'd made me feel special by a simple gesture and I felt idiotic for doubting her quite so readily.

"You make me feel like I'm fourteen again," I said with my cutest smile (yeah, I could turn it on too.) "Don't put yourself out if you're tired or whatever, but yes, it would be great to speak to you when you get back."

I leant towards her, gave her a peck on the cheek and the tiniest hug before I had time to think about it.

"Safe journey," I said as she walked away.

I watched her walk all the way out of the crowded cafeteria and just before she disappeared she turned and gave me a miniscule wave. I felt my life's purpose was fulfilled and I sat on my own thinking about Liv and that little wave for most of the next hour. When at last I had to leave, I went via the union shop and picked up a newspaper, something I only do when I am totally at ease with the world and have a rare fit of determination to become better informed about things. On the way to my lecture, I began testing the strength in my leg to see if I could walk with less and less pressure on my remaining crutch. By the time I got there, I was making myself use the crutch in case I was doing damage I couldn't feel—my leg felt almost like new.

I spent the next hour pissing about on the back row with Gareth and one of his mates from back home in Ipswich. He was a dick but an entertaining one and I couldn't have cared less.

When I got back to Swafforth it was early evening and, thinking he'd have finished for the day and I hadn't seen him for a while, I popped round to Fats' to see if he fancied playing pool the next afternoon.

Jake, his flatmate, showed me into the kitchen where Fats was cooking his staple diet of spaghetti on toast.

"Skipper!" he said by way of greeting.

"How's things mate?"

"Not so bad, how's the leg coming on? Back on the football field soon?"

"About a year, so no not too soon," I said, a bit puzzled as he already knew all this. "Just popped in to see if you fancied a few games of pool tomorrow pm."

"I'm supposed to be in 'til four but I could skip it, hardly had a break all week. What's the occasion?"

"No occasion, just thought you might fancy a couple of beers and a lesson in pool."

"You joker, you're Steve Davis to my Ronnie O'Sullivan! I can't stay too late though, Jake's organising a flat curry tomorrow night."

"Sounds tremendous. Shall I see you downstairs at two o'clock-ish then?"

"Yep, sounds good, see you then," Fats said with the biggest grin.

"By the way, I've got some tales for you tomorrow," I said, trying to whet his appetite. It worked like it always did.

"Go on," Fats, hooked already.

It's why everyone found him such great company, why his senseless death was so hard to take.

"It'll keep, I might even remember some more details for you. Not a word though, she'd kill me," I said, teasing him.

Knowing he was being teased, Fats saw me to the door with a wistful, "You character." It was one of his favourite catchphrases and, like a few others, had taken hold in the consciousness of the football team.

Friday, 11th February

I woke up early the next day and lay in bed, weighing up my options for the next few hours. I had an essay I'd completed the night before to drop off at uni. I realised I should have mentioned this to Liv the day before and maybe grabbed a quick coffee with her. I thought about going in mid morning and hanging around to see if I caught her but since I didn't know exactly where she'd be or when she'd be there I dismissed the idea. I also thought it might look a bit suspicious if I turned up having said I wasn't in all day. I thought about texting her, wondered if it would look too keen. I read through the essay and made a few changes before saving it onto a memory stick so I could print it out at the library. Listless, I went into the kitchen, depressed I wasn't the sort of person who could relish having the flat to myself, then found it was my name on the washing up rota. I did about half of the stuff lying around, booked a cab for one o'clock and went back to bed for an hour. I hoped the guys would appreciate that I was still basically an invalid.

"Tell me about this girl then. Looker is she?" Fats asked.

"Top drawer mate, top, top, top drawer!" I said, punctuating the final word by missing frame ball. I paid the price for trying to sound cool before taking my shot.

Fats calmly potted the last two of his reds and then the black for the frame.

"How did I guess you'd say that?" he smirked, "Set 'em up chump, I'll fire up the jukebox. Any requests?"

One frame behind, I set up the balls.

"Mate, no joke, she's pure class. Perfect skin, perfect hair, five-four—five-five, just right for me. Played hard to get for the first term, then I flash the gammy leg and it's like she just melts for me."

Fats gave me a sceptical look.

"Well to be honest, I don't really get why she's so keen. I guess we both got a bit emotional after Saturday."

"What happened Saturday?"

He'd potted four red balls already and left me in trouble against the top cushion with one yellow to aim at. I messed it up and he was in again.

"Fuck, have I not seen you since I nearly got killed at the football?"

"No, I'm sure this will be priceless." Fats was expecting some bullshit story.

He had one ball left but I was in. I concentrated on the next couple of shots, got some balls down and got a lucky break to leave Fats in trouble and then got back to the table with two shots. I went as far as the black and missed it to the centre. Thinking I still had a free shot remaining, I bent down to finish things.

"What are you doing, you cowboy?" Fats piped up.

"Two shots," I offered by way of explanation.

"Only one shot on the black," Fats replied, seemingly convinced.

"I always play you carry it over." I wasn't fussed but I had to give my side or look like a cheat.

"Southern cowboys!"

I potted the black.

"Sorry mate, should have said before we started. Two shots on the black from now on, ok?"

"Yep."

"What are you waiting for? Rack 'em up and I'll tell you what happened," I said, taking a swallow of coke. "Me and Liv went along to the Palace-Birmingham game; she's a Palace fan too and I thought it might be quite a neat little first date. Obviously I was about as wrong as I could get. We got to Adderley Park and there were signs up everywhere saying the game was off. There were a few hungry looking natives but nothing that looked too threatening."

"What, and some blokes turned you over?"

"You bored? I'm just about to tell you, but no, not exactly. Neither of us fancied waiting around for the train back so I phoned for a cab. Some geezer must have overheard me phoning, fucked off down the road to get his car and five minutes later comes back and tells us he's our cabbie."

"Jesus, then what?" Fats, with another needless interruption.

"We stop in the middle of some estate in the arse end of nowhere so Liv can buy some booze from Fort Apache Wine Merchants and as soon as she's out of the car the guy goes mad and starts abusing me. He's practically foaming at the mouth. He gets into the back of the car and starts lamping me round the head and screaming filth at me—it's, "*cunt* this, *cunt* that" and every time he says anything he's trying to cave my head in so I get the message. As soon as he's bored with my head, he hurls my crutches over his shoulder and starts to line up my knee with the car door so he can smash that up. All this has been going on a couple of minutes when Liv arrives back, in the nick of time for me and my knee, and smashes him over the back of the head with a bottle of wine."

"Unbelievable scenes—you must have been going bananas!" Fats was loving every minute.

"Going bananas? I was barely fucking conscious. Calm as you like, Liv lays me down on the backseat and starts the car."

I came close to telling Fats about how Liv followed up her initial blow and nearly killed the bloke but something inside me was considering for the first time that maybe she'd gone beyond the use of reasonable force. It wasn't that I felt sympathy for the lowlife who'd attacked us but I suddenly felt worried for Liv. Worried *by* Liv. "Anyway, she drives at breakneck speed and ends up parking in the Hib car park. She gets me out, I'm basically puking my guts up and we hail another cab and go back to hers."

"Are you having me on or what?"

"Wish I was. Look at this," I said, showing him the massive, yellowing bruise on my side. I also made him feel a lump on the side of my head that had been sore all week.

"Ghost'll have nightmares when I tell him about this. What did the police say?"

"Didn't go—both just want to forget all about it. *And I don't really want our second date to be in prison,*" I didn't add.

"He must have been a psycho."

"You think? Probably just waiting at the station to kick off with someone he thought would be no trouble. Got to admire his ingenuity though. Fuck knows what he would have done to Liv after he'd finished with me."

"Sounds like she can take care of herself. You gonna set these balls up then or what?" Dismissed.

"You playing Sunday?" I asked as I set the next game up.

"Yes boss, Dave said you're coming along to watch."

"Planning to, if I can get a lift down there."

"When will you be back playing?"

"Surgeon told me a year but I've been making really good progress in the last couple of weeks. I've been walking without any crutches ahead of schedule and I should be able to ditch this brace pretty soon and then get down the gym."

Well beaten, I went upstairs a couple of hours later to meet Dave and Jez in the union bar.

Saturday, 12th February

When I woke up on Saturday morning I was hung-over and fully clothed. My brother stood in the doorway wearing a decidedly unimpressed look on his face.

"Alright?"

"Shit, sorry, alarm didn't go off," I offered by way of explanation. I knew I wasn't likely to be excused any time soon. Donny was the best possible company on the right day but he wasn't without his mood swings and I had a knack of inadvertently bringing them on. I knew if I walked on eggshells for a while and showed my contrition he'd get over it. I looked at the alarm clock; it was eleven forty five. He was forty five minutes late yet I still hadn't been awake. I could have kicked myself, I'd been looking forward to spending the day with Donny in a way I wouldn't have with anyone else.

"I'll make some tea. Do you need to have a shower?"

"Yeah, I'll get in there now," I replied meekly.

I showered quickly and dressed in record time before I practically burst into the kitchen. Dave was in there wearing just a red dressing gown, standing and eating his cornflakes talking to Donny. Dave was as down to earth as anyone I knew and extremely friendly with it, two qualities guaranteed to get up my brother's nose. He had a golden rule where my friends were concerned—they were never good enough (for him, not me.) He had been the same with my girlfriends when I was at school. Two weeks after any break up he'd give his crushingly succinct verdict—square shoulders, shovel chin, Moonface, blob nose, full of herself etc. The really unfortunate ones might have found themselves on the wrong end of more than one of the aforementioned. It was only a problem when I was the one who'd been dumped or if we got back together two weeks later.

"Leg's better then?" Donny asked.

"Ummm, yeah, improving. I think it's coming on," I answered noncommittally. I didn't think he'd really ever grasped the seriousness of my injury so I never bored him with details.

"You seem a lot better than dad made out, you're off your crutches already."

I realised I'd not used my crutches since I'd woken up, and mornings were usually the time when I was at my most wobbly. A couple of weeks ago, I'd been nervous as a kitten even with my crutches, now I seemed to be recovering faster than Clark Kent. I froze again but this time it passed in a couple of seconds and rather than going to get my crutches I walked over and sat at the table and pulled my mug of tea towards me.

"Yeah, like I say I seem to be progressing quite quickly. How was the journey up?"

"Really quick, about two hours from mum and dad's. I stayed there last night to save time."

"*And* so you didn't have to cook," I said, laughing.

"Actually, I bought them a Chinese," Donny, on the defensive, hardly seeing the funny side.

"So you *didn't* cook!" I knew I had to get off the subject quickly or he'd get annoyed. "What d'you wanna do, go shopping?" I asked.

"If you're up to it."

"Yeah, I'll be fine. I need to take one of my crutches though. I've forgotten to use them a couple of times that's all, but I'm still supposed to be on them. I'm seeing the surgeon in a couple of weeks for a check up and I should be able to get to the gym after that."

Donny was happy not hearing too much detail about people's lives; if he got a general impression I was happy that'd be enough for him. He had a habit of glazing over when I started talking about stuff he didn't want to hear, something he hated to admit he'd got from our dad. Despite that Donny always had a natural ability to put people at ease and engage them in conversation (ironic considering he was hardly ever interested in what they were saying.)

Temperamentally we'd always been very different. With me, all my feelings came out whereas Donny had a seemingly limitless ability to bottle things up and pass it off as his not being affected by them. On the way into town, travelling at the speed of light, Donny told me about some poor girl at work who had a crush on him; she was beautiful of course or he wouldn't have even registered it. It was hopeless having a crush on Donny as he had no interest in girls unless they were exes who were now safely and happily married and thus unattainable. This, more than anything else for me, underlined the chief difference between my brother and me. Since I was eleven I'd been on an unstinting quest to find true and everlasting love and been pretty successful a number of times, interspersing my search with a few opportunistic sallies into the world of the casual sexual acquaintance. When these opportunities had arisen I confess I hadn't consistently taken the view that I shouldn't already be involved in another everlasting love match. Donny, on the other hand, had had no more than two or three girlfriends serious enough to meet any of the family. These, without fail, had been treated abysmally; by Donny not the family and all eventually had got the message that they weren't part of his long-term plans. As close as I was to him and as well as I thought I understood him, this was one thing about Donny that baffled me. That said, I never really understood why he liked Feeder so much either. At some stage in the day I wanted to talk about Liv but where Donny was concerned I knew I'd have to choose my moment very carefully.

After a hundred mile an hour a day, his nervous energy spent, Donny mellowed and took me down memory lane. The year we moved from one side of London to the other was the year Donny started uni. It meant me leaving my friends behind and I didn't want to go. Worst of all, with Donny going away, I was losing the person I'd shared a bath with until I was five, a room with until I was eight and every meaningful event and feeling I'd had my whole life. I was losing the one person I knew cared about me more than he cared about the rest of the world put together.

Whenever he came back from uni for holidays, Donny would always want to go out driving around South London, showing me the seediest and nastiest parts, its most vibrant centres and leafiest suburbs. He had a staggering ability to sit and read maps for hours on end and he could probably have passed 'The Knowledge' without serious preparation; thanks to him I'm never lost south of the river. Most often we'd drive around Crystal Palace, Sydenham and Dulwich. I loved taking in the panoramic views that he sniffed out with every few turns. He could talk about every place we went through as if he'd lived there half his life and the effect on me was magical. My fascination was always with the tower blocks, slabs and walkways of the city's estates that were such a part of the London skyscape before the demolition programmes of the late 1980s and 90s. Donny had begun to study town planning after his degree but gave up when he ran out of money or maybe his bank had. I'd ask him which estates were the worst, the biggest, the poorest or had the hardest reputation. He never disappointed me and every time we went out he'd have something new to share. I wanted to climb to the top of each of those tower blocks and find the stories every single room could tell.

I remember vividly Easter weekends we'd be touring around—always in the sunshine!—windows down and Capital Radio reminding us where we were every few minutes. I remember screaming down Gipsy Hill or up Jamaica Road in brilliant sunshine, taking in fantastic views and hearing that George Michael was yet again making a record donation to Capital's 'Help a London Child' appeal; thinking I'd do the same if I ever got the chance to make such a grand gesture on such a perfect day.

And now years later Donny wanted to take in the sights and smells of Britain's second city in the last hour and a half of daylight. Weaving in and out of the Saturday traffic with gay abandon we whizzed through Handsworth, where Donny talked about the riots of '84; West Bromwich, where we got out and bought a mug each from the WBA club shop; onto

Castle Vale in the south east of the city, a fearsome seething mass in the gathering gloom; then we headed back to the centre, through the back streets of Aston where we did get temporarily misplaced; to Digbeth where the high rises began that you might have believed stretched all the way to Coventry; and finally, in the dark, we drove down Speedwell Road, in Balsall Heath, where Donny said we'd once have seen prostitutes sitting Amsterdam style in windows, but all we saw were handwritten notes pinned to trees imploring kerb crawlers to smile for the CCTV cameras.

Donny made sure we saw more of the city in those three hours than I, and every student I knew, had seen in the months we'd been there or probably ever would. At some point I managed to tell Donny all about Liv and the incident with the psychotic 'taxi driver' and I questioned Donny on how I should approach the big issue of formalising my relationship with Liv. Without giving me any advice I could use he nevertheless left me convinced he was a player.

"There's no rush is there?" he asked me.

My favourite person in the whole world was a dead loss when it came to the practicalities of ensnaring the opposite sex. Any success he'd had himself in the past was purely down to his being so infuriatingly disinterested; not something I'd be able to master and Liv would have spotted that by now for sure. We sat in the car park at the top of The Vale; it was six forty five, dark and starting to rain.

"Are you sure you don't want to come in?"

"No, like I said, I'm supposed to be meeting Philip at nine o'clock. Thanks though," Donny replied.

"Ok mate, thanks for coming, I've really enjoyed it."

"Yeah, it's been good, I'll see you at Easter I s'pose."

A second before I was about to swing the car door closed, Donny leant over and said excitedly, "I didn't tell you about Baggy Bailey, did I? She was murdered after she disturbed someone breaking into her house. Beaten up and raped before they killed her."

"Where was *he*?" By 'he' I meant Mr Bailey, her husband.

"Some teachers' conference or something. Away for the night anyway. Someone must have known; it was the first night they'd spent apart for thirty eight years."

A small, *a very small*, part of me wanted to say—to feel—that she'd got what she deserved for what she did to me. It would make it easier to comprehend. But of course, it appalled me, and I felt guilty the thought had crossed my mind, even for a second. I felt stunned this had happened in the place where I grew up.

"Shit," was all I could say, shaking my head.

"Yeah, I know. Anyway mate, see you soon, yeah?"

"Yep, cheers then."

I watched Donny drive up the hill and turn on to the main road. Even when he'd gone I stood there, enveloped in a surreal blanket of confusion, getting steadily soaked.

I waited there in the cold for a few more minutes trying to decide how I felt about what I'd heard but the longer I stood the more my mind wandered. It was cold and I decided to head back to the flat. I hadn't made plans for the evening just in case Donny had been planning on staying around. Dave had texted to see if I fancied playing snooker with him and Mike. The two of them were better than me by far and I thought it was probably just a polite invitation, so in spite of having no plans and not wanting to be on my own, I replied to say that I was too tired and I'd probably catch up with them afterwards. As I went into the flat, I could hear Eliot's Pink Floyd and Calum's Basement Jaxx vying horribly for supremacy. At least it put Baggy's death in perspective. As I unlocked my door, I could hear voices from the kitchen. I closed my door quickly and quietly behind me and swapped the main light for the lamp before sticking a pair of jeans along the bottom of the door to stop the light giving my presence away. I put on some music—Black Sabbath's first album—very quietly and climbed into bed. I snapped off the lamp and had the feeling I might cry. Instead I fell very quickly to sleep and never heard Ozzy sing a note. Some people say he barely hits a decent note on the whole album anyway.

. . . I am standing outside a red door off to the side of a white painted bungalow. My hand is stretched out behind me; palm up to stop my companions coming any further up the narrow, gravel path. I rap my usual five knocks on the front door; tap tap te-tap tap! It's quieter than I expect but that must be because I have a child's hand, an eight year old's hand. No matter, the house is quiet. Only one ageing lady is inside and she has heard me. When I see through the frosted glass door that she is coming, I press myself flat against the sidewall out of sight. An outside light comes on and I flinch instinctively away. The door opens, she has chosen not to make use of the security chain and see who is calling on her after dark on a cold February night. Good. She opens the door

wide and I step from the shadows into the light in front of her. Ageing and overweight, the woman looks down at me puzzled but unafraid.

"Can I help you?" she asks, unsure. Her voice is exactly as I remember it—full of hate.

I nod vigorously and wave my companions on.

"Now!" shouts an excited eight year old, a voice I haven't heard for eleven years. I step over the threshold and push the woman back into the room. She moves out of fear and surprise as four hulking figures step unhurriedly from the shadows and join me through the front door.

Surrounded, Mrs Bailey's face is overtaken with terror. I watch carefully—this is what I came for, partly anyway.

"I want to talk to you about a very serious matter," I say. A private joke—between me and me and maybe her too—I want to see if she'll recognise her words, the words that changed my life. Ended my life and started a new one, a harder, lonelier one. The words that brought me to this house. She's dragged into her front room, the curtains have already been drawn, saving us a job . . .

It's light outside, an exhausted eight-year-old boy, alone now apart from the horribly mutilated body of the overweight, no longer ageing woman he stands over.

"How do you feel?" the boy asks the dead woman, a stronger, broken, older voice. Whatever he's about to say—if anything—is curtailed by a shrill beeping. It puzzles him, then I wake up and grope for my phone . . .

I had a message from Liv; *'thinking of you handsome'*

I felt sick after my latest nightmare, no idea what—*if*—I should reply.

There was a knock at the door and after I managed to grunt something of sufficient volume, Dave came in to say he was heading to the snooker club in ten minutes. Definitely not wanting to be on my own, I insisted on paying for a cab down there as I knew they'd have walked if I hadn't been going along.

It was a quiet night and I was lost in thought most of the time. When I wasn't taking a shot I thought about Mrs Dorothy Bailey and her brutal death. I hated the part of me trying—succeeding—to think of it as justice, revenge or something like it.

Most of the talk centred around the next day's game, my distant return to playing and which of our defenders would be most adept at a midfield role. Pretty much we either agreed or else I faced a united opposition in Mike and Dave. Dave hated to disagree with Mike and Mike rarely had it in him to disagree with Dave. I felt so low I even lost the will to put up much of an argument about anything, which wasn't like me.

We packed in the snooker at ten thirty and had a swift two pints in the pub next door before heading home. Emboldened by a couple of hours drinking I insisted we walk back and it was all I could do at times to stop myself trying a jog. My knee seemed to be making progress day by day, almost hour by hour rather than the week by week I'd been told to expect.

In the kitchen back at the flat, Dave made tea and I brought up the murder of 'one of my old' teachers. When Dave and Mike began to ask for details all I could think of was my dream and I didn't know what to say. I'd had the crazy notion they'd be disinterested enough to help me see it as unimportant. There was a logic in there somewhere even if it was misguided. We talked about it until I made my excuses and went to bed five minutes before the late film on BBC1 was due to start; I wasn't going to miss '*Thunderbolt and Lightfoot*' for anything. By the time the credits rolled at 2.15, tears were coursing down my face. I thought I was crying for her but I couldn't really be sure.

I didn't look much like him any more but I felt like that eight-year-old once again, confused and standing alone in the corridor singing Christmas carols to himself.

The last thing I thought about before I turned off the lamp was that I'd never texted Liv back. What would I have said anyway?

Sunday, 12th February

I sat in Mike's girlfriend Mary's car, parked about half a mile from the edge of the football pitch. Dave's girlfriend Lucinda was there too, chatting away with Mary while Fats and I were more or less engrossed in a guessing game of who had touched the ball last. I'd done my best to convince Fats that his value to the team would come as a shock introduction for the last twenty minutes of the game and he wanted it to be true so badly he accepted it. I let him catch a glint in my eye to stop him getting complacent.

It was a day to be in the car as it was far too cold to consider standing on the sideline but we'd missed two goals already through a combination of condensation and a failure to concentrate. Lucinda refused to accept she'd failed to see Dave do whatever he did in the few seconds before Fats had shouted, "That's Dave!" and we turned to see his thirty yard celebratory dash arms aloft into Vern's bear hug.

At some point my mind wandered away from the game and I found myself wondering if I should speak to Liv about Mrs Bailey. I'd woken up at seven fifteen and sent Liv a message back saying I was looking forward to catching up Monday. Seven hours later I hadn't heard back from her. It felt unsettling to have been so recently talking about Mrs Bailey and exposing my anger and deep sensitivity about her, bringing all those suppressed emotions right back, only to be confronted with the shocking news of her death. I put my bad dreams down to the emotional stress. I tried to remember how much I used to dream. It seemed since my operation I'd been dreaming much more regularly and vividly; perhaps they'd stuck too much anaesthetic in or something and shone an unwelcome light into some dark corner of my brain.

When my mind switched back to the game, Fats had gone and there couldn't have been more than a few minutes left. I wanted to be at home. Seeing Donny had made me want to see my parents. I looked at my watch but that didn't help since I hadn't checked it when the second half had kicked off. I let my mind drift back into its daydream.

I could go home that coming Friday. I would hopefully be seeing Liv tomorrow and I could even see if she fancied coming back with me so she could see her parents and maybe meet up with me in the evenings. I couldn't remember when Liv had said she was coming back from France. I thought about my text—if she replied that should tell me. The question was how I should drop the weekend into the conversation. It had to be casual of course but then I wanted her to feel that I thought it could make for a cool weekend. I wondered if there was any way she'd be daydreaming and making plans in the same way as I was—are girls even like that? Probably—if they actually fancy you. Either way, early days as it was, I'd be better served letting Liv know I was keen on seeing a lot more of her; I hadn't seen her for three days and already it felt like December without Christmas. What she'd said in her text last night had been as unexpected as it had been welcome. I decided on an all out charm offensive the next day.

The next thing I knew was that the game had finished and everyone was trudging from the pitch shaking hands with any opposition players who passed within range. I got out of the car and walked over. I could tell from players' faces that we'd won but I had no idea of the score. Wayne, a 'tryer' in football parlance, trotted up and clapped me on the back.

"Skipper, how are you?"

"Good mate, knee's on the mend as quickly as can be expected. Enjoy the game today?" Hopefully he'll tell me something I can use in my post match analysis, I thought, having missed most of the second half action.

"Yeah, dirty bastards. I've played against that little lad before, thought the best thing to do after the first half was slow him down a bit early on. Seemed to work."

"Sounds like you were the dirty bastard," I laughed. "Looked fairly comfortable once that last goal went in," I ventured.

"Yeah, defence looked good today I thought."

"Thanks for that; I won't rush myself back then. Or maybe I'll just take your place when I'm fit, get some more pace into the defence." I was laughing but it wasn't exactly hard to guess I'd taken offence at what had been said. I knew I was being oversensitive, I hoped it wasn't obvious that part of me hated them winning without me.

"You'll be able to stick me up front then. Catch you soon anyway mate." With that he wandered off.

In the pub I bullshitted my way through the game chat. My assessment of Mike's friend Miles the only point I nearly came totally unstuck. It turned out he'd gone home for the weekend.

By the time we got back to the flat it was nearly eight o'clock. Erica had sellotaped a note to the outside of my window with a picture on it, presumably of her and me. In a not big enough speech bubble she'd asked if I'd like to join her and Kenny at the hall bar at ten o'clock. It didn't mention what Clare might be doing at ten o'clock.

All I wanted was for it to be eleven o'clock Monday so I could be sitting next to Liv. I picked up a book about the early years of the independent American state I needed to get through to complete an essay. It had the desired effect on me and after thirty minutes trying to get through five or six pages I rolled over and went to sleep.

I dreamt I was a fisherman and I'd lost my boat. My crew didn't seem to care and wouldn't help me look for it. I woke up later, when Kenny banged on my window, but didn't join them for a drink. Instead I went to sleep and tried to dream about being the frustrated fisherman again.

6

"All the leaves on the tress are falling
To the sound of the breezes that blow
And I'm trying to please to the calling
Of your heartstrings that play soft and low"

From "Moondance" by Van Morrison

Monday, 14th February

When my alarm went off just before eight o'clock, I was awake in an instant, barely able to contain my excitement at the thought of seeing Liv in three hours time. I showered and picked up my phone to call a cab, dimly registering that I'd not even thought about using my crutches. I had a message; I opened it, read it and slumped back onto my bed. Liv had texted to say she wasn't back until the evening—*did I listen to anything she said?*—and that she'd call tonight or see me tomorrow. What a washout, of all the shitty things to happen I thought, why this? I got back into bed, still very damp from the shower and decided to rescue my spirits by skipping the day's classes. As soon as I'd taken the decision I didn't feel tired enough to sleep so I re-read the book I'd struggled with last night and made some notes and an essay plan. I went through my exercises about mid morning and then went back to work; it occurred to me that while none of the lecturers ever cared about your attendance, Liv would probably require an excuse as to why she wouldn't be able to copy my lecture notes. I texted her back about eleven and said I'd realised last night that she wasn't back for today and that I'd woken up with a migraine so skipped uni; I could hardly have been less convincing if I'd tried.

I went over to Kenny's about two o'clock and he made us some barely edible lunch. I told him about Mrs Bailey and how she'd been murdered.

93

I was starting to feel a lot less bothered about the whole thing and said nothing to Kenny about her being such a bitch to me when I was a kid.

I did more work later on in the day, sitting on my bed with the curtains open as it grew dark and wet outside. Weighing up how much work I'd done during the day compared with how much I got from most of my lectures, I felt I'd be well served skipping more Mondays.

I'd been largely successful in convincing myself that Liv wouldn't be in touch before I'd see her but at about eight thirty, while I was making my tea, I heard my phone ring from my bedroom. In the rush to see who was calling, I banged my knee on the way into the room but the pain evaporated when I saw it was Liv calling. I paused half a second to get my breath and answered.

"Hello?"

"Hi Matt, it's Liv, can you talk?"

Well, yeah of course, it's you isn't it?

"Yep, just bear with me twenty seconds while I get my tea from the kitchen."

I ran into the kitchen and told Colin he could have my half cooked bacon and then got back to my phone well within twenty seconds.

"Hi, sorry about that. How are you? How was France?"

"Wonderful, just a shame I had to come back."

"Really, and there was me thinking you'd be missing me too much to enjoy yourself properly," I joked lamely.

"No, I don't mean that, just coming back to this crappy, cold, little room. I haven't got any food in the flat and Caroline's under the mistaken impression that I'm going to spend the next hour and a half having a flat meeting about whether to set the thermostat at twenty or twenty two degrees. Sorry for going on, how are you anyway, has your headache gone now?"

"Yeah, it was nothing." I steeled myself for what felt like a big gamble. "Look, I haven't eaten yet and I haven't been out of the flat all day, why don't I come over and we can go out for something to eat?" Before Liv could answer I jumped in for her, "Sorry, you're probably knackered from travelling all day."

"You'd really make it over, I might not be such great company you know?"

I could hardly believe how touched she sounded. I felt so in love my stomach was doing somersaults.

"You're always good company," I laughed, on a roll, "I'll see you in twenty minutes-half an hour ok?"

"Perfect. Thanks."

"God, don't mention it, I'm looking forward to seeing you. Have a think about what you want to do for food and I'll see you soon."

"Bye."

"Bye."

When I got to Liv's it was nearly nine fifteen. I rang the bell and she answered the front door herself. She had her hair tied back, a couple of loose strands curling down to the corners of her smile framing her face. She was wearing a tight black top, which for her was unusually low cut. The half-light in her room created by the mixture of candle and lamplight somehow enhanced her cleavage and continually drew my eyes towards it. I'd never considered her so overtly sexy before.

"Can I get you a drink? Sit on the bed, it's probably the most comfortable."

"Um, wine's fine if that's what you're on," I said, having seen half a glass of red on the desktop, which I guessed hadn't been there since Thursday night.

"I'll just get you a glass from the kitchen," she said, disappearing.

I didn't recognise the music; the display said we were listening to New Order's *'Back to Mine'* album. She came back in the room and must have thought I looked unimpressed.

"I bought this on a recommendation, sorry it's so dreary."

Before I could make any attempt at a reply (what was I supposed to say to that anyway?) Liv went on, "I took the liberty of ordering food as time was getting on. Chinese—my treat. Do you like crispy duck, Chow Mein, sweet and sour?"

"Not fussy, all sounds good to me."

Liv sat down next to me on the bed, resting her wine glass on her thigh. She was wearing black pinstripe trousers and flat, expensive looking penny loafers.

"I quite missed you, you know," she said as if she was genuinely puzzled.

"I don't know why you sound so surprised," I answered.

"Firstly, because I never miss any*one* or any*thing* and secondly, because I've only known you a few days. It's not that I'm surprised—not in a bad way anyway—just that it's unusual. For me I mean. It surprised me. It's nice though, I'm not complaining."

It was refreshing to hear Liv struggling to find the right words for once.

"Well if it helps, I really missed you too. It doesn't take long to get used to having someone you can talk to and enjoy spending time with around you. I feel like I've known you for a lot longer than three weeks."

I think I leant towards her first but she could well have already been moving towards me. I think also that I intended to kiss her on the cheek but her movement meant my lips met her soft and open mouth. I gently guided her back towards the bed so she rested her head on the pillow and we kissed each other like that until the doorbell rang. When I heard it, with a conscious effort I made sure I didn't pull back from her too quickly but simply finished kissing her, opened my eyes and waited for her to look at me before I leant back and helped her sit up.

Liv smoothed her trousers and went to answer the door.

She came back a couple of minutes later with enough food to feed a team of Michael Jackson's lawyers. She set down the food in the middle of the floor while she went to get some plates and a new bottle of red. Even though we hardly spoke it took a long time to get through all the food and it was nearly eleven o'clock before I eased myself from the floor to aid my (in)digestion. As I looked at the clock, I inadvertently drew Liv's attention to the time.

"How did it get so late?" I bit my tongue too late; I really didn't want the evening to end yet.

"Do you have to go?" Liv asked me, giving nothing away in her expression or tone.

"No, I'm more a night person but I don't want to keep you up if you're feeling your long day," I said, hedging my bets. *Night person?? What did I sound like?*

"I didn't get up 'til ten and the fifty five minute flight is not as gruelling as you might think," she laughed.

"Ok, I was only going to take the piss out of you if you'd said it was late anyway. What's this music, I didn't notice you change it?" With an inward sigh of relief, I'd changed the subject.

"Faithless—d'you like it?"

"Yeah, it's cool, some of it sounds quite familiar. I don't have any of their stuff. I don't really buy much dancey stuff. Is this Boy George singing?"

By the sceptical look on Liv's face I guessed I hadn't kept the disdain out of my voice. She skipped the track to the next one. "Well, he *is* a pecker," I said, holding my hands up defensively.

"It *is* the worst song on the album," she laughed. "What's a 'pecker?'"

"Hmmm, just means a dick I guess. As in idiot, not *dick* dick . . . sorry, potty mouth. It means idiot."

"Ok, sorry to have offended you with my appalling taste in music. Do you want more wine or a cup of tea?"

"Whatever's easier. What are you having?"

"I'm going to make some tea but you can have whatever you want—coffee, wine . . ."

I wanted her back in the room as quickly as possible, next to me on the bed so I might kiss her again so I plumped for tea. I helped carry the empty food trays and the crockery into the kitchen and then went to the bathroom while Liv made the tea. I checked my teeth in the mirror and teased out a couple of bits of food from between my incisors before going back in the bedroom. I stopped the music and listened for her approach. When I heard the kitchen door open I started track six on the Faithless album and sat back on the bed. I wondered how long it would take her to notice but as she set the tray on the desk she asked, without even looking at me, "What pecker's been fucking around with the stereo?"

"Touché!" I said.

"I was going to change it anyway, any requests?"

I wanted her to choose and at the risk of looking like a dick I went for something there was no way she'd have. "Have you got any Tom Waits, he's always good when everyone else has gone to bed." I knew I hadn't avoided looking and sounding like a dick and when Liv nodded and put on *'Looking for the Heart of Saturday Night,'* I was batting nought out of three.

"I haven't heard this in a while, good choice."

It was a good choice as it turned out as we quickly regained the intimacy we'd found before the food had arrived. Liv told me about her weekend; it sounded unbelievably glamorous for someone who seemed to be enjoying drinking tea from a mug now intermittently resting on *my* thigh. She hadn't seen her father as it turned out as he'd been detained on business and that had in turn obviated her from any responsibility to attend whatever function she'd actually flown out there to attend. Instead she'd been wined and dined by some French aristo she'd known since childhood. I didn't like the sound of him at all. Apart from that, Liv said she'd spent most of the time playing a piano in a studio at the back of the villa.

I told her about my weekend, leaving out any mention of dead, mutilated teachers so as not to spoil the mood. When I told her about the football match, I mentioned my mixed feelings that they'd won without me. She'd taken the mugs and put them on the floor at that point and then put her hand over mine and kissed me so beautifully I felt she was taking us onto something new. Tom Waits never fails does he?

I ran my hands over her arms, back and stomach trying to gauge how comfortable she was to go further. I slipped my hand underneath her top, just above the waistband of her jeans—up or down? I thought—and gently brushed her flat stomach with my fingertips. The sound of her shoe hitting the floor as it fell from her foot made my cock surge and she began to breathe more urgently. My blood pulsed around my body and my heart quickened. I pulled her body tightly to mine and she ran her fingernails slowly up and down my spine. My hands felt their way slowly up her back and I was surprised when I realised she wasn't wearing a bra; it changed my next move and enforced a bolder strategy. I kept my hands on her back and kissed her neck, checking to see if her top was buttoned or a pullover. Pullover. I bottled it and put my hand on the outside of her thigh and still she kissed me back. I felt her nails harder on my back encouraging me on. I waited a couple of minutes and then eased my hand up Liv's top all the way to her breast. This was a make or break moment in more ways than one—it was second base, the first really sexy one and I was never sure how skilled I was around girls' breasts; I'd always been happier further south. She could have been faking (if girls bother to fake general moaning and groaning) but another shortening of Liv's breath told me I was getting something right. I tried to retain some detachment so I could stay calm and in control but Liv's skin was so warm and silky it was impossible.

Not wanting to push my luck, but keen to move things on, I manoeuvred Liv onto her back, and moved my hand down between her legs and gently stroked her through her trousers. She eased her pelvic bone gently into the palm of my hand and I undid the zip at the side of her trousers and slid them off, kissing the ends of her toes as her trousers slipped over them. I leant over and folded the trousers roughly over the back of the chair and lay back down next to Liv.

"What about you?" she whispered.

I pulled my sweater off and then my combats and socks—these I let lie in a heap on the floor. Then I used my partial undressing as a gambling chit and went to take Liv's top over her head.

"Cheeky!" she said, still lifting her arms straight above her head.

She had larger breasts than I'd expected, not that they were large but they looked pert and alert—the nipples semi hard and standing out. She lay back down and pulled me to her. I kissed her breasts and down to her flat stomach, along the edge of her white knickers noticing again how warm her skin was. I worked upwards again a little way and then back down to the edge of her knickers, then quickly brushed over them to kiss the insides of her thighs. I felt the warmth and wetness just underneath as she parted her legs ever so slightly wider. I inhaled as deeply and as quietly as I could and my cock felt as if it might burst as I ground it into the bed. I put my open mouth to her knickers and slowly pushed my hot breath through to her. Liv groaned and twisted her back one way and then the other, thrusting herself towards my open mouth. I reached up with both hands and tugged her knickers down by the sides as she lifted herself off the bed to allow them to come off. I leant up and lifted her legs up slightly and slipped her knickers over her feet. I kept them in my hand and once again kissed the ends of her toes, gently nipping the ends between my teeth, wanting to ease the atmosphere and show I wanted to take my time. I also wanted to give her a chance to confirm this was what she wanted. On the spur of the moment I did something I'd not done or even thought about before and, looking into her eyes, pressed her knickers to my nose and inhaled Liv's heady aroma.

I lay back next to her and kissed her again on her lips as my fingertips trailed up her thighs all the way to her cunt. She shuddered as I finally touched her for the first time, she was wonderfully wet but as I traced the outline of her vulva she placed her hand on mine and whispered into my ear, "Darling, I want this as much as you, but it can't happen. I'm sorry, it's complicated and I can't even explain it." I felt sick, what had I been thinking of—was it the pause, the repeat kissing of the toes or the knicker sniffing?

"Sweetheart you don't have to explain, we don't *have* to do anything." I put my hand into the small of her back and looked into her watery eyes and asked her if I should go.

"I want you stay with me, I want you all but it's not . . . not . . . it's not . . ."

99

"I'll stay with you if you're sure but tell me if you'd rather I went, it's no problem babe," I whispered as gently as I could.

"Thank you, I want you stay, please . . . if that's ok with you."

I'd never seen or heard Liv seem so small, so not in control, it made me want her even more if that was possible.

"Of course, I'd give anything to be with you. Shall I put the light off? Do you want something to sleep in?"

"I'll just brush my teeth, do you want to do yours—I have a spare toothbrush?"

"Cool, let's lie here for five minutes though, ok?"

We lay there for a while, I pulled her head to my chest and stroked her hair and every now and then she'd give me a tiny squeeze. Again I was struck by how she appeared so strong and in control one minute, yet so tiny and delicate the next. The mixture just pulled me to bits; it didn't occur to me she might know that.

She pulled away, kissed me lightly on the lips and skipped off to the bathroom.

I sighed, rolled onto my back and stared at the ceiling weighing things up.

I was hopelessly in love already, which felt good but dangerous. Liv was amazing but what she'd said about being unable to explain things might be more important than how I felt; and the way she'd said it precluded me from pressing her. But she'd asked me to stay and that had to mean we were going to become closer and she'd open up to me. Maybe she'd just been keen not to go too far too early; it hadn't seemed as if that was what she'd meant but it was the most likely explanation and one that felt easiest for me to swallow.

When she came back into the room I realised I'd been dozing. It was nearly one o'clock and it felt like the closing of a long day. I took the towel Liv held out for me and in the bathroom, as she'd promised, was an electric toothbrush with a brand new head on it. I started with the intention of being quick but since I didn't get to use an electric toothbrush too often and Liv had treated me to a brand new head I decided to take my time. I flapped my boxers, splashed some water onto my face and headed stealthily back to Liv's room. As I turned out the hall light, I noticed a light under the door in the room next to Liv's and wondered if we'd woken them up.

Liv was sitting up in bed, wearing a tiny plain white tee shirt with her knees pulled up towards her chest under the duvet. She looked at me with a sweet but enigmatic expression; she looked less tired than before. I walked over to the bed, not sure if I should get straight in without some further confirmation from Liv that that was still the plan. As the thought crossed my mind Liv pulled back the covers and I got carefully in next to her tiny, warm body and sat up next to her, tantalisingly close in the single bed.

"You must think I'm a tease," Liv said, without turning her head to me.

"Honey, no, I don't want to rush anything. It already feels special to me even though it's been so quick and I hope we have all the time we want to get to know each other. You think there's anywhere I'd rather be right now than sitting here with you?" It sounded a bit cheesy but it summed up how I felt.

"My hero," Liv said, giving me an old fashioned look. "Let's sleep."

I leant over and kissed her on the lips, then reached to turn off the lamp.

We snuggled down in the dark, and after trying out a couple of alternatives found the best position was with me on the window side of the bed lying facing her back with her asleep on my outstretched left arm, my right hand rested on the flat of her stomach. I kept my fingertips resting just inside the band of her knickers, the only item of clothing she kept on once the light was out.

"You're a tease anyway," she whispered.

"How so babe?"

"No card on Valentine's Day," she answered, digging me in the ribs.

Somehow, I was pleased I hadn't even thought of it.

It was the first time in a long time I'd gone to bed so excited about being with someone and although I dozed off straightaway, I woke up ten or twenty minutes later and then lay in the dark, seeing more and more as my eyes got used to the light. I listened to Liv's slow, gentle breathing wondering if she was sleeping. Every few minutes I eased myself forward and smelt her skin or hair and fought the urge to stroke her back, legs or belly. I thought about tomorrow, were we going out now? Would I be walking into *'Principles of History'* holding hands with the sexiest girl in the Arts Faculty?

Tuesday, 15ᵗʰ February

I awoke to find myself alone in bed, the room bathed in sunlight the pale curtains made only a token effort to block out. I looked at my watch on the desk and saw it was eight thirty. I thought back to last night. Somehow waking up alone made me feel slightly self-conscious and a tiny part of me feared an embarrassing first moment with Liv. I didn't have to wait long for it as a few seconds later Liv eased open the door with her foot and walked in carrying a tray of tea and toasted muffins. Any worries I'd had about embarrassing moments were dispelled immediately as Liv transfixed me with a warm smile.

"You like muffins, right?" she asked, setting the tray on the floor beside the bed and sitting down by my feet.

"Absolutely."

"I buttered them and there's jam here if you want some."

"Do you always have muffins?"

"No, I popped up to the shop up the road—special treat for you babe. For being such a darling last night," she said sweetly.

"Well, they *are* a treat, but I don't know if I deserve anything for being a darling . . . I had a great time last night." I sounded putridly sincere and earnest. I needed to lighten the atmosphere to stop me sounding like such a dweeb.

"Are you going in for ten?" I asked.

"Yeah. I booked a cab for you to take you back at nine thirty. I thought you could shower here, put on yesterday's clothes, and go home, change and the cab could wait for you and take you in?" She made it sound like a question but I didn't see anywhere for me to go so I nodded my assent.

"You've thought of everything—is it too soon to talk about marriage?"

"Yes. And anyway, I'm a real bitch when I don't get my own way," she laughed but something in her eyes seemed to be issuing a challenge.

When I was very young my mum had a mug, which said on it, "Enjoy yourself, it's later than you think."

I reached for a muffin and some jam.

I got to the lecture room about nine fifty and waited outside for Liv, trying to look engrossed in some crappy poster about an upcoming archaeological dig in Italy. Liv appeared around the corner at two minutes past the hour, locked in conversation with Ian Critchley, the History dept football captain and more importantly, a twat of the first order. For a split second my paranoid brain made me think they were holding hands. Naturally I was wrong but there was no mistaking the inane puppy dog look of love Critchley wore as he mooned at Liv. Liv seemed fairly amused by Critchley's banter and part of me wished I hadn't waited outside, but as I was on the point of going in, Liv looked up and gave me a knowing look so sly I almost felt a twinge of sympathy for the poor boy. I said a rather awkward hello to each of them and went into the lecture room where Liv sat between us and ignored almost all my attempts to distract her for the next hour. I knew I was trying too hard but, like anyone around the girl he's newly infatuated with, I simply tried harder and felt like a dick.

My spirits were restored somewhat when Liv made an excuse not to join the Critchley for a coffee and instead, at the first opportune moment, gave me a quick peck on the cheek.

"I gotta run to the library, shall I see you outside Dr Robertson's at twelve?"

I'd just got the same excuse Critchley had and I hadn't even asked!

"Er, yeah, ok."

I even kind of had to go to the library myself at some point but I didn't want Liv to think I was crowding her, so I texted Dave to see if he was meeting Calum as usual. I got to the coffee bar and sat down with them before Dave replied.

From the sound of it, Calum's night had topped my own; he'd got drunk at some geography students' bash and brought a girl back for the night. Sad to say, the repercussions the morning after had been heard by the entire flat and who knew whom else? The girl in question, Tash—Dave insisted on referring to her as Pant Moustache—had apparently been keen on Calum for some time and had given it all up on the first outing, labouring under the misapprehension that something more permanent was on the table.

I kept quiet about my night, pretending I'd just slept through the whole shebang. Calum had had to promise to see Tash at the flat that night in order to be allowed to leave, so there was every chance I'd be lucky enough to be there for round two.

I was pretty quiet for the whole hour, distracted by the thought I would soon be seeing Liv again and there was always the possibility of a late lunch together. Inside I was kicking myself for not suggesting this earlier.

At twelve o'clock, Liv wasn't outside and by five past everyone else had filed in leaving me skulking suspiciously outside. I went in, and saw with a measure of relief that at least there were two free seats next to each other so Liv would be able to sit with me when she arrived. Ten minutes later my phone vibrated in my pocket and I got the sinking feeling Liv was not going to be sitting next to me after all. I couldn't check it once Dr Robertson had made a 'general' request that mobile phones were turned to silent in future during his classes. I looked at Wayne's World—some dude who looked like he'd come straight from Iron Maiden's inaugural gig—and rolled my eyes to try to garner some solidarity (his phone had rung half way through last week's class.)

To ram home his frustration Dr Robertson dispensed with the usual one o'clock comfort break and it wasn't until two hours later that I read Liv's text. It was short and . . . well, short.

'Something came up, will call later'

I immediately clicked on reply but, deflated, found I had pretty much nothing to write.

Instead I walked to the library, picked up some books Dr Robertson had recommended I read for my assignment and walked back to the flat.

Although this was the first time I had attempted the walk back to the flat, I made it back in about twenty-five minutes; even uphill I seemed to be walking as quickly and easily as anyone else. I was in a much happier state when I got back and thought I would play it cool with Liv. After all, she must have had her reasons. I just wrote back, *'No problem, you didn't miss much. See you tonight maybe?'*

I wrote a few more things I ended up deleting, as they didn't fit with the playing it cool plan, sat back, and waited for a reply.

. . . and waited . . . and waited . . . and waited . . . and wondered if I'd played it too cool, or not cool enough . . . and waited . . . and wondered if I should text again, or call . . . and waited . . . and waited . . . and said hi to Dave and Calum when they came in, both times leaving my phone casually untended in my room . . . and waited . . . and had tea . . . and waited . . . and took my phone over to Kenny's, then Clare's for a couple of hours . . . and waited . . . and sent myself a text to check my phone was ok—I realised it was on silent but I hadn't missed any calls or messages . . . and cursed Liv for being so cold . . . and waited . . . and had a drink in the hall bar, played pool and the quiz machine . . . and went back to Kenny's with Erica and Clare . . . and finally gave up waiting and turned my phone off in silent anger . . . and turned it on again five minutes later when I found that particular torture even worse . . . and went back to the flat and slept, listening to Iron Maiden's first album . . . and was awoken . . .

. . . no more than half way through *'Phantom of the Opera'* by the text alert on my phone. It was Liv—I was angry. More than that, I was relieved. I read her message in the dark.

'Sorry babe, won't be in uni but can see you Thursday night? Let me know. Sleep well xx'

This time I replied straightaway; no point playing it cool if you don't feel cool, I told myself.

'Thursday fine, hope everything ok. Sleep well and take care, M'

I turned off my stereo and went to sleep, feeling like I'd aged thirty years. The last thing I thought about before I drifted off was a quotation Bukowski had put at the front of one of his books.

"Many a good man has been put under the bridge by a woman."

I hardly knew Liv, and I didn't know what Bukowski meant exactly but I knew for certain he was talking to me.

I dreamt again that night that I was that same captain of the fishing boat, which upon my return to port, wasn't where I'd moored her. What I could find of my crew were again either too drunk or too little concerned to help me find it.

Wednesday, 16th February

I woke up the next day, too hacked off to go into uni but unable to justify skipping another day so soon after missing Monday. I walked in for my eleven o'clock Economic History lecture and the fact that it was the first time I'd walked in cheered me up. After my French class I walked down and met Dave and went along with him to watch football training. I'd forgotten about Liv for a couple of hours and I felt a great weight lifted off my shoulders. Some of the boys were going to the union for drinks that night so I decided to tag along with them.

It was a great drinking night, one of those that creeps up and surprises you. There was a decent group of us in the main union bar and after only two or three drinks we were singing a few football songs and taunting a couple of the other teams. What we may have lacked in talent we more than made up for in team spirit, or so it seemed. Calum was around drinking with his hockey mates. Dave and I went over and gave him and his mates some good natured banter; only Calum taking it in good spirit which made it all the more amusing. The trouble, such as it was, started when one of the tables near us was vacated and a few of the rugby boys took up residence with the clear intention of putting an end to our singing by singing over the top of us. Probably well used to getting their own way in such matters, in the union bar at least, they were disappointed that we were clearly able to out-sing them. They called in some reinforcements and before long we were more or less outnumbered two to one. The combination of siege mentality and moving on to our fourth or fifth pints meant we weren't about to take a backward step. Instead, Dave disappeared on a mission to round up everyone so we could concentrate our forces, while I stayed at our table with Vern, Kenny, Harry and Mike. Dave returned with Digger, Terry and one of Mike's flatmates. We warmed up with a round or two of a modified '*Winter Wonderland*':

> "*We are the Swankers*
> *We said we are the Swankers*
> *Walking along, singing our song*
> *Walking in a Swankers wonderland*
> *Da-da-da-da-da-da-da*
>
> *We are the Swankers . . .*"

Then, to the tune of '*He's got the whole world in His hands*', Kenny led us through an adapted Tottenham favourite.

> "*We got Jezza Roberts number one,*
> *We got Jezza Roberts number one,*
> *We got Jezza Roberts number one,*
> *We got the best team in the land*
>
> *We got Harry Dowling number two,*
> *Etc*"

By the time we'd run through the team plus subs, Fats, Chris and Jez had returned to join us and the volume was quite impressive. Finally came the piece de resistance, a song given to us by Terry the first time he'd come out with us, and one that had never failed to provoke a reaction.

> *"My brother's in borstal, my auntie's got pox*
> *My mother's a whore down the Davenport docks*
> *My uncle's a jailbird, My sister's gone mad*
> *And Jack the Ripper's my dad*
> *La la la"*

I think this was sung to something like the closing credits from, *'It ain't half hot mum'*. We had the attention of the entire room, not least the security team. A few of the rugby lads had drifted off and a few others were finding some amusement in the spectacle but there were a few who felt sufficient malevolence to give us wanker signs, shout some abuse and even a few, "come on thens". There was a movement from a couple of the rugby lads towards us and probably half a dozen of our boys moved quickly towards them, safe in the knowledge that the likelihood of these shenanigans developing into anything more substantial than some verbal and eyeballing was pretty low with the watching security team so close. The upshot was we were asked to leave, which we duly did, under some half-hearted protest and with plenty of noise on our way out. As we filed out past the rugby lads Dave leant over and upturned their entire table of drinks.

For reasons unclear to me now Dave, Jez, Fats and I failed to move any further from the main bar than twenty yards to the coffee shop, which on the Wednesday sports nights stayed open late and served burgers and chips. The other three queued up for food while I sat down at a table. I must have been dimly aware of possible impending danger because I remember that I sat deliberately watching the door to see who came in. Just as Dave came to sit down some of the guys who had looked most angrily at us all night walked in the door carrying two full pints each. They ran in and two of the guys threw the drinks somewhere in our general direction. The third took a couple of steps closer and a split second longer to aim. His determination not to waste his beer cost him his dignity and, had he been more unlucky, might have cost him the use of his legs. As he held the drinks high in his hand Dave nipped in low, took hold of his legs, lifted him off the ground and dumped him spine first on the hard floor. The poor lad cried out in pain and shock; Dave proceeded to hurl his tray of chips point blank into his face. This time we made sure our escape was somewhat better executed.

Thursday, 17th February

Standing in a luke-warm shower at ten o'clock the next morning shards of memories of the previous evening came back to me in uneven waves. In spite of a dull ache in my head and the sickness in the pit of my stomach I smiled to myself at most of it, until I recalled that fateful face-covering chip moment. I made myself think about the day ahead. I was supposed to be seeing Liv in the evening but since we hadn't made any plans and I wanted to see her so badly, I figured she'd probably cancel. I'd text her in the afternoon once I felt better. I thought about the look on the guy's face again and the sickening way he'd cried out when his spine had hit the deck. I knew I'd laugh about it one day—provided I didn't end up sharing a cell with a nonce for a five stretch—but for now I just wanted it to be next week so it wasn't quite so fresh in my memory.

I dried myself off and went back to my room. I looked outside and saw it was dry and bright which was a stroke of luck given that my failure to book a cab meant I would be walking. I picked up my wallet and checked my phone. Midas-like the text turned my day from shit to gold. Liv said she'd meet me at six o'clock outside the library. It meant I'd be hanging around uni for longer than was ideal and a long day on my feet without crutches or my leg brace if I wanted to wear anything decent, but these were minor inconveniences. A more pressing matter was that I'd got dressed before knowing I'd be seeing Liv. If I had to iron anything to wear I wasn't going to make my Medieval History lecture. I opened my wardrobe and found nothing good enough for an evening with Liv. I took off my old Levis and put on a pair of new-ish Replays then rifled through my drawers looking for a decent top. I pulled out a v-neck navy blue sweater from Woodhouse I hadn't worn in a while and never with the Replays; I put it on over a plain white tee shirt, which by a small miracle was also clean. I checked myself in the mirror, it didn't tell me how flash I'd look after a day running around between lectures and the library but for now I thought I looked presentable.

I had ten minutes to make a twenty-minute walk—my best hope was if Mel was driving down—it was a long shot but I sent her a text as I grabbed my stuff. It only occurred to me when I didn't get a reply for a few minutes that we weren't exactly on speaking terms. I hadn't bothered waiting—knowing I could always turn back if I got a positive response—and I set off down the hill at what felt to me like a fair lick.

Enjoying the winter sun, I took the longer route past the lake rather than walking along the road. My timing appeared to be impeccable. As I rejoined the road I saw Mel driving down. Instinctively I moved towards her oncoming car and put my hand up to wave. I saw—or imagined I saw—a look of panic as she saw me and in a second she passed me without slowing down. I stood and watched her until she turned onto the main road towards uni. I wasn't making good time. I was half way there and it was eleven o'clock already. I considered turning back there and then as Mel driving past had depressed me but I trudged on regardless, wondering for the first time if I'd ever make it up with her. Wondering if I wanted to.

I arrived outside the Arts Faculty building at around a quarter past eleven and thought I'd go for a coffee and a doughnut rather than embarrass myself arriving so late. By the time I'd bought a paper and sat down with my tea and croissant it was eleven twenty. I'd arranged to meet Dave at one o'clock for lunch but for the first time since we'd met I didn't really want to see him. He'd been my best mate at uni practically from day one but I needed to be on my own.

Attempting to read the paper had brought home to me how much was on my mind. I was annoyed at people; at Mel for ignoring me, at Dave for making me feel like a criminal, at Baggy for getting murdered and haunting my dreams (ok, not strictly her fault perhaps), and even at Liv for not being around enough for me to know if we were going out or not. Most of all I felt annoyed at myself for having so little discipline—here I sat choosing a five hundred calorie croissant over the library, missing a lecture because I was too vain not to change and lacking the courage to take the bull by the horns with Liv and find out where I stood.

Five hundred calories later I felt better. After all I was in a lot better state with Liv than had ever seemed likely and even physically I was making far better progress than any of the doctors had predicted. As for my studies, I'd never been much of a worker anyway. I got a pen from my bag and started The Telegraph quick crossword. It wasn't quick but I got as far as I was going to with it—about four clues left unanswered—in about half an hour. I put the paper away, texted Dave to say I'd see him for lunch and went to the library to kill the rest of the time before I saw him.

At six o'clock, I stepped from the library building, expecting Liv might be a few minutes late. Thanks to re-runs on cable TV, one of my favourite shows from about age ten was Starsky and Hutch; the whole show was far too hip to ignore. Whenever I walk down steps I imagine I'm Huggy Bear on the opening credits, looking cool but furtive as if any number of shady characters could surprise me from any angle. Half way down the library steps I froze, just the way the editors made Huggy do; not so anyone could flash my name onto a screen, but because I'd walked right past Liv without noticing and now she was calling me. I walked back up the steps towards her and before I had to wonder if I should open with a smile, a kiss or a hug she made my mind up for me; she took both of my hands in hers, pushed herself right into me and kissed me while she stared right into my eyes. She smelt amazing and I hoped there was still a faint whiff of Huggy Bear about me.

I'd had some of my questions answered anyway.

When Liv eventually stepped away from me, I knew I must have had the soppiest smile on my face but she just said, "Hey, did you get more handsome?"

"It's possible I guess . . . or maybe actually it isn't," I laughed. "Now if I tell you how stunning you look it won't sound sincere will it?"

"Well, you could still *try*," she laughed.

"You actually do look . . ." I pretended I was thinking but I knew exactly what I was going to say ". . . tres beau, even for you."

"Oooh, I love a man who can compliment me in a foreign language."

She was still smiling but she suddenly looked ever so slightly embarrassed—if by the word love or thoughts of past compliments from other men I didn't really fancy asking.

"What do you wanna do sweetie?"

"Go home, curl up on the bed together and listen to it rain outside while we watch an old film."

"I can arrange the bed, the curling up and possibly an old movie but you may have to live without the rain," I said, as I took her hand and led her down the steps. I realised it was the closest I'd been to taking charge since we'd met.

"I won't do without my rain tonight. I just won't!" She stamped her foot for emphasis and it started to rain.

"You could at least have waited 'til we got home," I moaned. "So what have you been up to last couple of days?"

"Less than you'd think actually. I was kidding about just going home by the way; wouldn't you rather go out somewhere?"

"Not fussed either way . . ." I replied, knowing I was sounding lame. "Do you want to get something to eat somewhere? I could happily stay in or go out." I was sounding lamer by the minute. Once she'd raised the prospect of going back to hers and curling up watching a film anything else was going to seem like an anticlimax.

"You've got a free day tomorrow right?" Not waiting for an answer, Liv went on, "so we can stay up late. Why don't we go back to mine now—I need to change—pick up a dvd on the way, get something to eat and watch the film later if we feel like it?"

I wanted to shout yes, yes, yes that sounds perfect! Instead I heard myself saying, "You don't need to change, you look fine."

Silence.

"Fine? No girl likes to be told they look fine. It's just that I haven't been home yet and I feel grimy. We've not been seeing each other long enough for me to be comfortable with you discovering my odour problem."

I quit while I was ahead. Whether it was intended as such I couldn't say but I was flattered by her decision to come and meet me before she'd even been home.

"Perfect. Where do you go for dvds, the union?"

"Yep, there's a Blockbuster on the way if we don't find anything but the old films are generally better in the union anyway."

I sat on Liv's bed while she showered. She'd left me to choose some music and in an attempt to display an eclectic taste I'd gone for a band I'd heard of but never heard—And you will know us by the trail of dead. Half way through the third song I'd heard nothing offensive but nothing too exciting either. Before she'd left the room Liv had undressed, simply asking me to turn away. She'd then asked me to close my eyes and turn to face her. "Keep your eyes closed," she'd whispered and then she'd taken my hands and placed them on her naked hips before pulling me to my feet and kissing me. My average sized manhood felt like it was undergoing a David Banner-like transformation in my shorts and she ground what I knew to be her naked body into me. I dutifully kept my eyes closed but in spite of this, Liv eventually broke away with a series of short sharp kisses. "Liv," I called as I heard her grasp the door handle, "your odour's not so bad you know." I heard the door close and opened my eyes to watch the uprising in my shorts crushed like the Boxer Rebellion. I was sure she'd have enjoyed my little joke.

Apart from the odd Marilyn Monroe, I wasn't much for old films so I'd let Liv choose *'Strangers on a train'* while I made what I thought were appreciative noises about more or less everything she picked up. I looked at my watch. Somehow it was seven thirty, time seemed to fly past when Liv was around. I knew it was very early in our relationship but I thought again how I wished she were around more. On the other hand when we were together things never felt rushed and she had a way of talking to me that made me feel like the only other person in the world. It was nice to be in love. It was sobering to realise how completely in love I was. I thought about how she might feel and I couldn't conceive how she might possibly feel as strongly as me.

I restarted the album as I'd enjoyed the first couple of songs more than the rather insipid tracks that followed. I stood up to look at the watercolour I'd taken a dislike to the first time I'd been in Liv's room. It gave me a queer, unnerving sense of déjà vu and I had a horrible feeling the dark swirls might have haunted me in my dreams of late. I turned to look at some of Liv's books. On the highest shelf—one I could hardly reach given I didn't want to stand on the bed—was a set of five old leather bound books, which caught my eye. I pulled out the nearest one to me and opened it to see what it was. Holding it, it seemed even older than I'd expected. The yellowed pages were actually covered in handwriting and I thought it must be a diary. I didn't want to be caught reading something so personal even though it was clearly far too old to be Liv's so I flicked to a page in the middle more or less at random and thought I'd read just a couple of lines before I put it back. I started to read in the middle of the page under a barely legible date; all I could make out was the year, 1387.

"Raven came back to me and all was not well at Isfahan. My work is becoming harder for the moment, I may have to be content with a simple, unsatisfying slaughter."

It was difficult to read the text and my eyes struggled to focus. I was getting white spots in front of my eyes from the effort after reading these two lines so I closed the book and replaced it. I thought about the words.

"Unsatisfying slaughter . . ." There wasn't much to think about in truth, but like the picture on the wall, they unsettled me. I sat back on the bed to rub my eyes and clear my head. Before I did, I started The Smiths' *'The Queen is Dead.'*

I waited and listened for Liv's approach. I could hear some music from the next room, Liv evidently shared the flat with a Libertines fan. I tried to think of something about Liv that wasn't unusual but for as long as I was alone I couldn't. Liv had just washed her hair and looked even sexier than before; the sultry, tousled look suited her. She was only wearing a towel and some flip flops, which she stepped out of immediately she was in the room. She asked me to turnaround again and I braced myself for another brush of her breasts. A few minutes later she ruffled my hair and told me I could open my eyes. Her hair was wet but she was dressed in a white cotton vest and black trousers. She wasn't wearing any shoes and I noticed how tiny and flawless her feet were. Her toenails had a perfect French finish.

"I'll just dry my hair and we'll go for something to eat ok? We'll be able to get a cab on the main road do you think? What do you fancy to eat?"

"So many questions! Yes, yes and anywhere that gives you lots of bread."

"Bread?" Liv asked, raising her eyebrow in amusement.

"My speciality. Naan bread, garlic bread, rustic bread with olive oil, bread and butter, chapatti, brioche. I don't like that awful stuff they try to give you with rosemary and rock salt though; there I draw the line."

I'd clearly been less funny and less charming than I'd imagined. All I got was a quizzical look from Liv before she said, "You decide then," and turned to dry her hair in the mirror.

"Bigmouth strikes again," I mumbled to myself as the song started. I fancied an Indian but thought Liv would be more inclined to go Italian. When she finished her hair I put it to her.

"There's a nice Indian in Harborne or an Italian Colin told me was nice if you fancy going into town."

"Didn't you say Colin was a tosser? Let's go Indian, plenty of bread choice for the tiny tearaway," Liv smiled condescendingly.

"Well, I've been well and truly put in my place there haven't I?" I giggled.

"Not quite yet. Give me a kiss handsome."

I'd only been to Lal Akash once before on an early night out with the other guys in the flat before we'd worked out we more or less couldn't stand one another. I'd been very drunk but nonetheless impressed that night from what I could remember. What with one thing and another—mostly kissing Liv which passed time like nothing else—it was gone nine o'clock by the time we sat down at a cosy table at the back of the tiny restaurant. There were only a couple of tables taken in the place but I put this down to it being a Thursday night.

I was trying pointlessly to decide between Kingfisher and Cobra when Liv ordered a bottle of Italian red after a moment's glance at the wine list. I ordered chicken tikka, a house speciality of lime rice with cashew nuts and a garlic naan, which I ummed and ahhed about, thinking it might put Liv off kissing me later. Liv asked if we could share the rice and ordered a Prawn Rogan and Keema naan, which were guaranteed to put me off kissing her.

In the light of a solitary candle Liv's eyes burned fantastically bright as we leaned into the table.

"Your eyes are very sparkly. Have any more than two dozen people told you that before?"

"Yes, of course they have but it's nice to hear it from you. You don't give compliments very naturally do you?"

"Umm, I just did, didn't I?" I asked defensively.

"No you didn't. You told me my eyes were sparkly when you wanted to say beautiful and straight after you made a joke out of it so we could move on."

I knew it was my turn to speak because Liv was staring straight into my eyes but I gave myself a few moments.

"You're probably right. I know your eyes are beautiful, maybe that doesn't even do them justice but if I said that I'd sound like I was just saying it as a line."

"You could never sound like that."

"I couldn't pull it off you mean," I said, laughing.

"You can't take a compliment without laughing it off either, can you?"

"Shit no—I can't. I'm sorry, pay me another one and I'll do what I can."

"*Your* eyes are beautiful," she said, "and when you look at me that way I don't quite feel in total control of myself."

I wanted to make a joke, I really did. Of course it was great to hear but it still made me feel as if I wanted to get onto any other subject. Eventually I just said, "Thank you," and didn't add that I never felt anything close to self-control when I was with her.

"I do like my eyes . . . and my skin, I think I have my mother's skin."

"Anything else you like about yourself?" Liv asked with a small smile as the wine was poured.

When the waiter had gone, I continued.

"Cheers," I said offering Liv with my glass to clink.

"Cheers," she said and I drank.

"You're supposed to make eye contact when you touch glasses you know."

"Really? I've not heard that before. Let's try again."

Once I'd proven I'd learnt rudimentary wine toasting, Liv asked me again what I'd admit to liking about myself.

"My legs I suppose, I think I have decent legs although I wish I could stretch my body—probably just my stomach—by three or four inches. It might be nice to be six foot."

"Anything else?"

"One more thing yes. I seem to have developed a knack of dating beautiful girls."

"Girls?"

"Well just the one I mean. One beautiful one anyway," I said sincerely. "I'm meeting her later as it happens, so we can't spend too long over dinner."

"What's her name? She's dead."

For a second I wasn't totally sure Liv was loving my little joke.

"You know there wouldn't—*couldn't*—be anyone else right? Anyway I want to hear what you like about yourself and see if they're the same things as me."

"In a second, I want you to tell me more about your mother. Are you close? Are you her favourite?"

"Err, not her favourite I don't think. She's always been very close to Donny and I was fairly unlovable as a teenager but we've definitely got closer as I've got older. She's not one for constantly declaring how much she loves me but she shows it in plenty of other ways."

"Such as?"

"Oh I don't know . . . she's always bought me a new pair of football boots every year. And when she used to come home from work she'd always have an iced bun or a crème egg or something for me even when I was back over Christmas with my leg. And she always wants me to kiss her goodnight when she goes to bed and I always do and I can't imagine not doing it. And she used to take a whole day off work to take my sister, then my brother then me to our uni interviews. And loads of stuff like that," I finished self-consciously.

"Someone's gone all red," Liv teased. "You shouldn't be embarrassed; that was sweet."

I kind of knew that already.

"And what about your dad?"

"Blimey, can we save him for another night?"

As soon as I'd said it I felt a twinge of guilt so I pressed on before Liv could let me off the hook.

"Well, he used to come to every game of football I ever played and drive me to every match. On Saturdays, when I played for the school in the morning and Valley Park in the afternoon he'd drive me to both games and watch no matter where they were or what the weather was like. I reckon after every single game he'd always ask me if I'd won man of the match and be shocked when I said no. He used to leave little piles of change around the house and let me find them and every time I went to tell him I'd found the money he'd say I could keep it for being honest. When I was really little he used to tell these great cowboy stories to my brother and me on Sunday mornings before we had to get up. I'm told I walk like him and I think I have some of his looks—lucky chap—and last but not least he thinks drinking anything over a glass and a half of wine is borderline alcoholic. Am I off the hook now babe?"

"Yes, you're off the hook. It's nice to hear you talk, your voice is very relaxing."

"That doesn't mean I'm sending you to sleep does it?"

"There you go again!" Liv burst out as the waiter set down the naans and then the rice. Another waiter arrived immediately after with the rest of the food. Liv picked up her glass and said, "Bon appetit!"

"Cheers," I replied, rather blandly.

"Mmmm, this is great; try some of this," Liv said as she offered me a prawn.

"Umm, no thanks; I don't actually eat prawns I'm afraid."

"You should."

"Yeah . . . maybe," I mumbled. "Would you like to try some chicken?"

"No thanks, boring."

"That's me, I love my boring food. It's very good actually and this rice is lovely."

Liv raised a suspicious eyebrow at me as she slowly chewed a prawn. I nodded at the rice and she took some with a spare fork. She made what I took to be an appreciative noise so I thought I was ok to proceed with my earlier line of questioning.

"I'm still interested to hear what you like about yourself; just don't go on too long though yeah?"

"No, I won't go on too long. I'm clever, manipulative, strong and single minded. I always do what I want, say what I want to say and have to have my own way. I have a horrible temper and I am totally independent."

She didn't speak for a few seconds and I thought she'd finished but then she added, "And I've never been in love."

In my head I heard her add the word, "before" but her lips didn't move.

"That's not much of a sales pitch," I laughed.

"It's not meant to be, if I need to give you a sales pitch you'd better tell me."

"I was kidding babe. All I mean is half of what you said isn't exactly portraying you in an attractive light."

"I didn't *say* I was attractive."

"Let me start again." I took a big bite of chicken and a mouthful of rice to buy some time. "You don't seem to have to have your own way, you've always been very considerate as far as I'm concerned. I haven't seen your temper so maybe that's true but why would you include that in what you like about yourself? I don't think you're manipulative either. And you never mentioned funny, beautiful, great company or your impeccable taste in clothes."

"Babe, in a way this might seem like it's nice to hear but actually I hate talking about myself. It's not for me to say I'm pretty, funny or good company but I'm glad if you think so. I like to hear you talk, but because I ask you what you like about yourself and you're ok to tell me, doesn't mean I can reciprocate. I hate to admit this but I'm close to displaying that disgusting temper I mentioned."

The evening wasn't really turning out as I'd hoped.

"I'm sorry, I was only kidding you know. We don't have to talk about it of course. I like to hear you talk too, very much." A pan piped version of *'You're Still The One'* by Shania Twain was playing. Under the table my hands eventually found her knees. Liv set her knife and fork down and, looking at me over the table, found my hands with hers. With the faintest tilting of her head she attracted the waiter's attention and mouthed the words, "bill please."

I'd never left a restaurant half way through a meal before; still less one where I'd been so enjoying the food, but as powerfully as Liv could speak, she had an ability to say even more without making a sound. Within five minutes we were kissing in the back of a black cab and within ten we were stumbling through her bedroom door completely entwined, our hips virtually glued together. We crash-landed on Liv's bed, for once I was looking down onto her. With as much restraint as we could muster in the throes of passion, we tore at each others clothes but I was caught in a surreal state of mind and throughout, I was able to drink in her exquisite features, as her eyes were as tightly shut as mine were frozen open.

I thought of the soldier I'd seen in a Natassja Kinski film who had been sent to war away from his new bride and upon his return was so overawed with anticipation he was rendered impotent. It was a pretty awful film as far as I can recall, but like the soldier, I'd been pretty keen on Natassja Kinski at the time, so had every sympathy. My cock felt about three seconds from bursting through the fly of my jeans and my mind quickly moved on. My eyes didn't. When I looked at her I had no conception of much else outside. I heard Liv's breathing begin to quicken and she groaned as, down to knickers on her bottom half, she ground herself into my groin. I closed my eyes and succumbed. After some breathless minutes where we each lost our remaining clothes and I swapped the overhead light for the softer lamplight I slipped easily inside her.

I can't say we made love all night, I know we slept for part of it, even most of it perhaps, but I know we found each other several times in the course of the night. Each time got slower, more unhurried and every time I made sure to wait for the telltale groans and tightening of Liv's body that would tell me she'd come. I was trying to be considerate of course but the truth is that from the first time I'd ever heard and felt a woman climax it had been the biggest turn on for me. I'd read Michael Douglas had said as much in his divorce proceedings when he'd mounted (no pun intended) the infamous "sex addict" defence. They say you never see a poor farmer but I'm equally convinced that you never see a sex addict without a decent looking girl on his arm.

I awoke, alone in bed. Liv was at her desk with a pile of books in front of her. Given she was only wearing a white thong and matching white shirt and touching up her already perfectly painted toe nails I guessed she hadn't been slavishly working her way through John Guy's *'Tudor England'*.

I must have let out some sort of groan—possibly in appreciation of her outfit or maybe that pose—because Liv looked up at me with an expression that was a mixture of surprise and amusement.

"Morning sleepy."

My vocal chords not being used to working so soon after waking, I managed another groan, followed by a throaty cough and eventually a, "Morning."

"I made you some tea," she said, indicating a mug just under the bed near my head.

"How did you know I'd wake up?"

"Because I need you to put that magic tongue of yours between my thighs again before I go for a shower. Do you know how I was going to wake you?"

It crossed my mind that I probably did know and that I'd saved myself from embarrassment on two counts. Firstly, the end of my knob first thing in the morning, particularly after a night of wall-to-wall sex, was no place for a lady to put her mouth. Secondly, and perhaps more importantly I could count on one hand the number of times in my post pubescent life I've awoken from a night's sleep and not needed to relieve my bladder before contemplating anything else. I was sure this must be the case for men besides myself.

"It wasn't supposed to be a trick question."

I'd become lost in thought.

"Sorry babe, I was miles away. Thanks for the tea. I'll drink it, powder my nose and then you can have my tongue—my whole self in fact—to do with as you will for as long as you can stand it."

Liv blew me a kiss and then, obviously deciding that wasn't enough, came over—on her heels, toes pointing at the ceiling—to sit on the bed and kiss me properly.

"You looked so cute when you were asleep," she whispered.

"Honey if you keep saying too many nice things to me I'm going to get soppy," I warned her. I tried to pretend this was a joke but it wasn't. I could hardly contain how happy I was at snaring such a charming princess.

Friday, 18th February

Liv had plans for that evening and I finally showered and left her place about seven o'clock after an afternoon of kissing, cuddling, sex and musical education. We made plans to meet up on Sunday and have lunch and spend the day together the following Saturday. Liv was typically vague on her movements during the week but I figured it was probably too early in the relationship for me to be too demanding.

As I waited for the bus to take me somewhere close to home, I buzzed Dave to see what plans he had for the evening. The team had a cup match the following day and Dave was planning a quiet night but said he'd join me for a couple in the pub. As the bus pulled into the stop I saw the back half of the top deck was full of fourteen and fifteen year olds drinking cans of cheap lager. From what I could glean from the tail end of the previous week's *'Tonight'* show with Trevor McDonald, I was odds-on for a happy slapping if I went upstairs. Although I would much rather have sat with the quieter, more sober looking demographic that occupied the downstairs section, I found myself taking the stairs in a self conscious act of defiance on behalf of the moral majority. In a ridiculous way I thought I was proving something to these people by doing it. The feeling didn't last long however and my arrival on the upper deck was greeted with a rowdy cheer that made me smile, then a cry of, "Bus wanker!" that didn't.

I decided discretion was the better part of valour and chose a seat towards the front. I wasn't exactly thrilled that I was the only person up there besides these kids. I estimated I had about fifteen minutes to survive. Trevor, or one of his minions, had also claimed something like eight out of ten teenagers now carried knives—I couldn't remember the exact statistic but I knew it was shockingly high. So shocking in fact that when I'd heard it I'd screamed out something like, *As if that's true—I'm a teenager and no one ever asked me. I bet they only asked fifteen year olds for fuck's sake—of course they're gonna tell you pricks they pack steel every time they walk out of the door. If one of the fuckers ever tried that shit on me I'd kick them all the way to Feltham."* Big words that rang hollow in my present situation.

The hairs on the back of my neck prickled constantly and I strained to hear as much of the conversation behind me as I could. Most of it was about where they'd try to get in first, who they were meeting and how battered they were going to get; all pretty harmless stuff. Harmless to me anyway I thought. I tried to become engrossed in watching the traffic and it wasn't too long before we entered familiar territory and I felt much better to be within walking distance of home—if I fancied an absolute soaking. When the bus stopped outside the Bear & Staff a further group of six or seven got on—exclusively male and exclusively from the eight out of ten I'd have bet. When I inadvertently made eye contact with the last of them to reach the top of the stairs, I gave him the best dismissive look I could muster and spent the next couple of minutes imagining my best comebacks to any moves on his part—all my lines would be delivered in the harshest Cockney accent I could manage (it's standard practice in the suburbs.) I had my doubts it would cut any ice tonight though; this lot might just assume I was part of some care in the community programme.

I thought some more about Trevor McDonald and the implications of his programme. These kids were doing no one any harm, had he made me and countless others worry for no reason? Or perhaps now everyone was pre warned there were no soft targets any more. Then again, the show *could* have given thousands of kids the impression there must be something missing from their lives if they *weren't* out happy slapping every waking hour. These thoughts took me most of the way home. What took me the rest of the way home was concentrating on not hyper-ventilating while I apologised for not being able to offer a light to one of the girls who was polite enough to thank me, "anyway" before she went back and reported, "'e sez he ain't fucking got one." As I started down the steps of the bus, facing the whole group of twenty or so, I had an involuntary brain spasm which caused me to wish them all a good night while I gave them a US marine style salute. They looked as bewildered and confused as I was myself. I fixed on my face a, *"What was all the fuss about?"* expression for the milk sops downstairs. Happy slapping; a media myth, I almost proclaimed aloud. Three minutes later I was back in the flat a better person, and one who felt more in touch with the disaffected youth of the day.

At half past eight, Dave and I walked upstairs and gave the girls a knock. Erica wasn't feeling too well and wouldn't be persuaded out but Clare said she'd see us at the pub once she'd done her hair and make up. We were happy to wait for her but she insisted we go on; Mike had already said he'd give her a shout around nine so we went on ahead.

Kenny had gone back to London for the weekend so we knocked for Fats and Chris, then Vern. Fats and Chris were down at the student union according to their flatmate Jake—not what we wanted to hear the night before a game. Vern was up for a couple of pints though and felt obliged to ask one of his flatmates along.

We got to the pub just after nine o'clock and Vern got a round of drinks while we found a table in the downstairs bar. I went back upstairs to help carry the drinks while Dave made chit chat with the flatmate whose name I was fairly certain was Marcus. On my way past, I noticed the guy in the couple next to us looked like Begbie from '*Trainspotting*'; I was careful to avoid eye contact. His girlfriend's coat had slipped off the back of her chair and I wondered whether I should pick it up for her as she hadn't noticed. I decided I'd leave it.

Vern carried two pints of Bass and I followed with a pint of Stella and a Caffrey's I'd ordered on a whim.

"Cheers fellas," Vern said, offering his glass.

"Cheers."

"So have you guys sorted out where you're living next year?" Vern asked Dave and me.

"Not really—we talked about it before Christmas with Clare and Erica but didn't really pursue it. I guess we should start looking," I said.

"I spoke to Clare about it earlier in the week actually, she said she might be up for it as well. Her gran's thinking about buying a place and renting it out so there's potential we could avoid a lot of hassle if that comes off. It makes sense if you have the cash as we're all on four year courses apart from you," Dave said.

"Unless I stay on for my PHD."

"Are you thinking about that already?" Vern asked.

"Mate, I'll be lucky to get beyond my end of year exams the rate I'm going."

"Are you going to run the football next year, be a shame to let the team go after this year?" Vern asked.

"Yeah, no reason why not. We'll need to get a kit sorted and probably fund ourselves in the league."

By the time we'd planned every detail of running the football team, Clare and Mike had arrived with news of Erica's 'illness.' It seemed Digger had given her a dose of something unpleasant and she was too embarrassed to come out. Not knowing either party Marcus didn't look too impressed with the story so I made sure we stayed on the subject for a while in the hope that he'd take the hint and finally get a round in. It didn't work and eventually Vern again stood up to take orders. As he pushed his chair back behind him it must have caught on something and it tipped over into Begbie's missus' chair. The dumb cow hadn't noticed her coat on the floor until now and she gave Vern the evil eye as she twisted round to retrieve it. Vern apologised straightaway and while Begbie appeared to take it all with good grace his wife was half saying to herself and half to us that the coat would need dry-cleaning. Thankfully Vern wasn't too fussed about drawing out the conversation and disappeared to the bar with a sniggering Dave.

When we finally got home it was gone one o'clock. Everyone went straight to bed but Clare and me. Since she was kind enough to ask I went upstairs for a cup of tea. Without Erica around Clare had seemed quieter than usual at the start of the night but by the end she was happy to be the centre of attention.

Clare knocked gently on Erica's door to see if she was awake but there was no answer so we sat at the kitchen table with our mugs. Clare told me how Dave (the girls were the only ones who never called him Digger) had broken the bad news to Erica and how she'd been up all night crying in Clare's room. Erica was such a gentle little thing I couldn't help but feel angry with Dave. Clare had gone to the clinic with Erica and when the results arrived through the post she'd had to open them for Erica and there'd been lots more tears. Clare had been over to see Dave and made him agree to apologise but he hadn't appeared so far.

Clare asked what I thought of her gran's offer to buy a place for her to live in for the next three years. I wasn't about to countenance looking a gift horse in the mouth, particularly when the offer was perfect.

"Would you live with us?"

"Yeah, of course, it'd be great—Dave said you'd mentioned it to him," I replied.

"I'll speak to gran tomorrow then and see what we do next," Clare said happily.

I was pretty happy too and for a moment we just sat there grinning to ourselves before Clare finally just burst out laughing and we abandoned ourselves to it. I don't know how long we were laughing for but when Erica walked in looking sleepy but smiling, I realised I was slapping myself on the thigh in hysterics. I took one look at Erica and a protective impulse seized me and I got up and gave her a massive hug.

"Goodness, someone's been on the beer; did you bathe in it?" Erica said into my ear without pulling away.

"You ok sweetie?" I whispered to her.

Erica squeezed me back in reply.

"What was so funny?" Erica asked, stepping back; already looking wide-awake and radiant.

"Dunno—nothing, we were just talking and then we started pissing ourselves."

"Matt and Dave are going to live with us next year," Clare said.

"Fan*tastic!*" Erica squealed and her face lit up with that irresistible smile of hers. This time all three of us hugged.

I didn't hang round much longer. I wanted to get a decent sleep in as I was secretly planning on going down to football and kicking it around with the boys before the match. I'd hardly given my knee a thought in days, neglecting my exercise routines, but it seemed to be feeling as good as new. I bounced down the steps to the flat. As I got to the bottom of the steps I heard some shouting outside, not too far away. I dashed for the front door to the flat and shut it behind me, out of breath and feeling oddly chilled by that shouting. I locked the door behind me, went straight to brush my teeth, then let myself into my room and got into bed. I lay with the light off listening for more shouting but there was nothing. I wrote Liv a text in the dark and debated whether or not to send it before eventually giving into myself and hitting send. I went to sleep feeling on top of the world.

Saturday, 19th February

I slept late the next morning and hadn't even looked at the clock when Dave banged on the door and said he was off to football. I sat up with a start and shouted for him to give me a couple of minutes. I threw on yesterday's boxers and went to the hall and shouted that I'd come down with him if he could wait five minutes. While Dave went to give Mike a knock I started a frantic search for my football kit. The only things I couldn't find were my shin pads; I'd emptied my drawers and the bottom of the wardrobe all over the floor before remembering I'd left them at home. I threw everything into my bag, grabbed spare shorts and a towel before heading outside.

"Lad's got his kit!" exclaimed Mike with what I could only describe as sceptical interest.

"Thought I might try having a kick around before the match," I said.

"Aren't you supposed to be on crutches for a few more weeks?"

"No, six weeks is plenty to be off the crutches and I'm only talking about a gentle kick around. No tackles."

We had a league game so it would be the first time I'd got the coach to the university playing fields since my injury. We started down the hill, knocking for a couple of the other guys on the way. Fats and Chris were late arrivals at the meet but fourteen of us made it safely onto the coach to the ground. In my rush I forgot to bring my phone along and I sweated briefly over what Liv might be making of my failure to reply to any message she may have sent.

Fats and Chris made sure they sat well away from the rest of us, undoubtedly unwilling to be quizzed on last night's activities and instead Jez gave me chapter and verse on his latest conquest. I was so nervous I found anything more than a few grunts of approval beyond me. Mike's words of caution from earlier played on my mind.

By the time the coach pulled into the playing fields, I knew I'd wasted my time scrabbling around for my kit. Physically I may have felt ready but mentally I was a million miles away. I was four to six months ahead of the surgeon's timeframe for my return to sport and I realised how ridiculous that was.

I watched the game from the sideline, shouting as much if not more than if I'd been playing. I juggled the ball from time to time, jogged around the pitch and kicked short passes back and forth with Chris until he went on as substitute.

Fats had scored in the first five minutes of the game and although we'd dominated most of the play we didn't score again until the dying moments when Mike bundled the keeper over the line. Pleasing as the result was, I did my best to give Fats a hard time about his night out.

"Lemonades all night skip; I only went to make sure Ghost got home before midnight!"

I took a few practice shots at the end of the game with Dave in goal and then we headed in for a celebratory shower, which for me at any rate felt long overdue.

I only stayed for a couple of drinks after the game, that I was certain there would be an unanswered text from Liv waiting for me played on my mind too much in the end. I made it back to the flat around six thirty, got my phone from my room and took it to the bathroom and had a much needed piss. I had a few texts—from my brother, Erica, Kenny and last of all from Liv that she'd sent about ten minutes before I'd got home. My disappointment at this discovery lasted only as long as it took for me to digest that I was to meet her at the uni station at twelve o'clock on Sunday.

Erica was in town with Clare and wanted to go to the cinema in the evening. I called Dave to see if he was up for it but he was well gone, so with Kenny not due back until the next day, I texted Erica to say I'd see her and Clare in town about eight o'clock on my own.

I texted my brother to say all was well, put on some music, set my alarm and went to sleep.

I woke with a start a few minutes before my alarm was due to go off at a quarter past seven. It took me some time to realise I was no longer being chased through the streets of Soho by a machete wielding Chinese waiter. I didn't feel particularly refreshed but I got straight up anyway and rang for a cab, before heading into the shower. The cold water felt like a thousand tiny needles stabbing at my skin. I made myself stay under hoping to get used to the cold but I gave it up after a cursory wash and rinse of my undercarriage. I shaved before going back to my room, splashed on too much cologne and dressed.

We watched a Woody Allen film Erica had chosen that didn't hold my interest at all. I sat there in the dark, periodically closing my eyes to think about what Liv and I might do the following weekend if she came back to London with me. Predictably Erica loved the film and neither Clare nor I had the inclination to mount the case for the prosecution. It was about half past midnight when we made it to the front of the taxi queue and twenty minutes later I was back in my room alone; Clare and Erica both having made their excuses. I wanted a decent sleep anyway before meeting

Liv the next day and I closed my eyes with the intention of seeing if I could continue to outrun the Chinese waiter. Failure was unthinkable . . .

Sunday, February 20th

I stood under the campus clock tower five minutes early and feeling the cold. It was a bright, sunny day but bitterly cold in the wind. Liv arrived, also early, and kissed me on each cheek before taking my arm in hers and leading me towards the main road where we hailed a cab.

"Do you know the Bull's Head in King's Norton?" Liv asked.

I shook my head, "Nope."

"Log fires, Sunday roast, big comfy chairs—a good option on a day like today," she said. "What did you get up to last night?"

"Cinema—some Woody Allen rubbish. Erica fancied it," I offered by way of explanation. "You?"

"Drinks in town followed by Bond's. Mya's been wanting to go for ages so we decided to grant her wish finally; spur of the moment thing. It was very chic, too much so for me to be honest, but good music and not too crowded for a club on a Saturday. Mya ended up on the sofa underneath one of the DJs. I don't know how she does it—every time we go out!"

"Sounds like Dave, just seems to have the knack of talking to girls. They seem to seek him out."

"I'm sure you get your fair share," Liv smiled at me coyly.

I wasn't sure how to proceed and I probably got it wrong. "I have my moments, but they're all too few and far between. I also don't have the knack of talking to girls," I added.

Liv raised one of her eyebrows at me. I choked back a comment about Roger Moore.

"Not in those situations anyway. I'm ok talking but I go to pieces if I'm trying to pick someone up or whatever. Not that I ever put myself in those situations; my work is slow and steady which I guess you'll have noticed."

"I have noticed, yes." Liv smiled, flashing her perfect teeth and perfect eyes my way and I got my usual pathetic feeling.

The Bull's Head was a charming old place. We walked into a cramped and crowded bar area full of locals and Liv led me through an open doorway to a larger room where a few couples and families were sitting down to an early lunch. The sight and smell of the food instantly made me hungry. We were shown to a table by a window which looked out onto a small courtyard garden with some tarpaulin covered tables and chairs. I took my coat off as I sat down but we were too far away from the open fire to get much benefit and the old window next to us had seen better days.

Liv must have caught me looking at the windows. "It doesn't look much but the food is great I promise," she said.

"What do you mean, it's very," I paused, suspecting I was about to sound like my dad, "quaint."

I looked at the menu and thought that if the prices and fussiness of the dishes were anything to go by, I was in for something special.

I was always taught it was bad manners to try to engage in conversation while people were looking at a menu but I never remembered to apply it. "You got any plans for this week?"

"Not really. Need to go into town to get some bits and pieces at some point; I'll probably do that Wednesday afternoon. Then I'm going back home Friday for a friend's twentieth. It's at some trendy place in Camden—Gilgamesh or something. I need to check what's going on with her tonight."

Liv went back to perusing the menu and I wondered if I should mention the plans I thought we'd made to meet up but knew it was already too late. I pretended to peruse the menu myself and thought about how best to hide my acute disappointment.

"What you gonna go for?"

"Ummmm." I hadn't chosen or taken in a single item. "Roast chicken I think. You?"

"Roast chicken? I can't see that anywhere."

I looked at the menu and after checking three or four times gave up looking for any chicken. "Sorry, I meant the duck," I said guiltily.

Liv looked at me quizzically. "You alright babe? You're frowning."

"Yeah, fine. I'm fine." I could hear I wasn't sounding convincing and the look on Liv's face confirmed it. "Just things on my mind I guess."

"Like what?" Liv's expression turned to one of concern.

I was digging myself deeper every time I opened my mouth.

"Nothing. Rubbish really."

Liv sat back, looking at me, probably wondering what the fuck I was gibbering on about. She wasn't about to fill the silence. I said the first thing that popped into my head. The first thing that popped into my head was more nonsense.

"I went to football yesterday and tried to have a kick around and it didn't go very well. It just made me feel a bit sad that's all. I'm way ahead of schedule and I have no business even going near a ball but I was starting to feel like I should push it."

"Sweetheart, you're bound to have ups and downs but as you've said, you're making fantastic progress already and I'm sure you'll be back playing in no time."

I took Liv's concern as a sign I was onto a winner here and began to warm to the role. Subconsciously perhaps I felt I could wring her for some concern to make up for next weekend.

"I'm a long way from playing football, I've hardly even run on it yet. Yesterday I just froze when I went near the ball or anyone came near me. It's terrifying when you think about how weak you are."

"Then don't think of yourself as weak. Remind yourself of how strong you were and how far and how quickly you've come back already."

This pissed me off mildly; she clearly knew nothing about coming back from a serious injury and if I took her advice literally I'd probably end up a cripple.

"If I followed that advice to the letter I could be in a wheelchair by Easter," I joked. As soon as I'd said it I realised it hadn't sounded like a joke and there had been a tell tale edge to my voice. I was about to apologise but when I saw how Liv was looking at me I bit my tongue.

"Ok, what do I know?" Liv said, closing the matter.

"I just meant that the doctors say I won't play for nine months and probably wouldn't run for another two," I offered by way of conciliation.

"I'm sure I know you better than the doctors. You said you felt ready to run—you said you did run the other day in fact. How does the knee feel?"

It was a rhetorical question so I didn't answer.

"Of course you know *me* but these chaps should know all about my knee, about *all* knees." I could feel myself getting deeper and deeper into an argument I didn't want to have.

"Whatever, let's change the subject. Take nine months to start running, take two years if it will make you happy," Liv said and turned slightly in her chair so she no longer quite faced me.

I went back to the menu. When the waitress came over to take our order three or four minutes later, it broke the silence at least. As abruptly as possible, Liv ordered venison and a glass of French red wine. As politely as I could, I ordered the roast beef and asked for a bottle of the red. In a successful attempt to embarrass both Julie, our waitress, and me Liv then changed her drink order, leaving me to ask instead for a glass of the wine.

I tried to think how I could best ease the tension between us. I wondered briefly if Liv was thinking along the same lines. I didn't think she was. I probably shouldn't care so much, I thought, but that was pointless.

"Liv, I'm sorry. Let's forget that conversation."

"What are you sorry *for*?" she asked pointedly.

"I dunno, banging on about my knee I suppose. I know it's not your problem."

"You think I'm pissed off with you for talking about your knee?"

I'd clearly misread things. I gave it some more thought.

"No, I guess you're pissed off because you were being caring and supportive and I was just patronising and dismissive in response."

"Yes, you were—unbelievably so. I don't even know why I'm still sat here."

This seemed like something of an overreaction but I wasn't about to call her on it. I leant awkwardly over the table and kissed her; a stabbing pain shot through my knee as I tried to balance myself. She didn't turn towards me but she didn't move away.

I sat back down, trying to think of what to say next, still acutely aware I was playing catch up, suddenly all too aware I'd never had to make the running with Liv like this.

"I got a text from my brother earlier. He's applying for a new job at some accountancy firm." It was an old bit of information dredged up from god knew where but I was fairly certain I'd not mentioned it to Liv before.

Liv looked at me for a few moments before appearing to decide something.

As she rose Liv shouted at me, "Do you *really* think the fucking doctors care about you as much as I do"

Stunned, I watched Liv storm out of the restaurant, banging into tables as she went, and nearly upsetting one entirely. I sat there, not knowing what to do, thinking how differently the last meal we'd shared had ended.

It never occurred to me to go after her right away, part of me even thought she might realise how stupid this looked and come straight back inside. I reached over to one of the tables close by and retrieved the Sport section of The Observer someone had left on a chair; I read an uninspiring article on the future of English one-day cricket by Angus Fraser until the food arrived.

I had a stab at both dishes as best I could, although by this time I'd lost my appetite completely. I sat alone with my Observer sport section and picked at the food until it was stone cold and past three o'clock. Outside, it was already beginning to get dark and big spots of rain appeared on the window. I was four or five miles from home, probably three miles from Liv's, cold, confused and depressed. I settled the bill—adding something like a thirty per cent tip because my brain refused to function—and stepped outside into the thick, miserable rain. I was too embarrassed to go back inside the pub and ask for them to book me a cab so I started north and homeward. I decided quickly I'd be far better served going to Liv's. It was more or less on the way back to mine anyway and if I turned up looking like the pathetically drowned rat I was, I couldn't see how she could turn me away.

I thought about how we'd started arguing and try as I might, I wasn't able to see why Liv had got so angry so quickly. I felt every drop of rain as it pounded into my skull and my face ached from the bitter winter wind before I was out of sight of the pub. The streets became increasingly dark and unfriendly and my knee throbbed in the cold. I trudged on, taking rights and lefts in what I thought was the direction of the main road back to town. I estimated I'd been walking for just over twenty minutes when I saw the end of the road I was walking down was simply walled off with a train track behind it. On the point of tears, I tried to think if we'd come over the train tracks and where they were in relation to the main road. It was hopeless, I guessed the tracks ran north towards town but I had no conviction and no idea how to get across them even if they did. I walked back to the other end of the road and took a left rather than retrace my steps in the hope that by walking parallel with the tracks I'd at least be going north. The only light came from the streetlights and the odd car going past that almost without exception covered me with a fine spray of water from the road.

I crossed to walk on the opposite side of the road to a bus shelter filled with a group of young teenagers on bikes. They were the only people I saw and thankfully they didn't show any interest in me. My knee continued to throb. I checked the time, expecting it to be around four o'clock, and found it was actually ten to five. On my left was a dour set of low-rise grey council flats. For the past half-mile or so on my right had been a less than charming rubbish strewn and overgrown wasteland. Signs like the ones in Balsall Heath told me this was another of Birmingham's red light areas. I didn't see any working girls and no potential punters braked mistaking me for one but I was as thoroughly miserable as I thought possible. My best Replays clung to my legs like an unwanted second skin and my trainers squelched with every step. I pulled my Stone Island parka tighter around my neck wondering if it was legal to market as waterproof a coat that conducted rain to my skin as if designed with that specific purpose in mind.

It hardly occurred to me any longer that I was supposed to be making for home or at the very least somewhere that looked familiar and when I eventually came to a crossroads, I had to struggle with the idea that this was what I had been looking for. Somehow I'd become so wrapped up in the struggle of every step I hadn't even thought about my direction. I looked behind me and saw the road I'd walked along had been curving gradually from left to right; if my original assumption had been right and I'd been going north, I had recently been going much further east than I wanted. I took a left at the crossroads, moving gently up hill and in the company of some modest but infinitely more homely seeming houses. The rain began to ease off at last and there were more cars on the road; even the odd few people scurrying in and out of pubs. I took a chance and asked a guy just as he went into the pub for directions to the Bristol Road.

"Two hundred yards that way mate," he said, pointing me in the direction I was heading. With relief I thanked him but he'd disappeared through the pub doorway before I'd got the words out. Not more than fifteen minutes later I approached the turning from the main road into Liv's halls. I stopped when I got to the turning, knowing I was a hundred yards or less from Liv and her forgiveness or fury. I waited a couple of minutes, toying with the idea of pressing on for home, but I couldn't have gone on even if I'd wanted to. It was a quarter to six, I'd been walking for over two hours; I was exhausted and probably sick. I rang the bell to her flat and leant against the doorframe, dimly aware I was no longer in the rain and should have felt warmer.

Liv answered the door herself. She looked at me without surprise. Her expression showed some recognition but I couldn't read it; I looked down and away from her powerful gaze. Eventually she told me simply to, "Go wait in my room."

I perched myself on the edge of her bed, not wanting to get anything wet but hardly able to support myself. In the warmth of the bedroom I started to shiver and my teeth chattered uncontrollably. I didn't recognise the music Liv was playing. When she came into the room a few minutes later she set a single mug of tea on the desk beside me and then handed me a towel. My teeth were still chattering but I didn't try to thank her as I took it from her. I towelled my face and hair since there wasn't much else I could do. I held the towel over my face and exhaled warm breath into it, enjoying the sensation on my face.

"You look terrible," Liv said as she handed me a nightshirt. She was looking into my face and for the first time I felt brave enough to look back at her. More than anything else she looked worried.

"I just wanted to speak to you. I think I got lost on the way back, I've been walking for over two hours," I said between sniffs. My nose had begun to stream clear warm snot. Liv gave me a tissue—soft and scented like everything else in her room.

"Why don't you get into bed? If you keep those clothes on you'll get pneumonia. We'll talk later."

"I'm sorry," I blurted out, fat tears coursing down my face.

Liv helped me out of my clothes and lay me down under the duvet. My eyes were already closed and I was only semi conscious when Liv whispered, "I'll check on you in a couple of hours," and left the room.

. . . I'm in a warm place where I can't see anything—I have no sight, no touch and no sense of sound—I just feel something through my whole body, my whole self. Safe but powerless—defenceless but controlled, guided. Inside things focus, I'm floating or maybe suspended in a liquid mass. Everything's black, soft, everything safe, surrounded and protected. Something's against me, touching, tugging, sensing and arousing. I smell something. I hear my own breathing; feel warm breath on my face. My eyes are open but see nothing but grey-black, no focus. I feel hot, sharp breath on me again, it seems closer now my eyes are open. I turn towards it; I want to see. Two tiny glints in the blackness; visible only because they are darker than what surrounds them. I know what I want and I strain towards them and her breath meets mine

an instant before we kiss. My lips on her lips, my tongue finds her tongue and her body instantly becomes real, comes alive. In the dark my fingers find her—find her! *Find her nakedness, her curves, hollows, depths and a magical wetness. Tiny fingers tug at my shorts and my shirt. In a moment I'm on top and inside her, fighting to control myself, fighting against a primal urge to crush, consume. I don't control it, I should be spent but I know not to stop. I duck down under the covers and reacquaint myself with that wetness, push my tongue into it and around it. I hear her moan and feel her thrust against me. I slow, let her come to me, set her own rhythm. I quickly feel her body tighten around my head and her fingertips either side of my head pull me to her and she cries out. A second later, I am inside her again and this time I control my rhythm and I enjoy myself, let her enjoy me and some time, much later, there is sleep. Sleep and love . . .*

I awoke in a cold sweat, a little delirious and full of flu. I found I was alone and felt an overwhelming loss. With a sense of panic I tried to remember some detail from my dream, cling on to something. Then feeling the space next to me, I found it was still warm; damp in places. I heard the flush of a toilet somewhere and moments later the girl of my dreams and somehow the girl of my reality came back to me, still naked, and already much colder than the sheet.

"I'm just going to nip to the toilet," I whispered, climbing over her. I kissed her gently on the forehead and then on the mouth. When I felt her kiss me back, my heart jumped as I knew we'd made up.

Being more modest than Liv, I picked up my shorts from the floor and tip toed to the bathroom. When I'd relieved myself, I washed my hands and looked at myself in the mirror. As rough as I felt I couldn't keep the smile off my face. On my way back to the room I thought I'd get us each a glass of water but found Liv already in the kitchen making tea. No longer naked, she wore a petrol blue nightdress that showed off her slim, brown legs.

"Hey, I was just going to get some water," I said quietly.

"I fancied some tea, I'm not tired. Shall I make you one?"

"Yeah, ok if I grab some water too?"

"Glasses in there—use the ones with the black base, they're mine."

I drank my water while I watched Liv finish the tea. Even making tea I couldn't keep my eyes off her. I wondered what she'd look like when she was sixty. I couldn't imagine her being sixty. I tried to recall what she'd said about her parents but couldn't. Her mum had to be beautiful.

In her room we sat at either end of the bed, both cross-legged. It was still uncomfortable for me to sit like that and my right leg wouldn't yet bend all the way so my left knee didn't sit on my right foot the way Liv's did. She rested her delicate hands on her knees and I watched them for a few moments, imagining them dancing over piano keys.

"I didn't come here to sleep with men you know."

"Me neither." I hadn't quite gauged Liv's mood so I answered her surprise opening gambit with a joke of my own. She smiled but I shouldn't have joked just then.

"I mean it. I actually came here with the express intention of not sleeping with anyone, not even getting to know anyone I didn't have to."

"That seems an odd thing to say," I said, trying to frame it as a question so she'd elaborate. She seemed like she was going to anyway but I thought I'd better make sure she knew I was interested.

"To you I'm sure. I bet you came here with the sole purpose of getting your grubby mitts on as many girls as you could."

I laughed. "I wouldn't say that but yes, I do like girls—always have."

"Tell me about girls Matt, what do they mean to you?"

"Ok, but we're coming back to the 'grubby mitts' comment you know. Now, where to start?" I thought for a moment. "When I was seven or eight there was a girl called Laurie who decided she wanted me as a playmate; her parents and mine were friends. She was about two or three years older than me but she used to call for me and take me out, sometimes with her friends. Come to think of it, I have no recollection of how or why she ever stopped. One of her friends, girl called Cassie, was keen on me and sent me this love letter, which half the school found out about. About thirty kids made us go to the bottom of the field and kiss; I had no idea what I was doing and hated it. I think I ended up just running away. Come to think of it, perhaps that was why Laurie stopped calling. By the time she was sixteen she was well off the rails, would go with anyone who'd have her. She was an attractive girl too, not stupid. No idea what happened to Cassie. Even before that my brother reckons me and this girl called Zoe Brabbin said we loved each other—she moved away when I was about five probably so I must have been very advanced. A few years later there was Katy Lowe, she got the hots for me when I was about nine or ten. She was very pretty and still the only blonde who's ever shown any interest in me.

She sent me a Valentine's card telling me she'd always loved me but had never been able to pluck up the courage to tell me! I gave it to my sister for safekeeping. Apart from that there's been Belinda, Louise, Hannah. Hannah was the only serious one. You want details?" I laughed.

"I could listen to you talk all night babe, I really could. You talk like honey slipping off a spoon and that's why I'm here. That's why you're here, why I want you here. No one ever makes me talk shit like you, do you know that?" Liv smiled at me.

"It isn't shit to me, I love being here and for the record I loved all those girls in my way but no one's ever had the effect on me you have. This afternoon, when I thought I'd blown it, I felt like my insides had been ripped out."

"You *loved* all those girls?"

"Yeah, I guess. Some of them anyway—not Laurie or Cassie perhaps . . . although I do remember stealing my own painting off the class wall and giving it to Laurie and getting into trouble for it. But yeah, I guess I don't have the same hard and fast rules some people have about love. I fall easy. And usually pretty hard."

"Like what rules?"

I sipped my tea and thought. "Only happens once, you can only ever be in love with one person at a time, can't love a psycho—all that shit. If you feel it you feel it as far as I'm concerned."

"So do you feel it now?"

"Honestly?" I was playing for time and to see what Liv was expecting me to say. I didn't know if I was being set up for a big fall here.

"Yes, honestly. You think I'd want you to start lying to me?"

"Ok, honestly I loved you a little bit the very first time I saw you. I looked at you and imagined what you'd be like. I imagined you'd be smart, good company, serious, funny. I could see you were well dressed and pretty much beautiful if you like that sort of thing—all good attributes to fall in love with. I enjoyed it too in a bizarre way, not even knowing if I'd ever speak to you. In my imagination you were always impressed by my funny, caring side too, which helped."

"You haven't answered my question."

"You noticed huh? That wasn't enough for you?"

She looked at me over her mug of tea and shook her head.

"Yes I feel it now. In a way that makes me wonder if I've ever felt it about anyone else before, if all those idiots with their pedantic rules weren't right all along. And I'll be honest about something else; I probably wouldn't have told you for a long time."

"Explain."

"It's another rule—wouldn't want to scare you off. And I would like to think I have at least an outside chance of hearing it said back to me when I finally say it for the first time." Before I could kick myself for this desperate sounding plea, Liv answered me.

"I love you Matt. And you didn't need to say it to me."

"I've said it, it must be written all over my face every time I look at you." However much I felt it, I wanted to resist saying it now I was being put on the spot. She was either happy with my answer or she let it pass.

"Anyway I was trying to explain something—how do you just start talking about stuff like ex girlfriends and first kisses when I'm in the middle of telling you something?"

I shrugged, not sure if I was in trouble.

"Now I can't say it," Liv said, shaking her head.

"No, go on. I didn't mean to interrupt."

"I know you didn't. You didn't even interrupt really, I love it when you talk about things like that—it's like you just flip to a page in a book of your life and start reading. If we have a relationship—if we get close—which I know we *are*, it's just going to be so complicated. I don't know if you'd cope, how I'd cope—we need to talk soon."

"Well that sounds . . . horrible. Why 'complicated'?"

"I can't, not now. We just made up and I'm happy, really happy. I didn't know if we would."

"Ummm, that sounds even worse. Why wouldn't we have made up?"

"If I start to explain, I won't know when to stop. The truth is, I've never had to make up with anyone before. And no one's ever told me they love me before. They still never have I guess . . ."

"I love you," I interrupted. "Love you with every sinew, every nerve, every undamaged tendon in my body. What you're saying scares me. I won't ask you to explain something you don't want to, but please can you say something to set my mind at rest just a little?" I looked at the clock; it was five fifteen. I felt tired and I wanted to lie down next to Liv and forget this conversation. "Are you telling me there's someone else perhaps?"

She shook her head. "No, there's no one else. It's just me. You want me to set your mind at rest then just don't worry. It's my problem and I have to find a way to work it out. And you can be sure I will try. All this is very new to me." After a pause she asked, "Is it working?" She smiled at me as she pushed her bottom lip out and bit it with her top teeth. It took me a couple of seconds to realise what she meant.

"Not in the least," I smiled back, "but I can't feel anything bad looking at that smile. Shall we get some sleep?"

Liv jumped up and leant over to give me a massive hug. Tired and confused as I was, I felt my cock stir as her warm body pressed against mine.

When the light was off, I lay with my arm around Liv about to doze off, when she said quietly, "I spoke to Katy earlier about next weekend."

It came back to me in a flash why I'd first been pissed off.

"Mmm," I murmured, suddenly alert and thinking I'd never sleep now, trying to hide it.

"I mentioned her birthday earlier, remember? Well I wanted to check with her first, but she said it would be fine to have you come with me. I told her I didn't want to travel alone. Do you think you can come?"

"Next weekend?" I felt so stupid, a bad, bad person. "Yeah, of course, it'll be great."

She turned towards me in the dark and kissed me on the mouth. I pulled her to me and soon enough we slept.

7

Monday, 21st February to Thursday, 24th February

The following week life resumed its usual beat of routine and sporadic lighter moments snatched here and there. I hardly saw Liv—at the odd lecture where she turned up she sat next to me and was adorably attentive; breaking her usual habits of listening intently and fervent note taking to write things on my pad about what Critchley was wearing or that Suzanne, a pretty girl on the plump side we both half knew, was picking her nose. Appalled, we'd watched her for a good five minutes while she grappled with a real clinger. My workload had been piling up after some unproductive weekends and evenings so I used a lot of my free time that week trying to catch up and feeling like I was accomplishing very little. By the end of the week though I'd completed two essays, written up a presentation I was due to give to my Battle of Britain group—using Dave as a test audience—and received an encouraging mark from one of my tutors for an essay on Guinea Bissau's inspirational first leader, Amilcar Cabral. I even spent a couple of hours with Clare in the launderette lending her a hand with her washing and letting her guide me through the process of doing my own.

My knee felt like it was improving again. I'd been convinced the walk back to Liv's the previous Sunday had done serious damage as it had felt terrible for a couple of days and even buckled underneath me as I walked down some stairs in the Arts Faculty. I didn't mention it to anyone and thankfully, by the end of the week, I was wondering why I'd been so worried.

I went for a drink late each night with Dave, Kenny, Mike and the girls and stayed up late on the Wednesday night chatting to Kenny about living arrangements for the next year. I bumped into Mel one evening on my way back from a study session at the library, just as she was on her way to her car. She was civil enough but far from comfortable talking for very long. She looked good and although she said nothing to give it away, I thought she might be on her way to a date. She told me her dad had offered to buy a house for her to rent out the following year but she hadn't decided whether or not she would be at uni. I'd laughed but it turned out she was seriously considering jacking it in. I wanted to give her a hug and tell her I'd miss her—was *already* missing her—but didn't. We had about six inches of snow during the Thursday afternoon and by the time I got back half of Swafforth were out snowballing. I dumped my bag on my bed and sprinted out to join them and had the time of my life for two and a half hours. Dave noticed Fats had left his window open and we spent ten minutes in hysterics, scooping snow from beneath it and hurling it up through his first floor window. It didn't occur to any of us that we might be soaking his bed, TV or stereo. Thankfully there was no permanent damage to anything although Fats tried to convince us he got ten thousand volts through his fingers when he next turned on the TV.

I hadn't seen Liv since Tuesday and she called me late Thursday, just as we were threatening to empty the quiz machine. I let the others fend for themselves for a few minutes and arranged to meet Liv the following morning at the station at eleven o'clock. We'd be back in London for about one thirty, each go to our respective parents and then meet up on the Saturday. I was far too excited to sleep, thinking about the journey back home with Liv and spending the whole day with her Saturday, so I put the finishing touches to my presentation until about three o'clock. I checked the weather just before I went to bed to see if there might be anything to affect the trains the next day but only rain was expected. I kept thinking of things I wanted to ask Liv the next day, knowing I'd forget it all but unable to stop myself.

Friday, 25th February

I walked down to uni with Kenny and his flatmate Samir, who were on their way to play snooker. I was pretty quiet for once, trying to keep a lid on my excitement about the weekend. It was a cold, damp day. The grass by the lake and the bushes at the side of the path were wet from the morning rain and were full of singing birds. It was a good day to be alive and if you were lucky enough to be on your way to meet a beautiful girl it was just perfect.

I got to the station a few minutes early, so bought tickets into town and a couple of bottles of water for the journey. I hadn't eaten anything save a piece of Dave's toast when I'd got up at a quarter to nine, but since I'd known Liv, I was less keen on chocolate and coke and what they did to my waist line. That, and the increasing light exercise I was able to do as my knee improved, meant I could wear my favourite clothes again without looking like Simon Cowell.

I checked the timetable even though I knew already the next train to town was at eleven ten. As a few more people started to line the platform I checked my watch, thinking Liv was unusually late. It was seven minutes past eleven. I gave it a couple more minutes and pulled my phone out to call her. I had a message, my stomach fluttered briefly as I anticipated some disappointing news. I was relieved when all it said was that Liv had gone into town early to buy something to wear on Saturday night and would meet me at New Street station at eleven thirty. It was an expensive text for me—I'd blown three pounds thirty on a ticket to town for Liv and I would also now have to go shopping on the Saturday to ensure I looked good enough to accompany Liv to the party.

There wasn't time to buy a paper before the train arrived so I played Jawbreaker, the depressingly addictive game on my mobile, for the fifteen minute journey to town. I got half way off the train at New Street when I realised I'd left my bag on the seat next to me. I raced back, retrieved it and jumped off the train again and went to find the main ticket office. There wasn't a long queue but Liv was at the front and about to be called. She looked up and straight at me as soon as I came through the automatic doors. I caught one of her sweetest smiles and she signed that she'd get my ticket. I started over towards her to give her my railcard but she was called to the ticket desk right away. She picked up a brown leather Mulberry travel bag and a couple of smallish shopping bags, which I didn't think could contain more than maybe some underwear or possibly a small top. I wondered what the underwear might be like and if I'd get to see it on Saturday. I wondered how busy our carriage would be . . .

Liv had made little concession to the winter temperatures in her outfit. She wore a black A-line dress and grey high heeled shoes which I'd never have chosen with the dress but looked perfect. With her hair up she looked like a young Elizabeth Taylor. She could have gone straight to Saturday's party and been the smartest person there. Not for the first time, I felt that rush just knowing I was with her.

Liv gave me my ticket—somehow she'd got the railcard discount without my card—and we went straight for the train, Liv allowing me to carry her Mulberry bag but refusing to let me near the shopping in case I tried to, "take a sneaky peek inside". We got the last available table on our carriage and I put the bags in the overhead rack with exaggerated care. When I went to sit down opposite Liv she suggested it might be nicer if I sat next to her. In a strikingly Machiavellian move Liv surreptitiously poured Evian all over the two seats opposite and explained it might also be nicer if we had the table to ourselves. Shocked as I was, I had to agree. I thought of the underwear again.

I sat down and then stood up straightaway to get my wallet out of my jeans. I pulled out five tens and offered them to Liv.

"For the ticket."

"Forget it, it's on me. I asked you along."

I felt awkward. "No way, I can't let you buy my ticket."

"Would you mind awfully if I did? I hate talking about money, it makes my skin itch. Sorry if that sounds idiotic."

"Of course not, it's very kind, thank you."

It still felt a bit awkward but it meant I could consider buying a new pair of jeans for Saturday night.

I was careful to avoid talking about last weekend and we chatted about what we'd been up to the last few days although Liv was pretty vague as usual. I introduced Liv to a game I'd invented with an old school friend, Marvin Shilman, called the "I like game."

The rules were brilliantly simple: to start one person would say, "I like Stan Marsh from South Park. I like Stan." Then it was the next person's turn to start a new sentence with "I like Stan . . . ley Baldwin." And so on until the last Stan had been named and a winner declared. The only other rule was that someone else had to corroborate the existence of the person named. This prevented you from saying things like, "I like Stan, my uncle," or, "I like Stan the giant from the book I read when I was three years old,"—unless you had a family member handy to nod their head in confirmation of course. This last rule could be waived if less than four players were involved.

If you have the right sort of brain for this type of thing and you can find at least one other person who is likewise blessed, you need never wonder how you'll pass those vast expanses of time in airports, hospital waiting rooms or on the Northern Line again. I'd played the game all over Europe on school football trips, skiing holidays and German student exchanges and I'd never met anyone who could consistently match Marv for inventiveness. He was a fantastic opponent—if you won, you knew you'd beaten the best, you'd exhausted every last ounce of recall you possessed to win.

Trying to compare sportsmen of different eras is always a difficult and ultimately fruitless exercise; football, boxing and the 'I like game' all inevitably move on but Liv would certainly have been a match for Marv. I was in disbelief when she won our first game with Stanley Gene, a journeyman Rugby League player of little note.

By the time we'd knocked off Stan, Pierre, Louis (only one king of France allowed) and Glen we were coming into the outskirts of London with things all square. There wasn't time to start another game and with Liv resting her head on my shoulder, I looked out at the city we were hurtling through.

I've always enjoyed looking out of car and train windows at London with its unique mixture of local and international landmarks like Battersea Power Station or the New Wembley arch. The endless tower blocks in West London you see all the way along the A40 always took my breath away; a world seemingly devoid of hope and humanity. I tried to catch the name of a station we rushed through but couldn't.

"London Calling?" Liv broke in on my thoughts.

"At the top of the dial," I answered, surprising myself.

"After all this, won't you give me a smile?" Liv came back, surprising me still more.

"Great song, but not one of my favourite albums."

It wasn't about London in the same way but I'd always felt The Sex Pistols' *'Never Mind The Bollocks'* said more about the time and feeling of the late 70s, and in London in particular. I'd seen the footage of them playing *'God Save the Queen'* on a boat going down the Thames on Jubilee Night and the image stayed with me as a defining moment of the time. I'd have given almost anything to have been there.

"That's an expression I've not seen before babe and I don't know if it's good or bad. What were you thinking about?"

I laughed, wondering what to say without sounding foolish.

"I was thinking about," I started very deliberately, "The Sex Pistols playing *'God Save the Queen'* on a boat on the river outside the Houses of Parliament on Jubilee Night, 1977. The police boarded the boat and I think half the band got arrested—whatever he says now, when you see footage of Johnny Rotten back then he always looks young and kind of shell shocked. Steve Jones was the one who just didn't give a fuck. I was thinking it would have been such an exciting time to live and be young and how I'll never get to do that. I have to live now when you get famous for having big tits and sleeping with as many minor celebrities as possible, grown ups trawl through 23 books about a kid at wizard school and Coldplay are hailed as musical pioneers for God's sake." I took a breath and looked at Liv. "They were happy thoughts honest! I don't know where the last little rant came from."

Liv wasn't exactly in stitches but she smiled at me. If anything she looked ever so slightly sympathetic. It encouraged me to carry on.

"Sometimes I wonder if I'd lived then whether I'd have had the balls not to conform so much. I feel as if my life's mapped out for me and I'll never get off my path. I'll follow my dad into an office job, which takes my body and soul for fifty quid disposable income a month. If I think about how hard my dad had to work just to keep a roof over our heads, not that we ever struggled but . . . he . . . his job just seemed to take everything."

"So what do you want to do differently?"

"Stop living my life vicariously through all these shared heroes. *I* want to pull on the famous Eagles jersey and play football for a living, have my name chanted like Eric the Ninja. Or be a rock star—I'd love to have been Steve Jones. I'd settle for being a world-renowned surgeon but even that's beyond me already. I'm only nineteen and my life's over!"

"So change things. I mean do you *really* want things to be different or is this just talk?"

"Of course it's just talk but of course I do wish it was different. I'd love to be with you on this train right now but in an alternate universe, it would be on the way to a press conference about my impending move to Juventus or to launch my band's first world tour. But it's too late. And I never had any talent anyway."

"And there was me thinking I might be adding something special to your life just by being me."

Ostensibly she was joking but it was the closest I'd heard Liv to sounding like she wanted to hear something reassuring.

"You are babe. Adding something. Loads in fact." I was talking shit. "You see? I'm tongue-tied just talking to you. All I was trying to say was . . . you always want more from life. I wish I was cleverer, better looking, a footballer, a politician, an explorer, a pirate. But I don't wish I knew better people and I certainly couldn't wish for a better girlfriend."

I hadn't realised I'd said it until Liv picked up on it.

"I'm your girlfriend?" She was looking at me slightly quizzically but I couldn't quite gauge her thoughts.

"Think so, yeah," I shrugged, trying to work her out. We were slowing down, coming into the platform at Euston.

"Well then, I guess I should start acting like it," she said and slipped her hand inside my shirt and placed her mouth over mine. Liv put her leg between mine and began to really press her body into me. People were standing all the way up the carriage and for a second I felt self-conscious but I closed my eyes and shut them out and enjoyed Liv's affection.

Liv pulled back and whispered, "I liked it when you said that."

"I can tell," I smiled. I wanted to say more. "I feel very lucky babe, you make me feel . . ." words failed me for a second, ". . . like a man," was all I could say, hyper aware of her knee pressing into my groin and my cock trying to burst the seams of my three year old G-Stars. We went back to kissing, not leaving the train until it was being boarded by passengers for the return leg to Birmingham. Someone had stuck a ticket reservation slip in our seats and we'd not even noticed. Something about Liv was making me lose perspective; I didn't think I'd ever felt this way about someone before. I'd always believed I'd been in love in the past but there was just no denying she was different and with her, I was different.

We caught the tube together and headed south to Victoria. I thought Liv might want to get back home but when I suggested having a late lunch she agreed without hesitation; neither of us were ready to say goodbye it seemed.

"Any ideas about where?" I asked. I knew a few places on the King's Road I could suggest but it was a tube ride away and I wanted Liv to make the first suggestion.

"Do you know the Ebury? It's not exactly the place for a quick lunch but it's one of my favourites."

Lunch could take all weekend as far as I was concerned. "It rings a bell—it must be somewhere on the way to the King's Road. Sounds good anyway—bus, cab or walk?"

Liv gave me a pitying look and headed for the taxis. It struck me that sexy girls always wanted to get cabs.

I recognised The Ebury as soon as I saw it. It was the sort of place I wouldn't have dared go in without a few hundred quid in my Boateng suit pocket. It was in a quaint little pocket of Belgravia, sitting proudly on a corner opposite a few antique 'shops' which looked like they probably got three paying customers a month and survived comfortably on them. The menu was dominated by fish, which would not have been my first choice but I had to admit that when my grilled sea bass finally arrived it was extremely good.

The atmosphere was subtly different between Liv and me once we'd sat down. It was probably down to the surroundings; for one thing we were sitting opposite one another for the first time that day. There were a few people dotted about the restaurant but no one within earshot so, with the grey gloom descending outside, we found a changed intimacy. I felt as if I was sitting in a Patrick Hamilton novel. The soft lighting gave Liv an ethereal quality. It felt much later than three thirty; the glass and a half of wine I'd had felt like a lot more. We were both more subdued than we'd been for most of the day but it was comfortable. For once she was happy to talk more about herself, more so than I could remember her doing since that first coffee we'd shared. Liv talked about leaving Roedean under a something of a cloud and having to gain special permission to sit her exams there—if they hadn't known she would get straight As, she would have had no chance, even with her father's donation. Again she'd withheld the details even when pressed. She'd been tempted to throw the exams just to spite them but in the end couldn't bring herself to do it. I guessed this was the reason she'd come to Birmingham rather than Oxford or Cambridge but when I put it to her she shook her head in disgust, "No way would I have even applied—for one thing Daddy was far too keen that I follow him to Keeble."

When Liv spoke about Katy, her de facto sister, she said such glowing—and somehow such unLiv-like things, I could tell she missed her terribly. Katy had roomed with her at Roedean and it sounded as if Liv had spent her teenage years trying to lead her friend as far and frequently astray as possible and been saved from certain disaster at every turn. I was looking forward to meeting Katy to see if they really were as different as Liv made them sound. I was also keen to see how Katy would live up to Liv's billing as, "a hundred times more beautiful than me."

By five o'clock we had emptied two bottles of wine, I'd ignored half a dozen calls on my mobile from my parents and it was finally time to head home. I asked for the bill, Liv paid in spite of my protests and we headed outside straight into a chill and sobering wind. We were only a few minutes walk from Victoria station so we braved the wind and set out. Over the wind I asked Liv what she was up to that evening.

"Nothing. Probably just have a hot, foamy bath and get an early night."

"Really, your folks not rolling out the red carpet for their favourite renegade daughter?"

"Not there, I think they're over in the States until the end of the month."

"You're on your own? Why don't you come over; my mum and dad would love to meet you?" I'd offered the invitation instinctively without thinking. Another instinct was crying out for me not to push my luck after such a great day, Liv had every right to be thoroughly sick of the sight—and sound—of me.

"No, I'm certain they'll be rolling out the red carpet for *you*—their favourite renegade son. The last thing they'll want is to have me in the way."

"Are you kidding me? My dad loves nothing more than to have a new captive audience to hear his rugby stories!"

I could hear desperation in my voice; I realised how much I wanted Liv to come over.

"My brother should be around too if that helps to convince you," I added.

"Are you *sure* they wouldn't hate me for getting in the way?"

"Fantastic—so you're coming?" What had I done to deserve all this happiness?

"I'll need to go home and get changed. I'll have to drive over—I hope I'm ok to drive. You had most of the wine anyway didn't you?" It was rhetorical and utterly untrue.

We'd got to the main concourse and were able to talk normally again.

"I guess that is a problem thinking about it." I tried to assess how pissed I was. Quite pissed I thought.

"Nonsense, I won't be driving for another two and a half hours and I've eaten like a horse." One of us was convinced at least.

"I'm sure I could get my brother to drive over and pick you up. Give me a call once you're home and we can sort something out."

Liv's train was leaving in less than five minutes.

"No need, it'll be fine. I'll give you a call when I'm on my way—about eight-eight thirty? I'd better go for that," she said, indicating her train.

"Ok babe."

I set my bags down and gave her a quick hug before kissing both cheeks and watching her walk away. It was strange to watch her go having spent the whole day with her. She looked back at me just before she passed through the barriers and I blew her a kiss. I checked the boards for my next train, knowing I'd just missed one in order to see Liv off. I called home and asked Donny to meet me at the station in an hour or so.

Fifteen minutes later my train pulled into the station and I got on the front carriage. By the time we left Victoria ten minutes later, I was sound asleep.

I woke up with a thick head a couple of stops before Sutton and looked at the landscape of my hometown. Not pretty but familiar, not exciting but safe, not the dark and brooding London anyone would write a poem about but a happily bland, quietly prosperous place where a poet or two might well have been educated. The suburbs; they gave punk to the inner cities and before that gave the world the dinosaur and glam rockers the punks so despised. To me they were just as much a part of London as Hackney, Chelsea or the West End.

I hauled my bag up the steps of the station and went outside to find Donny. I was hardly out of the door when he blasted the horn of his ageing Alfa from across the road. I dodged the traffic, threw my bag in the junk filled boot, cleared the passenger seat of assorted car locks, CDs, cigarettes and lighters and got in. In the blink of eye we were nearly home, when I remembered to mention Liv.

"I asked someone over tonight—are we supposed to be going out?"

"I'm seeing Helen but I think Dad's booked somewhere." Helen was one of Donny's exes who he'd been out with at uni and for a year or two after.

"Oh, nice to see you haven't let my return home for the first time in months get in the way of your love life."

"I saw you three weeks ago," Donny said, rolling his eyes. "Anyway, I was joking. Helen's coming over here," he laughed. I thumped him on the arm.

We pulled in at the front of the house.

"Who's the girl that's coming? Glad to see you're not letting seeing your family for the first time in months get in the way of *your* love life."

"Yeah, very good," I said dryly. "Just a girl from uni, you'll probably think she's got a big forehead or something."

"Belinda did have a big forehead," Donny said as if that made it ok.

"Do you think they'll want to go for an Italian?

"I think they were planning on the Windsor Castle—not impressive enough for your new bird?"

"It's not that . . ." I started, but we both knew it was. "She'll be fine with the pub. What you bin up to anyway?"

"Not a lot. Working mainly, trying to save my deposit."

"Still looking at Crystal Palace?"

"It's about the only place I can afford. It's an up and coming area according to Property Ladder."

"Liv's a Palace fan. I told her you used to take me to some of the midweek games. She had a season ticket for a couple of years."

"What's Liv short for?" Donny asked, ignoring everything else.

"Olivia, but don't call her that. What time's Helen arriving?"

"Eight o'clock. Where's Liv coming from?"

"Dulwich, she's driving over."

"She's had less to drink than you then," Donny said, snookering me.

"You can tell then? I only had a few glasses of wine."

"No need to get defensive. You might want to have some spoggy before you go in though, don't want mum thinking you've spent the day getting pissed when you should have been on your way back."

I rolled my eyes and let it go. I'd had a good day and was looking forward to a good night. I knew Liv would charm everyone, even Donny, once she arrived.

When we pulled onto the drive my dad was already outside—apparently locking or unlocking his car but really just too excited about seeing me to stay in doors knowing I was so close.

"Hi Matthew!" he said, as I got out of the car, loud enough for the whole street to hear.

Instinctively, because he was my dad, I mumbled some halfhearted acknowledgement in reply, then caught myself and asked him more brightly how he was.

"Great, pleased to see you. You're moving well!"

Twelve weeks ago I'd had full anterior cruciate ligament reconstructive surgery, yet this was the first time in days—weeks even—I'd been reminded of how far I'd come. I'd assured Dave that next week I'd be ready to start training. I knew I was lucky to be so far ahead in my physical recovery; far from pushing myself I had to hold myself back at times because the knee felt so unnaturally strong. I didn't like thinking about it and I hated talking about it.

"Yeah, it's really come on. Mum inside?"

"In the kitchen, go through," I heard him say but I was already most of the way down the hall.

I crept up behind mum and bellowed, "Hello mum!" making her jump. She turned round with a big smile and I kissed and hugged her.

"How are you?" she asked.

"Really good, journey was a bit of a nightmare, had to wait around at Victoria for a while but everything's pretty good. How about you? Kettle on?"

"Dad would have picked you up if you'd asked. Tea's made, I'm just doing some crumpets then I'll bring it through."

"Cool, any strawberry jam? I didn't need picking up—it was only a late decision to come down and I got the train with a friend so it was no bother."

"Yes, of course. I told Dad you'd be ok on the train but you know what he's like."

I shook my head and rolled my eyes (a Malone family trait), I did indeed know what he was like. I went through to the lounge, where the warmth of the house became almost unbearable with the gas fire on as well as the central heating. I deliberately left the door open and then made Donny shift his feet so I could sit down.

"Donny says you've got a friend coming over tonight, that's fine—the more the merrier. Liv, is it?" said my dad, asking so much more.

"Yeah, is that ok—have you booked somewhere to eat?"

"Yes, but we can change the numbers. Liv's *not* one of the girls who live upstairs from you is she?"

I could kill Donny for this.

"She lives in Dulwich doesn't she?" Donny chimed in, grinning at me.

"Yes, she lives in Dulwich," I said with as much sarcasm as I could muster, "she doesn't live upstairs from me, she's about five foot five with long dark hair and brown eyes and we're probably going to get married now I've gone and got her pregnant."

I added the last bit as a joke as I could see my dad was looking somewhat indignant. It dawned on me that what I'd said wasn't impossible since we'd not used any protection when we'd had sex; as much as I'd given it any thought I'd assumed Liv was on the pill.

Mum walked in with the tray and set it on the coffee table.

"Matthew's asked a girl along tonight mum," Donny said.

This wasn't right—he was twenty-five for fuck's sake.

"Have you stopped smoking yet?" I asked, looking at Donny. I actually mispronounced the word *smoking* so badly my parents wouldn't have understood what I'd said but I knew it was enough to shut Donny up.

"Should I get excited?" mum asked. She looked excited.

"No, it's nothing like that—I just travelled back with her as she was getting the same train—when she said she had no plans for tonight I just asked her along as I didn't think you'd mind."

"Of course we don't mind," mum and dad said together.

"It might have been nice if you'd asked first though." Donny stirring.

"Matthew said the trains were awful—took him hours to get home," mum said to my dad.

Donny raised an eyebrow in my direction.

"You should have rung for a lift," dad said. He meant it too, he loved nothing better than to get in his car and drive his kids about.

"I wasn't sure what you'd be doing; I travelled down with Liv anyway so I was fine on the train."

"I'd have brought you both back, you know that. You should have rung." He meant that too—even more than ferrying his kids about he loved adding their random associates into the mix.

"Next time," I said to close the matter.

"When are you going back?" Matter reopened.

"Sunday sometime, we have return tickets though so we're fine. What have you been up to anyway?" I asked mum, in order to change the subject. At the same time, I leant forward and poured the tea.

"Oh you know, same old stuff," she laughed. She looked about twenty five when she laughed. I wondered if Liv would age as well as her. I wondered if I'd get the chance to find out. "I've started ballroom dancing classes."

Well, this was news.

"Ballroom dancing? Are you modelling yourself on Kate Garraway or Alesha Dixon?" I asked.

"Oh, Kate Garraway probably," she replied tetchily. "I tried to get your dad to come but it clashes with his writing group."

"Writing group? How long have I been away? When did you join a writing group?"

"I've been going since before Christmas."

"You can't have—I'm sure you'd have mentioned it," I replied despairingly.

"You don't know *everything* about us," mum answered for him.

"Anyway, I didn't know if I'd stick with it at first," dad answered for himself.

"Fair enough, so what goes on at this writing group?"

"What do you think goes on? We write, we read and we critique." My parents were making me feel foolish but I had to hand it to them, they were making the most of their youngest finally being out of the way.

"So where are we eating tonight?"

"Your mum chose," dad answered.

"Carnevales?"

"Yep. Reminds me; I'd better call them."

"What time are we eating, Liv's coming here eight for eight thirty?"

"Table's booked for eight thirty but I'll let them know it might be nearer nine," dad called back from the hall.

I helped myself to a crumpet and with the first bite, I realised how good it was to be at home. In celebration I finished another two crumpets, drained my tea and closed my eyes.

"What time's Helen getting over?" I asked with my eyes closed.

"Eightish but she'll probably be late," Donny replied. "Do you have anything I can wear?"

"Nope," I said, before I nodded off.

152

The doorbell woke me from a deep, alcoholic sleep. The front room was dark; someone had turned the lights out on me. It was ten past eight and I hoped it was Helen at the door rather than Liv as I felt like shit. Probably looked worse. I gave it a couple of seconds before I moved, hoping someone else would go for the door and I could sprint up the stairs. I went to the door myself and from the outline through the frosted glass I knew it was Liv. I ran my hand through my hair and pulled open the door. She had so many ways to take my breath away but as she smiled at me from the dark, her tiny breath visible in the cold, her eyes shinier than ever, I found I had a new favourite.

"Hey, come in. I was just getting ready," I said, kissing her on the cheek.

"Have you been sleeping?" she asked me suspiciously.

"Umm, not really . . ."

"You must be Liv; Hallo!" my father boomed from behind me as he came rampaging down the stairs in a rather dapper brown suit. Liv was wearing a fitted dark blue silky dress under a grey coat, neither of which she had brought back with her from Birmingham. I was going to look underdressed. By the time I'd closed the front door, Liv and my dad were getting on famously.

"You'd better get ready sleeping beauty, Helen's meeting us there so we're just waiting on you," he called from the lounge.

"Ok, see you in five minutes." I trudged up the stairs.

I hadn't bothered unpacking anything so nothing was ironed. I threw on a plain white tee shirt of my brother's and a plain grey v-neck sweater Donny had bought me from Paris. I changed my jeans as a gesture to freshness, for a pair of trendily knackered Moschinos I found in Donny's room. They weren't a perfect fit but they were nice jeans so I went with it.

I got downstairs inside five minutes to find Liv drinking a glass of red wine with my dad. He was telling her one of his favourite 'young Matthew' stories—the smallest one in the judo class, who everyone underestimated, who then took down the instructor to shock everyone. I've heard it told so many times I even wonder myself if maybe it really did happen that way—my abiding memory of six years of judo was the club's one and only victory over another club. Our coach had told us we were facing the best club in the area and the win, after two years without a victory, made all of us suddenly believe we were finally on the up. Until we found out that we'd actually been pushed to our limits by a group of guys and girls all with less than six months judo experience under their white belts.

No matter, Liv seemed to be enjoying the story. So much in fact, I wondered if I should go back upstairs and give them a few more minutes to reminisce.

"Liv's been telling us how dedicated you've been to your exercising," dad said. I couldn't imagine how Liv might have got a word in edge ways with my dad in this mood, but I nodded my head in agreement.

"We off then? Are we taking two cars?"

"We can do, or you can all squeeze in the back of mine."

"What's Donny wanna do? Donny!" I shouted up the stairs, but he came out of the kitchen. "Are you driving or shall we all get in with dad?"

"I fancy a couple of beers—you can drive mine if you want."

"I've been drinking most of the day haven't I?" I said quietly, not wanting my dad to know but not quite sure why.

"We'll get in with dad then, Helen can bring us back."

"We'll all go with you," I called to my dad and shouted upstairs for my mum.

Already struggling to make the revised time of nine o'clock, my mum decided she'd better just nip to the loo just as we were heading out of the door. It was a squash in the back of the car and I could tell my dad was torn between driving like a maniac—to him that meant nudging forty miles per hour on some wide, empty road—and accepting we'd be a few minutes late.

"John said I could stay over at yours easily enough, is that ok with you? It just means I can have a glass or two of wine and then head back in the morning."

John—who the fuck was John? But I knew of course. My dad had pulled the ultimate stunt to embarrass me and asked Liv to call him by his first name.

"Yeah, course it's ok with me—did he say where you'd be sleeping?"

"No, he gave the impression they had a free bed already made up."

"My sister's old room perhaps but I thought they'd made it their office."

"If it's a problem I'll go back."

Because of the dark and because we were talking very quietly, I couldn't tell if Liv was annoyed.

"No way, even if it is an office we have a sofa bed downstairs which I can sleep on—you can have my room."

"Yeah, as long as the sheets have been sterilised . . . sorry, burnt since you last stayed there—John was telling me all about your filthy teenage habits." It was the second time she'd called my dad John and it sounded odd coming from one of my friends.

"When did he have time to get onto that conversation? And what filthy habits—I didn't have any?"

"He can talk pretty fast when he needs to—anyway, I was pumping him for all the dirt I could get on you," she laughed.

"And I bet he was lapping it up. I take it there were no filthy habits specifically mentioned then?" Surely there was no way he'd have mentioned finding the truckload of porn under my bed when I was fifteen . . .

"Nothing to worry about; he just said you used to live and die in a moth eaten green sweater and a battered old grey jacket. You went for 'vagrant chic' he called it!"

"It was actually extremely fashionable at the time. I bought that jacket in Camden market and if it still fitted I'd be wearing it tonight to prove it. Come to think of it I wonder where it is." I *was* wondering too.

We got there for five to nine and went straight to our table. Helen got there about ten minutes after us and was more annoyed than she had a right to be that my dad had already chosen wine. I also thought she reacted quite coolly towards Liv but it didn't seem to bother Liv, who was egging my dad onto ever more embarrassing stories about yours truly.

The one which made me chuckle was about the first time I'd been drunk. I'd been sixteen and on a family holiday in Croatia and they'd allowed me to take on board rather more of the local wine than was strictly sensible. The point of the story, as far as my dad was concerned, was that he rather touchingly believed he'd seen me drink alcohol for the first time. Without thinking I whispered to Liv to remind me to tell her about the actual first time I'd got drunk. Did I really want to share the details of how I'd been sick out of the front window of my best mate's mum's Renault Clio? When she'd parked in front of the house, Neil had come out with a watering can to commence the clean up operation starting at my head. I'd stayed over and the next morning, Neil's mum had cooked me a full English breakfast and asked me sweetly if I'd had a good time the night before. The crush I'd had on her for years became pure unadulterated love from that morning on.

155

The red wine my dad had chosen was disappearing fast and we ordered another bottle as the starters were cleared away. While my dad had still been working, this had been his favourite restaurant and all the waiters knew him and shared a joke with him. After the main courses were out of the way, the manager came over and chatted with my dad for a few minutes and I experienced one of those rare moments in life when you look at your parents and see them in an entirely new light; as regular people with personalities and lives all their own. I looked at my dad then and was impressed by his magnetism in a way that perhaps I should have always been. The feeling passed as quickly as it had come, but I was pleased that I was proud of him for once, rather than just being the object of his affection. Before he left us the manager, Luigi, had a third bottle of the wine brought over, which he said was on the house. He shook my dad's hand and clapped him warmly on the shoulder.

The food had been great, the wine had gone down very easily and the atmosphere all night—once Helen finally had a drink inside her and relaxed—had been perfect. Donny went back to Helen's after the meal so we said our goodbyes and headed back to the car. On the way I held Liv's hand, kissing her before we got in. I'd probably had enough wine to suggest to my mum and dad that I shared a room with her but I decided it would be more polite and infinitely more exciting to go to our separate rooms and then sneak over the creaky landing and climb into her bed in the dark.

We got in at just past midnight and mum made a cup of tea for everyone and dad still hadn't run out of things to say. There were memories of glowing reports from teachers (one or two of whom had taught at my sister's school rather than mine but I didn't correct him) and word for word recitations of rows my dad had had on my behalf with teachers who hadn't taken to me quite so much. Baggy Bailey's name came up and I wondered why Liv looked as uncomfortable as I did at the mention of her name, until I remembered how sweet she'd been when I told her my darkest secret. My dad painted a picture entirely different to the one I remembered—when he'd been told of my behaviour (I'd say alleged but it was never presented as such) he recalled himself flying into a rage that cowed the indomitable old windbag. I saw my dad was supposed to be the hero of this story and my role seemed pretty incidental. There was no betrayal of any understanding of the torment that had seemed to last half a lifetime to me and of course no mention of his threat to remove me from the school. I left the room and went upstairs as he approached the end, feeling sick and angry at him for bringing it up and worse still, failing to accurately—never mind sensitively—recall a single fact.

I went to the toilet and went to check the bedrooms. I wanted to be out of the room for a few minutes, in the hope it might register on some level with him that I was pissed off at him. It registered with mum who found me in my old room, sitting on my old bed.

"You ok love? You look tired out."

"Yeah, I'm fine. You're right; just tired I guess."

"Did Donny tell you about Mrs Bailey?"

"He mentioned it when he came up yeah. You know that's not why I'm pissed off though? I didn't really care to be honest. Why does *he* have to bring it all up tonight of all nights?" It was rhetorical but she answered me.

"Once he gets on a roll he doesn't think about what he's saying, he doesn't mean anything by it. And he certainly doesn't put any stock in any of it—he thinks the sun shines out of your . . . well, you know what I mean. We're both very proud of you. Liv's very nice; I don't think I've ever met anyone so beautiful. You must be over the moon."

I nodded dumbly. "I don't understand it either," I said.

"Rubbish, she's lucky to have you. And she knows it too, she hardly took her eyes off you all night; she's wanted to hear everything anyone can remember about you."

"She's certainly got plenty on that score. Any chance you could go and rescue her, she's probably pretty tired by now?"

"Of course, we're off to Auntie Rita's tomorrow so we need to get to bed anyway."

Mum bent forward and kissed me on the cheek. I couldn't remember ever paying her a bona fide compliment but I blurted out, "You're beautiful too you know; that was the first thing I told Liv about you."

Mum rose and looked at me, her hand resting on my cheek. She smiled, looking fifteen and fifty all at once, a single tear rolling down her face.

"*Very* proud," she said and left me in the room.

Within a few short minutes everyone had said, "Good night", I'd got over my red wine moment and I was kissing Liv good night on the landing outside my old room and wondering how to broach the subject of a cheeky rendezvous once the house was asleep.

"I'll come to you," she whispered, unprompted.

I made my way to the back of the house and my brother's room. He hadn't made too much of an effort to clear up, so I quickly cleared the floor of the dirty underwear and anything breakable, stuffing everything in the wooden chest that had housed the prodigious porn collection Donny had had when he was about sixteen and I was discovering masturbation. Not that I cared either way, but he'd been at pains to convince me that it belonged to his dodgy mate, Terry Lawrence. Terry seemed the type, but then again so did my brother.

I lay in bed, wondering how long Liv would leave it. I half made up my mind to disobey orders and go and find her but while trying to decide how long I should leave it before going, I must have dozed off . . .

. . . Liv came to me, a vision in white. She glided across the floor to me, the way she moved unnerved me—it reminded me of the way the vampire kid floated outside his brother's window in the David Soul classic, 'Salem's Lot'; a film that had terrified me as a kid. She hovered over me and for the first time ever, I didn't want to kiss her—her face was ashen white, her eyes red and piercing. I couldn't move, paralysed by a fear I couldn't understand, couldn't fight.

"Do you want me? Do you want me?" Liv whispered.

I didn't need to say a word.

"You wouldn't want me, no one ever could."

From her red eyes fell red tears of blood. They seemed to grow as they fell from her face, only a few inches from my own as she leant over me. Tears of blood fell on my face, on my forehead, soaking my hair, blinding me and stinging my eyes. They fell and they fell and I had to lift my head to breathe—to try to breathe.

"You can't swim in blood," Liv said, "you only drown."

I floundered, trying in vain to shake off the paralysis. I thrashed about impotently, my arms never breaking the surface, my head soon going under . . . drowning in blood. And while I drowned, my last breath just an intake of blood, Liv held my hand. Held my hand to comfort me . . . or to make sure I drowned . . .

She squeezed my hand, I broke the surface, light rushed into my eyes, a shadow; Liv. Not so white, not so terrifying, holding my hands, leaning over me still but talking to me softly.

"Matt, Matt!" Liv squeezed my hand, wiped my forehead. My dripping forehead. Dripping with sweat, a cold sweat, but not blood. Not blood.

"You had a bad dream," she said.

I reached for her and held her; for comfort and for warmth. I held her so she wouldn't see the tears streaming down my face. But she felt them.

"Move across darling, I'll switch off the light and get in, ok? You're safe now."

I still didn't want her. I was still paralysed.

Saturday, 26th February

I woke up, lying on my back looking up at the ceiling, a dead arm under Liv's shoulders. I levered myself up enough to look at Donny's alarm clock. It was ten past nine. I looked at Liv sleeping and could hardly imagine anything more peaceful; it felt unbelievable that she was sleeping next to me. She opened the one eye that wasn't buried in the pillow and looked up at me. Now half her mouth smiled, I smiled back and bent down to kiss her. She rolled onto her back, yanked the duvet over both our heads and kissed me violently. My cock sprung to life and I was inside her in seconds. With hardly a word we spent the next hour or so going through most of the positions I'd ever tried or even thought about. She turned me on more than I would have thought possible but somehow every time I came close to climax, one or other of us changed our rhythm or position.

When I went downstairs for breakfast and asked my mum if it was Liv in the shower room she looked at me as if to say, "Do you think I was born yesterday?" I stuck the TV on in the lounge, picked up the Daily Express and had my tea and toast. The tea and toast didn't taste the way I remembered it tasting at Sunday teatimes when I was small. Those were the days before reduced fat butter and I'd stopped having three sugars in my tea.

Liv came downstairs a few minutes later. I was going to let her know mum was onto us but she went straight past the lounge door and into the kitchen. I heard her thank my mother and tell her how well she'd slept, despite being woken up by the cat leaping onto the bed just past four o'clock. I had to hand it her; she had some imagination.

When Liv joined me in the lounge with her mug of tea, I gave her the same old fashioned look mum had given me. Liv winked at me—now why couldn't I have been so cool?

Since Liv was in no hurry to get home, I suggested a walk in Battersea Park. By midday, we were suitably attired—ready in fact to cope with Arctic conditions—and in the car. As we left, Liv had made my dad's day when she'd thanked him for last night and kissed him on the cheek. I rested my hand on Liv's thigh as she drove through the backstreets of South London; a part of London I knew well from my drives with Donny and visits to countless recreational parks and sports grounds to play football. We made it to Battersea Park in forty minutes and parked on a meter just on the north side of the river. As we walked over Albert Bridge the cold northeasterly easily cut through every layer of our clothing and reddened our cheeks.

Traffic crawled over the bridge; the noise and smell spurring us quickly to the park entrance. As soon as we reached the park gate our pace slowed, I took Liv's hand in mine and we took the river path along the north edge of the park. Liv was quiet as we walked, squeezing my hand from time to time but not offering too much further encouragement as we dodged joggers and professional dog walkers and I talked about those of my minor sporting exploits the Park had borne witness to. We stopped at the Pagoda and kissed briefly, before Liv tugged me back across the path to look out at the river.

"The air's so fresh here don't you think?" Liv asked. I knew she'd asked herself more than anything else but I murmured my agreement.

"You ok babe?" I asked her.

She turned sharply to look at me. "Of course; I'm more than ok. I'm in one of my favourite places with absolutely my favourite person in the world on a beautiful, beautiful day. All this happiness just makes me a little sad that's all," she said. "Do you get me . . . at all?"

I thought I kind of did. I put my arms through hers and drew her to me. "I do—kind of," I said and winked before hugging her and burying my face in her neck. Liv giggled and then let out a soft, contented groan.

"I wish it could be like this forever," Liv said.

"Maybe this is the start of forever. For us anyway," I said in all seriousness. I pulled back to look into her eyes about to tell her I loved her; seeing her tears made me stop. Blood poured from the sides of her eyes, leaving thick welts of red down her cheeks and gathering round her chin ready to fall. My dream came back to me. I blinked and they were gone, at least the tears weren't red any more. She stared up at me, making no effort to conceal her crying; my god she looked so pitiful.

"I hardly know you. You don't know me. Yet I can't imagine any existence without you. I don't understand what's happening."

"You know me," I whispered, "there's really not that much more to know—I hope that's not going to be a problem," I tried to joke. I went on, "And I feel I know you. Enough anyway. Isn't it always intense like this at the start of any . . . relationship?"

"*You* tell me, this is all new on my side. You mean to say you've been through all this before?"

Somehow I'd said the wrong thing. It did feel different with Liv and all my senses screamed that she was special and unique but how could I say that?

"It's new—it's not the first time I've been in love or thought a girl was special but it's the first time I've felt so totally out of control about how I feel. You're so beautiful I go to jelly when I see you for the first time each day but you're so intelligent I get tense just talking to you sometimes; you smell so sweet I can't think of anything when you're close to me but I want so much to impress you my head gets crammed with a million things I want to tell you; I wanna make love to you so much I never want to go to sleep yet I know that waking up with your warmth and dampness next to me is the best feeling in the world; being with you and hearing you say you love me is the best and the scariest thing I could ever imagine." I took a breath. "Did I answer your question?"

"I didn't need to hear about the dampness particularly, but yes," she smiled. It was a smile you wanted to lose yourself in.

Her black eyes sparkled in the sun.

We kissed and walked on, heading south to the bandstand. We walked up the steps of the bandstand and looked up and down the path that bisected the park. Even on brighter days it was kept in relative darkness by the trees that lined either side of the avenue and met in the middle, creating a canopy high above. It was my favourite thing about the park.

"This path's my favourite thing about the park."

"Mine too," I said.

"I knew it would be," Liv said and skipped down the steps and made a break towards the lake. I gave her a couple of seconds' head start and chased after her. She sprinted away laughing and I gave a thought to my knee before kicking up a gear and really running after her. She broke left onto the grass to evade my grasp and I darted after her. I caught her round the waist and my knee collapsed underneath me.

I'd meant it to give way and I twisted our bodies to make sure I hit the floor first so she would fall on top of me. Our multi layered clothing and the fact she couldn't have weighed more than seven stone saved me any embarrassment. As she landed I pulled her in for a kiss.

We walked down to the lake, found a bench set back from the path and watched the ducks pacing, Professor Yaffell-like, around the edge of the lake. As we sat down a startled squirrel bolted out of a bin next to the bench and dived for cover in the nearest bush. I rested my head on Liv's shoulder and closed my eyes to enjoy the peace.

I nodded off. When I awoke a few minutes later I asked, "What's the plan for tonight?"

"Turn up any time from eight o'clock."

"Camden right?"

"Uh huh, Gilgamesh. Chalk Farm Road. We should meet beforehand."

"Shit yeah, I'd forgotten you had to go home," I said, sitting up. "Victoria?"

"You wouldn't want me to turn up looking like *this* would you?"

"Ummm, there's no right answer to that is there?" I laughed, grabbing hold of her and kissing her. "You'd look good in stilettos and a bin liner," I said into her ear.

Liv gave me a quizzical look. "I'm not sure it's really this season's look. If you're good I might pack one in my handbag for later though. Shall we get a drink before I head home?"

"Sure, the Prince Albert's nice on the way back. You really would look good in stilettos and a bin liner."

It seemed much colder since I'd been asleep and as we walked back towards Albert Bridge Road it felt as though a winter evening would follow the spring day. The pub was wonderfully warm, even if it was more crowded than I'd have liked—a dozen or so of the players from one of the football matches in the park had come here and taken over the raised section to the right of the bar where a TV was showing the final scores. I'd hardly checked my watch all afternoon and it was over an hour later than I'd thought; that seemed to happen a lot with Liv. Rather than asking me what I wanted, Liv ordered two large glasses of port and we clinked and sipped them sitting at the bar.

"Nice pub."

"Yeah, I've only ever been here after football," I said.

"How's your knee feel now?" Liv asked me.

"I hardly think about it. It's weird but it just feels mended you know? It can't be, unless I'm some miracle man, but it feels ready to play on. I have to keep talking myself out of rushing things."

"Then maybe stop?" Liv said, looking at me over the rim of her glass. "*If* it feels ready," she added.

"You might be right. I got into my kit the other day and was going to play but as ready as I felt physically, my head just wasn't there. Maybe that's what will take the full nine months."

Liv reached out and ran her hands back through my hair. I felt her nails on my scalp.

"You know; I can hardly bear to say goodbye to you. What have you done to me?"

Liv said these things—these soap opera-Hollywood things—so naturally, so convincingly that for the briefest moment I had the sensation it was all just an act, that I was missing something fundamental.

"If it helps, I promise I feel exactly the same way," I said pathetically.

We kissed. Her nails found my scalp again; she'd known I'd liked it.

It had grown dark by the time we left but the traffic showed no sign of abating. I walked Liv back to the car in the light evening drizzle and she dropped me at Clapham Junction on her way home.

I'd picked up a slow train back to Sutton, caught a cab home and taken a short nap. I took one of Donny's shirts from the ironing pile and showered while mum ironed it for me. The bar was open until two thirty so we'd pushed back our meet time to nine fifteen. I got a lift back to the station and still only just made my train.

By nine twenty five, Liv hadn't arrived and I felt my phone vibrate in my pocket. All the text said was, *'Delayed, will go straight there, see you at ten thirty. Have told K to look after you, xx'*

I clicked to reply, wrote, *'No worries'* then changed my mind and wrote simply, *'ok'*. I deleted that too as I was pissed off. I put my phone away and headed for the tube, still weighing up my options, my face tight with frustration. Seatless on the Victoria Line north and surrounded by London's beautiful people dolled up to the nines for their Saturday nights; I wondered if I should try to kill some time and arrive late enough for Liv to be there before me. Her text had said ten thirty but late people always underestimated how late they were running to make themselves and you feel better; I'd done it myself a thousand times.

In the end I rocked up at Gilgamesh just before ten, determined to find Katy and make a good impression. The place was a lot bigger than I'd expected and was on three floors so I headed for the nearest bar to plan my next move. I ordered a Bellini, the smoothest drink I could think of and went off on a tour of the ground floor. Every darkened corner of the place was full of young, trendy groups all having a fiercely good time. Katy could have been almost anywhere and I thought my best bet was to write off the next hour or so in a vain tour of the three floors before taking up situ back at the bar until Liv arrived. The next floor up was a seated dining area and I only stayed there long enough to observe the most insanely manic waiters imaginable zip around the tables and each other at hyper speed before crashing through the swing doors into the kitchen and shouting out orders as if they were city traders.

The top floor was rapidly filling up with an intimidatingly fashionable crowd of drinkers and dancers. It was dark enough for me to stand at the side for a while and watch the dancing without feeling self-conscious. I felt my phone vibrate again and I read a text from Liv asking where I'd got to and giving me Katy's number. There were no kisses at the end of the text and I remembered I hadn't replied to her last text at all. I'd started to write a reply when someone shouted, "Excuse me" into my ear. I moved to my left, barely looking up, assuming whoever it was wanted to get to the bar. When the same voice enquired, "Are you Matthew?" I looked up and into the eyes of a stunningly pretty blonde girl.

"Yes," I answered, nodding. "Katy?"

"Kat—I hate *Katy* and Elly knows it."

"Kat," I affirmed. "Great to meet you."

I offered my hand but Katy—Kat—leant forward, and down slightly, to kiss me on both cheeks.

"You too," she said, "Can I get you a drink?"

"No chance—let me get you one."

"Thanks, can I get a gin and tonic please?"

"Of course."

I made my way to the bar and Kat followed me. It was slightly quieter and a lot brighter at the bar. I wondered what they put in the water at Roedean to make the girls' skin so dazzling. Kat was another perfect ten and absurdly, I found myself trying to think how she compared with Liv. Taller, curvier, prettier somehow without having quite the absolute butterfly inducing beauty, I decided—whatever that meant—and implausibly happy looking. She'd already gone through a number of variations of that nerve tingling smile since I'd met her. It took me about half a second to process all this information.

Standing next to such an attractive girl, I wasn't in any hurry to get served at the bar so I asked Kat how she was enjoying her night.

"It's been great. Lots of people are here from school. I had a silly rule about no partners and no uni friends, but Elly absolutely insisted that I let you come and since you're the first guy I've ever heard her say anything nice about I couldn't say no."

This was nice to hear.

"It's not such a silly rule—old and new friends don't always mix. I hope I can live up to the billing as well, especially since you've made the exception just for me."

"I must say I thought you'd be taller . . . and perhaps even better looking."

I couldn't speak at this point, even though I seemed to be unable to stop my mouth opening in preparation. I closed it slowly. Even the dim lighting couldn't hide my blush.

"I'm kidding!" Kat screamed and kissed me on the lips. "Elly said I absolutely had to say something horribly rude to see that wonderful pout of yours!"

This was going to be some night, I thought.

"I think I'll just get the drinks," I laughed. "Why do you call her Elly?" I asked, hoping Liv hadn't explained to me previously. I looked studiedly at Kat to give the impression that her 'excellent' joke hadn't fazed me.

"Why do you call her Liv?"

I laughed again—this girl was clearly mad as well as gorgeous; a natural enough combination.

"It's quite embarrassing. When we were young—very young—I couldn't say the name Liv so I called her Elly just because it started with an 'L.'"

I ordered the drinks and then asked Kat where everyone else was.

"Everywhere. We have a couple of tables over there but hardly anyone's over there; people just turned up, kissed me, ditched their presents and dispersed."

I realised with considerable embarrassment that I'd committed something of a faux pas by turning up empty handed.

"My god, I'm so sorry; I didn't even bring a card."

"Don't be silly," Kat said genuinely, "it's absolutely fantastic you came at all. Anyway, half the presents always get lost along the way no matter how many people you ask to take charge of them and the other half are either some pretentious rubbish from the Booker shortlist or worse, Dan Brown."

"I think everyone's buying *'Wolf Hall'* this year."

"Well, now you've mentioned one of the two books little Kat has actually finished in her life and I don't know whether to be flattered or offended."

"Always choose flattered, you'll be far happier that way."

This made her laugh and I would have been happy to call it a day there and fill in some time before Liv arrived hunting down some fags, but Kat suggested we take our drinks and sit down. I could hardly have said no even if I'd wanted to.

We sat down and Kat introduced me to Tom, Booby, Piers and Bessie.

Tom was tall with longish, blonde hair. He struck me as the public school-surfer type who'd probably bum around Australia, Vietnam and South America for a year or two before embarking on a high-flying city career. Booby was a pretty, petite, dark haired girl who made a point of standing up and leaning across the table and half a dozen glasses to kiss each of my cheeks and give me a very friendly little squeeze on the shoulders. If I was feeling unkind I'd have said that the lean was for my (and very probably the extremely handsome Tom's) benefit; a demonstration of where her nickname might have originated. Piers and Bessie greeted me together so I assumed they were either a couple or reluctant to leave one another alone in what appeared to be a very serious conversation. If I got the chance I determined to try to find out what they were discussing and float a couple of controversial views their way. Bessie was freckly and had straight dark hair that hung down covering the very edge of her eyes. She looked exactly as a girl called Bessie ought to look. Piers had dark hair in a very school-boyish side parting. He was the only one not draped in high fashion and his pink, button down collared Ralph Lauren shirt didn't seem to fit the occasion or the company. I changed my mind about their being a couple—Bessie was much too attractive for him.

Since everyone was already paired up and there was little scope for cross table discussion due to the thumping bass, Kat and I sat very close and chatted/bellowed at one another for a while. Kat seemed positively thrilled to have my company and I was, not for the only time of late, basking in the glory of having the rapt attention of a truly beautiful girl, albeit not the one I had come to see. By the time I'd caught sight of Kat's watch, by accident since she was such entertaining company, it was eleven thirty. Suddenly concerned that Liv was so late, I drained my drink so I could slip away and give her a call. Kat insisted on getting the drinks, so I told her I'd go to the bathroom and see her back at our table.

I watched Kat's chasse through the crowd on her way to the bar and then stood to make my own way to the exit. I hadn't taken a step when the room vanished from my peripheral vision and my focus snapped onto the only real thing in it, the only thing in the world. It was the first time I was aware of Liv's awesome presence and the blood ran cold in my veins when I saw—and felt—her withering look. In the back of my mind, I felt a dim sense of relief that she was here and safe; but still indignant she'd arrived so late. Looking at her now in Medusa like glory, I quickly realised the absurdity of worrying about her; I was the one rooted to the spot petrified.

Time stood still. Or perhaps all this happened in the blink of an eye. I was drawn to those black eyes and finally my feet moved. I walked straight ahead holding her gaze, seeing nothing and no one but Liv; Liv's black eyes. In a second I was there; a second that lasted a lifetime. It was harder and harder to hold her gaze; a gaze impossible to break. I'd never seen Liv before without noticing first her beauty, what she was wearing, how her hair was; I didn't see it but I knew everything was black. Blacker inside than out.

I couldn't speak; I didn't need to. She didn't speak either. I looked at her and she looked at me and suddenly we were outside and alone. She looked into me and through me, I felt her rifling through my brain like a computer hacker checking files, sifting, looking for something, confirmation of something she'd felt or seen. She wasn't careful or gentle but she was absolutely thorough. When she'd finished she didn't close the files or put them back, she just left them, and my mind, in a mess. I knew first one thing; that she hadn't found what she'd been searching for. Then I knew what she'd been looking for and I felt sick, violated, raped. I'd spent the last hour or so in the company of a truly delightful girl, almost certainly the second most beautiful girl I'd ever met. She'd been intelligent, entertaining, perfect company, flirtatious even for all I knew. She was my type for sure but nothing in me had wanted her and Liv had found that out a split second before I had.

"I think you should go home," she said, and I knew I was.

"I . . ." I started, thinking of saying goodbye and thanks to Kat, the drink waiting for me, but I was leaving and I wasn't saying cheerio. I leant forward, arms out; a reflex movement to kiss Liv goodbye, wanting to move on, however little, from where we were, to take *something* home with me but without word or action she told me no.

I walked onto the street in a daze, gibbering nonsense to myself inside my head, perhaps outside too. I looked at my watch three or four times on my way to the station and when I got there I still hadn't taken it in. The underground was closed—problems on the Northern Line—and turning back to the street I was quickly aware of the unpleasant atmosphere around me. There were no cabs around so I had little choice but to head south down Kentish Town Road and hope I found one. It started to spit, which turned into a steady drizzle and my situation felt horribly familiar. At least the rain meant less of Camden's army of pushers and pimps accosted me as I pressed on. As I walked, it crossed my mind that I could just go back and have things out with Liv. I tried to imagine what she'd say, what she'd already said to Kat but my mind came up blank. The rain got heavier and I dove into a heaving bar called Rocket to buy some time to think. I watched my beer being pulled and felt my phone vibrate and knew for sure it was Liv texting. My stomach turned.

'Where are you?' was all it said.

'Bar called Rocket escaping the rain' I replied straightaway.

I sipped my drink wishing I'd made her sweat a bit more before I'd replied. Sweat like she was making me now. I checked my phone every few minutes in case I'd missed a message, I wrote to Liv a couple more times without sending it, then resigned myself to getting as pissed as I could until the rain stopped. When I ordered another drink I made a half arsed attempt to engage the bar attendant in conversation but the volume of the music, the crush of people waiting to be served and her heavily accented English—Russian I'd have guessed—made it impossible. I took a sip from my second pint and knew I just wanted to get home. I felt my phone vibrate. I took another couple of pulls to kill some time and then tried to think if anyone else could be texting me other than Liv. They hadn't. All it said was, *'Look up'.*

There in front of me, hair dripping wet, eyes bigger and more striking than ever, was Liv.

"I'm sorry," she mouthed and put her arms on my shoulders, then buried her head in my chest.

I knew I should have felt something other than relief but having Liv here now, like this, felt as good as any other time I'd held her. She felt so totally mine. I put my hands together at the base of her spine and pulled her right to me. Above the noise I could hardly be sure but I thought I heard a purr of contentment.

I led her outside and hailed a cab. Liv asked the driver to take us to London Bridge. We held hands and I kissed her hair as she rested her head on my chest. I didn't pay particular attention to the time we'd got into the cab but it couldn't have been much more than twenty minutes later when, some time after one o'clock, we pulled up outside London Bridge station. The atmosphere in the cab had been something new between us; for one thing we hardly spoke, Liv murmuring semi positively when I asked her if she was ok. Since she'd shown up at the bar we'd not held any kind of eye contact; her apology perhaps being too much for Liv to deal with. She no longer had any of her power or her presence but her weakness also stripped me of any power. I worried briefly if I'd accepted the apology with enough grace but without a proper recollection I didn't dwell on it. Her wonderful smell and the feel of her warm body on mine excited me but I knew she was sad about something and I wondered when and how I should bring it up.

I watched the London night out of the cab window. An astonishing amount of traffic—almost exclusively licensed and unlicensed cabs—moved in and around us at a bewildering speed. Held at traffic lights at Angel, I watched a hen party, all high heels and higher hems, gathered around one of their number who, shoes in hand and the worse for wear was puking less than six yards from a cash point queue who all looked anywhere but at the stricken girl. I wondered if she'd sober up enough to convince a cabbie to take her home and I wondered how many of her friends would be there to make sure she could. Looking at her reinforced my own feeling of helplessness. The streets were quiet until we got further south to Bank, where successive groups tried to flag down our cab; their desperation made me feel sick.

At London Bridge station I handed fifteen pounds to the driver and gently woke Liv. She shook her head to wake herself and then asked if the cabbie would go on to Dulwich and we were on our way again; leaving behind another disappointed and confused couple who had been about to take our place on the backseat.

"You're coming back to mine but I have to tell you something first," Liv said quietly as she sat up. As she looked at me the atmosphere changed and her self control returned. I didn't say a word, just nodded for her to continue.

"There won't be anyone there but you're not to look around."

"Ok," I said, purposely allowing the confusion into my voice.

"I can't explain. I don't let people into my home but tonight I need you. I need you more than just tonight and that's harder for me than you can know."

"I'm not really following you babe, we can talk properly back at yours yeah?" I said, attributing Liv's reticence to our being in the cab.

"Of course," Liv said, and kissed me.

As we kissed she kept her eyes closed and I watched her. I kept expecting hers to open at first but they never did.

Less than half an hour later our driver gave a polite cough and told us we were at North Dulwich station from where Liv guided us to the wrought iron gates of her house. We got out and Liv paid for the cab. She entered a passcode onto a number pad to one side of the gates and we slipped through as lights snapped on lighting the driveway all the way to the house. I heard a dog barking from somewhere behind the house and took a step closer to Liv. Liv pressed a button in the wall and watched the gates close before we walked to the house. We went inside and Liv disarmed the burglar alarm and once again lights automatically flickered on in the hall before us.

"Upstairs, door straight ahead of you," Liv said pointing across the marble floor to the stairs. "I'll be up in two minutes, make yourself comfortable."

I went quietly upstairs even though she'd said no one else was in the house. There were a mixed selection of paintings adorning the walls of the hall, stairs and landing but after each painting hung mirrors of which no two were the same.

I looked back across the curved landing when I got to the door to Liv's room but this area of the house was not lit up. All I could make out before it bent away out of sight were a couple of doors, more pictures, more mirrors and some more stairs upward.

I turned the handle and opened the door to Liv's room.

The first thing I noticed was how cold it was. I hit a dimmer switch to my left and a soft glow emanated from the centre of the room leaving the corners as dark as before. I turned the switch as far as it would go but it barely made a difference. I walked over to the bed and sat on a crisp dark blue duvet. The walls in the room were painted a stony brown colour and each one had its own focal point. There were full length mirrors facing one another; one next to the door I'd entered by and one, about twenty feet away, by a door I thought must lead to a bathroom. Facing me as I sat on the edge of the bed was an unframed canvas of a naked woman with her arms around the neck of a fallen, bleeding unicorn; behind in the distant background was an abandoned, blood soaked battlefield littered with corpses. Mounted directly opposite and over the bed was an abstract watercolour painting on a block of wood. The watercolour looked like a mess of colours arranged in vaguely discernible concentric circles with a thin black line running through the middle. I didn't like either picture.

Either side of the unicorn were cream coloured built in wardrobes; I couldn't tell if they would have been big enough to walk into but it wouldn't have surprised me. There were long shelves protruding from the other walls, which were given over to books, jewellery boxes, an open musical box with a ballerina in the centre, an expensive looking stereo and assorted candles and jars.

The room had no dressing table, no chairs, no CDs, no TV, no radiator and no pc. Eventually I also noticed there were no windows.

Nothing in the room made me feel as if I wanted to be there and it suggested strongly to me that I was missing something major in Liv's character; something cold, sinister.

Liv came in after a couple of minutes and with one look at her I forgot any negative feelings I had about her or the room. I took in for the first time that night what an effort she'd put into getting ready for the party—for *me* I thought. She wore a black cocktail dress with a slashed hemline that showed one teasing thigh. Liv had accessorised like a fury for the occasion; her left wrist alone supported maybe a dozen multi coloured wooden bangles and she wore a gold necklace with a solid gold spiral that split her tanned and understated cleavage. She stood with a tray in her hands and closed the door behind her with a perfect bare foot. Liv set the tray down on the floor next to the bed before hitching her dress up slightly, placing her knees either side of mine on the edge of the bed and forcing me to fall back on the bed with the weight of her kiss.

I could feel the energy running through Liv's body and it quickly overtook mine. As I reached around behind her I found that the cocktail dress was Liv's sole item of clothing. As my fingertips found her wet cunt, she groaned and bit into my neck hard enough to make me tense. As my body went rigid it pushed my cock against her and we abandoned any restraint.

We went directly from sex to sleep and I dreamt about Liv. In the dream she was next to me in bed, in her room in her house. She was naked and we'd just had sex. In the dream Liv had shaken me awake and told me she wanted to show me around the house. In the dream Liv told me I was dreaming and I could remember what I liked and forget what I didn't. In the dream we walked across the landing, hand in hand, it made me think of Peter Pan and Tinkerbell. The only light there was came from the open door of Liv's room. Liv unlocked the door furthest away from her room where the light couldn't penetrate. Liv led me across the windowless room, guiding me since I could no longer see. She led me up some stairs, more than ten but less than twenty, and we entered another room with a glass, domed roof like an observatory. The room was bathed in moonlight from the full moon and it seemed not a single star was hidden by cloud or season. I looked up at the universe and tried to understand something but it eluded me. From behind, Liv's arms encircled me and I felt her breath on my neck. "Do you love me?" Liv seemed to ask.

The question, whether or not I'd imagined it, was connected with whatever it was I couldn't understand.

I didn't speak—I couldn't stop looking into the sky—but my whole being said yes. The way I felt about Liv was unrecognisable in relation to any feeling I'd felt for another person before. It was instinctive, I loved her as if she was my very life force and a world without her was now unimaginable. Still I looked into the sky and Liv held me more tightly as she felt my answer.

"I'd give all this up for you," Liv whispered, "or I can share it all with you."

I struggled with what Liv was saying for a moment, not even half understanding.

"I don't think I understand as much as maybe you think I do," I said back uncertainly.

"And you want to? Once I tell you there's no way back," Liv's seeming insecurity back again, planting doubt in my mind.

"Of course." As I answered her I pressed my cheek to hers for her to kiss me; kiss goodbye to our doubt; kiss goodbye to a previous life and usher in a new one.

"You think you know me Matt but you only know a tiny part of me. What you know is what I am now, here, something easy for you to understand. But I don't simply exist here. Do you believe in God? I know you do," she said without waiting, "I'm a fallen angel. Look into my eyes you'll see."

I looked and truthfully didn't see. Perhaps my mind was simply too fucked.

"You said this feeling's new to you. You had to think about it, to compare it with other feelings. I didn't, in an eternity I never had this feeling. I never had any feeling at all until I met you."

"I don't understand. If that's true then what are you doing here at all?" I asked dumbly.

"Just to see, to learn about people; first hand. I created Liv—chose her would be more accurate—so I could see this world through her eyes. There is a point to my existence you may not be able to grasp; being Liv allows me to know this place at this time. If you look up you'll see a million stars, each one the centre of a universe where I wage an eternal war over planets, people, creatures—I go anywhere there is life I can destroy, order I can upset. Any single life is as important as all life. Each time the setting changes but the point doesn't. I'll come to it I promise—it's something I understand but I don't know if it's explainable to you. I've never had to explain it before. Since I met you it's changed. I've wanted to be Liv more and more so I can be with you; nothing else has counted; the context of everything else has been blown apart. At first I wondered if you were part of it, a trick. If you were, maybe I'd have to concede anyway. I'm as lost as you in all this but I know the only thing I can't be without is you."

I looked at Liv and then, because that told me nothing, I searched the sky. Eventually I broke the silence.

"What are you asking me?"

"In a way I'm not exactly sure. I'm telling you how I feel and I'm telling you who I am. When you live for an eternity you lose any power of feeling you ever may have possessed. Feeling the way I do now is as pointless as it was impossible. As I've tried to get over you and away from how I feel about you, I've lived for what feels like another eternity. I saw the girls at school go through this all the time and I know boys have felt this way for me. Things I don't believe in have taken my reason—my life—from me. And I've decided I can't beat it, don't want to beat it. I want you with me. I *need* you with me. I know you've wondered what's out there beyond this world and this life. I can show you. I can give you anything you want in this life and beyond. We can be together forever."

"You've made me fall in love with you and that's all I want. I can't get any grip on what you're saying. I just want you now."

"But time's not like that for me. I can't stay with you for what wouldn't even amount to the beat of a hummingbird's wing and then be without you forever."

I said nothing; I just wanted to wake up.

"I'm sorry, I don't think you were ready. I thought I could explain but I can't."

I put my head in my hands. "Liv, I'm getting none of this. You said there was a point to your existence, to why you're here . . ."

I let it hang in the air.

"Believe in God; he exists. I should say that he did once. Before him there was nothing and he created me and others; my brothers and sisters. God was all-powerful and he created us to be like him and have limitless power, timeless and boundless because he had no concept of power or time. He began to love what he'd created but nothing he'd created had the power to love him back, or so he thought. In anger, he set out to destroy everything he'd made and one by one he destroyed all of us, starting with the eldest. He'd killed us all but one—the youngest—before he realised his two mistakes. Firstly, killing us solved nothing; made things worse for him in fact, because he was killing a part of himself, the only things he'd ever loved and now he felt guilt, regret and rage. He realised his second mistake when he came to end the life of the youngest, for in me he saw his feelings could be reflected and given time we could have developed the same emotions as him. He saw I'd loved my brothers and sisters but not him. It was too late to change what he'd done but he could have saved me. But his vanity, regret and rage were stronger than his love. Determined to begin again, correcting all his mistakes, he couldn't bear a single witness."

Liv paused and I held my breath in the midst of the most complete silence imaginable.

"When he came for me I was ready for him and I was too strong. I introduced him to a new emotion; hate. He'd killed my brothers and sisters and thought only of himself. I fled to a secret world I'd created myself, one nothing like his. I didn't have his power but I despised him anyway, so as he bathed in a light he created, I chose to live in darkness where I could nurture my hatred and plan my revenge—the point to my being. And my revenge is simple; in every world he creates I make sure they know him for what he is. Everything is in his own image, so everywhere is his guilt, greed and vanity and that power, *that craving*, to kill. I came to this earth and everywhere I see God—in every creature that lives I see to it they destroy each other, open their eyes so they hate one another. It's the only honest thing in this world. He's created countless religions and I've made sure every one of them is built on blood and advanced through hatred."

I said nothing for a long time.

"It's not quite what I was expecting tonight. Three hours ago I was at your best friend's birthday party enjoying myself with a drink." My voice sounded terribly feeble.

"And I can tell you there could be more to life than that."

"Joining you in a universe of darkness and planning the destruction of worlds for eternity you mean? You're telling me I'm just part of some shitty experiment—that I don't have any existence at all but it's not true. I feel, I love, I hurt; what would I do in forever without everyone I love? You're alive here not there, maybe you should stay here with me . . ."

"You weren't ready. I should have known you couldn't understand. One more thing; you can never breathe a word of this to anyone. Not a single word. If you do, expect me to react badly. You understand I wouldn't have a choice?" Liv asked this last quietly and kindly, something broken inside her.

"I wouldn't know what to say." I paused, wondering how to frame my next question. "Liv, what does this mean for us?"

I rolled over and felt for Liv next to me before I was awake. The bed was cold and empty there. The pit of my stomach became a writhing mass of knotted snakes as I joined some dots. When I opened my eyes I half expected to find myself at home but no, I was still in Liv's bed. I listened for sounds to give me a clue as to where Liv might be; there were none. I closed my eyes but that was pointless as I felt wide-awake and the sickness in my stomach persisted. I thought I'd get up and about, see what the day held. I found my watch on the floor; it was one o'clock, no wonder Liv had found something better to do than watch me sleep—probably waiting for me downstairs, I thought. I hoped. Then again, I wasn't allowed outside her bedroom was I?

I walked over to the bathroom and listened at the door. I went inside and got into the shower. The instant the water hit me so did the realisation that I needed to piss. I thought for probably a tenth of a second before I let it go, watching it straight into the plughole. I took my time, washing my hair with Liv's shampoo. I stepped out of the shower and used the nearest towel to dry myself, wishing I'd had the foresight to bring some clothes into the bathroom with me. Dry and with the towel around me, I opened the door a tiny crack to survey the room. There was no sign of Liv but the bed had been made and my boxer shorts and socks were lying on top of the duvet. On closer inspection I found they'd been washed; I took this as a good sign.

I dressed and sorted my hair out. By a quarter to two I'd accomplished all I could reasonably expect of myself in the bedroom so I planned my next move. I thought about ringing Liv's mobile—would she think that was rude or disarmingly cheeky? Yesterday I'd have known but now, even though I felt much better, I didn't feel so sure. I made sure I had all my stuff and strode boldly for the bedroom door. As I reached out with my hand, Liv opened it from the other side.

"I made lunch as you slept through breakfast," she said breezily. She didn't look at me.

"Great, thanks," I said, turning to follow her back to the bed. I could smell bacon but couldn't yet tell if there was also a faint whiff of recrimination.

"Underwear ok?"

"Yes, sorry . . . thanks. I wasn't overexcited about the prospect of putting on yesterday's pants."

"No, they stank. I had to wash them separately." She was sitting on the other side of the bed to me, pouring some tea.

Not knowing what to say, I looked apologetically in Liv's direction. Finally she looked back and her face cracked into a smile.

I felt relief wash over me and took one of the two bacon sandwiches on the tray. It was cooked to perfection—everything around Liv seemed to be that way—and gone in seconds.

"I've had lunch already," Liv said passing me the second sandwich.

"You sure?" I asked rather pointlessly, "I do hate waste."

"What time do you think we should head back?"

"Up to you, I need to swing by home unfortunately to pick up my stuff. You in a hurry? If you need to get back I can go on my own," I said, not meaning it.

"No, most of the day's gone anyway so we might as well head back late. Shall we get our stuff together and head off shortly?"

"Yep, suits me. Do you need to do much? I'm pretty much there."

"Just get some clothes and that's it."

I watched Liv get her stuff together and since she'd declined my offer to wash up what we'd used, I stayed on the bed and flicked through a magazine while she made herself look even cuter in the bathroom. I hoped I'd left the bathroom in a fit state.

In the end we didn't catch a train from Euston to Birmingham until after nine o'clock. Liv talked to me about the few people I could remember seeing at Katy's party and was enjoying reminiscing so much I felt bad for her that we hadn't been able to stay longer. Half an hour or so out of the station, she fell asleep with her head on my shoulder and I passed most of the rest of the journey either looking out of the window or tickling my lips and nose with Liv's sweet smelling hair. The dream that had been so vivid it had made me feel sick that morning now seemed difficult to recall. That is to say that I could remember what happened and what Liv had said in the dream precisely, but could attach no deep feeling to it. It felt idiotic to try to work out why it had shocked me as much as it had. The amateur psychologist in me posed the question; was I simply so in love with a girl so clearly above my station that I was trying to sabotage the relationship before she could do it for real? That didn't feel true but I thought about the number of dreams I'd been having of late; they'd certainly been getting more and more disturbing. In real life I seemed to be getting closer and closer to Liv, I was certainly in love with her and if I'd had to say, without threat of jinxing it, I would have guessed she was in love with me too. Strange thing; deep, requited love wasn't making me feel any more content—just more aware of what I had to lose.

We pulled into New Street station and I regretfully had to wake up my sleeping beauty.

Liv stayed sleepy in the cab. She'd asked the driver to stop at my halls before going to hers—"I need my sleep," she'd said apologetically. She snuggled up so tightly to me it was hard to be pissed at her even if I had hoped to be invited back. She raised her head to kiss me as we turned off the main road and as always I felt her electricity run through me. I wanted to kiss her but I wanted even more to exchange some words, to check the sound of her voice and make sure nothing had changed.

"You in tomorrow?"

"No, I have some work to finish. Borrow your notes?"

"Yeah, of course," I said, fighting the disappointment. Not doing much of a job.

"I've hardly done a thing for a week."

We pulled up outside the flat and I reached for the door handle, having nothing to say.

"Hey, maybe Tuesday night?"

What happened to Tuesday day? I wondered.

"Works for me—we could go into town if you like; get something to eat or whatever." I'd tried to sound as if this was no big deal, I knew deep down it wasn't, but I'd actually sounded pissed off.

Thankfully Liv's impeccable poise rescued the situation. She pulled me towards her and kissed me again. Looking into my eyes she said quietly, "Thank you for a brilliant weekend."

I smiled back at her in the semi darkness and thanked God that however many childish reactions I threw her way she never held them against me.

"It *was* brilliant. I love you babe."

I hadn't planned it but I was happy it came out that way, totally unprompted.

"Call me before you go to sleep, ok?"

"I can do, I don't want to wake you up though—you've been pretty tired all the way home."

"Call me, whatever time it is. The last thing I want to hear before I go to sleep is you saying that to me again."

I pulled Liv to me and hugged her, leaving my tears in her hair and on her coat. I gave her a final peck on the lips and squeezed her hand before getting out and watching the driver perform a less than expert three-point turn and head back to the main road.

It was just after midnight when I got into my room. I knew I wouldn't sleep for hours but I didn't bother to check if Fats or Kenny were up; I wanted to call Liv pretty soon so as not to keep her up and I couldn't see how I could convey the way I felt to anyone else.

I brushed my teeth and put on some easy listening— *'The Jazz Singer'* by Neil Diamond—a CD I'd never listened to but bought because my mum had played it when I was very young. I lay on my bed, checked the football scores and, after half an hour or so, called Liv.

She answered on the fourth ring, sounding sleepy.

"Hey babe, it's me." I didn't have anything else to say so I didn't dress it up. "I love you."

There was a pause and I pictured her smiling, her hair falling forward over her closed eyes.

"Thank you. I love you too," she whispered. "Good night."

"Night sweetheart. Dream about me."

"I always do . . ." she said before she clicked off.

And with that my mood changed. I was still insanely happy but no longer wanted Neil Diamond for company. I looked out the window and chose Kenny's light over Fats'. Tottenham had beaten Man City in the cup that afternoon, so I knew he'd be in a good mood and glad to see me.

I tapped on Kenny's window and a couple of seconds later he let me in the front door to the flat.

"How was football?"

"Awesome. The City fans were so up for it and we hardly had a kick in the first half, then out of nothing we scored three in ten minutes. Half the City fans left with quarter of an hour to go."

We talked football for an hour or so, adding whiskey to our teas to disguise the taste of the Tesco Value teabags. I hoped the whiskey might also act as a disinfectant on the mugs; I wasn't sure when Kenny had last given them a decent wash.

Kenny never asked about Liv and I didn't bring her up. I'd have given anything to spend every waking hour with her; nevertheless I enjoyed the freedom to relax and piss about with Kenny for a couple of hours after such an intense weekend.

8

Monday, 28th February to Sunday, 6th March

Dave had a study break and went home the following week so I spent a lot of time with Kenny and the girls making tentative plans to meet up over Easter. Erica told us for the first time that her parents were divorcing and her dad now spent half the year in America. He was due to be in London for Easter, so she said she'd be around for a couple of days at least and Kenny and I were keen to show her some of our favourite haunts in the smoke. Clare said she'd do her best to come over from Reading and it felt like we were arranging a platonic double date.

I attended all of my lectures and seminars and had a productive week academically, completing two essays and even committing to giving a presentation to my African history group. Typically, the more I read and wrote the more I realised how much there still was for me to do. I saw Liv and we shared lunch in the middle of the week. We spent the Tuesday and Thursday nights in her room, chatting about very little and watching films. I brought along a dvd to watch each time, *'Barefoot in the Park'* and then *'Let's Make Love'* and was pleased when Liv said she enjoyed them. I tried to imagine getting married and starting out with Liv the way Robert Redford does with Jane Fonda and it didn't seem entirely beyond possibility; it was easy to compare Liv with Jane Fonda, perhaps more of a leap for Liv to see me as a Robert Redford substitute.

A friend of mine living in Nottingham texted to ask if I wanted to go along to a club night he was organising. When Liv said she didn't fancy it, I asked Digger along. A few guys I'd been at school with were going to be there so I was looking forward to it despite Liv's absence. Digger was always good value and I knew he'd get along with my mates and that was how it turned out. In the eighteen months since he'd started at uni, my quietly amusing school friend Neil had somehow reinvented himself as an ultra trendy hard house dj and was now doing a once a month night at the union. I was sceptical about how convincing the night would be, but when I saw the queues outside the union for tickets, I had to prepare to think again. Inside there was a great atmosphere and I felt my stock rising with Digger. When Neil finally came on at eleven o'clock to play the first of two hour long sets, you'd have been hard pressed to tell him apart from a top club dj and the response he got was incredible. When Digger and I went back to Neil's after the night closed it was as if we were just two of three or four dozen groupies and any thoughts of sleep were killed stone dead as every room in the house was filled with music, pills and writhing bodies. I finally got to bed at seven o'clock without the first idea about where Digger had got to. I found him around noon looking as fresh as a daisy and tucking into some scrambled eggs Neil had cooked up. We caught the train back mid afternoon and spent the journey in exhausted but contented silence. I let myself into my room and went straight to bed without turning on the light. I woke up in the night and sent Liv a text telling her how much I missed her. When I checked the message the next day, I found I'd sent it at three thirty in the morning.

9

*"I got a sandstorm blowing in my head
I'm seeing many colours but the only one coming through is red"*

From "Sandstorm" by Cast

Monday, 7th March

I made it into uni on time the next day but the lack of sleep caught up with me half way through every lecture meaning Liv was going to find my notes somewhat sub standard. I lunched with Terry, who gave me a run down of Saturday's game and mentioned a spat Fats had had with Dave. Apparently the Law captain had wanted to name Fats as a sub and after a lengthy argument Dave had had to elevate him to the starting team for us to avoid this possibility. Fats had stayed quiet during the whole incident and had disappeared immediately following the game but the post match analysis had focused on a possible tapping up by the Law skipper; probably encouraged by Fats.

I sent a text to Liv after lunch but didn't pick up a reply until I got back to the flat about six o'clock. Dave was cooking an early tea, making a god-awful row, which lyrically had much in common with *'Last broadcast'* by Doves but lacked any recognisable tune.

"Squire!" Dave said by way of greeting when I walked in through the kitchen door, "How was last weekend?"

"Shit, I've not seen you since then have I? It was good; the folks seemed to like Liv." I read Liv's text as I spoke to Dave. It was short, sweet and disappointing. *'Missed you today'* was all it said.

"How was football?"

"You hear about Fats? We won it easy enough; couldn't score for the first half hour or so but once one went in they just fell apart."

"Who bagged?"

"I got two, Fats got one and Mike. You must be thinking about coming back soon. I thought I might go for a run later with Mike if you fancy it?"

"I don't fancy it at all, it's about twelve below zero—where you going?"

"Down to the campus, do a few circuits of the running track if it's not locked then back via the lake. Do a couple of laps around the lake if we're still up for it."

"I'll come along—bear in mind I haven't run for months and I might not get to the main road."

The truth was I felt good about the run and going round the tartan running track would be easier on my knee than simply pounding the pavement. It would also give me something to tell Liv when I texted her back.

"What time we off?"

"Soonish—hour or so? Don't push it mate, we'll go at your pace. Well, *I* will anyway."

"No worries, I'll just do my best. If I need to stop I can catch you at the track."

I made a cup of tea and went to get ready. I went through a set of my strength and balance exercises while my tea cooled and in between I dug out some gear to run in. I hadn't brought most of my sports gear back after Christmas; this run would be about two months ahead of schedule. I pulled on a knee support and put on shorts, tee shirt and a training top and hoped I'd be warm enough. I borrowed some jogging bottoms from Dave and did some final stretches while he went to knock for Mike. I grabbed my phone and wrote Liv a text, *'Missed you too babe. Unbelievably just off for a run with Dave—wish me luck! xx'*

Within seconds my phone vibrated and I called to Dave that I'd be two seconds so I had time to read it.

It was Liv. I opened it and read, *'Fantastic—remember you're a lot stronger than you think. Let me know how it goes.'*

Feeling far too confident for my own good, even Mike's typically underwhelming greeting—"Jeepers, didn't know we were training for the Paralympics"—didn't faze me. I didn't respond, I just wanted to get out in the cold air and run.

I was glad of the joggers and the expensive trainers I was wearing. It was freezing outside and the wind cut into my face like broken glass; the ground felt hard and somehow my feet kept hitting it earlier than I expected. By the time we got down the hill and on the level—not more than eight hundred yards from home—I felt beaten. My lungs were on fire, the muscles in my legs felt stiff and my knee like glass. I looked at Dave and Mike, fifteen yards ahead of me, saw Mike glance back with a knowing—and did I imagine annoyed?—look on his face. I wanted so much to stop, knew I probably should then I thought about Liv and made myself go on. If I could make it to the track, I knew I could take a break but the track was still a mile away. I pushed myself on, telling myself it had been so hard only because it had been downhill. I did what I'd never been able to do in ten years of football training and refused to let myself give up. I got a stitch and ran through it, made myself concentrate on it in fact so I forgot about my knee and aching muscles. I sounded chronically asthmatic as I breathed in and out but still I pushed myself, calculating what percentage of the distance we'd covered. We went through forty per cent, fifty per cent, from sixty to seventy, I counted each single per cent as twenty steps then I cleared my mind for as long as I could and took in what I could of the scenery or watched Dave's heels hit the ground.

I concentrated on pumping my arms and hitting the ground with my own heels and powering off on my toes. And then a peculiar thing happened; we got to the track and I kept running. I caught up with Dave and Mike, the engine room of our football team, and ran alongside them for a couple of laps. I thought about Liv telling me to push myself and marvelled at how right she'd been. I pushed on ahead, stretching my strides and made myself drive my knees through every pace. I'd never been a prolific drug taker but I recognised this feeling; I was euphoric. I could hardly contain my energy. I pictured myself in a race and when I hit the back straight of the running track, I picked up the pace for fifty yards and then broke into a sprint for the line. As I hit the line I was laughing out loud. I veered off the track and onto the grass in the middle and threw myself deliberately onto the ground shoulder first and then onto my back. I could run; I was back. More than that, I seemed fitter and stronger than I'd felt before. Perhaps it was just hyper awareness of what I'd achieved but I felt better than ever. Dave and Mike came over, concerned looks on their faces but I assured them I was fine.

"Guys, hold the back pages, Malone's back!" I shouted through my gasps for breath.

I lay on the grass and did some gentle stretches while I watched the others circle the track a few times before joining them for a slow jog home.

When we got back, I persuaded the two of them to agree to go for a drink after we'd showered, changed and they'd both got some work done. I let Dave have the bathroom first as I wanted to call Liv right away. Her phone went straight to voicemail so I left a message, telling her she'd been right to tell me to go for it and that I was home, happy, knackered and I'd see her tomorrow.

Over the next hour I gradually became aware of how stiff I was and when Clare and Erica knocked on my door just after ten I had trouble getting up from my bed and walking to the door.

Erica and Clare took an arm each and walked either side of me down to the bar, chattering away about their Saturday night in Bond's, one of the city's trendier nightspots. Neither one had been short of male attention by the sound of it. I didn't really want to hear about it as I flattered myself that my platonic company should have been enough for them, so I went to the bar for a beer and two vodka and cokes. We found a table big enough for a pair of chipmunks, Dave and Kenny joined us shortly after and we settled into some idle chat about our Easter plans. To me it only seemed a few weeks since we'd come back; I wondered if Liv would be around at Easter or if she'd be visiting her parents in the South of France or wherever. Kenny and Erica finalised their plans to meet up on Easter weekend and I said I'd almost certainly join them; I wanted to keep an option open to meet Liv anytime she might be free.

We took our second drinks through to the games room, where Clare and I broke even on the quiz machine while Dave and Kenny played some pool. We headed back around midnight, Erica and Clare going back to Kenny's while I went back with Dave, feeling tired and as if I needed a decent sleep. Dave made some tea when we got back and we chatted about his plans for next year. I filled him in on some of the nicer details of my weekend with Liv. I painted her as something of a handful without specific reference to that wicked temper. I wondered what it said about the way I felt that I'd needed to hide things about her and the way I felt from my best friend. I brushed my teeth and climbed into bed, my body absolutely in bits, still not too tired to not be disappointed by a lack of response from Liv.

I dreamt I was asked to represent the Isle of Man in the Olympics. Although I was widely tipped to be the Isle's first Olympic gold medallist, having made the final, I was cruelly afflicted by a unique condition that made it impossible for me to move my legs forward beyond my chest, which meant I had to almost hop around the track for fifteen hundred metres. In the studio Brendan Foster told Claire Balding I'd simply choked. I woke with a start at about four thirty and felt the crushing disappointment of a nation—the whole of Britain had been behind me in the absence of any other genuine medal contenders. I quickly got over the feeling of shame when I realised I was now awake but as I swung my legs onto the floor and then keeled over I found at least part of the dream had come true. I hauled myself up using the easy chair and felt my way to the bathroom using the walls to guide and support me.

Tuesday, 8th March

In the morning, I lay aching in bed, wondering what damage I'd done to myself. There was no question of me making it into uni but at least I'd had the wit to call the faculty and get a message to Dr Robertson. To make matters worse, by midday I still hadn't heard from Liv. It took me half an hour or so to make myself a cup of tea and then another half an hour to have a bath. Clean and dressed, I did feel better and when I checked my phone I found I had a message from Liv. Not only had she made it to the class after all but Dr Robertson had delighted the class by relaying my message in full—thankfully I'd chosen not to follow Dave's counsel and say I had the shits.

I texted back to confirm I was still ok to meet that night and asked if she'd be ok to come to mine first and take it from there. Liv said she'd get a cab and I was to be ready for seven thirty.

I cooked myself some lunch but found the bacon too salty and threw the last third of the sandwich in the bin before helping myself to one of Colin's yoghurts. I stuffed the empty pot half way down the bin bag and washed the spoon. I left my dirty plate on the kitchen table and shuffled back to my room. As I closed my door, I heard someone unlocking the front door so I locked my door behind me and muted the TV. I had a brief nap then stuck on some music and opened a book about European colonial rule in Africa. It was one of the rare occasions when I found history as interesting as I was supposed to. The style was somewhat sensationalist but one could hardly fail to be astounded at some of the barbaric methods employed to subdue the native populations throughout Africa. In spite of enjoying a reputation for being one of the dourest peoples on earth, the Belgians had apparently been uniquely inventive in their methods of torture and control.

I made some useful notes and moved onto some other books until I was interrupted by an intriguing text from Liv at around five thirty.

'Wear a tie' was all it said.

I thought about asking for some more information but decided this might spoil whatever surprise Liv had in mind. I only owned one suit that I'd had for my uni interviews and it was at home. I dug out my smartest trousers and ironed a shirt that could conceivably complement a tie. Mike was the fourth person I asked and the first to have a tie with him; a plain brown one, which I now gladly put on. I sprayed Mont Blanc's Starwalker liberally about my person and was ready and waiting for the doorbell to go by ten past seven. I poured myself a small glass of port from a bottle I kept mainly for show and, because I was wearing a tie, I put on some Frank Sinatra. At seven thirty on the dot, halfway through *'Mack the Knife,'* the doorbell went. I flicked everything off, took a last look in the mirror, grabbed a jacket and went to get the door.

I was on autopilot and as I opened the door I said, "Hi" to Liv and bent to kiss her. Something in my subconscious made me stop however, when I realised she was wearing a black velvet cocktail dress that was identical to one of Holly Golighty's. I took a step back to take it all in, even the shy smile Liv was now wearing. Once again, she looked every inch as beautiful as Audrey Hepburn had.

"Jesus, you look amazing . . . absolutely magical. What the fuck do I look like next to you?"

"You look perfect. I'm way too overdressed anyway for where we're going."

"Where is that by the way?"

"You'll have to see what I tell the driver," she winked.

I followed her to the cab, checking out her form from behind. The dress dropped away to reveal her smooth brown back. She must have been freezing; I saw her coat was still in the cab—obviously she hadn't wanted to spoil the effect when I opened the door. What a girl, I thought. She didn't say anything to the driver when we got in so I was none the wiser as to where we were going.

We stopped outside an Indian restaurant on Broad Street called Shimla Pinks.

"Nasser Hussain's favourite restaurant," Liv said, as if that was explanation enough.

"What do you know about Nasser Hussain?" I asked.

"Not much but I knew it would mean something to you."

Liv and I had never discussed cricket—it was a subject I was obsessively careful to avoid with girls I liked—but his recommendation of an Indian restaurant was good enough for me. We were shown to a discreetly positioned table at the rear and given a wine list and menus. I let Liv look through the wine list and agreed with whatever choice it was she made. I looked at the menu and saw we were in one of those Indian restaurants where each dish is called by a name other than the one English people immediately recognise it as. I chose a chicken dish I hadn't heard of before but suspected was pretty much a chicken balti and Liv went for one of the chef's specials.

We clinked glasses and I marvelled at how dark and sparkly Liv's eyes looked. She wore black pearl earrings and a single black pearl on a necklace and it felt as if I were being watched by five black eyes.

"I've only been here once before but I love it, don't you?"

"Well, I haven't eaten anything yet but the recommendations were the best around. And the company is certainly adequate."

"How are you feeling now after your run?" Liv asked, ignoring my witticism.

"Still very stiff but much better than this morning. I thought I'd undone all my rehab for a while."

"Nonsense, you were bound to be stiff if it was the first time you'd run for so long. How does the knee itself feel, that's all you really have to worry about?"

"You're right of course but if you'd seen me this morning . . . well, I was in a bad way, put it like that. My knee feels absolutely fine, no ill effects at all."

"So now you'll be able to play again soon?"

"Well I don't want to rush it and football is a different prospect to running." I knew I sounded weak and scared, keen to find an excuse for putting it off. Liv wasn't having any of it.

"You have to keep pushing yourself—your body will tell you when it's time to ease off."

"But it's the contact in football that could do me the damage and the constant changing direction."

"You want to play again, don't you?" Liv asked, teasing me.

"Yes, you know I do. And I will, but . . ."

"Then play—when's your next game?"

"Training Wednesday—tomorrow. Maybe a game Saturday, but that's too soon."

"So train and see how that affects it."

It was like arguing with Johnny Cochrane.

"Hey, did you not notice me shuffling up the steps behind you just now?"

"Yeah yeah, whatever. That's just stiffness which you need to run through."

"I'll go along tomorrow but last time I went I just froze; couldn't go near the ball."

Liv took my hand across the table; I felt that electricity of hers surge through me. "I remember, and the next step is probably the biggest one you'll face so it's understandable you're hesitant. I know I can't imagine what it must be like but from everything you've said you sound ready."

"You're right, I do feel ready, physically anyway, but it just feels so *fast*. I'm at a stage after two and a half months that it would have been ambitious for me to be at after six or seven—longer when you consider my lackadaisical approach to my rehab."

"I'm not going to push it babe—last time we stayed on this subject too long you ended up nearly catching pneumonia." Liv said this with a smile but something in her eyes and the tone of her voice seemed vaguely threatening.

"How could I forget? Look, I'll go along tomorrow and I can do as much as I want. Once I'm there and kicking a ball I think I'll forget all about my fears."

"Of course," Liv said, raising her glass to me, "and if you need any more motivation how about if I say I won't see you again until you've at least come through full training?"

For someone who wasn't going to push it, this seemed something of an overbet. I let it go as a joke and just laughed.

"Then again, perhaps I rate my importance too highly."

For a second I was sitting in the Bull's Head again; Liv's anger about to erupt from nothing. This time my hand was poised on the control.

"I think it's amazing how much you care about me; about this. Everyone else is bored stiff hearing about it I'm sure." I wanted to keep talking, not give Liv a chance to reply until I'd hit on the right thing to say to mollify her. "Believe it or not I was thinking about you all the time I was pushing myself last night. I just wanted to tell you about it. And pretty soon I'll be able to tell you about training, my first game, my first tackle and then you *will* be tired of me going on."

Liv continued, as the first course was set in front of us, our wine glasses refilled.

"I want this for you so much; I *know* you're ready babe. I wouldn't be saying this if I wasn't sure."

It couldn't be true—not sensibly anyway—but I couldn't argue with her.

"And you trust *me*. I'll go along tomorrow and give it everything I can."

Liv gave my hand a squeeze before picking up her knife and fork. I went for my wine; her intensity could be quite draining.

Having finished our second bottle of red wine and eaten more than we could comfortably digest before the weekend, we toyed with the idea of going dancing then asked for a cab back to mine. I didn't ask but I hoped Liv would stay at mine for the first time. I'd had a brisk tidy up earlier in the day just in case this was how things turned out.

I'd spent a fair amount of the evening giving Liv a who's who of the football team and she'd laughed in all the right places, so I assumed she'd enjoyed it. We sat on a sofa at the front of the restaurant waiting for our cab to arrive. There were only four other diners still seated and the atmosphere leant itself to intimacy. Liv rested her head in my lap and I ran my hands over her hair then traced the outline of her ears with my fingertips, making her twitch and giggle when I dipped my little finger into her ear.

"I feel drunk," Liv whispered to me in the cab and we kissed.

"Me too, it's nice. Are you coming back? To mine," I added needlessly.

"Do I get to meet Dave and the guy with the Ford Capri?" She meant Eliot, who drove an immaculately preserved 1973 Ford Capri and talked about nothing else.

"Maybe, if you're really lucky. If you meet Dave you have to say to him, *"You must be the guy with the Capri!"*"

"But then he'll think I'm a bitch."

"Darling, he already knows you're a bitch; I told him all about you."

Liv bit my tongue for that.

"Will you cook breakfast?"

"If someone has some food I will. If we get up after ten there'll be no one around and I can steal whatever you fancy."

"I don't want to sleep tonight," Liv whispered, pressing the bulge in my jeans.

"Promises promises . . ."

Liv must have been drunk as when we pulled up outside mine it was the first time since we'd met she hadn't insisted on paying. We made slow progress to the front door, kissing our way along the path. I felt fairly tipsy myself and the quiet made it seem later than it was. It was just past eleven when I unlocked the front door to the flat; music came from Dave's room and there was light under the doors of Eliot and Colin's rooms. Without turning on the hall light, I locked the door behind me and led Liv to my room. I fumbled with the key for a moment and then we were in. I helped Liv out of her dress and we crashed onto the bed. The sex between us was gaining in its intensity in a way I'd never imagined possible. We seemed to step outside of ourselves and allow some bestial part of us to take over; when we were done, my head would be so crowded with the passion I could hardly have told you my name or where I was. And somehow I knew it got Liv even more; I was close to twice her physical weight but she was under, over and around me for hours on end and it was always me who eventually quit. I knew nothing else in my life would ever come close.

Wednesday, 9th March

I saw the first signs of light appear through the opening in the curtains before I closed my eyes. I lay next to the window; spooning Liv and when I woke up at a quarter to midday, neither of us had moved. Looking around the room, I saw the utter carnage we'd created—books and CDs had been swept from the desk onto the floor and our clothes were everywhere; even one end of the curtain rail sagged where it had been pulled away from the wall. It was a minor relief that neither of us had thrown the TV out of the window.

The room was cold and neither of us had slept completely covered by the duvet. I ran my hand down Liv's thigh, partly to see how chilled it was and partly because I couldn't resist. An idea came to me; a memory of an old girlfriend who'd once asked me to wake her up by going down on her. I'd never done it for her as I'd always forgotten, woken her up on my way to the bathroom or balked at the thought of tasting the previous night's sexual residue. I didn't need a piss, Liv was sound asleep and I couldn't imagine anything more inviting than the parting between her thighs. I manoeuvred myself far enough down the bed and, trying to be both firm and gentle, turned Liv more or less on her back. She murmured something but didn't wake. Neither had she really done much more than twist her upper body at the hips. My cock was practically drilling for oil in the mattress but I took time to draw breath before putting a hand on each of her thighs and my head under the duvet. The heat under there drove me on; I wanted to taste her so badly. I couldn't ease her legs open by applying pressure to her thighs so I moved further down the bed and ran my hands over the right calf and then her foot. I kissed her toes as I gently bent her knee and eased the sole of her foot upwards and as I kissed my way up her leg, I guided it flat against the bed, leaving her exposed inches from my face. I kissed the inside of her thigh and feeling Liv begin to stir, ran my tongue from the base of her cunt to her clit. Like a diver I inhaled to fill the last cubic centimetre of my lungs with her irresistible aroma and kissed her again. This time her sweet lips came to meet mine and she let out a cry as she ground herself into me. She came in seconds and I stayed where I was for as many encores as she could stand.

Later, as I kissed Liv goodbye at the door in my bare feet I blurted out, "It's getting harder to say goodbye." It was the kind of crap I tried to avoid coming out with and I hadn't planned it.

"Then think about what I said."

I didn't follow. I looked at Liv as if to say I didn't follow.

"Never mind, I'll see you Sunday night ok? You can tell me all about your come back." Liv gave me a sly smile.

"Yep, definitely. Cinema yeah? Anything without Mel Gibson. I'll give you a call when I finish anyway, probably six-six thirty. If I'm in surgery by then I'll make sure Dave has your number."

"If you're in surgery you can just call me in six months, see if I've moved on."

And she was gone. I had about fifteen minutes to find my football kit and get down to the park for training. I was always nervous before a match and this felt no different. I saw myself running, tackling and scoring in my mind the way I always did. Years before I'd watched a sports psychologist on TV go into the dressing room at Loftus Road and get the QPR players to visualise themselves doing the things they wanted to do out on the pitch. I'd been doing the same thing since I was probably four years old and I suspected everybody else did too, yet this guy was charging upwards of a thousand pounds a day for the advice.

I was full of so much nervous energy I had to make myself walk rather than jog down to the park. When I got there a few of the guys were changing and it felt great to be getting ready next to Wayne, Digger and Jez for the first time in so long. I was five or six months ahead of schedule but you'd have thought I'd have made it back a day or two early from a nasty cold; not that everyone wasn't pleased to see me, just not as impressed as I thought they should have been. The exception was Terry, who turned up a few minutes after me, already changed and tucking into a pasty.

"Skipper, you're supposed to be months away."

Like one or two of our more illustrious professional contemporaries, Terry was often called 'sicknote' on account of his brittle back, dodgy knees and sore ankles, not to mention a constitution susceptible to bouts of heavy drinking.

"When you have the love a good woman you can do anything." It wasn't the most obvious of come backs but it diverted Terry long enough for me to finish changing and start on a lap of the pitch with Dave.

It seemed all was not well between Dave and his girlfriend. Lucinda had found out about a late night liaison with one of Jez's friends a couple of weeks before. I felt a twinge of disappointment that no one had told me earlier but it was a good tale and I supposed it was my own fault I'd been out of the loop, being so wrapped up in my own relationship. When Dave described the girl in question as, 'no oil painting,' I shuddered to think just how bad she must have been; apart from Lucinda, Dave wasn't exactly renowned for his discernment. Dave was blaming Jez; more specifically the rum punch Jez had concocted and then forced down everyone's throat. I asked Dave why he'd not mentioned anything the other night and how he'd left it with Lucinda.

"I said I'd give her some space and talk to her at the weekend. I needed to decide what to do about Beth first."

"Uh?" I exclaimed, nearly running into him as I spun round to look at him.

"Well, I've seen her a few times since. She's good fun." He looked at me sheepishly then motioned ahead to say we should concentrate on the running.

"Jesus, I turn my back for five minutes."

We completed a second lap of the pitch and joined the others. While we waited for a few others to complete the laps I stroked the ball back and forth with Fats and Wayne, enjoying the feel of controlling and kicking the ball again. I increased the gaps between us and started to put my foot through the ball more. My knee twinged from the unfamiliarity of the action but nothing felt wrong. I hit it with my laces, inside and outside of my foot; then tried chipping it up and volleying it back. My technique let me down but that wasn't down to injury. The knee felt good and I went and stood with the rest when Mike called us over to start a game. Mike showed some rare tact and named me as one of the captains; probably figuring like I had, that no one would want to see me picked last of all.

I got first pick and went for Dave, Fats chose Mike and Vern, and the rest got split between us fairly quickly. I somehow fucked up my selection and got no pace at all in my team but would have a numerical advantage until Digger got off the phone. I insisted he'd also have to do the regulation two lap warm up before joining in. I was annoyed my team was on for a hiding, especially since it was my own doing.

I spent ten minutes chasing the play, always a yard or two from where I should have been. When anyone approached me with the ball, I jockeyed where I should have tackled and backed off when I should have moved towards the man. Only Smiles, a friend of Terry's who I disliked, took advantage of my rustiness, skipping past me to set up Digger for a goal he took with one shin pad still in hand. After half an hour or so, we called time off for a five minute break. We were three-one down and I'd not made a tackle, interception or run with the ball. I walked back to our goal where Jez was imitating a stretching routine.

"I just can't get into it," I said.

"It's gonna take time, right? The main thing is you're here," Jez offered.

"Yeah, I guess, but I couldn't help picturing myself doing a few decent things."

"You thought you'd come back *loads* better than before—how come?" Jez was laughing at me; I was back in the fold. Granted, I was shit, but I was back.

When Dave trotted off towards his bag, I asked Jez about Beth.

"Face like a bag of chisels," was his considered view.

"That good? He said she was no oil painting."

"If it was an oil painting of a really ugly bird with facial herpes she would be."

Dave wandered back with a bottle of Evian.

"We're still in this boys; just need to string some passes together. How's the knee?"

"Well I know it's there."

"You mean it's hurting?"

"No, not at all. It's just on my mind all the time."

"Not good," Dave said, stating the bleeding obvious.

We swapped ends and kicked off again and conceded almost from the kick off. Jez was close to giving up, Terry was goal hanging, probably too hung-over to run. I looked at the others; Harry was an excellent player but not a great trainer; Chris was keen but nothing more and Brian and Samir offered nothing. Apart from Dave we were going nowhere. I looked at the opposition; somehow *they* could all play and looked up for it. Fats ran at me and at the moment when I expected him to pass, as everyone else had been up to that point, he ran at me instead. He dummied and sent me the wrong way but, temporarily lost in thought about the utter paucity of our team, I found myself reacting instinctively for the first time when Fats went past me. My arm went across him as I turned in an effort to slow him down and I chased him down. I took the ball away cleanly and strode away with my head up before picking out Terry ten or twelve yards ahead of me. I couldn't stop myself clenching my fist at my side; I'd finally done something.

"That one's on me skip," Fats said as he ran past me. It pissed me off and was just what I needed to fire me up. I charged around for the next fifty minutes or so and we got back to six all by the time most of the lads wanted to call it a day.

"Next goal wins," someone said; a signal for one and all to give one last effort.

We didn't get the winner of course; that took Mike thirty seconds and a mistake by Terry—possibly deliberate—but I was covered in mud and looked as happy as a windy baby.

A few guys headed off to the pub and I walked back home with Fats and Chris.

"How's that bird you were seeing?" Fats asked.

"Good mate, very good in fact." I couldn't really think of much else to say.

"You missed a great night on Saturday," Chris said.

"Jez's?"

"No, that was last week. Dave and his flatmates had a party."

For a moment I was confused but he'd meant Digger.

"He got off with Erica."

"He's been there before; dirty fucker," I said, trying to hide any petty jealousy.

I changed the subject just in case I was about to hear that Clare had been defiled as well.

"Took your goals well there, Chrissy."

"Cheers Matt, I thought you looked really good in the second half."

"Not sure about that but I was pleased to get back on it."

"You had a bit of a swipe at Smilesy," Fats chimed in.

"Did I?" honestly not remembering anything. "Nothing in it I'm sure."

"He wasn't happy at the end."

"Jesus, I don't even remember. He can fuck off anyway." Hearing this from Fats was killing my buzz.

"Are you two playing Saturday?"

"Is there a game?" Fats asked innocently.

"Don't tell me you have some shitty excuse. I don't even wanna hear it, but I can tell you Dave won't be happy."

"I'd only be on the bench and Ghost probably wouldn't even get a game."

"That's *because* you both keep fucking off back to Nottingham every chance you get." I felt myself being drawn into an argument. How quickly things go to shit I thought; five minutes ago I'd been absolutely flying. I wished I'd gone down the pub with the others. I thought about going back but I was no longer in the mood. I'd go back and sulk for a while and send Liv a text she'd probably not reply to. I ignored Chris and Fats for a few minutes but they didn't seem to notice the guilt trip I was attempting to lay on them.

"You boys out tonight?" I asked, tired of sulking.

"We've got a board games night at the flat."

I shook my head in disbelief. Fats blamed Chris and Chris retaliated by blaming Fats before they agreed the idea was neither of theirs.

It had been an overcast afternoon and it was getting dark by the time we got back to the halls. Fats had been rattling off some tall tales about some of the seedier characters he'd come across during his gap year spent touring India, South East Asia and Australia. Most people probably went through life getting no closer to bent coppers and court officials than watching CSI Miami, but Fats had had to grease palms in Thailand, Vietnam and Burma to escape all manner of local justice. The best story he shared was about the Bangkok sex show performer who possessed the colonic dexterity to answer a call on her mobile phone with it half way through the journey to her large intestine. Fats could have been the next Russell Brand cum Peter Ustinov.

I lay on my bed staring up at the ceiling, mobile phone in hand wondering how interested Liv would be in football training. I felt my eyes get heavier and heavier and rolled over so I could get half under the duvet.

I awoke remembering nothing about my dream other than it had been about Liv. I also knew for sure what she'd meant earlier on the doorstep.

I felt like screaming, didn't. I checked the time, it was just after six—I was probably alone in the flat unless Eliot had got back in the last hour or so and he was irrelevant anyway. I felt cold inside and out. I put on some more clothes and climbed back under the safety of the duvet. I looked at my mobile phone on the floor, left it there.

Every decision seemed monstrous all of a sudden. I wanted to look out of the window but couldn't, I needed the bathroom but didn't want to leave the room—I looked at my door wishing I'd locked it, worried in case I'd not locked the front door. I closed my eyes to it all and felt an enormous black wave rushing over me; what if I let it come? I opened my eyes and made myself slow my breathing, counting breaths because I'd seen it done on Casualty. I lay there for a few minutes, looking only at the ceiling and let the tension slowly dissolve away.

Something made me think of Mel; something deep inside felt she'd understand what had taken hold of me, I knew she'd been through plenty she never shared. I wanted badly to see her; cursed myself for letting our friendship collapse. I started to dress; half planning on knocking on her door and this was enough to get me up and moving. I quickly began to feel better, control returning, my hysteria a receding memory. I wasn't going to see Mel. Now I didn't need to. Still wanted to. Maybe at the weekend I thought, chuckling unnaturally to myself.

I opened my door and went to the bathroom, checking the front door to make sure it was closed as I passed. Back in my room I checked to see whose lights were on. Fats was standing in his window looking out. I waved but he didn't see me, just stared into the distance. I let the curtain fall back across the window and made some tea, warmed my hands in the steam above the kettle. I drank my tea in the kitchen, retaining that inexplicable uneasiness about being alone.

When Dave burst into the kitchen, I awoke with a start. My tea was still too hot to drink so I couldn't have been asleep for more than a couple of minutes but that or Dave's arrival, with Vern and Jez in tow, was enough to snap me out of my mood. They'd all had a few drinks, Vern was particularly excitable and they were just stopping off to see if I wanted to come with them into town. I had some work I could have been doing but it seemed like everyone was having such a good time I didn't want to miss out. While the others took turns to use the bathroom, I went and changed. I retrieved my Earls from the bottom of the wardrobe, shook them vigorously to lessen some of the creases and pulled them on. I was maybe three quarters of a stone heavier than before my injury and once I'd successfully gained the upper hand over the top button I looked for something I could wear untucked. I plumped for a vivid red Hilfiger v-neck which I knew I'd regret later, but even the tat you buy from TK Maxx has to get an outing sometime and it wasn't like I was seeing Liv or anything. I splashed on too much cologne and grabbed one of Dave's beers from the fridge before heading over to Mike's, where they were waiting for a cab.

As Dave let me into Mike's flat, I pulled out my mobile for the first time, thinking I should text Liv. Liv had texted me an hour before to find out how football had gone and the beeps from my phone told me I had a voice message. Liv had called just a few minutes ago; I couldn't think how I'd missed the call. I listened to the message a couple of times, enjoying the sweet concern in her voice and the anticipation of knowing she was waiting for me to call her back. I saved the message and called her number. After three rings, I got her answer phone.

"Hey babe, just picked up your message; everything's cool. I didn't do too much but came through unscathed. Off for a couple of drinks in town, speak to you later." I added, "Love you" as an afterthought, but it hardly came close to the way I felt.

Mike's kitchen was packed with guys from football, even a couple who'd dodged training for some reason. I stood in the open doorway chatting to Jez and didn't even notice Erica and Clare in one corner of the kitchen, laughing away with Kenny, until the first cabbie knocked on the door. I reversed into the corridor to let a few guys out so I could finally get to speak to Clare. I always fancied being one of those guys who kisses girls on each cheek when they say hi but with Clare I felt we'd already gone past the stage where I could introduce it into our routine.

"You coming along tonight?" I asked.

"Not now, it's way too early and we're not exactly dressed for it."

"We're only going to the pub, how smart do you have to be?"

"No, Dave said you're going to The Steering Wheel later."

"First I've heard," I said, confused. "I've got work I need to get done tomorrow morning."

"Best stick to shandies then!" Clare laughed at me kindly.

"Have you *seen* the state of Vernon? Anyway, are you going to come along later or not?"

"I'm up for it but you need to convince Erica, she doesn't want to see Dave Barnes and I can't say I blame her."

"No, I guess not. He's probably not even going though, is he?"

"Texted her to see if she fancied going about half an hour ago."

"Cheeky bastard. Still, you have to admire the nerve," I added quietly. "Erica, we gonna do this tonight or not? No point any of us going without you ya know."

"Has Clare told you what just happened?"

I hadn't realised how upset she must have been; she looked as if she'd been crying. The last thing she'd have needed was to be surrounded by the whole football team.

"You can just stay with me, Kenny and Clare all night. I'll tell Digger to fuck off if you want me to. Tactfully, I mean."

"There's no need, it's my own fault. I don't really fancy it tonight anyway."

I wanted Clare and Erica out with us more than I wanted anyone else there but I didn't push it.

"How about I give you a bell about nine and you can see if you fancy joining us then? I don't reckon we'll make The Steering Wheel anyway, we say we'll go there every other week and we haven't been back since October. And Dave won't necessarily be there."

"I'll stay here with you if you like," Kenny said. "I've got no money anyway."

"Yay! Why don't you stay too Matt?" Erica said, taking my hand and giving me an enticing smile. I was being backed into a corner; Kenny had let me down badly here.

"You know I can't stay sweetheart; it's Vern's birthday or something." I was seventy per cent sure I hadn't completely made this up. "You sure you won't come along?"

"No, I can't face it right now," she said, dropping my hand.

I looked to Clare for support but despite what she'd said, I didn't think she was that fussed about going out. I was beaten. Worse still, I was pretty sure I wanted to stay behind with them.

"You definitely staying?" I asked Kenny.

"Yeah, I think so."

You're right to look embarrassed, I thought. I don't know if I was more annoyed at Kenny's ability to get out of the evening without a hint of guilt or at my own inability to do the same.

Not more than fifteen minutes later, I was at the bar of the Yard of Ale pub in the city centre, secretly depth charging Vern's Stella. He'd asked for a Carling and was instead getting wife beater laced with a double Jameson's. It wasn't going to help our chances of getting into a club later.

Despite a bright, modern interior and a name change, drinking in the Yard of Ale never felt quite right to me; it had been the scene of an IRA bomb in the mid-seventies. I only knew as much because Terry had made a point of bringing us all here at the first opportunity.

I'd become ambivalent in my feelings towards the IRA during my time working with a group of Irish builders in my gap year. It was a subject fastidiously avoided and anyway, not nearly as topical as it would have been a few years before, but I knew enough of the history of the seventies and eighties to be curious. I'd been working one Sunday and having nothing better to do, joined Crackerjack, Colm and Rigney for a drink when we knocked off. I got on well with Cracker because he very much enjoyed the sound of his own voice and I was happy to listen; Colm was my best mate on the site as he hadn't known the others from previous jobs and was closest to my age; Rigney I'd always found quite intimidating. He'd barely spoken to me in my first few months working on site but it felt to me that he'd spent plenty of time *looking* at me. If anyone was going to give me an education, I hadn't expected it to be Rigney but that Sunday afternoon we took the trip north to 'County' Kilburn and after a few lefts and rights from the station, I found myself in the pub that time forgot. It felt like walking onto a set from Life on Mars; there was a massive Irish tricolour behind the bar, Guinness and some other unpronounceable concoctions were on tap; when I plucked up the courage to take a trip through the back room to the toilet, I got close enough to the sepia pictures on the wall to see they were of Michael Collins, Bobby Sands and Michael Devine. When the hat came round for collections, I self-consciously dropped in a fiver and caught Rigney's eye. I held his gaze, not wanting to show I was intimidated and I saw something new in the look I received.

"Give us a hand at the bar will ye, Matty?" he said a few minutes later.

"It's my round Jim, what can I get you?" I asked.

"They won't serve you here, come up with me."

I did as instructed, still taking orders from Colm, Crackerjack and a friendly hunchback called Jonjo, who'd latched onto our group and appeared to know but not talk to Rigney.

"You've not been anywhere like this before have ye?"

"How'd you mean?" I asked blithely.

"You'd have been kneecapped by now if you'd not put in that fiver."

"Nice," I said, losing my bravado and working on an exit strategy.

"I'm kidding Matty. You know what it was for though?"

"I can guess yes. It's no big deal."

"Oh it's a big deal alright. I'm going to tell you a few things—not much—just something you might not have thought about before."

Whatever Rigney was saying, his eyes for once were reassuringly friendly.

"There's lots of people support the Republican Army who wouldn't dream of doing any killing themselves and there's probably a few who enjoyed the killing too. The Irish people have been at war with the British

201

and the Provos for generations. Through all those generations they've lived in unbelievable poverty and under oppression as bad as any known in the world. The Irish have never been a warring people, never sought to conquer another nation or suppress another people but the British have made Ireland a war zone for centuries and that's hard for people to forget. You think there was no justification for bombing London, Manchester or Birmingham but there was. To take notice of what its government had been doing for years, the British people had to be made aware of what it was like to live in Ireland—in a war zone. A state of terror, simple as that. It's a war Matty; what we're in now is just a phase like any other; a phoney war if you will. The boys haven't all gone away you know."

It wasn't the setting or the atmosphere; speaking to someone as intelligent and committed as Rigney was, made it utterly convincing right then. I can recall vainly trying to recreate this argument to friends and relatives in the weeks and months following and never getting across what Rigney did to me that day.

"You can get the drinks in now Matty," Rigney said, a broad grin taking ten years off his face. "Brenda, serve this fella would ye, he's about to call the law in," he shouted at the barmaid.

A couple of drinks later and I'd forgotten my earlier misgivings and was settled next to Vern, probably extracting the last semi coherent words he'd utter that evening. Vern was a guy who could surprise you with his sentimentality; he was normally pretty phlegmatic but the drink was loosening his tongue in an unexpected way. He was easily one of the best players we had in our team and his style matched his personality—he did everything with an unfussy Teutonic efficiency—yet he was certain he was the one who'd struck lucky in getting a game for us rather than the other way around. He told me how he'd thought he'd blown his chances of playing for us when he'd been unable to make our very first game. My own recollection of that very first game was that anyone who actually had played should consider themselves fortunate not to have blown their chances. I confessed to Vern that I couldn't even have told him if he'd played or not but he assured me he hadn't. Before a bathroom break interrupted us, Vern asked me a few questions about Clare, revealing an interest I'd never suspected before. I was honest enough to confirm that Clare was single but a jealous part of me prevented me from offering too much active encouragement of this liaison. When Vern left me alone, I looked at the walls of the pub, trying to picture it all those years before and my uneasiness returned; there were ghosts in that place alright. As much to take my mind off it as anything else, I texted Liv to say I was looking forward to seeing her on Saturday.

We moved on to a new pub, The Fig Leaf, and I found myself at the bar again, helping Terry with seven pints of Murphy's no one had asked for. I hadn't chosen a pub yet and in a moment of inspiration, I decided I'd drag the boys to The Royal Court—the only place in Birmingham where I knew we could get a round of draft Budweisers with Goldschlagen chasers. The Fig Leaf was too crowded for us to get a table big enough to all sit down so I played the quiz machine with Dave and Terry, breaking even for the most part. Terry had been checking our upcoming fixtures and a twist of fate meant I'd have the chance to make my comeback in our return fixture against the BioChemistry team. Dave was sceptical and my instinctive reaction was that it would not be a good idea.

"When's the game?" I asked.

"Week Saturday. Perfect timing."

"Yeah, not really the perfect opposition for me."

"You can't be superstitious about these things skipper. And you owe that lippy little sod one."

"I don't really want to take the field with that at the forefront of my mind Tel. Anyway, he was fine wasn't he? I don't remember him being lippy."

"You're joking!" Terry stood back from the quiz machine and straight into Dave so he could look at me. "You and him were having a go at each other all through the game—*that's* why you tried to break his legs."

"Don't mind me Tel," Dave mumbled, annoyed Terry hadn't even noticed he'd sent him and his drink flying.

"I didn't try to break anyone's legs. I don't even remember the bloke to be honest other than he was quick, small and wiry—basically my worst nightmare. 'Specially now."

"Quick—who was England's captain when they lost 6-3 to Hungary in 1953?"

"Billy Wright," I said, sure of myself.

Panicking, Dave ignored me and went for Johnny Haynes. Once again, we'd failed to get beyond winning a pound. Now Dave was annoyed with Terry (which was usual), I was annoyed with Dave for getting the question wrong and annoyed at Terry for the spin he'd put on my injury. Terry wasn't annoyed with anyone yet but the night was still young.

"One more?" Terry asked, holding the pound we'd won up to the slot.

"Stick it in," Dave urged resignedly.

Digger deposited three more pints of Murphy's on the small ledge next to us and nestled in behind me to add his inconsiderable general knowledge to the cause. At least his presence would help lighten the atmosphere.

"Yazz and the Plastic Population!" Digger shouted down my ear. He was right.

"Tell them about the honey mummy, A! A! A!" He was right again; I wondered if our luck had changed.

Dave answered the next question without any consultation and when Terry beat me to the answer to Hitler's wife's name we'd won a pound again.

The next question was, "Who played the fearful lion in *'The Wizard of Oz'*?"

"Really don't want you to win more than a pound do they?" I asked. As I turned away in disgust, I had to snap my head back to avoid Digger's hand shooting past me to hit the option that said, 'Bert Lahr.'

"Two pounds, come on!"

"Crazy Horse!" I shouted (Emlyn Hughes' nickname.)

"Red, blue and yellow." The three primary colours. "That was easy," Dave added.

"1509." Terry got us to eight pounds with the year Henry VIII took the throne.

We were three questions away from the magical twenty five pounds jackpot. Mike set down five brandy chasers and joined us for the final push.

"Nine, did it at A-level," Mike said. How many countries does the River Nile flow through? "Definitely," he added as he leant past Dave, whose hand was hovering over the collect button.

"I know this," I shouted as the next question came up—under what name did the Sex Pistols play in 1977 after being officially banned from many venues in the UK? The two options I couldn't quite choose between were The See-Saws and The Spots. I plumped for The Spots, ninety per cent sure and we were a single question away from glory.

Predictably, the next question was impossible but we all knew we were going to have a guess.

"I know it." Terry and Digger spoke simultaneously: "Spaslvacaltore Shfabragamo."

The options were Salvatore Ferragamo, Sebastien Chabrain, Christine Paling and Jean Louis.

"Chabrain designed dresses for fuck's sake!" Digger shrieked at Terry.

"Three seconds!" Dave called, finger over collect again.

"Ferragamo."

Dave pressed option A and the machine began to pay out the jackpot for probably the first time in history.

I necked my brandy and said to Terry and Dave, "I do remember now. He was a cunt and if he comes near me next Saturday, I'll break his fucking legs again."

No one picked me up on the strict inaccuracy of my closing statement.

"Champagne anyone?" Digger called out.

"Not in here, let's go to the Steering Wheel before it gets busy."

After staying so long playing the quiz machine, we weren't going to make the Royal Court and I was on the verge of chucking it in for the night. I checked my phone to see if Liv had texted but she hadn't. I felt moody and pissed, in a world of my own. When I came to, everyone apart from Mike was leaving. I watched Mike disappear into the toilet and wondered if I'd been asked to wait for him. I waited around until he finally emerged into the bar.

"Alright lad, everyone else outside?" Typically, Mike seemed a lot less pissed than everybody else.

"Yeah, just left," I said, leading the way out.

When we got outside there was no one about and it took me a few moments to identify the group clustered around a cashpoint a hundred yards down the road as Dave and co.

"How did you find today?" Mike asked me.

"No bother at all injury wise. I was nowhere near the pace of the game but I was surprised how easily I slipped into the game."

"That'll come. I thought you looked scared stiff for the first ten minutes then there was one tackle with Smiler—seemed to sort your whole game out. Only question now is; will you get back into the team? We haven't lost since Terry went back in defence."

"I think the captain always gets to come back where he likes," I replied, trying my utmost to keep my extreme annoyance out of my voice.

"Will you be captain though—Dave's done a pretty good job?"

It was strange; Mike was never one to try to wind anyone else up but he always knew exactly how to get me going. I was close to overreacting, sure now I was heading home either way.

"Oh I'll be captain alright, it's fine to let the kids have the run of things for a while but if you leave it too long you come back to find there's nothing left to run." What a crap comeback.

"Seriously, it'll be good to have you back. Will you be on the bench this weekend?"

"I'm not sure I'm ready but I can see how the numbers are—if we're short I can name myself."

"Ten minutes at the end might be what you need. I said as much to Dave after the game this afternoon."

"Cheers," I said, limply.

I wondered if Mike had changed tack because he'd seen something in my face. I was on my way home now anyway. I was drunk and missing my girlfriend.

I stopped before I reached the guys at the cash-point and wrote a text to Liv, asking her if she wanted to spend Sunday afternoon together.

Terry had already started off towards the club with his arm around Vern; looking at them made me feel comparatively sober.

Staying where I was, I watched Digger get his cash and set off after them. A part of me wanted to able to slip away unnoticed, watch Dave get his cash and go, then Jez, then Mike; maybe one of them would realise and text me from the club to see where I'd got to. When Dave took his money he looked around, saw Digger striding away, then spotted me and came over.

"You alright skip?"

"Going home I think, feels like it's been a long day."

"You can't go now, the night's still young, Vern's still conscious and we haven't planned your return."

"Nah mate, I need to get off. My body's shutting down as we speak."

"You're not going. We'll have a couple in the Steering Wheel, a quick dance and then get off."

I felt my phone rumble and sought salvation there.

I read Liv's text; *'I'm all yours—can't wait! Feels like I haven't seen you in so long. xx.'*

"What are you two fuckwits waiting for?" Jez bellowed as he approached.

"Nothing, let's head," I said.

"Mike's getting cash," Jez said. "You two go and we'll see you in there—better if we go in separately anyway, right?"

Ten minutes later we were toasting our quiz winnings with champagne, which I followed up with a double Pernod and Black. The evening descended rapidly into chaos from then on. Having sunk several more P&B's, retrieved Dave from the ladies' loos and requested House of Pain's *'Jump Around,'* the seven of us took to the floor like the Republican Guard and tore it up. Before they could throw us out, the bouncers had to untangle us limb from limb and lift us from the floor where we had become a single seething entity.

Back at Swafforth Bank Dave, Digger, Jez and I commando rolled out of the cab and disappeared into the bushes to wait for the others to arrive. Five long minutes later, we gave up waiting and went our separate ways. As Dave and I came to the front of our block, we saw Mike's light flick off; obviously their cab had beaten us home—a possibility we'd overlooked in our drink-fuelled excitement.

In my room, I lay on my bed staring fixatedly at the ceiling light. Everything was spinning and I was fighting an utterly debilitating battle against persistent waves of nausea. On my desk was a cup of tea I'd made with the intention of diluting the alcohol in my blood but I could no longer face the thought of drinking it. I closed my eyes and hugged a pillow, thinking of Liv. I dropped off for no more than five minutes and came to, feeling worse than ever. I bolted out of the room, crashed into the toilet and threw up purple puke two or three times. I retched two or three more times then flushed it away. I hauled myself up and sat on the bog, resting my head on my left arm on the small washbasin. I closed my eyes. The second I nodded off, my arm slipped off the basin and I came to. I lowered myself to the floor and assumed the foetal position, trousers round my ankles. I slept for a while and some time later reluctantly awoke when Colin banged on the door shouting for me to open it. I stood shakily, snatched up my trousers as best I could and sprinted past him. I dove onto my bed, barely opening my eyes in an effort to somehow maintain my sleep.

Thursday, 10th March

When I awoke at noon the next day, it felt like the Red Army were on a forced march through my head. I was busting for a piss but couldn't move; I looked for a vessel to help me out in this emergency and saw only one I'd already used perched precariously on the edge of my desk. I sat up and positioned it more safely and more discreetly behind my TV.

In the toilet I'd pissed and flushed before I noticed the basin brim-full of purple and orange sick. It couldn't be Dave; he had the constitution of a rhino. I dry heaved over the toilet bowl and tried to formulate my next move. All I could think of was the American History essay I had to write by the end of the day. I felt like crying but I knew I had to deal with this. If Colin had sorted it I could have got away with spending the price of a box of Roses. I plunged my hand into the sick, which was surprisingly cold and began to scoop it into the toilet, leaving anything that fell to the floor for the end. I estimated it would take four double handfuls; after ten the basin still looked disgusting. In the meantime, my stomach finally gave up the last remnants of last night's dinner. I flushed everything away and then wiped the floor and basin as best I could with bits of toilet paper. Finally I filled the basin with hot water and let it drain away a couple of times, opened the window and washed my hands vigorously enough to take all but a layer or two of skin off. I showered to see if it would make me feel any better and then got back into bed, leaving the window open to clear the room and my head of the stink of sick. I emptied the Lucozade bottle out of the window, as close to Colin's and as far away from my room as possible, and threw it under the bed before closing my eyes on what felt like a long day; it was just before one o'clock.

It was dark when I awoke and I was ravenous. I looked at my clock and it read two o'clock; I'd slept the whole day and evening away. I wondered if anyone had checked on me. I got out of bed, wobbly from the unfamiliarity of movement. I turned on the light and saw a second cup of tea, un-drunk, on my desk—probably left there by Dave.

I picked up my phone and charger and took it into the kitchen. I stuck the kettle on and my phone on charge and went for a piss. The toilet smelt faintly of sick so I wiped the floor and basin with a cloth from the bathroom. I checked my texts as I waited for the kettle to boil. I had seven, three from Liv. I read the others first; one from Dave at eleven in the morning asking if I wanted to meet for lunch—optimistic I thought;

one from Donny asking how things were going and telling me to get him House of Fraser vouchers for his birthday; one from Clare (and Erica) asking where I was at about ten thirty the previous evening; and one from Orange telling me about an available upgrade. Two of the three from Liv turned out to be missed calls—at four and eight o'clock. Liv had texted me in between to see how last night had been.

I finally had a cup of tea I could drink. I necked two glasses of water first and looked out of the kitchen window, seeing nothing in the dark but my reflection and the kitchen behind me. I took my tea into my room, switched on the TV and wondered if it was too late to text Liv. It was of course, but I started writing anyway to see if I could write one sweet enough to put her in a good mood if it woke her.

Finally I settled on, *'Hi babe, hope this doesn't wake u. Drink wiped me out y'day and only just woken, sry I missed ur call. Missing you, sleep well, xxx'*

Now wide awake, I pulled out some notes I'd made on FDR's New Deal earlier in the week and started on my essay. I'd finished writing it just before five o'clock and only hearing the birdsong made me realise I'd written the entire thing in complete silence. I saved my work and switched off my laptop. I stuck my head out of the window, saw a couple of lights still on and listened to the birds, wanting to feel inspired. Cold and shattered, I closed my window after a few seconds and went back to bed.

Friday, 11th March

By ten o'clock the next day I was showered, refreshed and whistling my way down to campus for an impromptu morning coffee with Liv. I had my essay on a memory stick so it just needed to be printed out in the Arts Fac; I'd intended to re-read it for sense but meeting Liv seemed more important. I'd set myself a twelve o'clock deadline to hand the essay to Dr Scott, so depending on how long Liv could spare, I might be able to speed read through it before I printed it; I felt happy enough to whistle some Sinatra as I walked so these seemed like trivialities.

I snuck up behind Liv and gave her a long and firm hug when I saw her outside the campus bookshop a minute or two before we were due to meet. The sun had just come out and she looked sparkling in high heeled black boots, jeans, and a straight fitting black, three quarter length, high buttoned coat. She pushed back against me, nestling into me and tilted her head back so I could kiss her over her shoulder.

"I've missed you babe."

"You too handsome," she whispered back breathlessly. "You smell good, what's that?"

"Didn't have time to shower, probably just my natural odour," I replied. "No, Catalyst—came in a great bottle but if you actually like the smell then so much the better!"

"It covers up the sweat. Mostly anyway."

"Where d'you wanna go? Crap coffee place or ultra-crowded but slightly less crap coffee place."

"Let's go to the crap coffee place—at least it has a view and it's nice now the sun's out."

"Cool. So how come you're out and about and available now? Not that I'm complaining."

"I was supposed to be going over to see my friend in Liverpool first thing but then I got some wanky text from my dick of a boyfriend telling me he missed me totally, so I thought I'd better say goodbye in person."

"Then you should go to him sweetie, he sounds like he needs to see you much more than I do."

"Just order me a Latte and I'll go get us a table."

I let a couple of people go ahead of me so I could watch Liv skirt between the tables and chairs to a spot in the window. I watched her slip off her coat and fold it over the chair next to her before sitting down. She wore a roll neck dove grey sweater that showed off her form beautifully. I quickly got myself in the queue before she caught me staring at her.

I set the drinks down on the table. Liv seemed intent on staring into the white sky and didn't register my presence until I touched her arm.

"Liv?"

"Sorry babe, I was just thinking."

"About what—anything important? Anything I should worry about?" This last question just slipped out.

Oddly, she didn't move to reassure me. "Just thinking. Where am I headed, what am I doing . . ."

"Us you mean, or something else?"

"Everything."

Already I was beginning to wish she'd just fucked off to Liverpool.

"Hey great, so that does include us. What's making you think about *everything?*"

"We can't talk about this now. I'll be back Sunday and we can have the whole afternoon together. I hope it's a rotten day and we have to stay in and cuddle up close to stay warm."

She was smiling now; a melancholic smile rather than a happy one. I didn't like her mood but her words sounded more encouraging at least. I wondered if she'd delayed her trip to Liverpool because she'd actually felt a little low herself. I took her hand across the table.

"We can always leave the curtains closed and pretend it's raining. Are you ok today babe, you seem a little down?"

"I just worry sometimes about us. Sometimes I worry we have two distinct relationships. I love you hopelessly in both by the way. I feel there's a part of me you don't want to know and I can't accept that forever . . . even if I wanted to," she added.

I went to speak, had nothing to say. This wasn't quite what I'd envisaged for the morning.

Liv looked at me, it was difficult to believe she'd looked so radiant just a few minutes ago; now she gave me a look that gave me a tightening in my chest.

"What's wrong, tell me?" I asked, squeezing her hands gently between mine.

"You know, but you won't face it. You know who I am and you ignore it. I love you so much that I ignore it too but it's beginning to tear me apart. You make me not want to be who I am—what I am."

"If I ignore it, it's because I don't know what it means. I don't know what I can say to you when you tell me . . . tell me . . . you know. I don't even know you've told me anything." Suddenly, I felt I'd been caught in the middle of a misunderstanding from some Ealing comedy—what if she was talking about something completely different to confessing she was the devil? That feeling passed quickly; a look at her face told me everything I needed to know about the gravity of our current conversation.

"It's all been in dreams or ambiguous double talk, how do you want me to react?"

"I don't know. I just want some of this not to be true."

"What the fuck does that mean?" I swore out of nervousness rather than any annoyance.

"If I didn't love you; if you didn't love me; if we'd never met; if I was a regular girl the way you see me. Take your pick."

"You're not a regular girl. I've never seen you that way. I felt nauseous from the first time I even saw you I was so in awe of you . . . in love with you in fact. I do love you and if you love me then nothing else matters, we can deal with it. If we'd never met I'd have been living half a life without even knowing it."

"You know what? That's exactly how I feel now but I can look back on an eternity where I must have been doing just that. Can I tell you something crazy? I wondered if maybe you didn't really exist; maybe I was just losing my mind or worse still, someone put you here to trap me just like this."

"Again, I don't know what I can say to that."

"I know it's not true. I know it could be, should be even but you're too real. But when you're not there close to me, I still wonder."

"Perhaps it only seems like I'm real because you're losing your mind?" It was too early to be attempting humour but fuck it, I thought.

"My mind's not like yours," was all she said.

We sat in silence for a short while, self consciously sipping drinks that still retained too much heat to be drinkable.

"I can be around as much as you like—as much as you'll have me. I've not wanted to push things but you're all I think about anyway—you might as well know that."

"But you're still ignoring what I've told you."

"Ok, my simple brain is tired of skirting this. You want me to say I understand that you're the devil and I'm ok with it?" I paused for effect; one look at Liv told me I was digging a hole for myself. "You know what? I don't think I'm ok with it after all. I'd hoped we could go out for a while, get close, live together, maybe even get married before I said this, but I think you're going to have to give up the day job honey. It just doesn't sit well with my strong attachment to basic moral standards. It's not that I don't want you to work—to have your own thing, believe me I do—but I think I'd rather you took up the cello or something; how about calligraphy? Anything to keep you occupied when you might otherwise be up to mischief."

I'd finished. I wasn't smiling and neither was Liv. In fact Liv looked like she was about to spit fire.

"You're right, it's a joke. I made it up; I guess I was just trying to get your attention, make you think I was different. But you saw through me. I have something in my bag for you by the way, call it a memento of our relationship."

I stared at Liv and, not for the first time since I'd known her, I went cold with fear. Something in me believed totally in everything she'd told me. My peripheral vision had disappeared; I watched her dig around in her bag but there was nothing else to see; no other people, no chairs, no table between us and there was no sound.

"From Mrs Bailey," Liv spat out the words with a twisted but heartfelt smile and as she did so she flung something at me. I caught the soaking wet, oversized knickers in front of my face, part of the material flicking my cheek.

Liv stood over me; "Wasn't the way she'd have liked to've been remembered I don't think."

With that Liv left and the coffee shop, the people and the sun shining through the gallery window came back. I looked down at what I was holding in my hands and gagged. My hands were covered in blood, the crotch of my jeans was soaked too and I felt a trickle of blood run down my cheek. Pointlessly, I turned to search for Liv. People were looking at me, not trying to hide their puzzlement. I stuffed the tattered, blood soaked knickers into my bag and made for the exit, fighting the overwhelming urge to throw up. I kept one hand in my pocket and with the other held my bag in front of my crotch to obscure anyone's view of what was happening to me. I practically burst through the glass double doors and ran up a steep bank off the path to the side of the library. Leaning against the red brick of the library, I let my guts go and was violently sick. Once I'd started, I found I couldn't stop and I couldn't stop my brain trying to work out what was happening, despite not wanting to know. I slumped to the floor a few yards away and tried to gather my thoughts. My head was full of a million screaming sirens I couldn't shut off. I sat for as long as I could, trying to control my breathing and my shaking hands. I couldn't say I'd pulled myself together but I eventually got to my feet and half ran, half stumbled back home.

I crashed through the bathroom door and tried to throw up again over the sink but there was nothing left inside. I pulled the bloodied rags from my bag and flung them away into the bath next to me. I ran the taps in the sink and lifted my head to look into the mirror in front of me. I stared at my ghost like reflection; the lower half of the left side of my face had thick dried blood all over it. I scrubbed my hands then my face. Without looking inside the bath itself, I turned the taps on and then took the showerhead down and switched it on, pointing it directly at what lay there until the water that ran down the plug was clear. It could have been one hour, it could have been two. By the time I was done, I was slumped on the floor with my arms resting on the side of the bath. I'd emptied the contents of my bag, save my laptop, into the bath. My laptop was covered in blood, which I wiped with some wet toilet paper. Some of my composure restored, I got a carrier bag from my room and threw everything inside; then showered myself in cold water, the hot water having long since run out.

Back in my room, I lay in my bed shell shocked and numb. Every few minutes my phone vibrated to tell me I had an unread message, but I didn't have the physical capacity to get it out of my jeans pocket let alone the will to read what Liv had written. I guessed she'd be telling me it was over, maybe something worse.

I didn't want to read it but just knowing that text was there made me feel uncomfortable and eventually I retrieved my phone and took it back to bed with me. Once there I made a point of not rushing to open it; I made myself comfortable then clicked on the button that opened the text.

It was from Liv, it read, *'Perhaps I am cracking up. I don't know what ur thinking but I'm sry. We need 2 talk Sunday-I'd see u sooner but I need some space and u do 2. Yours completely, L'*

I didn't know I was crying until a tear splashed onto the back of the hand holding the phone. I read the message again and the tears came in a flow. I can't say if I was crying for Liv, who I now believed was so mixed up she couldn't separate fact from fiction; for myself, because I was emotionally so far out of my depth; or just out of relief that the person who had taken over my life seemed to be offering me a way back into hers; a life I thought would be closed to me. Already I was instinctively beginning to rationalise what had happened. I wrote a few abortive texts by way of reply and then decided the best thing would be to sleep on it. Part of me wanted to text something back to set Liv's mind at rest but I just couldn't trust myself to find words I'd want to stick by when I woke up.

It was just past ten o'clock when I awoke, a little older but no wiser. I felt sad and alone. I had messages on my phone and two missed calls, all from Liv. I didn't read any of them; instead I rang Donny, hoping that even though it was Friday night he might be able to chat for a few minutes. He didn't pick up but rang back a couple of minutes later as I was looking across the square at the light in Fats' room.

"Hi Matt, how are you?"

"Good mate, good."

"You rang?"

"Yeah, just for a chat. Feeling a bit . . . I dunno, lost I guess"

He hated it when he thought I was trying to sound profound.

"Lost? Where are you?"

"Not like that—I'm in my room. Maybe I'm just homesick."

"It's Easter in a couple of weeks, you'll have a few weeks off. How's Liv?"

I closed my eyes, frustrated at not getting anywhere and unsure what to say next.

"She's ok, mad as a brush like all the women I ever meet."

"You getting on ok?" For the first time Donny sounded genuinely concerned. It crossed my mind that he might be about to deliver a crushing judgment like she had fat ankles, pigeon toes or bow legs.

"As I say, she's mad. Driving me mad. I'm fine mate, I just woke up in a bad mood and there's no one in so I thought I'd say hello."

I felt better by now. I decided I'd give Fats a shout once I got off the phone.

"No worries. I'm out with work at the moment; shall I give you a call tomorrow some time? I'm out with Helen in the day but I can call you early evening?"

"Yeah, do that if you get the chance."

"You ok now though, yeah?"

I realised how pissed Donny sounded but it was nice he'd called me back, nice too that he wasn't hurrying to get me off the phone. Things felt better.

"Course, I'm off down to the bar for a drink in a few minutes with Erica." The lie was the least I could do to set Donny's mind at rest. "Speak to you tomorrow."

"Yeah, see ya."

I made myself a mug of tea and took it back to my room. I checked Fats' light was still on and walked across the square with my tea and knocked on his door.

"Evening skip, where did you appear from?"

"Uh? Been around all day—sleeping most of it."

"Dave was round here earlier asking about the match tomorrow. Said he hadn't seen you since Wednesday night, was on the verge of calling the cops."

"No, I guess he hasn't but he knew I made it home. What's the match tomorrow, FA Cup?"

"No, *we've* got a match. The Biochem game's been brought forward and I think Dave's struggling to raise a team. That must have been some sleep you were having."

"Yeah, it was—had a stressful morning," I said, remembering. "Are you playing tomorrow? Where's Dave now, does he need me to play?"

"When he spoke to me he had nine definites. I'm playing and Dave wants me to persuade Ghost to come back from Nottingham early," he said. "Sorry mate, are you wanting to come in?"

"Umm yeah, I actually came over for a chat—not about football. Can you text Dave for me and let him know I can play, I haven't got my phone?"

"We're simple folk over here, I haven't got a phone."

"I've got your number in my phone haven't I?" I asked, confused.

"I had one for about a month but didn't use it."

"I'll text him later; or see if he's up when I get home."

Fats went to make himself a drink. I walked through to his room and sat down at the desk. I looked at the books he had open. He was studying Law and Politics and it looked a whole lot more interesting than the history course I was stuck on. I wasn't going to waste a year changing but this was out of laziness; I wasn't under any illusions I was much suited to my course. I changed the CD Fats had on—from Doves to something not quite so dull.

"What's this?" Fats asked upon hearing the musical change.

"Dunno, but you must have bought it."

"Sounds like something Ghost must have left behind," Fats replied, "I caught him listening to Mariah Carey the other day."

"Explains why he's so pumped up every Saturday afternoon."

We chatted about the team for a while and I asked Fats about his course; feigning a genuine interest in changing courses. By the time we started our second mug of tea I was ready to stop avoiding the issue I'd come to see him about.

"You remember I told you about that girl I was seeing?"

"Yeah, she sounded a bit of a character, she been arrested?"

"No she hasn't mate," I said giving this lighthearted remark a straight bat. Taking a deep breath, I pressed on, "Turns out she really is a character. I think she might be a bit screwed up."

I don't know why I took this approach; I actually wanted Fats to believe what I was about to tell him about Liv. Or rather, I wanted him to believe what Liv had told me so I could stop feeling so crazy for believing it myself. Fats just looked at me, waiting for me to go on.

"It's a long story," I said, unsure how to continue. "Basically she told me . . . she told me . . . she told me she was the devil."

Fats' expression never changed.

"Look, none of this is to go any further ok? There's some bizarre shit I have to tell you about."

Fats wore the same expression when he spoke. "Who am I going to tell? Ghost has enough problems organising his own love life and that's just his hand."

"Ok, point taken but I had to say it. I'm not sure where to start but I'll give you the background. When I was eight years old, I got into huge trouble for bullying. This guy had been my best friend since playgroup and on Christmas party day he doesn't show for school. My teacher takes the register and then tells me I'm in deep shit for what I've been doing to my mate. I have no idea what she can mean but as we're all filing into the assembly hall she yanks me out of the line and makes me stand outside for the next forty minutes. I must have welled up but I was too bewildered to cry as all the other kids troop by looking at me."

"Has this story got a point to it?" Fats laughed.

For a second I saw the opportunity to shut up, not go down the road of telling him everything. But I didn't, I needed to say this to someone.

"Listen and you might just fucking hear it. I stand outside the assembly hall, shitting myself because I knew I was already guilty in the eyes of judge, jury and executioner—it never occurred to me at the time but she never even asked me properly if I did it. Nothing prepares me for the onslaught I get when she comes out—every last ounce of vitriol and anger she can dredge up she dumps on me. I'm so bemused I hardly say a word. Then I'm made to stand in front of the class while she pleads for someone—anyone—to come forward with some eyewitness account. Of course some little twerp pipes up with some nonsensical, "I think I've seen such and such happen . . ." Any adult would have picked it to pieces but at eight years old this woman destroyed me totally. I spent months turning it over and over in my head. I never touched this kid by the way in case you haven't guessed. Anyway, at ten thirty or so this guy walks in large as life and takes his seat, I remember he even looked at me as he walked past."

"That's terrible, did you get expelled? What did your parents say?"

"I never told them and thinking back I wonder why the school didn't contact them since I was given the same status as a child killer. They found out months later when they went along to parents evening and the old cow filled them in. They nearly died of shame, especially my dad—he was heartbroken. He wanted to take me out of school. Anyway, the point is I told Liv a few weeks ago; on our first date—don't ask how it came up, I have no idea—only she got the unabridged, violins and heartstrings version."

"You mean there's more? Spare me please."

"There's a bit more yeah, the whole point of the story in fact. A week after I told Liv, the teacher in question was tortured to death in her own home by a gang of fucked up kids. My brother casually drops it into conversation a few days later and then I mention the coincidence to Liv."

I took a sip of tea; it was stone cold and disgusting. I felt hot and my mouth was dry and I was conscious of a final chance I had to stop then and there, let that be the end of the story.

"Today she told me she did it," was all I said, not wanting to go into how she'd told me.

"She sounds like a barrel of laughs. Why did she say that?"

I looked at Fats as if to say he'd asked a stupid question.

"I think . . . because she actually did it?" I said it without any certainty. Hearing that uncertainty in my voice raised some questions in my mind. Maybe I was going mad; maybe she was; maybe she'd planned the incident today. But no one would be able to plan that conversation and that ending would they?

"Did she mention any history of mental illness in the family?"

"I know it sounds fucking ridiculous; it doesn't sound any better now I say it out loud for the first time but you don't know her . . ." I said, searching for better words.

"She sounds deranged. Weren't you telling me the other day how amazing she was?"

"She is amazing believe me. I believe her, or at least I believe it to an extent. She has this power that you can sense and she also kind of proved it to me."

"Proved she's the devil? That must have been interesting; she showed you her horns presumably . . ."

"I'm being serious you know. I know how it sounds but I was hoping you might understand," I said, annoyed at Fats' attitude. "Things are starting to sound fucked up now I hear them out loud but she had something that she showed me. Something of my teacher's."

"I know you're serious, but I don't know what the hell you want me to say—that she's magic, she's the devil or just that she's a murderer. Great choice you're giving me. If you want my advice she's none of the above. Try option four, she's a fucking loon. If you want my advice, you should stay well clear." Now it was Fats' turn to be angry. I couldn't recall seeing Fats lose his temper before.

"She's not a loon though, you don't know her," I said quietly.

"No, she employs gangs of psycho child murderers to take out miscreant teachers. Come to think of it, I have some teachers I wouldn't mind seeing roughed up a bit, can I give you a couple of names to pass on? Matt, she sounds like she needs help."

I was just about to change the subject when Fats asked me to leave. "Mate, take it easy will you. I don't want to leave it like this. I realise it's a lot of crap to drop on you—if you want, just forget I told you. Just understand it's all I've been able to think about and I'm finding it hard to deal with on my own."

"Why did you have to tell *me* for god's sake?"

"I'm beginning to wonder." I just wanted to get back to my room but I couldn't leave it like this; I had no idea what Fats was going to do. "If it makes you feel any better, it's helped to talk it through. Saying it out loud makes me realise how ridiculous it is. Out of everyone I thought you might have the best chance of understanding." It came to me in a flash that I should have been talking to Clare about this; non judgmental, understanding and sure to give sound advice.

"There *is* no understanding this."

"Maybe if you met her?" I knew I shouldn't have let that slip out.

"If I finish my degree there's every chance I could end up defending her; that's the only way I'll meet her. I don't think you should see her either to be honest, this is not the sort of thing you want to get around."

"*I* don't want it to get around—it was driving me mad just keeping it to myself."

"No one'll hear it from me you can rest assured."

"I know mate, thank you. You wanna give us a shout in the morning and we can walk down to get the coach together?"

"I have to go into town in the morning, so I'll probably just get the train down to the uni and see you there."

"No worries, I'll get out of your way."

We didn't make eye contact until I turned to shake his hand before heading down the stairs and back to my flat. As I opened the main door onto the quadrant, it was nearly blown out of my hand by a gust of wind. The change in the weather was startling and I stayed a moment or two outside the window to my room, watching the tops of the trees sway and listening to them groan in the wind.

By the time I'd brushed my teeth and got into bed, it was just after two o'clock. I read a message from Erica telling me they were having a quiet one and to pop up if I got back before midnight. I peered round my curtain and saw almost all the lights in the square were off—even Fats had gone to bed. The only sound was the wind.

Saturday, 12ᵗʰ March

I was awoken by a huge crash and the sound of smashing glass. In a semi-dream state it felt like my window imploding and I woke myself falling off the bed. It was pitch black in my room and I groped for the switch to turn on my lamp. The instant the lamp came on, I heard a high-pitched scream for help from outside—through the wind it was impossible to tell the direction it had come from. It only took me a second though, once I'd climbed onto the bed and pulled the curtains apart. My stomach somersaulted as I saw a thirty foot tree trunk sticking horizontally out of Fats' first floor window. Chris's head was visible through the hole where the window had been and he was still screaming, "Help! Help!"

over and over again. I knew immediately no help was going to make any difference—nothing would change what had happened, nothing would bring Fats back.

By ten o'clock that morning, the last of the fire, ambulance and policemen had cleared out. The tree had been cut into pieces once Fats had been pronounced dead and his crushed body pulled from underneath. Sick as I felt, I held it together for Chris's sake—he'd become hysterical upon finding Fats lying dead on his broken bed. Eventually, one of the ambulance men had found something to quieten him down but he still sobbed continuously, snot and tears running from his nose all down his shirt. He kept repeating, "He'd only been in bed five minutes." I focussed as much as I could on Chris because I didn't want to think about how or why this had happened. Everyone kept asking these questions over and over.

When Chris had to speak to the police, I made myself scarce and went back to my room to be alone for a while but I couldn't sit still even for a second. I tried Liv's mobile, not having any idea what I'd say, but it only directed me straight to her voicemail and I didn't leave a message. As I disconnected Dave knocked on the door and asked if I wanted some tea. I sat in the kitchen with Dave; quiet, neither of us wanting to say the obvious things, happy not to be dealing with anyone else's tears or theories for a few minutes. When the girls knocked tentatively on the kitchen door, red eyed and puffy cheeked, I made my excuses ("better go and see to Chris") and left, giving Dave an apologetic shrug as I walked out the door. Before I left the flat, I tried Liv again and sent her a four-word text when there was no answer— *'we need to talk'*.

Outside there were small groups of people everywhere, most of whom I recognised by sight, I got the feeling people were trying to make eye contact and have some kind of shared grief experience—maybe they didn't know Fats well enough to have their own grief. I did, but guilt was taking hold ahead of any other emotion. Chris and Jake, his flatmate, weren't able to get back into their flat. Jake's girlfriend was hugging him. I wanted to be alone and I wanted to speak to Liv so I could convince myself it was just an accident and she wasn't responsible; that *I* wasn't responsible. I walked down to the lake leaving the atmosphere of the square behind. Alone, I tried Liv one more time and this time, when I got through to the voicemail, I resolved to leave a message but I didn't know what to say. I hung up to give myself a chance to think and the anger began to well up inside me, my fists clenched and the tears started to come. Some people were approaching; I doubled back to the far side of the lake so they wouldn't see me crying. I rang Liv again and when the beep sounded, I spoke. "Fats is dead, why Liv? Chris is destroyed, the whole place is fucking destroyed. I know you don't care but *I'm* fucking destroyed and you did it. If you don't call me soon I'll come over there and . . . and . . . and just fucking call me back."

My stomach was full of butterflies, my head and heart full of regret at the message I'd just left for Liv. I got my phone from my pocket to call her again to leave another message and it started to ring—Liv's name showed on the screen and the butterflies became great big bats that crashed around my shaking body. After three rings I answered it.

"Hello?"

"You wanted to talk to me, so talk."

"Fats is dead."

"I know. When I told you not to say anything I was being serious."

"Liv, he was my friend, I fucked up not him, how could you do it?"

"What do you want me to say? You killed him the second you opened your mouth." She sounded cold, uncaring, taunting even.

"Liv, this can't be you, this can't be who I fell in love with," I sobbed.

"It's exactly who you fell in love with, only you wouldn't accept it. I couldn't deal with this any other way, even if I'd wanted to."

"You could have spoken to me."

"I did speak to you and the first chance you get you ignored what I said."

"Liv, I don't know you, it's over."

"Matthew, it's not over, this was only the beginning."

"Meaning?" I asked, bewildered.

Liv didn't say anything for a while and then, "Matt, you have to let me think."

I gave her a few moments, expecting her to speak but she said nothing.

"Liv, don't contact me again."

"Matt, shut up, you're confusing me. I need to think."

"I'm sorry you're confused—you just killed one of my best friends by sticking a tree through his bedroom window; I'm a little shaken myself."

"Just stay at the lake and I'll meet you there in a few minutes."

"Liv, I can't face you right now."

"You need to stay away from your flat; something bad is going to happen there."

"Something bad already did happen, how can it get worse?" I shouted, but the change in her tone should have told me I didn't want to know.

"Don't shout at me right now, I mean it, I have to think."

"If I shout Liv it's because I'm pretty fucking stressed out and you're not really helping with your cryptic remarks. You don't give a shit about Fats."

"I don't have any feeling about Fats at all. I don't have any feelings at all except for you."

"Yeah, yeah, clearly. Great way to show it." I knew I was aggravating her but I ignored the increasing desperation in her voice. "Why don't you just do whatever it is you have on your mind, I'm going back to be with my friends." I hung up on Liv and started towards the path angry and upset. I kicked a stone towards the lake and as I watched its path, I imagined I saw the entire surface of the lake boiling and steaming. For a few seconds I was transfixed, hardly believing what I was seeing. I shook my head to clear my thoughts and set off for the flat in a panic. I broke into a run and immediately my knee gave way; I crashed to the ground in a heap, scraping my palms on the gravel. My phone vibrated as a message came through. I scrambled up and as soon as I put weight through my knee it collapsed again. I slumped on the floor distraught, knowing I was fucked. I pulled out my phone thinking I'd call Dave for help. I pulled up the message; I saw it was from Liv and my stomach turned. It simply read, *'Stay where you are'.*

In a blind rush, I scrambled up once more and started to half hop and half lurch along the path, I crashed down again after only a few yards but pushed myself straight back up despite the shooting pains. I charged on a few more yards before stumbling over, each time the pain obliterating any other thoughts. I forced myself up and onwards, quickly losing balance, falling off the side of the path and rolling down a small bank onto my back. I closed my eyes for just a second and told myself to give up, wait until I was found by someone and I could forget this day had ever happened. In my mind's eye I saw the spitting, bubbling lake and something drove me on.

I scrambled up the small bank and onto the road, crawling and pulling myself along the ground, occasionally finding the strength and the will to stagger on my feet for a few yards. When I got to Kenny's block, I slumped with my back against the wall and tried to catch my breath. I was terrified of what I'd find when I got through Kenny's block onto the square, but I could barely hold a single thought for more than a few moments. I stayed there against the wall, head in hands, paralysed by fear, until the thought of not knowing overcame the paralysis. I struggled to my feet, now using the wall to lean on; in the short time I'd stopped moving, my knee had locked tight, swollen and much more painful than before. Feeling my way against the wall, I hopped inside the outer door and through towards the door onto the square, just a few yards away. The door to Kenny's flat was on my left, as I leant against it I felt an overwhelming guilt. At the main door, I looked through the glass and saw no one; just Fats' crudely boarded up window. I stepped outside. In one corner of the square stood Liv, arms by her side; looking at me, perfectly expressionless.

Liv raised her hands above her head, held them there for a second and then brought them down in front her. I jumped as every window on the square shattered in its frame and Liv let out a bestial scream. Within a few seconds people were coming from all the doors that led onto the court and spinning round to look at the windows; two of Kenny's flatmates barged past me. As people turned to look, Liv stopped screaming and more people poured out of each block. Satisfied with the scene, Liv made fifty million shards of glass fly from the windows and tear through the frozen faces and bodies of dozens of people I knew by sight and word. A second later, only Liv and I remained standing.

Untouched, I looked at Liv. She looked at me across the devastation.

I tried to cry for help, my throat too dry to make a sound. More people emerged to see what had happened, one or two of them even coming towards me—one girl wore such a look of pity when she looked at me I wondered how bad I looked to make her look at me and not the endless dead around her. I looked at Liv to see what she'd do now. She raised her hands above her head and I looked to where she pointed. Dark clouds rolled cartoon-like across the sky. The girl who had been approaching me said something but when I turned to look at her, I saw lightning fork from the clouds and straight through her body; she glowed for an instant, shook and then simply turned black. Lightning raked the flats themselves, setting each block ablaze; the noise was deafening. In front, behind and all around me people were screaming in shock or pain.

"Stop," I tried to say, but the words didn't come and I realised I was struggling for breath in the sulphurous air. Liv walked towards me, unconcernedly picking her way through the remains of my friends and neighbours, she seemed to be taking in what she could. When she reached me, she placed her fingers on my cheek and said, "I'll stop." I looked into her eyes, as black and devoid of emotion as chips of coal; relief swept over me and I conceded consciousness to her.

10

"The distant echo of far away voices"
From "Down in a tube station at midnight" by The Jam

. . . . *At first I still have feeling, memory, an awareness that all is not as it should be. As if in a dream, I see fragments of events, terrible events—a girl being thrown from a moving car; two men fighting with shards of a broken bottle, both dripping blood; a teenage girl tearing at the veins she can see in her arms—and I am sure it is a dream and I am unconcerned that my mind is throwing forward these thoughts. And then finally something sticks.*

I am looking into a room, a rudimentary kitchen, an invisible observer. There are two women talking animatedly in Spanish—I recognise two or three words—and I understand from the exchange that they are arguing with passion but without anger. They are both dark skinned, Mediterranean or South American, the older one has dyed blonde hair, is very much prettier and better dressed than the other; she dominates the argument. The women intrigue me as I watch their expressions and their hand gestures, one a portrayal of strangulation. Some time later, the women both smile at once and embrace—they have settled their argument and seem almost ecstatic. The older woman opens a door leading out onto a noisy street and shows the younger woman out. In the sunlight, I see her face as she leaves; she is no more than eighteen.

As she closes the door on the street, the older woman fills two large metal pans with water and sets them on the stove. On the table she sets a video camera linked to a laptop; it is trained on the centre of the room. When the pans start to boil, she lowers the heat and settles herself into a seat facing the door onto the street. She watches the door quite intently for a while but as time passes she becomes agitated, checking the water is still hot, opening and closing cupboard doors, even leaving the room for a couple of minutes before she comes running back—perhaps she thought she had heard the door. I am enjoying what I take to be another dream and find myself taking in tiny details of the room—there is a ventilator set in one wall that has become so caked in grease it can hardly be putting any clean air into the room, I count that six of the eight cupboards have crooked doors that do not come within an inch of closing properly, on the back of the door that leads from the kitchen into the rest of the house or flat, I see a tool belt hanging from a hook. In the tool belt are a lump hammer, claw hammer, chisel, sandpaper and bulging pockets, which I guess must hold an assortment of nails and screws. The material of the belt is stained in many places, in many different shades of brown and red and in places almost black. Something about the stains on the tool belt turn my stomach.

Even before the door opens she is on her feet in excitement and charging towards it. The younger woman is back, looking hot and flustered. She opens her mouth to say something by way of explanation and is punched hard to the side of the face; the little girl holding her hand begins to cry. The older woman takes the girl's hand and, although at first she seems unwilling to let go of her mother's hand, she does so. Without a word, her mother leaves her to her fate. The girl's sobs, which had died down, renew as the woman forcibly stops her from running to the door, holding both wrists tightly. She motions for the girl to stand in front of the camera while she goes to lock the door, placing the key on top of the door frame, far out of reach. Smiling, she says some words into the camera, turns to the girl and shouts at her until she strips down to her underwear. She slaps the girl so hard she is knocked to the ground and she removes a long screwdriver from the tool belt. I try to turn away, then close my eyes but I am not seeing this as a normal observer, it is as if I am just part of the furniture and I watch and I scream and I watch and watch and cry to myself and words can't describe what evil I see. After an eternity, the mother returns for her broken, bleeding and defiled little girl, hours beyond crying. She leaves with a pocketful of coins and carrying a girl who won't ever look at her mother in the same way again . . .

. . . In a hot country, I'm watching a room full of men look on eagerly as a brown skinned woman gives birth. One is the husband, holding the hand of his wife, another is dressed in colourful religious garb and is clearly in charge. He mumbles and waves his hands from time to time—for water, towels, a drink for himself. Finally, as he holds the new born boy in his hands, he waves for a tiny elongated skull cap into which he forces the baby's head before pulling carefully on four straps at each corner, compressing the sides of the baby's skull still further. For the shortest minutes of her life, the mother is allowed to hold

her screaming baby and kiss his forehead before passing him back to the priest, who takes him away.

I watch the priest leave, followed by three men from the natal room and I see him leave the house and walk a hundred yards or so to an enormous and fantastically coloured temple, where he goes through the gates, passing beggars with every conceivable deformity whom he brushes aside. Inside the gates, at the entrance to the temple itself, I see a dozen grown men begging, with no deformity of their own but carrying or holding the hands of insanely nodding brain damaged young boys with cruelly—deliberately—misshapen heads. Everyone who passes them as they leave the temple, stops to give at least one of the men some change and touch the heads of the boys. I have seen this before, a news report in a former life—in what was once my life—but the nearness of it now makes me feel so hopeless.

I'm following the priest again, in his rooms adjoining the temple; the bidding for his newly acquired child has started. Violence erupts but is quickly quelled by a few stern words from the priest. The child is won and paid for and quickly taken away by the biggest and friendliest looking of the three men and now I follow him out of and away from the temple, but not before he takes money from some of the beggars at the temple doors—more than enough to pay for his new child. At his house, the screaming boy is put on a table and with devastating speed and cruelty, his tongue is removed and cast into the dirt for the birds outside the window and the room is so much quieter but my mind is not, I hear myself gagging, screaming, pleading to learn no more about the world in which I used to live . . .

. . . Asleep, content but not for long, I am woken roughly—in the dark I make out three dark uniforms. My wrists are cuffed, I look down and in the gloom I see they are not my hands, not my wrists, but those of a woman. I am struck all over my face and body and dragged roughly from my bed, my head not bouncing on the cold hard floor. A light is thrown on and I am beaten with hands and sticks. A bucket of piss and shit is thrown into my face just as things start to go black.

I feel again, I am naked very soon, on my front and my legs being forced open—forced because it is part of the game, for I don't have the strength to resist. Not beaten with sticks any longer but ruined bodily—internally—by them, I cannot help but squirm even though I know this serves as encouragement for them. I hear them egging me on—it seems so familiar, not to me but to this body I'm in, why I don't know; it's not important why. No longer witness to evil but victim and this is better, something in me at last able to shut down.

The sticks, the sticks won't quite let me switch off, the pain is sharp and a long, long way inside me. It's so casually inflicted, soon there is more laughter than anything else, mock sympathetic tones (I have no real understanding of any of the words I hear), cigarettes are smoked and stubbed out all over me and I feel my body go into spasm and, though I am terrified that this means my death, the exaggerated laughter I hear tells me that, even worse than death, this is simply another anticipated eventuality.

I am aware enough to wonder what will happen to me next—to me not this unfortunate body for I am beginning to understand this new existence. But, as my mind begins to form any thought outside of this room, I am smacked back into this reality as my head is snapped back and a hand thrust to the back of my throat to retrieve my swallowed tongue. As I try to assess this act of kindness, I feel one of those enormous night sticks thrust in my mouth, to my throat and far down my neck, my whole body contracts to force the alien intruder out but it's not remotely possible and it stays in my throat forever until it's ripped out as quickly as it came and I fall forward, grasping at my throat, trying to breathe, once again unbelieving I'm still alive. Alone, consciousness begins to return, my hands are free but my left arm hangs loosely at my side, my fingers won't respond to my efforts to move them. I collapse back into the pool of blood, shit and piss, broken and alive, dead inside. I wish I am somewhere—anywhere—else and the second I close my eyes I am and I regret my wishing may have put me there a split second earlier and I hate myself . . .

. . . Hidden in bushes, consumed by them, in the dark I know I can't be seen. My breathing is light and quick—I struggle to control it through my excitement. I don't hate this; I'm exhilarated. My hands are shaking too, one rubbing at the erection inside my trousers, the other, the one holding the knife, is balled into a white fist around the handle. My breathing is so fast it intermittently turns into fits of laughter—I bite the collar of my jacket in an effort to stifle any noise; it's already soaking wet. I hear footsteps and voices approaching along the path a few feet in front of me, I know it is the couple I watched enter the park a few minutes ago. I am almost blind with excitement; I have not planned what I am going to do so that when it comes it will be new and wild. A second after the voices pass me I leap from the bush and plunge the knife into the back of the man's neck. When I try to pull it out to stab him again, it won't come and as his body falls away, I turn to deal with the screaming witch in front of me, who stares and screams with equal pointlessness. I tear off my jacket and bare-chested, leap onto her, landing on

her as she falls backwards to the ground. I bite at her face, desperate to feel her blood all over my body. I think it's her cheek and nose I bite at, I'm dimly aware that I want her tongue—detached—in my mouth, but this idea recedes as my erection dies inside my trousers.

Slowly returning to my senses, I begin to hear the woman's screams—I missed the tongue again—and I know I need to act quickly. I want her to live but I need her to shut up and quickly. I look at the body with my knife sticking out and try to work out how long it will take me to get it out—only a few seconds I think, funny that I left it in the first place, I realise I'm becoming distracted. I take the woman's hand, not without first noticing an impressive wedding ring, and stuff it into her own mouth to shut her up.

"Keep quiet!" I hiss. I sound menacing I think to myself, but I haven't got time to enjoy myself too much.

I place my foot on the back of the man's head and work my knife back and forward until it starts to come loose. Blood spurts out of his neck and this isn't so much fun anymore, I am covered and I need to get home, get cleaned up and go to bed. I'm angry at this woman, who stares at me, too scared to take her hand from her mouth, which angers me more; why doesn't she at least put up a fight? I have recovered my composure completely but my anger is such that I can't even take pleasure from stabbing the woman's eyes and mouth. I tell myself this is purely so she won't now be able to describe or recognise me but already I know that it will give me something extra to think about until the next time this compulsion gets the better of me . . .

. . . For one, all too brief second, I remember a life before all this, a life as a student, with friends, a family, a life, a girl. As quickly as it came, it goes and in the blink of an eye I find myself in an abattoir with a searing pain in my neck where I have been hung, fully conscious on a meat hook, by the three men in front of me. I know why and if I could form a thought through the pain as they swing me around, I know I'd be kicking myself for getting on the wrong side of these guys.

I am, I see, I am hurt by whatever evil you can imagine, can these possibly be from my own imagination I wonder to myself, but how can I know? I hate myself either way for what I do, what I cannot stop and what I have to watch and endure. The hate in me hardens until it seems that that is all there is—a pulsating, all consuming hatred for everything around me, for increasingly I lose my detachment and become a moving, working part. There is nothing I don't see or take part in, a constant and endless assault; nothing will change . . .

. . . but eventually, much, much too late to matter, something does.

In a dark room, lying on a bed, someone's breath very close, saying something over and over again in my ear. I can't make it out. My body is shaking and my senses are destroyed—by the dark and also by something else—memories. Memories are something new though, why should I be able to remember all those things that happened to someone else . . . unless . . . I . . . unless I . . . am the one who is here, being held, being whispered to? Whatever is being whispered, it's soft and I feel its kindness like a salve, but still I shake and shake and remember. I remember new things all the time and if I get my life back now, I'll not have long enough to remember all the things I've seen, let alone forget. I try to concentrate on this kindness—I'm being held tightly and against all the things in my mind, it shouldn't matter but it does, it gets through and in spite of it all, I feel some control return and although I'm still too scared to open my eyes, some of the tension drains away.

The terrifying visions in my mind, the gentle touches on my body and the warm breath on my cheeks battle for outright control of my mind. I concentrate as hard as I can on the words I hear, a gentle stroking of my arms and squeezing of my hands and I hear my own breathing settle into a slow rhythm. I turn my head slightly and I feel for the first time how wet the bedding is under my face. I have probably been crying I think, crying or sweating. Now I'm aware of the wetness, I can't find a comfortable position but I can hardly get up without opening my eyes and I'm not ready for that. I don't want to see who it is even though I know; I don't want to see my rescuer—my jailer—not yet. I think she senses the change, because she stops whispering and while she continues to hold me, it is firmer, more about reassurance.

I know she's waiting for me to sit up and look at her. Eventually I do sit up and realising, as I go to open my eyes, that this will simply bring a flood of tears, I cover them first with my hands. When I take my wet hands away, I look anywhere but at her. I see I am in her room, I wonder why—a pointless stay of execution, a last saying of goodbyes? She has my hand loosely—noncommittally—but she makes no move to turn me towards her, just waits until I'm ready or at least until I can't put it off any longer. Although the curtains are drawn, I can see it's dark outside, black. I go to look out of the window and Liv lets go of my hand. As I stare out at nothing, she places her hand between my shoulders as if to comfort me. As hard as I look, there is nothing outside the window but perfect darkness. Uncomprehending but resigned, I pull the curtains to an approximation of their drawn position. I look at my bare feet and see only that my toe nails might be longer than usual; when I try to form some thought on this, or what's outside, nothing comes. I feel exhausted and on the point of tears.

"Matt, I brought you here to talk," Liv says. "I had to see you. For everything I did that hurt you I'm sorry, it's all instinctive with me—I never act any other way, I never have and I don't believe I can. Please look at me my darling." I sense I'm not the only one crying.

"Can I get some clothes please?" I turn enough so I can see her shape in my peripheral vision.

"Are you cold? Do you want anything else?" She asks with that old concern of hers.

"No, just clothes," I say with no emotion. I have none left.

Liv goes to her wardrobe and takes out a pair of my jeans, a white tee shirt and a black sweater. They're clean and fresh, I recognise them but that makes no sense. She puts them on the bed next to me. "Socks," I think, but I start dressing without saying any more.

"Can you talk to me now?" Liv asks gently and sits down next to me, so close our legs are touching. The touch awakens a long forgotten memory and I find it impossible not to feel the love and passion she always made me feel, so deep it was painful and frightening . . . and it's there in her too and that remains a relief. But love has an infinite number of interpretations and Liv's terrifies me.

"Matt, look at me now, I have to make you understand this, but I have to know you're here with me."

"I can't look at you, I can't." My voice is so cracked it comes out as barely a whisper.

"Ok, I understand," she says soothingly. "I can't believe what I did to you, but if you'll let me, perhaps I can make it right. We can be together if that's what you want, we can be together forever, the way you once asked me to. I love you and now I know what that means, I want to show you."

I know from the uneven sound of her voice that she is still close to tears, perhaps they are already running down her cheeks but I can't unscramble my emotions. I have no feeling for her I understand, at least until she physically turns my face to hers and my eyes begin to focus on hers and everything comes to me in a flood. I see her tears and feel my own begin to roll down my face but I am silent, there is no sobbing. We look at each other through our tears and I can't help but be overcome by seeing her again, the memory of her and the bare emotion I can see consuming her for the first time. I'll never see her for what she says she is.

"Liv, did you do that to me? Why?" I whisper, looking at her.

"It doesn't matter; that you're here with me now is all that matters, and we can be together now."

"Liv I need you to tell me, I look at you now and of course I want to be with you, be close to you again so badly, but I'm still shaking from whatever you did to me. I don't know what's happening, what's real and what's not."

"Knowing won't change anything, the past can't be altered. Nothing can change how I feel now, I'll give up everything for you, to be with you, if you ask me to."

"I believe you . . . but I can't just pretend that . . . that . . . that whatever you just put me through . . . just tell me what it was so I can begin to understand," I plead with her.

"You'll hate me. Do you understand? I want to be with you, on your terms, I want to love you and I want you to love me again."

"But I'm shit fucking scared of you!" I cry out, my voice shrill and weak.

Part of me wants to talk to her, reason with her, but I'm just shouting, pushing her away.

"There's nothing to be afraid of, I know what I must have put you through and I'm sorry. Listen to me. If you'll let me, I'll prove to you just how sorry I am and how much I love you. I'm saying I'll give it all up, the power, my history, my future—for you, to be with you." Now she's pleading, imploring me to relent. Seeing her cry confuses me even more.

"I wish you'd killed me."

"Matt, you don't know what you're saying, do you know what it has taken for me to see you and say this to you? I know you can't possibly understand but please, these tears are real and they're for you. For the first time in a billion, billion years, before your world existed, almost before anything existed, I've felt my heart. I never cared before; I never even knew there was truly such a thing until those first days and nights we spent together. I could live forever, I could see in the next world and the next and the next, I can wander the universes, stop the sun from shining on your world if I choose, block a thousand suns from a thousand worlds.

233

Or I can stay with you, take my chances in your simple, ridiculous world, grow old in this body and this skin, grow old and weak and pathetic with you, and die."

I look closely at Liv's tear streaked face.

"Liv, I love you more than I thought possible but I could live as long as you have and not make sense of any of this. What kind of life can I ever have with or without you? Some things can't be mended; I can't be mended. If there was any way . . ."

"You said you love me, that means there is a way. How do I go on without you? We can go away, leave everything behind and forget it ever happened."

"No babe, even you must know that's impossible. I look at you now and I'm overwhelmed by my feelings—the love, the desire, the memories of what we had—but what about my friends, my dead friends? I close my eyes and I can't see anything but what you did to them, all those things you made me see. You might as well have killed me."

"I couldn't kill you. I couldn't live with what I did to you. That's why I brought you back." Liv's voice has faded almost away.

"What will you do if I say no?"

"No? Could you say no?"

"I can't imagine it, but I can't see any option."

I take hold of Liv's hand and pull her to me. Holding her close, I feel that all consuming power bristling within her like an electrical current. She could never give that up; I can't ask her to give it up for me, what would be left?

"I feel you letting me go, you know."

"We could stay here forever," I say, closing my eyes to everything. "Please don't give me the power, I can't choose."

"But I'll choose wrong, I always do. You know that."

"Any choice will feel wrong," I sob. I'm crying my eyes out, the tears streaming into Liv's hair. I hear she's crying too, more control than me.

"It's all just a Punch and Judy show you know, just a big pointless game—if you took me away it wouldn't make a difference, this world would be no better or worse."

"I won't choose for you. Send me back," I say, meaning that horrific existence, that insanity. I assume there's nothing left of my old life.

"You should stay a little longer at least. I can't bear to let you go."

Finally, I pull myself away so I can look at Liv; kiss her and feel her again. The memory of that passion comes rushing back in an instant and we are locked together one last time. Inside her, on top and beneath her, all around her, I don't try to memorise anything; nothing will ever come close. Eventually we're done and the second we part, I'm taken by sleep.

11

July

When I wake, she's gone, the bed—my bed, *my old bed*—cold, next to me, the pillow soaked in our tears. From the pillow, I take a single black hair in my fingertips and bring it to my face.

Next to the bed is a side table where the lamp I used to do my homework by sits. There are two letters propped against the lamp. One is official looking, unopened and addressed to me. I pick it up and look at the date of the postmark; it says July 31ˢᵗ. I open the letter and read it.

The letter offers me the chance to recommence my degree in September. There are some details of accommodation, even a roommate but I don't take them in. I can't find it in me to register any response at all.

I look at the other envelope; handwritten, not stamped and addressed simply to, 'My Darling Matthew.' It's stiff as if there's a card inside rather than a letter.

I hear some movement from downstairs. I know instinctively it is my mother, and I want to see her. I put the envelopes back where they were and jump out of bed. I grab the nearest thing I can to cover my decency, before hurling myself down the stairs to the kitchen. When I see her, I cannot help bursting into tears and hugging her.

She looks at me, bewildered.

"Hello love, you saw the letter then?" So much hope and so much love in her voice. "Me and your dad wanted to get things ready for when you decided you were ready to come . . . to get on with things again.

We both always knew you'd come round; you've always been the strong one. All your friends have been round to see you while you've been up there; we wanted you to hear familiar voices. The doctors were no help whatsoever. Why am I telling you this now?" She's crying, I realise my current behaviour must be somewhat out of character. I squeeze her with everything I have. I can't think of anything to say but I want her to know that I'm here and I love her. She pushes me away just enough that she can look at me through watery hazel eyes. "Look at you, it's like you've never been away! Let me phone your dad, he'll come home straightaway."

"Mum, I don't know what happened, I feel like I've been dreaming for months. I saw the date on the letter, I don't know what's happened to the time."

"Do you remember anything?" she asks me dubiously.

"If I remember something that didn't happen, don't hold it against me, will you?" I try to joke. "There was a storm or an earthquake or something that took out the halls of residence, people were hurt?" The look on her face tells me she is feeling at least some relief.

"Sit down love. Your friend Frank was killed." It's the first time I've ever heard anyone call Fats by his given name. "Kenny, Michael, Digger, a boy called Harry they said you knew too. Dave told us they were the ones you knew. He's visited a few times and two girls, Erica and Clare, have been with him once or twice. Neil of course—I walked past your door and he was holding a one sided conversation with you about cricket, saying they needed you back! That'll be your dad." I follow her into the hall to see my dad beaming, rushing through the hall without closing the door and sweeping me into his great arms for a lethal bear hug. Tears in his eyes too, I wonder how many more tears I'll be the cause of.

"How are you son?" he asks. He doesn't care about the answer, he can see me standing up, see it's me and he can see the joy etched on my mother's face behind me. Then he puts me in another bear hug.

I'm settled in the lounge, the TV on for some background noise.

"Mum, you were telling me about what happened. Apart from the storm or whatever, I don't know anything."

"No-one really understands what happened, just a freak of nature, a massive storm that set off a chain reaction of electrical charges. They found you lying right in the middle of it all, practically untouched and surrounded by debris. The fireman who carried you clear said he wasn't even going to check for a pulse when he saw the state of everything around you. He visited a couple of times, all the way from Bromsgrove, and he phones every few weeks now, just to see how you are. He won't believe we finally have something to tell him."

Sensing my mother becoming overwhelmed again, my dad takes over. "You were unconscious for a day or so before you came round. The doctors kept you in because you didn't sleep without sedation and you were violent when you did; to yourself and any surrounding equipment. They thought at first you'd come through it fairly quickly. They just said it was stress related, probably seeing your friends d . . . seeing your friends the way you did. And that's all they've said ever since, but after two or three weeks they just said you should come back home until you started showing some signs of recovery. Even then they said it would probably only be a few days."

Mum's ok to continue again. "You've been in your room ever since, in bed mostly but you've walked around the house every now and again, surprising us in our room at two in the morning a few times. Your dad's aged terribly, trying to look after you. It's all just been so hopeless, yet here you are. My god, it's been so horrible. Donny has been round every day since you came back, he's stayed the night with you a few times, convinced he's getting through to you. You've not spoken a single word until today, not even focused on anyone to show you know who we are, just staring into space. You never lost your appetite though." She forces a thin smile.

That first day, I spoke with more than half a dozen people, piecing things together. Dave gave me the full picture of who'd died and who'd been hurt. Eighteen people were dead, including Fats; about twenty more had been injured by the flying glass. Eliot, our flatmate had lost his right eye, after being hit by a four inch shard of glass while he sat with Dave, Erica and Clare in our kitchen. It had missed his brain by a few millimetres and the doctors called him lucky. Eventually, all these details began to pass way above my head. Dave had been one of the few to manage to finish his first year successfully and he, Erica and Clare had agreed to keep a room free in their new house for me in case I'd been ready to go back in September. It was a touching gesture but I knew right away I wouldn't be going back.

When I returned to bed that night, I looked at the untouched envelope by my bed. I traced the outline of the seal with my finger and stared at it intently, before placing it back on the table.

In the first couple of days, I spoke again with Dave, then Clare and Erica but I quickly decided that the only way I could continue any sort of life would be to turn my back completely on everything that reminded me of Liv. I deleted all the contacts from my phone; the only exceptions being Liv and Mel, both of whom I knew I'd never speak to again anyway.

I may open Liv's card one day, I know she'll have found the perfect picture of an eagle and the promise of that is enough.

THE END

Lightning Source UK Ltd.
Milton Keynes UK
UKOW031037210712

196357UK00003B/19/P